Survival of the Fittest

Genesis

Therese Pal

Open Leaf
Media

Survival of the Fittest: Genesis
© 2025 Therese Pal

A CIP catalogue record for this book is available from the British Library.

Travel Edition 2025

Published by **OpenLeaf Media**
www.openleafmedia.com

ISBN: 978-1-9192163-3-1
Cover design: Vincent Sebastian
Book design: Abhijit Pal

For information, please contact:
OpenLeaf Media
Email: publisher@openleafmedia.com
Website: www.openleafmedia.com

To Abhi, for walking beside me with love through two decades

and to my parents, who walked ahead of me, lighting the path.

Contents

Prologue

Wayanad, India: 25 years ago

The first cry of the infant was feeble, reluctant—an unwilling declaration of her arrival into this strange, dangerous world. Minutes later, her twin brother echoed her sentiments with shallow breaths and folded fingers. Their mother lay flaccid on the table, ghostly pale and equally lost, oblivious to their arrival. Through the invisible thread that bound them, the twins had known the trials their mother had endured, had tasted the salt of her tears, and they expected nothing but the harshness of the treacherous world.

Dr. Mathew, the gifted gynaecologist at Maria Mission Hospital, was sweating profusely beneath his mask and overalls. His fear for the woman on the operating table was apparent. Her pallor had grown progressively worse, her long, elegant eyes were closed in surrender. His hands trembled as he lifted the second baby. No excitement or jubilation accompanied their birth, aside from the frenzied heartbeat of the surgeon; he alone knew the peril that waited to swallow them whole.

"Keep them safe," Mathew whispered, handing the baby to Nurse Tina, his longtime friend and the only companion he trusted that night.

"She has lost too much blood. The vitals are not good. We need to transfer her to the medical college hospital. We're not equipped for this," Tina said, wrapping the babies in clean towels and placing them gently in a cot.

"Yes," Mathew replied, his voice strained. "An ambulance is being prepared for the other accident patient. We will send her with him, but quietly."

His heart grew heavier as he glanced at the adjacent room. It had been a tragic day. Life and death had passed through his hands in the last few hours, and he battled the sinking feeling that more was to come.

Tina rushed to see to the transfer, leaving Mathew alone to wrap up. They were acutely short of staff due to the impending Christmas holidays.

As Mathew worked alone, his mind flashed back to the evening's startling events. It had begun with all the promise of a blissful night. The air was filled with soulful music, a Jugalbandi of Veena and Flute—forever entwined and heavenly, lifting his heart too in its soft embrace, calming his mind. It was the first day of his holiday, and he watched the travelling theatre group's latest play, "Krishna Leela", at the open ground with a feeling of contentment, a feeling that was rare to him in the recent months. The accompanying music then quickened, the Drums and Mridangam adding a sense of dramatic anticipation.

The majestic stage was charged with the presence of Kamsa, the evil king of Mathura, awaiting to kill his sister Devaki's eighth child, prophesied to end his reign, just as he had with all her previous newborns.

In the dim-lit room, Devaki's son was born. A beautiful baby with skin a dark and divine blue, akin to the darkest cloud about to pour down. He was adorned with thick black hair and big, beautiful eyes—a perfect baby. Yet, no delight, no wonder, remained on his parents' faces, only dread, a reflection of their breaking hearts, knowing the imminent fate awaiting their child.

Suddenly, the stage lighting changed; a clap of thunder and a flash of lightning filled the air, making the entire stage seem to shake. The walls collapsed and guards buckled and fell. Lord Vishnu appeared in all his glory beside the newborn, his most powerful avatar, intended to bring joy and justice to the world as prophesied, an answer to the prayers of the oppressed.

His booming voice reverberated throughout the room,

Therese Pal

commanding Vasudeva, Devaki's husband, "Take the infant away from Kamsa's eyes to the Yadava king—Nanda and his wife Yashoda, across the Yamuna River. This infant is to be called Krishna; he will grow up as their son and become the protector of all, the god of love and kindness…."

At that moment, Rajan Master, the director of the play, had hurried to Mathew with a bewildered expression. "Varkey is looking for you. He's in a rough state but wouldn't tell me anything!"

Mathew rushed out immediately. Varkey, his godfather, had been reclusive since the devastating landslide that claimed the lives of his wife and daughter during the torrential monsoon, six months ago. Mathew shuddered at the thought of that doomed day, the pain of his own loss resurfaced, like a waking sea monster, gnawing at his heart.

Varkey was waiting alone at the far side of the ground, under the cover of the old mango trees lining the compound. The news his godfather brought knocked the ground out from under his feet. He clung to a tree trunk for support, staring at Varkey, unseeing, as he struggled to process the information.

"I am sorry I couldn't tell you the truth earlier. I had my reasons. What we need right now is your help…Its urgent…" Varkey looked away, worry lines etched deep into his age-hardened face. Misery and sorrow darkened the hollows around his eyes, his pride lay forgotten.

Mathew knew he owed his life to his godfather, his father's lifelong friend. Their bond had endured through thick and thin. But this revelation was outrageous… Varkey knew how he had felt about her… and to let him suffer through all that agony! He wanted to swear and scream. A lifetime of respect for his godfather choked him from inside. "What in the hell happened in the last six months?"

Before Varkey could respond, one of the actors from the play appeared, still in his elaborate costume of Putana, the demoness sent by Kamsa to kill the infant Krishna.

"There was a call for you, Dr. Mathew. An emergency at the hospital," said the actor, casting a wary glance at Varkey.

Mathew turned and saw Varkey, staring at the costumed man.

"Oh, never mind his atrocious looks. He is one of the actors, playing a demon today!" Mathew continued hurriedly. "Bring her to the hospital at once. I will wait."

Mathew turned and rushed to the hospital, his heart a tumultuous mix of fury and relief.

****

Dr. Mathew gazed at the pale figure before him. How quickly fate had turned—he was on the verge of losing her once again, before he even had a moment to savour her return. The attached machines glowed ominously, displaying figures that indicated her vitals were plummeting. Fresh dread enveloped him like a hurricane. Her babies slept silently in their cot; he must keep at least one promise to her...

He moved to check on his earlier patient in the private room. The woman was still not fully awake from the sedatives. She seemed comfortable, her breathing steadied, blissfully unaware of her loss. Her decade-long struggles and hopes had once again ended in ruin.

"Cruel fates," Mathew thought bitterly.

An SUV screeched to a halt outside the compound, directly below the room. Mathew saw harsh headlights streaming through the tiny gaps in the curtains. He peeked out cautiously. A heavy-built man emerged from the driver's seat; his face hidden by a grey woollen balaclava. Matted, dirty long hair spilled out from under it, cascading onto his back. His skin was ink-black, as if painted. He crept towards the back gate of the hospital.

Mathew sensed the danger before his brain processed the information; the figure was disturbingly familiar. He needed to act fast. He hurried back to the operating room and locked it from the inside. The new mother—closer to death than life—and her tiny newborns in the cot beside her were in mortal danger. He shivered under the weight of the promise he had to keep. His mind raced through the options. The hospital was thinly staffed at this hour, and an ambush was imminent.

He moved to the side room to check the doors. It held a cot with another two infants, curtains drawn shut around them. They looked so tiny in their cot, their skin having turned blue, losing the battle before it fully began, before they had a chance to bask in the love awaited them.

A memory flashed in his mind—another infant, lively and divine blue. Flashes of lightning and claps of thunder echoed in his thoughts—this time, tinged with a ray of new hope...

Therese Pal

Part 1

"We all belong to an ancient identity. Stories are the rivers that take us there." - Frank Delaney

1. Sitayanam

Cambridge, UK: Present Day

She was all alone. The dark forest closed in around her like a suffocating shroud. Gnarled ivy twisted around ancient trees, their roots clawing at the earth beneath the high rock she perched on. Below, a lonely river snaked through deep ridges, its banks lined with jagged rocks and dense thickets. Her face was buried in her knees, arms wrapped tightly around her legs, her long hair cascading like a veil. Tears streamed down, soaking her velvet skirt and the silk shawl she clutched protectively over her belly. The encroaching darkness seeped into her very soul.

A few hours earlier, she had been surrounded by comfort and adoration. The dancing ghungroos, celebratory music, and vibrant decorations of the much-awaited homecoming now felt like a distant dream. The coronation day of the rightful heir seemed like a mirage compared to the frightening depths of the lonesome forest around her.

Born a princess, she had married an heir. On her wedding day, she had solemnly promised to be his companion for life. From that day onwards, she had followed him to the ends of the earth, like a shadow. She hadn't left his side in sickness and in health, through the luxuries of the palace and the frugal existence of their exiled life in the forests for the past fourteen years. Her dedication did not waver, even after she was taken, confined alone in the fortress of the demon. All she ever asked in return was her husband's love. She knew he loved her, even now. But he chose to be the king first—a king without blemish, without her—the subject of accusation and gossip. He would set an example for the rulers to come for eons, to be known as the most righteous king of all, even if it meant personal sacrifices.

But by sacrificing his love, he sacrificed her life too! He had left her when she needed him the most. Where was the justice for her? Where was his justice for their unborn child, his own heir? Wasn't he supposed to be the right and just king for them too? His silence broke her heart into a thousand more pieces. Her grief knew no bounds, and she wept uncontrollably...

Jane Banks woke up abruptly, drenched in sweat, her body tense with grief. She was weeping for real, still feeling the sorrow and loneliness from that desolate place in her dream. Who was that woman? Why did she feel her misery as her own? She switched on the bedside light. A stash of sheets fallen from the bed, the script she was reading right before she fell asleep. The title embossed on the scattered pages shone in the light: Sitayanam – The Reimagined Story of Sita.

The phone which pulled her out of the nightmare went silent again on the far table. Jane blinked rapidly, trying to shake off the lingering haze of her dream, her heart still racing. It felt so real, the desolation of the character drilling deep into her heart. She had read that script many times during rehearsals but rarely thought of the protagonist in that heart-wrenching way until that dream forced it on her. In the corner of the room, her elaborate dance costume was stacked in the overnight bag.

She peeled herself out of the dream and swung her legs over the side of the bed. Two missed calls glared from her phone; she must have been deeply asleep to miss both. The phone vibrated again in her hand, startling her. It was James, her twin brother.

"You're not on the train yet, are you?" James's voice was a mix of concern and exasperation.

"James, You Ok? I missed Mum's call too!" Jane's voice trembled slightly, betraying her anxiety. Her mind raced through possible scenarios, both plausible and far-fetched, as was her habit. The dream had intensified her dread today.

"Shouldn't you be on the way to London already?" James chided gently.

Jane sighed, "I know, I know. I'm running late. What's up?"

"Mum and Dad won't be able to make it to your performance today. Something came up."

Jane detected a hesitation in his voice, a telltale sign he was holding something back. He knew her well... too well.

"I'm coming instead. My friend Olivia is rather fond of Indian classical dance."

Jane paused, considering. "You should stop counting on cancellations for free dates!"

"If you impress her, I'll get a season ticket, I promise!"

"Ha! So, there's hope for at least a season with your new friend. Good to know..." she chuckled.

"Of course." James said plainly, refusing to be drawn into the probing. "I'll come with you to Kent this evening if you're still planning to stay with Mum and Dad for the weekend?"

"Okay. I must leave now if I'm to reach the theatre on time. See you this evening." She hurried to get ready, her mind buzzing with the urgency of the hour. She had a final dress rehearsal at the venue before the performance tonight.

Jane's studio apartment in Cambridge was scarcely furnished, clothes stacked haphazardly on the corner cupboard, her desk overflowed with books, reflecting her chaotic life. Fabrics and jewellery boxes lay scattered, remnants of her late-night costume preparations.

Jane freshened up quickly. She chose a simple white

shirt, bright blue jeans, and a pair of comfortable boots and pulled her short thick black hair into a ponytail. She had a natural brilliance about her, and her large almond-shaped eyes, lined with dark kohl, were pleasant and bright.

She was looking forward to the evening, to take part as one of the support casts for the SivaLakshmi Dance Academy's show at the renowned Royal Albert Hall in London. She was eager to finally meet Siva and Lakshmi, the legendary couple who founded the Academy. Based in Florence, their Indian classical dance drama group had garnered accolades and followers for its tasteful adaptations of classics and powerful storytelling. Jane had trained at their London academy during her school days. After busy but lonely research years at the University, she seized it when an opportunity arose to join their latest production.

Jane hurried to finish packing, leaving the storage bags and jewellery boxes strewn across the floor to tidy up later. It was still raining outside. The intermittent rain had started in the night, making the late autumn leaves on the footpath squelchy and slippery. The train to London was running late; the announcer attributed the delay to unruly autumn leaves on the tracks. "That pairs well with the wrong kind of snow last winter," Jane thought ruefully.

When she reached the venue, the group of performers were already in costume, ready for the dress rehearsal.

"Hurry up, right here..." her friend Rita called out from the backstage dressing room. Rita helped Jane get into costume and makeup in record time. The vibrant colours of the costume felt at odds with the grey fog of unease that still clung to Jane after her dream. As Jane's fingers brushed over the intricate designs, she felt a connection to her heritage that she was only now beginning to appreciate.

"You're practically unrecognisable and look beautiful for a change!" Rita laughed, dragging her to the waiting group.

Evening descended swiftly, and the audience settled

Therese Pal

into their seats. James and Olivia sat among them, reading the synopsis from a decorated brochure: *Sitayanam*. The dance drama retells the story of Sita, daughter of Mother Earth, adopted by King Janaka, who grew up as the princess of Mithila. She married Lord Rama, Prince of Ayodhya, after he surpassed the valiant test set by her father to choose a suitable groom for his precious daughter, only to endure the trials of life and emerge as a feminine power reflecting the strength of her mother.

The lead dancer moved with elegance, her performance poignantly conveying Sita's journey. Her feet and hands created classic postures and mudras in perfect harmony. Her face beautifully reflected the emotions: the playfulness of a child, the dreams of a young woman, and the guarded optimism of a bride-to-be. A graceful male dancer joined her, portraying Prince Rama and enacting the Swayamvara scene. They moved in unison, their synchronized movements mirroring the love and adoration between the young prince and princess, transporting the audience to a timeless scene of romance. Beautiful Gandharvas and Apsaras—the divine performers—welcomed them to their enchanting world, worthy of the gods.

The audience was captivated. James reached out and took Olivia's hand in his own. She gave him a radiant smile in return, taking in his oval face, beautifully framed by flowing hair, his thick eyelashes lining his deep black eyes. Her face was set in deep emotion, as if transported to the enchanted world, with her own prince looking at her with adoration. The depth of his intense gaze made her cheeks flush. James held her hand and gently kissed it, silently promising her his own devotion.

On stage, the play moved on to Sita's life in exile and her lonely existence. Jane waiting at the wings, thought of her dream, reliving the experience through the dancer; shards of Sita's broken heart piercing her own once again. Maybe Sita was that mirror, reflecting her own heart, and its deepest scars, still raw behind the veil. She pondered Sita's resolve to endure and fulfil her karma for her children; After all, Sita was the daughter of Mother Earth, the goddess of infinite endurance.

The audience erupted in a standing ovation at the end. The dancers held hands, bowed in unison, thanking the audience and invited guests.

Backstage, all performers were graciously welcomed by the enigmatic founders of the group. Lakshmi, with her toned, slim body and elegant features, looked every bit the timeless dancer. Siva, older with greying hair and beard, exuded an air of melancholy, as if the lines of the heart-wrenching play had etched themselves into his soul. Jane thought of her mother; she would have enjoyed their company very much.

Jane went to touch Lakshmi's feet for a customary blessing, but Lakshmi hugged her instead. "You look just like my daughter," she said quietly with a gentle smile. Jane felt an instant connection to the artist.

"Of course, with this makeup and outfits, we all could be identical siblings!" Rita quipped, drawing hearty laughter from the group.

Back at the dressing room, Jane removed her makeup hastily. "James must be waiting outside."

"Oh, why didn't you mention that earlier? I would have danced better!" Rita was fond of James just as much as Jane, having spent their childhood together. She had a crush on him during school days but had given up eventually; James never seemed keen to change their close friendship to anything else.

"He is with a date apparently!" said Jane.

"What kind of doctor is the new one then?" asked Rita, rolling her eyes

It was a standing joke between them, and Rita never

missed a chance to tease him endlessly for his repeated choice of his colleagues as dates. His reasoning was simple enough. He rarely ever had time to socialise outside work. The only women he met long enough to ask on a date were either his colleagues or his patients and dating the latter was apparently illegal!

Rita tagged along with Jane to meet James. They saw him waiting at the side of the now empty main hall talking attentively to a young woman in an elegant black dress and matching shoes. She was incredibly attractive and carried an effortless charm.

James came forward to give Jane a bear-hug and high-fived Rita as was their custom.

James beamed at Jane. "You were amazing!"

Rita turned to his pretty companion to shake hands, "I am group dancer number 33. And you are Dr.?"

"Olivia. Olivia Russel!" she looked at James in surprise.

Rita was grinning peevishly. James grimaced at her.

He put his arm around Olivia, protectively. "No, she is not my colleague, if you must know," he clarified. "She works at the Medical Research Laboratory at Cambridge. I met her at a conference few months ago."

"Oh, that is the reason I got to see you more often recently!" Jane exclaimed with a mischievous smile and greeted Olivia warmly. "Hope you enjoyed the evening?"

"That was absolutely splendid! The performance was simply exquisite," Olivia exclaimed in admiration.

Jane smiled warmly, enveloping her in a hug, noticing how happy her brother looked with Olivia.

"Have you been roaming in royal circles now? She sounds very aristocratic to me!" Rita asked James in a muffled voice as she poked his rib discreetly. He ignored her jibe.

"Are you ready to head to Kent?" He asked Jane as they walked out together.

"Yes. What was it you weren't telling me this morning?"

Jane asked, her voice filled with sudden gravity.

James frowned slightly but nodded. "Let's talk about it on the way."

Jane couldn't shake the feeling that her dream was more than just a figment of her imagination. It felt like a connection to a past she couldn't fully understand, a past somehow intertwined with her present. The echoes of Sita's story lingered in her mind, blending with the rhythms of her own life. She wondered if there were answers waiting for her, hidden in the pages of time.

It was midnight when James and Jane left for Kent, unaware of the intense storm gathering in their horizon...

2. The twist of fate

"I love your car. How come Mum and Dad gifted you one and not me?" Jane reclined her seat, her tone teasing.

James smirked, eyes glued on the road. "You hate driving, remember? No, I am being polite - You are a terrible driver! Besides, they helped you buy your apartment."

"I can drive fine. I couldn't say that about the parking though!"

"And who gets sick on long drives?"

"Not if I'm the one driving! I just like to hold onto something."

"Me too, when you drive... my dear life!"

Jane made a face, then settled back, glancing at him sideways. "Olivia seemed nice."

James glanced at her; eyebrows raised. Jane was a keen observer, always sizing people up. Gaining her trust was a feat few managed.

"She is nice," James said, nodding. "And yes, I do like her."

Jane smiled, understanding that was all she'd get out of him for now.

The drive to Kent was quiet, the late hour ensuring light motorway traffic. Jane, exhausted, half-closed her eyes. James, lost in thought, finally cleared his throat.

"I wanted to tell you in person. Mum hasn't been feeling well. Her symptoms weren't great, so I insisted she get tests. That's why they couldn't come to the show today."

Jane sat up, alarmed. She had sensed something was off with her mum, though Lissy never said anything to keep her children from worrying.

"She thinks it's cancer."

Jane's heart sank. Lissy Banks was their rock. Her unwavering presence and optimism had shaped Jane and James into who they were. Their father, Richard, a finance executive, was often away, leaving Lissy to anchor the family.

As they neared their parents' house, a handsome two-story brick home at the end of a tree-lined private road, Jane felt a knot tighten in her stomach. Lights glowed warmly in the living room, and the driveway lanterns cast a comforting light.

Inside, Lissy was reading in her favourite armchair, a colourful blanket snug over her feet. She rose, her face lighting up. Short and plump, with greying hair framing her kind face, Lissy exuded warmth.

Jane hugged her tightly, fighting back tears. James joined, kissing his mother's forehead. Though they towered over her, she matched it with her love.

"How many times have we told you not to wait up this late?" James chided gently.

"I napped in the afternoon. How was your performance, Jane? I was so looking forward to it. Gutted to have missed it!"

"It was great. Met Siva and Lakshmi too... But how are you feeling, Mum? Really?"

"I'm fine, just a bit weary."

"We'll talk in the morning Mum. It's really late, you must get proper rest." James insisted.

Lissy reluctantly agreed, kissed them both goodnight before heading to her room.

Jane tossed and turned in her bed, worry gnawing at her. Anxiety wrapped around her like a suffocating fog. She finally drifted into a fitful sleep, haunted by dreams of death and demons.

The next morning, breakfast was lively. Richard, home for the weekend, was in charge, serving steaming mugs of tea, fried eggs, and bacon on toast. His receding hairline was speckled with grey, and a faint stubble shadowed his usually clean-shaven face.

Lissy looked determined, almost cheerful. "I got my test

results yesterday. The initial diagnosis was correct—it's breast cancer," she said matter-of-factly.

Jane and James hugged her tightly. Jane wiped her tears, trying to stay strong.

James asked about the treatment options while Jane clung to her mother, warding off dark thoughts. Lissy was their protector, who kept the demons at bay, and her presence itself always had a calming effect on her.

"Don't worry, it's early stage and treatable. I recognized it early," Lissy reassured them.

"But there's something you should know. My mother died of breast cancer as she was diagnosed too late. My grandmother also died young; no one knew the cause, medical facilities were scarce then," Lissy said gravely.

James caught on. "You think it's hereditary?"

"Yes. I've checked with my doctor." Turning to Jane, she added, "You should get tested to see if you're at risk."

"Why worry about it from now? I'll face it if it comes," Jane said flatly.

"There are preventive measures you could take," James urged.

"I'll think about it," she replied noncommittally. The nightmare of cancer loomed over her, staring at her mother, possibly eyeing her too. She shook her head to clear the thoughts.

"James has a new girlfriend," Jane announced suddenly. "Someone outside his usual bubble!"

Lissy and Richard looked at James with interest. He was known for having no serious girlfriends, always blaming his busy schedule.

"Olivia is lovely. It's early days though. And Jane, stop using me as a diversion," James said, smirking. "What about you? Found anyone good enough, or are all men still vain and imperfect?"

Jane scowled at him and busied herself clearing the

table. She carried the plates to the sink, away from any potential conversation about her own life.

She thought about the crowded but lonely halls from her Cambridge days. She thought of Steve Chang, a passionate political researcher and outspoken activist. His fervent speeches about global injustices had captivated her, his unwavering commitment to the cause stirring something deep within her soul. She remembered the heartache she felt when he made the decision to return to Hong Kong to join the movement he believed in so fiercely. To him, his calling lay not within the pages of textbooks or the hallowed halls of academia, but in the gritty reality of activism on the ground; His profound anguish for his people overshadowing any comfort or hope for a bright future.

As she grappled with her own feelings of rejection and despair, Jane sought solace in the boundless expanse of the cosmos, immersing herself in the study of physics. The vastness of the universe provided a welcome distraction from the pain of her fruitless affection, offering a sense of perspective that brought her some measure of calm again. Finding the insignificance of humans and their irrational feelings in the vastness of the universe was oddly comforting!

She couldn't shake the feeling of déjà vu, the feeling of emptiness and rejection left as remnants from the dream. 'I'm in a select-few club!' she thought wryly as she washed her hands. 'How many could claim they were spurned for a philosophical rival such as one of true public duty! Maybe Sita was one of the first, and I have felt her predicament all my life without even knowing her!'

She gazed into the window glass without seeing. A silhouette of a weeping woman, an embodiment of despair and abandonment remained stamped in her mind, her silent whisper clearly in her ears - "Where is the justice for me and our unborn child?". A sudden gust of wind rattled the glass, making her shiver involuntarily.

3. An unforeseen storm

A week later, James called Jane again, urging her to take the test. Reluctantly, she complied, if only to get him off her back. Another two weeks passed before she was asked to meet the doctor in person. Jane felt a knot in her stomach as she trudged through the rain to the grey office. The consultant, an older woman who resembled her grandmother, greeted her with a quiet, whispery voice, barely audible over the din of the medical equipment in the background.

"Please, take a seat, Jane. I'm Dr. Rosin Jones. First, the good news: you are not more likely to get cancer than any other young woman of your age."

She also sounded like her grandmother!

"Then why not just say that over the phone?" Jane asked, her voice edged with apprehension.

"The thing is…" Dr. Jones hesitated, her eyes intent on Jane's face. "Your DNA doesn't match your mother's."

Jane felt the world tilt. She had braced herself for one deadly disease or the other, but never this…

"What do you mean? That's got to be a mistake!"

"We checked it… twice."

Blood drained from Jane's face. Her lungs tightened, making it hard to breathe. She felt an unfamiliar tension in her chest and a churning in her stomach.

Dr. Jones handed her a glass of water. "Drink this. Take deep breaths. It's just the shock."

Jane obeyed, her hands trembling. The foundation of her identity seemed to crumble beneath her feet. How does one navigate such a revelation? She felt adrift in an endless ocean with no oars or anchor, her thoughts whirling and clattering in her brain. Sobs threatened to escape her.

"You could take another test with fresh samples. Also talk to your family. There might be an explanation," Dr. Jones suggested gently.

Eventually, Jane's anxiety settled into a steady ache, allowing her to speak.

"Yes, I'll do that." She stood, shook the doctor's hand, and left. Her steps were unsteady, her vision hazy. She sat on the steps of the sheltered passage, staring blankly at the pattering rain on the pavement.

After what seemed like ages, her methodical mind kicked in. 'Mum wouldn't know about this; she was the one who asked me to take the test. Neither would James or Dad. They both were there. It must be a sample mismatch. Yes, that's it... James would know for sure!'

She called him. He picked up on the first ring.

"I was just about to call you. Did you get your result?"

"I did. But I need to talk to you in person."

"Is everything alright?" Concern edged his voice.

"Just some technical things. I need your help to clear them up."

"Okay, come over. Right now."

When she arrived at the apartment James shared with a friend, he was reading on his laptop. The place was unusually tidy for two busy young doctors. Jane knew that was James's doing.

James looked puzzled by her sombre mood. Jane grabbed a bottle of water from his fridge, fidgeting. Finally, she decided to mimic Dr. Jones's approach and pulled out the stack of papers.

"The good news is, I have no higher chances of getting cancer," she said with a forced smile.

James looked relieved, but Jane's heart ached. She felt a great love for her brother but also a pang of dread—what if she were to lose that link too? She quickly chided herself— 'It's not blood that makes us close, it's our shared soul.'

"But there's something confusing. My genetic record doesn't match Mum's," she said quietly. "Maybe it's a sample mistake, but I wanted to check with you before talking to

Mum and Dad."

James frowned, scanning the papers. Finding no mistakes, he grabbed his work laptop and started typing furiously for reference data.

Jane watched him silently. Shared mannerisms, like the way James screwed up his face in concentration right then, reassured her of their bond. They were too alike—same black, almond-shaped eyes, same olive skin tone, even though much paler than their Mum's rich brown. But their features resembled their mother's, or so she thought until now.

When she looked up, James was watching her solemnly, probably reaching to the same conclusion.

"Maybe it's a sample mix-up, but let's do another test to be sure," he said. "It might take longer through the usual route, but Olivia has access to test facilities for her research. Let's get a sample to her."

Jane agreed, relieved at the quick turnaround plan. James called Olivia, who agreed to help.

"I'll get fresh samples from Mum and Dad. I don't want them to worry until we know more," Jane said.

James gathered at-home blood collection kits, took their samples, and labelled them correctly. He handed a kit to Jane to collect samples from their parents, so she could take them all to Olivia in Cambridge.

"I'll meet you there tomorrow evening. We'll see Olivia together once she's had time to do the tests, okay?" James said.

Jane nodded, feeling relieved he would be with her, no matter the outcome.

Late evening found James and Jane arriving at the research centre where Olivia worked. Darkness had fallen, and November's sleet and gusty wind followed them inside. They signed the visitor register and asked to see Dr. Olivia Russel. She appeared a few minutes later, her step light despite the serious expression on her face.

"We have brought a storm for you," James said, shaking off his drenched coat. He pecked on her cheek lightly while keeping her at arm's length to save her from the wet clothes.

She led them to the top-floor cafeteria, warm and filled with the inviting aroma of fresh coffee.

Olivia fetched them hot mugs of coffee, scones, and cakes. A few sips brought colour back to their cheeks.

"You know my brother well; the way to his heart is definitely through his stomach," Jane said, watching James's contentment as he munched on a scone.

James smiled, embracing Olivia warmly, now that he was dry and content. He was charming and intense at the same time and pulled her to him to kiss her passionately. Colour warmed her cheek as she returned his kiss tenderly with a shy smile.

Olivia's face turned serious when she looked at Jane.

"You managed to run the test then?" Jane asked noticing it.

"Yes. First things first, your genes match, so you are indeed full siblings. However, Dr. Jones was correct about your parentage; neither of your parents' DNA matches yours," Olivia said quietly, aware of the graveness of her pronouncement.

Silence fell in the room suddenly. The wind shrieked outside, splattering rain on the wide glass windows. A lonely, leafless weeping willow swayed incessantly in the middle of the wet lawn. Thunder echoed in their hearts. The coffee remained forgotten; the cold had seeped into their souls as well.

4. Memory lane

Kent, UK: 15 years ago

The little girl stood tall, her fingers entwined protectively around her brother's arm, who cried silently. He seemed more apprehensive about what was to come than about what had transpired. Another boy lay sprawled on a heap of snow in the schoolyard, wailing loudly. A cluster of ten-year-olds formed a circle to witness the scene, one of them helping the fallen boy to his feet.

"I'll show you, just you wait," the boy yelled as he stormed off with his friend to the headteacher's office. After a brief interval, an office assistant appeared to escort the two young accused. Owen exhibited his scraped elbow to the stern-faced Ms. Stapleton, his tear-streaked countenance and snow-dusted hair painting a convincing victim.

"Jane, I'm deeply disappointed to hear about your reckless behaviour," the headteacher admonished sternly.

"He started it, Ms. Stapleton. He called my brother a 'butter chicken brownie'," Jane retorted defiantly.

"You pushed him down the steps?" Ms. Stapleton inquired incredulously.

"It was just a bit of snow," Jane looked mad again, sorry that it was only snow!

Ms. Stapleton turned to James for clarification, but he remained silent, staring at the ground and fidgeting.

"Jane, this isn't the first time you've lost your temper. He could've broken a bone!" But Ms. Stapleton's tone softened, the anger dissipating.

Jane remained defiant, unable to comprehend why anyone would prioritise bones over feelings. Why couldn't they see how distressed her brother was? Later, Jane observed the teacher talking with her mother upon collecting them after school. Lissy showed no sign of anger during the journey home. However, after dinner and a warm shower, she gathered her children close, enveloping them in her armchair beneath her fragrant blanket.

"James, would you care to share what happened at school today?" Lissy inquired gently.

"It was nothing, Mum. I'm sorry we caused you trouble," James replied, shooting Jane a warning glance to prevent further escalation. He abhorred confrontation of any sort.

"And you, Jane?" Lissy's gaze held concern, prompting Jane to unburden herself. Perhaps she and James needed assistance, and Mum could set things right.

"Mum, Owen was terribly mean to James. He's been taunting us for ages..."

"It's just childish behaviour, both of you know better than to pay it any mind," Lissy reassured patiently.

"But he made fun of us. He said we smelled like butter chicken, and everyone laughed!" Jane's floodgates opened, and she couldn't stop herself.

"I know you chide James for lingering in the shower, but he scrubs his skin so hard, it often turns red. He is that afraid of smells of any kind," she continued.

Lissy embraced them tightly, sadness clouding her eyes as her heart ached for her children.

"I'm sorry you both had to endure that. Some children can be unkind, especially when they're ignorant or insecure. But remember, their shortcomings are not yours. Embrace your differences; they make the world more beautiful and interesting. Your hopes and dreams are nurtured in your hearts, unaffected by appearances. What matters is the spirit you cultivate within yourselves to realise them. You are what you believe, not what others perceive. If you aspire to be the best version of yourselves, you will become just that. And remember this in your heart, our family is made with love, and you will always have abundance of it in our home..."

Lissy kissed them both on the forehead, tears glistening.

They sat together for a long time, wrapped in each other's embrace. Lissy hummed an old lullaby, weaving a sense of tranquillity.

> *'Omana thinkal Kidaavo...*
> *Nalla Komala Thaamara Poovo...*
> *Poovil Niranja Madhuvo,*
> *Pari poornendu thande nilavo...'*

Jane and James eventually drifted off to sleep, clinging to their mother, dreaming of a serene, lotus-adorned pool bathed in moonlight, nestled within a fragrant garden resonating with the melodies of nightingales and the dance of peacocks.

5. Truths that cut deep

"Families are made with love; it doesn't make any difference how I feel about our home..." Jane said aloud, but her voice wavered, her fingers gripping the seat. The road stretched endlessly ahead, mirroring the uncertainty gnawing at her heart.

In the quiet of their journey to Kent, James stole a glance at his sister, his brow furrowed with worry. They had spent the week grappling with the daunting task of revealing the devastating truth to their parents. But now, as they neared their destination, apprehension hung heavy in the air.

Richard welcomed them with a weary smile, the lines etched on his face deeper than they remembered. "Your mum's resting," he murmured, leading them to the kitchen. "She's feeling rough these days, mostly the effect of the chemo. I took a month off to be with her. I'm also thinking of retiring. I just feel it's time," he explained as they gathered around the kitchen table with a pot of tea.

Jane couldn't bring the image of her father's retired self. "Retiring, Dad? No more business targets? No more strategies?" Her words held a note of disbelief.

Richard's gaze lingered on the swirling steam rising from his cup. "It's time for a slower pace," he confessed, the weight of years spent chasing success suddenly evident in his weary tone.

Richard had been a busy executive for a long time, with a special penchant for numbers and a dependable leadership style. He felt the burnout creeping in, like a waning candle losing its vigour. He realised his work no longer held the same purpose it once did, and he felt increasingly irrelevant in a sea of younger colleagues. Fog and bewilderment clouded his once-crystal-clear mind. A complex feeling to battle at this confusing stage of his life, past the prime. Only the fear of the unknown, of a life outside the regular routines and familiar

Therese Pal

work, had kept him going as it was. Lissy, too, had reached a similar crossroad. She had always believed the primary purpose of any living being was to bring the best of the next generation, so life would go on for the better. Every parent owed that much to their offspring, to the nature, to the circle of life. Now, with their children grown and independent, she felt the vacuum of purpose slowly encroaching upon her. The sudden illness only served to underscore the fragility of life, prompting both to prioritise their time together.

James, who always understood the world of emotions better, nodded in agreement. He had witnessed countless instances of life priorities shifting in the face of illness, and he knew firsthand how drastically perspectives could change.

Taking advantage of the time alone with Richard, James broached the subject they had been dreading.

"Dad, we have something to tell you…" His voice faltered slightly as he struggled to find the right words. "Jane did a predictive test for the possibility of any genetic transfer of cancer. She's all clear. But in the process, we found out both of our genes differ from yours and Mum's… It means we couldn't possibly be your biological children…"

A stunned silence followed; Richard's disbelief mirrored in his children's faces.

"How could that be? Maybe some mistake?" he questioned, his mind racing to find a logical explanation.

Then he recalled Jane's insistence on obtaining a blood sample from them the week before, under the guise of ancestry research, a fun project with Olivia.

"You've double-checked, haven't you?"

"Yes, we have. We didn't want to worry Mum and you before we knew for sure," Jane said, her face etched with worry.

It took Richard some time to process the information, his concern adding shades to their worried faces. In the silence that followed, Richard's thoughts drifted back to a distant memory.

"Lissy was with her aunt, Sister Frances, in India at the time of your birth, few weeks earlier than expected. I was in Paris on a work trip. When I got news of her aunt's death, I set out at once, not knowing about Lissy being taken to the hospital that evening - reaching the very next morning after your birth. Lissy was weak and drowsy due to the complications during delivery; but you two, the most beautiful babies I had ever set eyes on in my life, were doing well..." His voice trailed off as he reminisced about that joyous day. "We've never left your side since. We moved to a city hospital the next day and returned home as soon as your passports were sorted through the British Embassy."

"Why did you move to a different hospital?" Jane inquired.

"The hospital said her routine doctor was unavailable. He had been called back from his planned holiday just for the emergency delivery. I wanted to ensure she, and you, had the best facilities to recuperate."

"Do you think Mum is strong enough to take this news now?" James asked, his concern evident.

"She's a strong-willed woman. Of course, it will be a shock, but I think she will cope, given time."

Jane went in to check on her Mum. Her parents' bedroom was spacious. Cream coloured, floor length curtains were drawn open and tied neatly to the side; the huge West facing windows framed the pine trees lined up in the enormous garden. Lissy was sleeping; her face was paler than usual, and her hair was greyer. The bedside table had an oak picture frame with all four of them laughing under the blooming wisteria arch in the garden. Jane sat on the easy chair next to her bed, looking at her mother affectionately. She had been their constant pillar of support, witty and fun to be with. She often told them to view life with humour and not be too intense, though Jane never mastered that particular trait. Her mother evoke the feeling of a calm and serene lake, whereas hers was a raging ocean most of the time and she needed her mother to bring it under control. Whether they shared genes or not, Jane couldn't think of anyone else as her mother.

Lissy seemed to have sensed her presence and woke up. She greeted her with a warm smile, a reminder of her uncomplicated love. Tears threatened as Jane held her tightly, cherishing the moment a little longer.

When Lissy and Jane joined the family in the kitchen, Richard sat next to Lissy, held her hand and gently relayed the news. At first, she thought he was joking, but every face she turned to, was solemn. As reality dawned, confusion clouded her eyes, and her tired body trembled with emotion. She pressed her hand to her chest, as if her heart was being ripped off by the howling thoughts... Richard held her close and waited for her spasms to subside... Jane and James came around to wrap them in an emotional embrace. Tears streaked through all their faces. Time went still in that kitchen. Silence extended its hands to wrap around their grief.

After what it felt like hours, Lissy looked up from behind the curtain of tears, at the miserable faces of her children. The grief she saw in them broke her heart once again. It was still full of love for them, as it had always been.

"You two are what we had always dreamed of... Nothing would change that for me, whether you share my genes or not; you have and will always share my soul," she reassured them, her love unwavering.

Tears flowed freely as they embraced, grief and relief mingling in their hearts. Yet, amidst their sorrow, a silent question loomed large - what next? How would they uncover the truth of their parentage, and what secrets lay buried in their past?

As questions gave birth to more questions, Lissy

struggled to recall. An infinite swathe of cobwebs seemed to have shrouded those memories. She found it hard to draw them back, certain of the monsters lurking on the other side....

She was in the small chapel, softly lit with candles, which seemed to shift right in front of her eyes; she felt her limbs freezing and her muscles pulling hard. The seat was soaked, as was her clothing. It seemed dangerously familiar, but it was not supposed to be so this time. She was nearly at the finish line; she needed to cross it anyhow, she must not quit... Not now.... She was sobbing all the while she shouted for help.... She saw the outline of a white habit rushing towards her; or was it an angel? She wasn't sure. Then she fell...

6. Hope

Kent, UK: 26 years ago

Lissy had endured six miscarriages in the past decade, each one a crushing blow. As she neared forty, hope dwindled, replaced by resignation. Adoption seemed the only viable path forward, but for an interracial couple like themselves, that journey too was fraught with obstacles and the waiting list remained long and far. Repeated disappointments strained their marriage, eroding the once vibrant love between Lissy and Richard.

The dinner table now bore witness to silence, broken only by the clink of cutlery. Arguments erupted over trivial matters, leaving behind a heavy stillness that neither of them could bridge. Lissy found solace in food. As she looked at her reflection, draped in baggy clothes, she thought about her once colourful wardrobe, now gathering dust in the closet. She couldn't remember the last time she felt alive or even remotely happy. Food was her only comfort, the only thing that didn't let her down. Richard had buried himself in work, seeking refuge in the familiar embrace of spreadsheets and business meetings.

Then, a beacon of hope emerged in the form of an early morning call from Sr. Frances, Lissy's aunt, a devoted nun in India.

"Lissy, it's been too long," Sr. Frances said, her voice a soft balm over the phone. "And perhaps… you could try adopting a child from here. It might be easier…"

Lissy remembered her first visit to the convent, the warmth of Sr. Frances' embrace… Sr. Frances had been her rock since childhood, the one constant in her tumultuous life. Her father, a military man riddled with trauma, depression, and spiralling alcoholism, had left the fourteen-year-old in the care of his older sister. Sr. Frances had nurtured her through adolescence, supported her through school and college, and building a career. When Lissy met Richard in England and fell in love against all the odds, it was Sr. Frances who offered her blessing, her unwavering support a testament to their enduring bond. She was reaching out again with a rekindling light.

She applied for an extended leave from work; the renewed hope brought her cheerful self, back from the brink. To their great relief, Lissy and Richard had managed to rescue their marriage during that period.

Their reunion in Kerala, was a bittersweet affair. Amidst the lush greenery and idyllic surroundings, Lissy and Sr. Frances reminisced about the old days, about her long-lost grandparents, about the times when Lissy was happy by her mother's side, when her father was respectable, sober, and present in her life. In these borrowed times, Lissy relived her younger self through her aunt's memories, through which she found the revered connection to their shared roots.

As they flipped through the pages of the old family album, memories flooded back. Her mother, so content with baby Lissy. She picked up another photo of her father in an army uniform standing in front of a snowy mountain. He was very handsome and determined. Looking at that face, she wouldn't have guessed such a man could have left his only daughter and sunk to the bottomless pit of drinks and oblivion. She couldn't even remember his face now. Sorrow and loss filled her heart, all over again.

"Count your blessings," Sr. Frances counselled, her voice tinged with the wisdom of age and experience. She made Lissy register for the adoption process and verification, introducing her to the charismatic Dr. Mathew at the mission hospital to add a recommendation to her adoption papers. Lissy was impressed by the young and extremely efficient doctor.

In the next few weeks, her aunt's condition worsened. Lissy left everything else to attend to her aunt and make her remaining days as comfortable as possible. When the older woman felt better, Lissy wheeled her to the chapel, where they both found solace and peace in silent companionship and in the presence of God.

Amidst all this, Lissy had forgotten about herself. She hadn't noticed the swelling on her feet or the roundness of her belly. She had given up on the scales a long time ago, too preoccupied with her aunt's deteriorating condition to notice the weight gain. Her period hadn't been regular for years.

During one of her hospital visits for her aunt, Dr. Mathew's professional eye detected the change in her. She underwent scanning on his insistence, revealing that she was pregnant and had been for nearly six months. This time her womb had succeeded beyond any of its earlier trials. Maybe her body was free from the weight of expectations to produce an outcome, far beyond all her hopes and dreams put together.

Richard was exhilarated at the news when she called. "Truly?" he kept asking, as if not daring enough to hope. Sr. Frances seemed to have energised from the happiness radiating from her niece in the months that followed. She helped her niece relax, meditate, and look forward. But the reprieve was short-lived, like a flame burning brightest before it goes out. She died peacefully, three days before Christmas.

After the funeral, Lissy sat alone in the chapel, tears falling freely down her cheeks, the loss of her rock and the last of her family finally registering. It was late into the night, the darkness outside thickened, bringing with it a chill that seeped into her bones. Her body was too tense, her stomach felt constricted. She felt the wetness before she saw the pool down the bench and on the stone floor. It was early, too early, she thought frantically, shouting for help, barely registering it herself. Panic began to settle in as she realised, she couldn't feel her babies anymore. There was a sound of running steps before she lost consciousness.

7. A leap of faith

Lissy sobbed quietly in the comfort of her kitchen, memories flooding her mind. Richard's arm was wrapped tightly around her, offering silent support. Jane and James listened intently, absorbing every word. These were details they had never heard before; Lissy had locked away the painful memories, hiding the key even from herself.

"You went to your aunt all those years ago hoping to adopt?" James asked, a hint of comfort in his voice.

"Yes, that phone call saved our lives in more ways than one," Richard said firmly.

"You made it to the hospital in time?" Jane asked, bringing the conversation back to the original thread.

"I had an emergency delivery at the Maria Mission Hospital. When I woke up, Dr. Mathew was there, holding the cot with both of you wrapped in blankets, sleeping peacefully." A loving smile returned to Lissy's face, momentarily dispelling the shadows of sorrow.

"I arrived the next morning," Richard added. "She was holding you both, one in each arm, beaming. It's still the happiest moment of my life."

"Mum, the only time span we don't know about is from when you were taken to the hospital until you woke up that night. Was there anything unusual?" Jane pressed gently.

"Dr. Mathew looked unusually dishevelled and tired," Lissy recalled. "The nurse later told me he'd had a rough day with back-to-back emergencies after being called back from his holiday."

She paused, lost in thought.

"When he handed me the babies, I thought I saw tears in his eyes. Maybe I imagined it; I was tearful myself with happiness. He brushed his fingers tenderly on your cheeks and asked me to promise to keep you safe. I thought it was because he knew my struggle to be a mother. I didn't think anything was odd. I was overjoyed to have two healthy, beautiful children, answers to all our prayers. He was relieved to find me happy and said as much. He apologised for having to leave to take another patient to the medical college hospital for urgent care. He looked sad and worried, like he wanted to say more, but he was then called away by the ambulance driver. The nurse though stayed with me all night."

The room fell silent, the unspoken realisation hanging heavy in the air: Dr. Mathew might hold the key to further answers. Jane began searching for the Maria Mission Hospital on her laptop, but no Dr. Mathew Joseph was listed.

"It's unlikely he's still there," Richard remarked. "He was highly accomplished even then; he must have moved on."

"Do you have any family or friends we could contact?" James asked.

"My aunt, Sister Frances, was my last family link. I've lost touch with old friends over the years. There's no one else," Lissy replied.

"Can we just let it rest until we know more? You two are our children, no matter what we find out," Richard said, his voice steady.

"That night, I thought I had lost our children. What if that was true? What if there was a swap without the knowledge of their birth parents? Just like us? What if they had to go through the unimaginable pain instead of us? Or what if our children survived? How do we know how their lives are now? What if they're in dire need of help?" Lissy whispered, her voice trembling.

The questions churned in their minds like a relentless roller coaster. Numerous what-ifs made the ride more precarious. The only way to stop the ride was to find the answers.

Jane knew they needed to find the truth to return to normal life. Lissy and Richard deserved to know what had happened to their children. The uncertainty was tormenting her mother, evident in Lissy's tired face. Jane and James needed to find their roots, to settle their identities. The weight of it all descended heavily on her.

"Mum, you need to take it easy until you complete your treatment. I have some time before I start my job; I could plan a trip to find more information," Jane suggested, liking the idea of having a plan.

"I'll go with you, Jane. I need a break from work. We were planning a trip next year; why not now? I'll arrange it with the hospital," James said.

Jane's gaze locked onto his determined expression; a silent vow evident in his eyes: he wouldn't abandon her in this quest. They had always made a formidable team, but now faced the daunting task of unravelling a truth shrouded in mystery for 25 years, amidst strangers in a distant land. Their destination remained unknown, a labyrinth thousands of miles away. The prospect of navigating this emotional maze had weighed heavily on Jane. She felt a sudden relief knowing James would be with her, no matter what...

Therese Pal

8. To the unknown

James took time to set things in order, getting his leave approved and arranging the travel details. Jane meanwhile gathered as much background information as possible. Lissy struggled to recall names of other doctors or nurses from her consultations, remembering only the bubbly duty nurse, Sister Tina Mary, whom she hadn't seen after the delivery. Attempts to contact the convent revealed that her aunt's successor and the two senior nuns had passed away, and others had moved on to different states.

James reached out to colleagues to search the Indian medical register but found no current record of Dr. Mathew Joseph. Jane called the Kalpetta Hospital, where a sympathetic receptionist initially promised to check but later became abrupt, repeating that they had no current information on Dr. Mathew and the patient information couldn't be shared without authorisation. Jane sensed caution in the receptionist's apologetic voice, as if she was being careful not to go beyond the script. She couldn't shake the ominous feeling that something was amiss. Her meticulous nature usually involved careful planning, but for this important quest, there was hardly any information available to her.

Lissy got a similar response from the government office when she tried to check the birth and death registers from 25 years ago, this time with no apology but a quick dismissal. Anticipating further red tape, Lissy drafted and signed letters of authorisation. She knew the kind of bureaucracy in those office corridors, which Jane and James couldn't even imagine, having grown up in altogether different setup.

The night before their departure, Lissy went up to Jane's room and found her sorting clothes.

"I think it's sensible to carry some Indian clothes, so I can blend in?" Jane asked.

"Sure, but only until you speak," Lissy laughed. She had

made it a point to teach both her children Malayalam, but they spoke it with a strong accent.

"I've been watching movies and catching up on local news to improve," Jane replied in the local dialect.

Lissy was impressed.

"I shouldn't let James speak at all! His accent is even more pronounced since he started dating Olivia," Jane joked.

"You are fabricating tales!" James said, frowning at the open suitcases. His were neatly packed and already in the hall downstairs. He didn't like leaving things to the last minute, a constant argument with his sister.

"What did Olivia say about your trip?" Jane asked, trying to divert his attention from her rumpled skirt in the stack she forgot to iron!

"She wished to come but the short notice made it impossible. Her research is currently in critical stage." James' voice reflected the loneliness he felt. It was the first time he was going to be away and far from her and that too for a considerable time.

"So, you're serious about her?" Lissy asked, noticing his miserable face.

"Oh, he's head over heels, if that counts as serious!" Jane teased.

"Nothing of the sort, Mum. It's early days," James said quickly, hiding his brightened face. Lissy decided not to pursue the subject further.

"Listen, be careful out there. Something might have gone wrong that night. I knew Dr. Mathew, so did my aunt. If he was involved, something dreadful must have happened. Remember, India is still conservative about families and relationships. Be discreet on your enquiries," Lissy warned.

"I doubt there's any need for concern, Mum. It's been decades; any dangers must have cleared by now, even if there were any to start with." James beamed at her with his typical belief in the goodness all around.

"Not necessarily. If it was done on purpose, family matters can go on for generations," Lissy cautioned.

"That's true anywhere. Most wars in history were originated on family honours or wronged relations. But don't worry, Mum, we'll be discreet," Jane promised.

"Knowing is half the battle. That's the only reason I'm letting you go," Lissy said, her voice heavy with concern.

As the day approached of their departure, a sombre mood settled in the house, matching the weather outside. Lissy and Richard lay awake, trying to drown their worried thoughts. Lissy felt as though frost had crept inside her, nesting in her heart. A sense of foreboding filled her. Was she sending her children into danger? It had been so long since she had been to her homeland; things could have changed. They wouldn't know much about the land or the people. The last thing Dr. Mathew said to her was to keep her babies safe; did he foresee any peril, or was it just a figure of speech?

9. Onboard

In the morning, Richard drove Jane and James to London Gatwick Airport. They were set to take an Emirates flight to Dubai and then transferring to a flight to Kochi, Kerala. Richard had insisted on getting them business class tickets for their first-ever trip to the land of their birth, a place now intertwined with more connections than they had ever imagined.

"We should have taken you both for a trip a long time ago", Richard said, his voice tinged with regret "The least I can do now is help you have a comfortable journey. Try to have some fun while you're there. Kerala is beautiful, especially at this time of year" he continued, attempting to mask his worry.

Richard's hands gripped her a little too tightly. Jane noticed the furrow in his brow. She knew he was not happy to let them go on their own on this voyage into the unknown. Beneath all his unwavering support, Richard harboured concerns about the complexities his children would face. 'May the land of mystic lead you, soothing your senses. May the spiritual essence of the country grant you the composure you need.' His said a silent prayer as they said their goodbyes.

Jane and James checked in at the desk, breezed through the 'by invitation only' gates, and completed security checks in no time. They had few hours before their flight and found two comfy chairs in the lounge. The hot food counter looked inviting, especially to James, who immediately opted for chicken tikka masala and rice.

"From now on, I could get used to having curry every day!" he said happily, his eyes lighting up at the sight of the fragrant dish.

"For that exact reason, I'm having a Cornish pasty. I doubt I'll see that again any time soon," Jane remarked, helping herself to a big portion of fries too.

After lunch, Jane pulled out her notes on possible lines of inquiry. They didn't have much to go on yet and had agreed that their first stop would be the hospital to check the birth records and track down Dr. Mathew Joseph.

"We need to verify the birth register too, in case there are other births recorded on the same day," James suggested, prioritising finding the real Banks' to ease their parents' worries.

"There must be staff at the hospital who know Dr. Mathew's whereabouts, don't you think?" Jane said, trying to sound more hopeful than she felt.

"Let's hope so. Mum mentioned there were other emergencies that night. Someone must remember, if they're still around," James replied, reassuring her.

They boarded the plane shortly after. James took the window seat, leaving Jane across the aisle. A cheerful steward offered them drinks, and soon they were airborne, leaving the gloomy London skies behind.

"I'm going to catch up on some sleep. It's been a busy week," James said, reclining his seat and slipping under a blanket.

"Alright, I've got a few things to read," Jane replied, settling into her seat with her footrest up. She had picked up some books on Kerala as part of her research. The state's history piqued her academic interest, particularly its unique political, literary, and health movements.

'The state of Kerala is situated in the southern peninsula of the Indian subcontinent, a narrow strip of land guarded by an almost unbroken wall of the Western Ghats. The mountains rise to 8,000 feet above sea level on the eastern side, with the Arabian Sea on the west. The 360-mile-long coastal land is believed to have risen from the Arabian Sea, possibly due to geological events in ancient times. However, according to local legend, it emerged from the sea when the valiant *sage Parasurama, the sixth Avatar of Vishnu, threw his axe from the northern mountain of Gokarna up to Kanyakumari. Over 40 rivers originate from the mountains, most flowing west towards the sea, making the plains very fertile. Long monsoons keep the region lush and green all year round. The steep Western Ghat highlands are full of thick forests, creating a natural fortress for the state, resulting in a distinct individuality in culture, history, and politics. On the other hand, it has been constantly influenced by the rest of the world through its ports and long-established sea routes from the Mediterranean and European countries.....'*

"Ma'am, would you like some tea or coffee or a snack?" A courteous steward interrupted Jane's reading. She realised she was hungry, having declined lunch earlier. She accepted a cup of tea and a sandwich. James was still fast asleep. The flight map showed they were flying over Iraq. She looked out of the window; it was dark outside with no lights in sight. She peered into the darkness, willing it to reveal the secrets it held to its chest and lighten the sorrow she had carried for so long.

Suddenly, there was commotion in the cabin behind. The crew hurried down the aisle with a medical supply box. A steward who had served Jane earlier approached her.

"Ma'am, your title said Dr. Banks in the passenger list. Are you a doctor? We have a medical emergency on board."

"Oh no, my doctorate in Physics is no use there... my brother, he's the real deal," Jane said, gently tapping on James.

He awoke quickly, still disoriented. "What happened? Which patient?" He rubbed his eyes, clearly thinking he was at the hospital. It took a moment for him to realise where he was.

"I'm sorry, doctor, but a young woman cut her hand on a broken baby food bottle. We've cleaned it up, but the bleeding won't stop. Could you please take a look?"

"Sure, just a minute." James put his seat back up, washed his face with cold water, thoroughly cleaned his hands, and went with the steward to the back of the plane.

A young woman, pale and terrified, was holding a baby in one arm while a crew member held her other hand over her head, pressing it with a thick cotton swab soaked with blood. The cabin pressure was causing the excessive bleeding.

James approached calmly, asked the steward to take the baby so the woman could relax, and examined the cut on her palm for any residual glass fragments. He applied a thick absorbent gauze over the cut and then a pressure bandage to secure it.

"This should stop the bleeding. We'll keep an eye on it, but don't worry," he said reassuringly.

By the time he returned to his seat, the injured mother had been upgraded to the empty seat next to Jane. She winced with every movement of her injured hand. Jane offered to hold the baby, who was soon laughing and pulling her shiny earrings.

"Thank you so much for your help. My name is Anita Raj. I teach in a school in London. My dad took ill suddenly, so we took the trip on our own. He's a retired doctor from Kozhikode Medical College. He would be glad to know another doctor came to my aid. He would say it was karma!" Anita said gratefully.

Upon landing, medical staff boarded the plane, alerted by the Captain, to attend to Anita. Before being whisked away, Anita thanked Jane and James once again and gave them her parents' address and phone number, reminding to call upon, if they ever came to town.

The night was cool in Dubai. Jane and James went through security again to reach the connecting flight gates and lounge. It was well past midnight, but the airport was alive with passengers, either hurrying to their flights or wandering through shops. They found a quiet corner in the lounge with lie-flat sofa beds and settled in to catch some sleep for a few hours. James, accustomed to catching sleep whenever possible, was soon out.

Jane woke up after a short nap, unable to fall back asleep in the unfamiliar surroundings. She envied James, who was still comfortably asleep, hugging his leather backpack like an extra pillow. Early morning light painted the skylines, casting a soft glow through the windows. Their flight to Kochi was in a couple of hours. Jane got a cup of tea and resumed her reading.

An elderly man sat alone in the next bay; his side table cluttered with books. Jane smiled, reminded of her own desk. He looked over seventy, dressed in khaki trousers and a sleeveless sweater over a t-shirt. His hair was white, his face lined, and his big-framed glasses magnified his tired eyes.

"I see you're reading Professor Sreedhara Menon. A good reference on the history of Kerala. It's unusual to see young people with a history book nowadays," he said with a warm smile. "I am Gopal Sreenivasan. I was a history professor myself, retired after a long service at Maharajas College."

Jane shook his hand and introduced herself and James, who had just woken up. James mumbled a sleepy hello and went to freshen up. He returned with a cup of coffee and a plate of croissants from the food counter.

"We're visiting the country of our birth for the first time, so I wanted to learn more about it," Jane explained. "Are you traveling alone?"

"My only son lives in the US. It's easier for me to travel than for him to visit, with his work and family commitments. I'm free now, having retired. My wife passed away a couple of years ago, and now my books keep me company."

'Sure enough', thought Jane. He seemed to be travelling with his library.

"Have you got family in Kerala?" He asked,

Jane glanced briefly at James.

"Our mum is from Wayanad. Her parents were originally from Kodungallur, but we don't have family there anymore, as far as we know. Do you know the place?"

"Yes, Wayanad is beautiful, right on the hillside. Many Christians migrated north from southern Kerala after the second world war. The widespread belief is that St. Thomas, one of Jesus' apostles, came to Kerala in AD 52 and started the Christian Church. He's believed to have landed in Kodungallur, your mother's place. Kerala had an established sea route from the Mediterranean, and records show Aramaic-speaking Jews settled there at the time. Some modern historians think early Christians came from Persia in the fourth century with another Thomas, Thomas of Cana. Either way, when Europeans reached Kerala in the 15th century, starting with the Portuguese explorer Vasco De Gama, followed by the Dutch, French, and British, they were astonished to find an established Christian church perfectly amalgamated with the local culture. All Indian heritage but with distinct Christian names and traditions evolved in the two millennia!

Kerala has a rich heritage in literature, politics, and economic growth, with diverse cultures and religions. The drive for total literacy, achieved in 1991, is a famous case study. Kerala also has one of the most robust public health systems in the country. The state has deep literary roots, with many poets and writers, which expanded through theatre and cinema," he continued as if he was back in his old history class.

Jane nodded, absorbing the information.

"Statistics are one thing, but you'll make your own observations during your visit," the professor smiled, surprised to find them still receptive to his long lecture.

"How is the state doing now?" James asked.

"There's a rise in crime, political nastiness, and corruption. Growing intolerance is also a concern. A mountain range or forest can no longer isolate a land from external influences, with the world at your fingertips," the professor sighed.

He gave them his contact details in case they needed help. Jane and James thanked him, appreciating the openness and willingness to help. Little did they know how much they would come to rely on perfect strangers to get to the bottom of their quest—and to stay alive...

— Part 1 End —

Part 2

"You can't connect the dots looking forward; you can only connect them looking backwards. So you have to trust that the dots will somehow connect in your future" - Steve Jobs

10. God's Own Country

The connecting flight to Kochi was uneventful. James caught up on his sister's research, finding her summary particularly useful. He read through the marked pages of the books she recommended. Years of speed-reading journals and research papers came in handy for him to quickly grasp the information.

The first glimpse of the land was magnificent. It lay sleeping between the foggy Western Ghats and the Arabian Sea. The blue sea softly merged with the lush green land, dotted with red-tiled buildings. The white sandy coastline stretched long and straight, giving way to several backwater inlets that formed tiny islands. The long, winding river reflected the bright sky and tree lines, following them all the way to the airport. Everything looked serene and peaceful like in a masterpiece of oil painting. The twins' faces glistened with mixed emotions—the strong pull of their birthplace and the mysteries shadowing its enchanting silhouette. Jane's heart skipped a beat at the sight, a mix of nostalgia and anxiety.

The ultra-modern airport was unexpected. Gleaming white tiles reflected the numerous ceiling lights, and traditional art adorned the expansive walls. James and Jane collected their luggage and stepped out into a bright and warm day. They took a taxi from the airport to the railway station. The hustle and bustle of the city enveloped them. The roads were busy and noisy with midday traffic. Horns blared intermittently, as if holding their own conversations. Brightly painted buses sped past each other, leaving barely an inch between them. Students from the nearby college walked in groups, chatting with carefree ease and full of laughter. Men sat on benches around outdoor tables in front of small tea-shops, sipping hot, frothy milk tea from tall glasses, and engaging in heated political debates.

James asked the driver to look out for a suitable place for lunch along the way. After a few miles, the car stopped in front of a traditional-looking restaurant with a tree-covered courtyard in a quieter area. The restaurant's walls were decorated with replicas of famous paintings from Kerala. They found a table beneath a painting depicting a very pretty woman in a sari, looking wistfully at a swan perched on top of a marble plinth.

"This is one of Raja Ravi Varma's works, 'The Swan and Damayanti,'" James said with an air of authenticity as he took the seat.

Jane looked at him with admiration. "I didn't know you were into art history of Kerala!"

"Oh, don't sweat. I just read the small print," he grinned to her groan.

Their traditional meal arrived, a large plate of brown rice surrounded by numerous bowls of vegetables and curries.

"Mum used to make some of these for Onam festival," Jane noted, a touch of nostalgia in her voice.

"But she never made these many dishes!" James was enthusiastic, always a fan of Indian cuisine. By the end, he was thoroughly satisfied.

"There's traffic building up; we must hurry," the driver said, rushing them into the car and they crawled through the long queuing traffic.

Jane glanced at her watch, worry creeping in. "We might miss our train."

"There's a smaller station nearby; You won't miss the train."

"That's perfect, thank you," Jane said, relieved.

At the station, the train was already pulling in. Porters helped with their luggage, and James barely had time to pay them before the train began to move.

A porter shouted something to the ticket inspector, two compartments behind them, a peevish grin spread on his face. A portly man with a thick gold chain and numerous rings on his fingers, his belly straining against his uniform soon appeared at their seat.

"Tickets, please," he demanded.

Jane handed over their booking.

"Your ticket is from the next stop. You're traveling without a ticket from here," he stated, eyes gleaming with opportunism.

"We had to divert here due to traffic," Jane explained. "Can we get an extension now?"

"No, you should have bought it at the station. You'll have to pay a fine for traveling without a ticket and for boarding the first-class compartment without a reservation," he growled and quoted an exorbitant sum.

"That's more than the full fare we paid! And it is just 15 minutes to the next stop!" Jane protested.

"Or, for half the amount as a gift, I could delay the inspection for fifteen minutes," he suggested, eyes glinting with greed.

Jane's face hardened. "Write the fine and give me a receipt," she snapped, writing down his name from the tag on his uniform.

The inspector's demeanour shifted. "I was just trying to help," he muttered, hastily writing a lower amount, and retreating.

James shook his head in amusement. "The professor mentioned the good and the bad. It was bound to happen at some time!"

He pointed out the basic human tendencies towards

easy gain if circumstances allowed it without any repercussions to themselves. It depended on the other spectrum of people who chose to avoid raising issues to make the problem go away, the ones who simply accepted the idea of bribe as a way of life, having seen it all their life.

"Corruption spreads like cancer," Jane fumed. "How can they not see that it will make their lives harder day by day until it ultimately kills the society's progress?"

The rest of the journey was more pleasant. Their compartment, separated by thick curtains, housed four sleeping berths. The other berths were empty, and in-house pantry services offered lunch and tea.

The passing stations were a world of their own with hurrying passengers, porters, and hawkers. In every station, there were small tea stalls with a constant supply of tea and coffee along with various hot snacks. A selection of cool drinks and sweets of assorted colours and shapes decorated the tiny glass windows, partially obscured by accumulating dust. At most stations, hawkers with their various menageries in baskets got onto the train to trade local specialties, made quick sales, and jumped off when the train started moving.

The hotel had arranged the taxi to pick them up from the railway station. Thankfully, the driver was right there on the platform when they arrived.

"I'm Gopi, your Sarathi for the duration of your stay at the hotel. I am as seasoned as these Western Ghats," he introduced himself with a grin, helping them with their luggage.

Gopi looked formidable with a muscular body and a rough voice. His large face was characterised by the thick joined-up eyebrows and a matching moustache. But his eyes lit up when he smiled. It was difficult to guess his age.

"Sarathi?" James asked, clueless.

"It means charioteer, from old times. Lord Krishna was

Arjuna's charioteer in the battle of Kurukshetra, which made all the difference!" He grinned at James.

"From the Mahabharatha? India's very own epic?" he added, seeing James's bewildered look.

Jane laughed, knowing James's limited reading preferences.

"You might have better luck with Sushruta Samhita," she teased.

"Oh, that I've read for sure. Sushruta is considered the father of surgery. One of my professors had recommended it after an interesting lesson on ancient medicine..." James said, laughing.

Gopi loaded their bags into a newish Tata Sumo car. Its panels gleamed in the evening sun. The seats and floor were spotless.

"You keep your car well!" observed James.

"My wife complains I love my car more than her. But I spend most of my time in this car; we make true companions!"

He navigated the car effortlessly through the busy traffic. Few seemed to care for lanes, overtaking dangerously close to oncoming vehicles. Gopi, untroubled, anticipated these erratic behaviours as the norm and maintained a smooth pace.

"You're fond of books," Jane struck up a conversation.

"Most people here are. I have a degree in English Literature, but jobs are scarce. So, I started this specialist tourist taxi business," Gopi explained.

"How come there aren't enough jobs for such an educated population?"

"Too many reasons. The landscape and politics don't favour industry. Small farm owners stopped active farming due to labour shortages and high costs. Farming isn't profitable anymore. Governments change every five years, it reduced corruption but long-term plans are shunned for short-term policies of the vote-bank. The education system hasn't evolved to promote business culture or entrepreneurship. Most young people leave for better opportunities," His voice held a tinge of disappointment.

"Let me know if you want to go sightseeing. Wayanad is beautiful with lots to see. Ooty and Kodaikanal are also close by," he added.

Jane noticed the sudden change of subject but did not mention it. He seemed more pragmatic than to idly reminisce about things he couldn't change.

Once out of the city, lush green hills and plantations came into view. Neat houses in unique designs dotted the farmlands. Darkness had fallen by the time they reached the hotel. James arranged for dinner to be sent to their rooms, aiming for an early night. They were both tired from the long travel.

James showered, unpacked, and neatly arranged his things in the cupboard before going to the adjacent room. Jane was on the phone, her case open on the floor, clothes scattered on the bed.

"It's Mum, if you want to speak!" Jane pretended not to see his annoyed look at the mess.

It was still afternoon back home. Lissy was relieved to hear they had arrived safely.

"Take care and stay safe," concern etched in her voice as she said good night.

11. A rocky start

James woke up early to a warm, pleasant morning in Wayanad. The sky resembled a wide palette filled with a thousand soft reddish hues, spread beyond the tall coconut treetops. His first task was reading an email from Olivia. It included contact numbers for her Bangalore colleagues and conveyed her longing and regret for not being with him. He sent a quick reply, promising to call later, knowing it was too early for her time zone. She must be snug under the duvet, fast asleep now. He imagined her sweet sleeping face, framed by the golden strands of her hair, a faint smile possibly lingering on her lips from a dream. He sighed deeply and went to take a cold shower.

Jane joined him for breakfast in the restaurant downstairs. Gopi was ready with the car at the front door to take them to their first stop, Maria Mission Hospital.

The receptionist, a young woman barely over twenty, shuttled busily between the constantly ringing phone and the long queue, which was already growing even at this early hour.

When their turn came, Jane stepped forward. "My name is Jane Banks. I have a pending inquiry about one of your former staff members, Dr. Mathew Joseph. We need to access some old records."

"So, you are THE Jane Banks... I recognized your voice. My name is Ancy. Sorry I wasn't more helpful over the phone earlier," she said apologetically. "I can send you to the hospital manager, Father John, who can help you. Please sign this register. Do you have an ID card?"

Jane produced her driving license and signed the register. The receptionist asked a security guard to escort them to the manager's office. They walked through long corridors, smelling of disinfectants typical of hospitals. Long benches in front of the out-patient rooms were occupied by people, their faces cloaked in varied shades of worry. After several turns and stairs, they finally reached the room labelled 'Hospital Manager – Fr. John Kottayil'.

The security guard knocked on the door.

"Come in…" A soft voice called out.

The room was minimally furnished with a high-back chair and a wooden desk. An old computer, a phone, and a thick stack of files took up most of the desk space. There was a large filing cabinet on one side. The only luxury the room boasted was a wide window with views of the magnificent hills beyond. Father John looked to be in his 60s, his head and beard of white hair contrasted against his dark, wrinkled skin. His gaze was alert and intent. He shook their hands warmly and invited them to sit.

"Our receptionist told me you were requesting details about Dr. Mathew Joseph. I understand you called multiple times from abroad. May I ask why you are seeking him?"

He was straight forward with no preamble. Father John invited confidence and forthrightness. Jane and James exchanged a look, deciding to return it. They needed his help.

"Father John, we were both born in this hospital 25 years ago," Jane started.

James watched the priest intently. His face lit up with a genuine smile.

"Dr. Mathew Joseph was our mother's gynaecologist and attended her delivery. Recently, we discovered that our parents are not our biological parents. We are seeking the doctor to understand if he knew something our parents did not. He was the one who handed us to our mother when she woke up after the delivery."

Father John's expression turned to astonishment. He assessed them silently.

"We confirmed the DNA results. We must have been swapped at birth; we can't see any other possibility. Our parents had taken us to England soon after our birth."

"That wasn't the introduction I expected…," Father John said after a pause. He sounded sad. "When I heard someone was inquiring about Dr. Mathew after all these years, I hoped for new information on the whole tragic case… I understand this isn't the news you hoped for. Dr. Mathew Joseph died in an accident 25 years ago."

The twins were shocked. They hadn't expected to close in on their search for Dr. Mathew so quickly, but death was not a scenario they had considered. They saw a chasm open right in front of them, leaving their quest on the other end, farther and unreachable.

"25 years?! What date exactly?" Jane recovered first.

"He died on Christmas Eve. His car collided with another on the treacherous mountain pass in the early morning and crashed down the cliff, causing both drivers' deaths."

"Christmas Eve?!!!! That's the day we were born!" the twins exclaimed together, disbelief colouring their voices.

Silence hung in the room, absorbing the oddity of the events that had just unfolded.

"Why were you hoping for more information from us?" Jane frowned.

"There was a police case at the time. The other driver who died was the nephew of a police officer suspended over a complaint from a local youth—a college student brutally assaulted in police custody. Dr. Mathew insisted on registering the formal complaint with senior officials. He was horrified by the student's injuries when admitted to this hospital by his distraught mother."

"But the case was closed. An eyewitness said it was Mathew's car that crashed into the other, not the other way around. He had attended back-to-back emergencies that day and was uncharacteristically agitated and tired. The police closed the case, recording accidental death."

"But you had your doubts?!" James insisted.

"Dr. Mathew was one of the most competent doctors

I've seen. He had attended countless emergencies, sometimes did 24-hour shifts but remained alert and attentive to his patients. That day, he started his holiday and returned to help with a couple of emergencies, nothing he couldn't handle."

Father John sighed, looking through the window at the tree lines, bright with sunshine, still and silent, no breeze in the air.

"I was only an assistant to the hospital manager then, so I don't know all the details. But most of the hospital staff felt the police were eager to prove the doctor was fatigued and caused the accident. They summoned all hospital records and questioned staff about workload and duty patterns. It seemed they wanted to close the case quickly, perhaps to protect one of their own from further investigation."

"Now, if what you say is true, it adds an angle no one knew. I can't fathom how such a thing could happen."

"Our mother said Dr. Mathew handed us to her and asked her to keep us safe. He ensured a nurse stayed with her all night as he left to attend another patient. Could there have been any other births that night?"

Father John was thoughtful. He picked up a couple of files from his desk, yellowed with age and tied securely with a string.

"I asked the hospital's archival room to retrieve these files when Ancy first mentioned your calls. Forgive me, I asked her not to give any information over the phone unless the details were verified. After all, it was a police case."

One file contained the hospital birth records from that year. Father John looked up the date and found the records.

The first entry for December 24th was theirs. 'Twin birth, male and female, @ 00:15 AM, Mother Mrs. Lissy Banks'

That was the only entry for that day. Another entry was for December 23rd. 'Single Birth, Male @ 07:00 PM, Mother

Zubeida Suleiman'.

The twins looked up at him enquiringly.

He shook his head. "I know that family. They've been local residents for generations. The entry is of Samir, the grandson of Suleiman who runs Kalpetta Café. It's unlikely there's any link. There are no other entries in our records."

"Is there any staff from that time still working here?" James asked.

"25 years is a long time; staff move on to better or bigger hospitals. Our head nurse, Sr. Girija is the only one who stayed that long here."

He called the nurses' office and asked for her.

Sister Girija walked in after a few minutes. Slightly overweight, her hair pulled back tightly into a bun, and wearing a crisp white coat, her steps were purposeful and quick.

Father John offered her a seat and introduced the visitors, mentioning they were born in the hospital on Christmas Eve 25 years ago—the night Dr. Mathew died.

Her face lit up; the severe look disappeared in that single smile.

"What a surprise! I was with you and your mother all night. You two were so tiny, and now look at you!" A maternal look crossed her face.

"You remember our mother?" Jane said in disbelief.

"Oh, I remember your father too. He was the first Englishman I ever spoke to! He rushed to the ward, looking for his wife, short of breath and worried, but still had a bouquet of flowers. He came straight from the airport, only knowing about your mother being in the hospital when he reached the convent where she was staying."

James and Jane felt a connection to her, knowing she was there on their first day of life. It brought hope. She might unravel the events of that night.

They explained what they found out about their parentage and possible swap.

Sr. Girija looked concerned, vouching it couldn't be true.

Was there anything unusual that night? She couldn't tell; it was a long time ago. She struggled to trace the events of that night.

She was in the operating room earlier with Dr. Hema, attending an accident case—an older man with a severe head injury. His jeep hit a tree and overturned. Delirious, he couldn't remember his name but called for his daughter repeatedly. No one else was found in the vehicle. They performed an emergency operation to stabilize him and referred him to the medical college hospital.

Dr. Mathew called her for assistance in the maternity ward to look after a new mother and her babies. Glad for the quieter environment after the rushed, traumatic evening, she found the exhausted but happy mother cuddling her babies. They all seemed fine. But Dr. Mathew had insisted she stay alert with them all night and not leave their side at all, no matter what. It seemed odd for him to worry about post-delivery care; he usually trusted the nurses' instincts and duty of care. Later that night, Lissy had told her how she still couldn't believe she was finally a mother after a long wait and repeated disappointments. She expressed how happy she was to hold the tiny babies, especially after such a scare the previous night. Then she understood—Dr. Mathew wanted to spare the new mother from any more worries, and she thought nothing more of it.

"That morning, we learned Dr. Mathew had died. The hospital didn't tell your mother to avoid distressing her. She was told he was on holiday."

"Who assisted Dr. Mathew during the delivery?" James asked.

"Sr. Tina, his regular assistant. They were a great team, and good friends."

"I don't know where she is now...," Sr. Girija added. "She left the hospital shortly after his death, deeply affected. She didn't keep touch with anyone."

There was call for Sr. Girija from the hospital floor, she gave the twins a tight hug before taking leave and hurrying down to her office.

"Two road accidents on the same day, isn't that uncommon here?" Jane asked.

"Not really. The mountain terrain is treacherous for road users. The roads are busy nevertheless, they connect three states and tourist spots. So, we see a lot of vehicle traffic and unfortunately accidents too," Father John explained.

"Where is Dr. Mathew's family now? Sr. Tina might be in touch with them," James suggested.

"He left behind a wife and young son. Mrs. Mercy Mathew remarried and settled in Ooty, a hill station about 100 miles from here. Their son was six years old then."

Fr. John gave them Mrs. Mathew's address. The twins thanked him and left their contact information, asking him to inform them if he uncovered any new details.

12. Puzzle pieces

The sun was blazing hot when James and Jane stepped out of the hospital. The queue had grown longer, and the receptionist was barely visible over the crowd. They walked quickly to the shade of an ancient Mango tree in the corner of the ground, away from everybody.

Their discovery so far was a big setback. All roads seemed to be heading nowhere, with the doctor dead, no hospital records of any unusual admissions or births, and no one knew where nurse Tina was. Their only lead was 100 miles away—perhaps Dr. Mathew's family could help them find her.

"I know Fr. John said there was no link to Samir, but I think we should make a stopover before heading to Ooty," James suggested.

Jane thought for a second and agreed. They walked over to the car, where Gopi had parked it in the shade. It was cool inside. He was reading another book.

"You know Kalpetta Café?" James asked Gopi.

"Ah... you heard about the Kalpetta special already? They make the world's best Malabar Parotta and Beef curry. Many tourists take a detour just to devour them. Do you want to take an early lunch now?"

"Yeah, we will take your word for it. An early lunch is right on the cards," James replied, his spirit lifted.

Kalpetta Café was half a mile away from the town. A narrow red dirt road along the green manicured tea plantation took them to a courtyard bordered with a shoe flower hedge. A traditional single-storied building with red tiles and a long, circular veranda stood on the vast ground, lined with honeysuckles and roses. The restaurant's name, 'Kalpetta Café,' was artfully printed along with a logo of green and red coffee berries on a twig on a wooden board. A wide wooden arch covered in vines and flowers offered a warm welcome to the guests.

Gopi parked the car and got out. He called out to the man sitting behind a counter, inspecting a logbook.

"Suleimanikka, you have visitors from England. Looks like your Parotta and beef curry was mentioned by the BBC!"

"Ha-ha! CNN reached out only yesterday for an interview," Suleiman returned the humour. He spoke with the peculiar Mappila dialect influenced by Arabic.

He came out to greet them with a wide grin on his face. He was very thin, with a receding hairline and a long angular face. His big, irregular teeth, misaligned in a haphazard fashion, gave him a comical look. His smile was genuine, and his general mannerism was very engaging and open.

James shook his hand and said, "We just learned, we are also birthday buddies of your grandson Samir. My sister and I were born here in the Maria Mission hospital on the same night as Samir. Fr. John just told us."

Suleiman's grin widened. He invited them inside and took them to his special booth next to the rear veranda. An old jasmine plant was artistically trained around a pergola, providing a fragrant canopy. It reminded them of their mother's garden back home, with its wisterias and climbing roses.

There was a good-sized vegetable garden to the side. A big, two-storied house with arched windows and balconies stood partially hidden behind a high-walled garden a short distance away.

"That is my house, and it is my daughter Zubeida who planned all these gardens. Samir runs the kitchen. He is great. I wanted him to do his higher studies, but he said he just wants to stay here and run the café with me," Suleiman said proudly.

He called out to Samir. Despite his small frame, his voice carried a long way. A young man came up to their booth. At once, the twins could see what Fr. John meant by no links—

he was a younger copy of his grandfather with the same long angular face and big teeth. His teeth were aligned though, likely from braces when he was younger. He was terribly shy around them; the only conversation he seemed confident in was about food.

Samir glanced at the front door and excused himself, mumbling about attending to regular customers and lunch deliveries as more people streamed into the restaurant for lunch. But Suleiman stayed back to chat, clearly fascinated by England.

James took the opportunity to inquire about Dr. Mathew.

"If it weren't for Dr. Mathew, both my daughter and grandson would have been long dead!"

"How come?" Jane leaned forward with keen interest.

"Zubeida spent her entire pregnancy in tears over a thug... her useless ex-husband!" Suleiman spat out the words. "She was back with us in four months after the marriage. He divorced her while she was pregnant with his baby! Just because I refused to write the house I gifted to my daughter in his name! I would rather have my daughter home safe than with such a jerk, mind you! Who knows what else he would have wanted next!

My wife—she is no more now, bless her—was so adamant about a home birth for Zubeida, just like she had and her mother before her. Stupid woman wouldn't listen. Even after hours of Zubeida being in labour, exhausted and screaming. I couldn't bear it. I broke in and took her to the hospital. Dr. Mathew was called in from his holiday to attend to her. After the delivery, he said we were just lucky—it would have been very tragic if we had waited any longer; the baby was breech. Immediately after, he was called in for another emergency. It must have been your mother as I heard nurses later talking about the foreign family with twin babies."

"You saw him later that night?"

"When my daughter had settled in the room for the night, I went out to get supplies for her. There was an accident case with a man bleeding all over, who was brought into the hospital right then. I saw Dr. Mathew coming out of the delivery room and rushing to him. The man was grabbing the doctor's hand in panic. He was begging him to save someone. I thought he was talking about himself, but Dr. Mathew handed him to the emergency duty doctor and left quickly. I saw his car tearing down the road while I was waiting at the medical shop. There was no streetlight, so I wasn't sure if it was really him or not. In the morning, we heard he died in a crash. I still don't know if I had seen him driving to his death that night!" He looked crestfallen and dejected.

"What time was it? Do you remember?" Jane asked.

"I was hurrying; the medical shop was about to close when I reached. That store is owned by my neighbour—they always close it by 10:30 at night."

"Dr. Mathew was at the hospital at least until after midnight. We know that from our birth record. Our mum had spoken to him too. Obviously, you did not see him on his way to death," James consoled.

Suleiman returned a sad smile.

"Has anything come of the police investigation?" Jane asked.

"All locals thought that was a farce of an investigation. The other car was driven by the nephew of the former Police Sub Inspector Raman Poduval. Do you know the story? He had been suspended from service based on Dr. Mathew's testimony on a police custody injury case just a few weeks earlier. They took the word of an eyewitness, Vareeth Kappan, that it was the doctor who crashed into the other car in the front. Apparently, he was right there at the site, returning late from the 'Krishna Leela' play to witness the accident! He said the hospital ambulance was close in the hairpin bends ahead and he tried to get help but failed to get their attention as it sped away. For all its worth, it was super fishy. This Kappan was a known crook and was already in trouble with the police for illegal liquor trading. How would anyone know he wasn't a false witness to win a favour from them!" Suleiman was sceptical.

"Did you know the doctor's family?" James asked.

"That woman, his wife, was nothing like Dr. Mathew. I had heard all the rumours... she married him only for his brilliance as a doctor, thinking he was going to be rich and famous. But she did not like the good doctor's dedication to his patients, his long busy hours, or his refusal to start private practice as she wanted. I once heard her saying to her friend—here in this very cafe—that she married the wrong man, and he did not care for her!" Dislike lined Suleiman's last words.

"She married a rich hotelier in Ooty within a year after her husband's death. His 'Lakeview' resorts probably had higher stakes than a poor honest doctor! She now lives in a big manor house next to the resort!"

"What about his son?" Jane asked.

"Oh... Joey... He is a fine man." Warmth returned to Suleiman's face. "He turned out to be just like his father after all. Well-spoken and a handsome young man. His mother had sent him to an international boarding school. I made it a point to visit him at school now and then, the only way I could return the gratitude for his father's kindness to my family. He still comes and sees me here if he travels this way."

"You have his number?" asked Jane.

Suleiman called a Bangalore number. It went unanswered. "I don't have his new mobile number. He could be at his mother's house; he mentioned visiting her."

The steaming Parotta and curry were delivered to them. Seeing James's delighted face, Suleiman grinned again and left them to enjoy their lunch.

"Oh, it's everything I hoped for, and more!" relished James.

"I should have asked them to go a tad low on the heat in mine!" Jane dabbed her watery eyes and nose.

Over lunch, they pored over the latest information they had so far. The accident victim Suleiman had mentioned corroborated what Sr. Girija had said earlier. But why would Dr. Mathew come out to meet him when he was supposed to be in the delivery room with their mother? An accident case didn't qualify for his area of expertise. Was it really him, driving out immediately after? What had transpired between 10:30 PM and 00:15 AM, their birth time as per the hospital records? No one seemed to have given much attention to the delirious man's lament before; but what if there was a daughter indeed? Nobody, including the police, thought the earlier accident was anyway linked to the doctor's death apart from the fact that he was accompanying him to the medical college when the accident happened.

They could not find any other obvious connection.

Jane had ordered a dessert to cool down—a bowl of sweet payasam made of lentils, rich and creamy with chopped coconuts and cashew nuts. It felt heavenly after the hot curry.

The restaurant was full by the time they finished lunch. Jane smiled at a happy young couple who were eagerly taking the seat in the booth next to them, as soon as the earlier occupant finished his lunch, nodding curtly on his way out, clearly irritated by their rush.

James asked for the bill, but Suleiman would not hear of them paying for the food. "You are connected to me in this universe from the time you were born!" he declared with much drama. "So, you are forever welcome to my home."

They said their goodbyes with a companionable feeling. James surreptitiously dropped the cash in the charity box at the counter.

Gopi was talking to someone on the phone. They walked to the pretty garden away from the crowd.

"Sr. Girija had said the accident victim was referred to the medical college hospital. Someone must have gone with him from the hospital if he was in critical condition," James said with hope.

He pulled out his phone and dialled the hospital number and got transferred to the head nurse. James asked about the hospital transfer.

He could sense Girija was trying to remember the day.

"I was to go with him, but I suffer from bad motion sickness, especially on those winding roads. Tina volunteered to go with the patient in the ambulance. We swapped duties, and I went to your mother's aid. Dr. Mathew said he would also go with them to the medical college hospital, to spare an extra staff during the hectic holiday period. But he chose to follow the ambulance in his own car. He was planning to travel on from the city the next day for his delayed holiday."

"The ambulance driver passed away, not too long after that," she answered his question about who else could be traced from the journey.

"Dead end again!" Jane said when he came off the phone. "Sr. Tina remains the only one who holds the key! And no trace of her!"

They had promised to call their parents as soon as they had anything. Lissy picked the phone up on the first ring and put them on speaker. They could hear her calling out Richard. Lissy was speechless on hearing about the doctor's death. She felt uneasy; something did not quite fit, but she couldn't say what. Richard thought something was very fishy about the many deaths on that very day.

That's when it clicked for Lissy. "But Dr. Mathew had said he was accompanying his patient to the medical college, and she was critical. He was a gynaecologist! There must have been another patient who wasn't in the hospital records! Where did she go after? Could she be the one the injured man was lamenting about? What if she was in labour?"

"The accident victim—who was he?" Richard asked.

"Sr. Girija said he couldn't remember his own name to enter into the hospital admission records," Jane replied, her excitement building. "But Fr. John mentioned that the police had all the records from that day. They might know who he was. There was his jeep, right? That could have been traced!"

"Yes, it's possible," James said, cautious. "But I'm not sure we should make an official record of our hunches about that night, especially since the case involved police mishandling. All accounts so far paint Dr. Mathew as an impeccable person. There's not enough evidence to reopen the case."

Lissy nodded, her thoughts troubled. She didn't want to drag Dr. Mathew's name into another investigation, especially after learning he died that very night, after helping her.

"That's okay," Jane said confidently, a plan forming in her mind. "We don't need to tell the police about the swap or any link to Dr. Mathew now. All we need to do is find out the identity of the accident victim."

13. Missing person

The local police station was a new building in a big compound with high walls. A blue and red board announced it as 'Janamaithri Police Station.' An old Neem tree with twisted branches and dried broken bark stood in the corner, contrasting sharply with the new structure.

Gopi was puzzled when they had asked him to take them to the police station. That wasn't the normal tourist route he had seen with any of his passengers. So was the hospital visit in the morning. They told him they were looking for some long-lost family relations during their visit, a sort of family tree search.

"What does 'Janamaithri' mean?" James asked Gopi.

"It means community relation. It's an initiative by the police department to increase community collaboration and trust. Traditionally, our police were feared by the public who avoided reaching out if they could manage. There was a common belief that decent people shouldn't get entangled in police affairs unless something awful had happened!" Gopi explained, his voice a blend of curiosity and caution.

"So, have the views changed now?" Jane enquired.

"You will see," he said noncommittally and opted to stay put in his car.

The small reception room in the front was sparse, with a wooden desk and a few straight-back chairs. A big hall could be seen behind it, with several narrow desks cluttered with files and papers. The chairs were pulled out and empty. They could hear the hubbub and laughter from a closed room on the near side of the hall, most enjoying their lunch break.

A solitary young constable staffed the reception desk. His name tag read PC Ranjith. The young man looked up questioningly when they entered, his eyes darting nervously between Jane and James.

Jane stepped forward confidently, extending her hand.

"I'm Jane, and this is my brother James. We're here about a missing family member."

PC Ranjith hesitated, clearly not used to such direct interactions, especially with women. The young man hesitated a moment before shaking her hand. He pulled out a missing person report form and began taking their details. Jane provided the hotel address and phone number.

"Okay, who is it you are looking for? Need identifications and details including their last known locations. And a photo?"

Jane handed over an old photo of a man in an army uniform, standing in front of a snowy mountain.

"It is our grandfather, Abraham Varghese. He is a retired army officer. Our mother is his only child. His sister was a nun in the Kalpetta convent. When she passed away, our mother tried to reach him, but he was out of station. Nothing was heard about him afterward. His last known location was Bombay."

"This photo looks old. For how long he has been missing?"

"Twenty-five years," her voice did not falter.

"Twenty-five years?! That is a long time! I am not sure what we can do," he shook his head, his scepticism palpable.

"I know. You see, we were born here in the Kalpetta hospital 25 years ago, on the day of our great aunt's funeral, just before Christmas. We learned from the hospital today that there was a man with a severe head injury who got admitted that night. We think it could have been our grandfather. He might have received the message about his sister's death after all and was probably coming here for the funeral. We just want to know if it was our grandfather and what happened to him. You might have someone still working here who would know the details?" Jane's voice was calm but insistent.

James adopted a pleading expression, bolstering Jane's narrative. He couldn't help but admire her knack for crafting such a convincing story on the fly. If he didn't know the truth, he might have believed it himself. Their real grandfather had abandoned his teenage daughter at the convent fifty years ago, leaving her in the care of his sister. His whereabouts had been unknown ever since, and his heavy drinking most likely to have led to an early demise.

"I don't think anyone would have such a long memory!" the constable said again, shaking his head vigorously.

He got up and went into the lunchroom. There were several people in uniform sitting on red plastic chairs around a long folding table, enjoying loud banter and lunch from take-away boxes with the distinct 'Kalpetta Café' logos. He returned with an older man, whose remaining hair on the sides of his bald head was all grey. His big moustache and eyebrows matched in colour. He gave them an assessing look, but his overall demeanour was kind.

"Our young Ranjith here says you are after a history lesson! I agree with him, 25 years is a long time. But let me hear what it is all about before I say, 'No idea!'" He waved off the young constable who happily rejoined the lunch.

"I am the 'soon to be retired' head constable Ravi Nair and I am as old as the Neem tree outside." He shook their hands with a grin and nodded to Gopi through the doors. Gopi acknowledged him with a wave; they obviously knew each other.

Jane repeated her request.

"There are so many accident cases over the years. I will have to see if the archived records can be pulled into the computer to have a look. But it will take time and need approvals," Ravi said, scratching his head.

Jane was not one to concede easily. "Sir, the day we are talking about was the day before Christmas 25 years ago. We heard there was another accident later that night, resulting in the death of a well-known doctor from the local hospital and another man. We heard there was an enquiry of some sort due to the tragic double death, we were hoping someone might remember the day."

Recognition dawned on the older man's face this time.

"Oh, that one," he sighed. "That night was one of the most tragic and the deadliest. I was the first to reach the bottom of the cliff to find the wreckage of those cars and the broken bodies of the unfortunate two. That scene I will not forget for as long as I live. It was a sheer drop of hundred feet into the boulders and bushes. They had no chance."

"Was it an accident?" James asked cautiously.

"It could only have been a murder-suicide if not an accident. We did not find any reason for them to kill themselves or each other. The doctor was a gifted gynaecologist and well known. The other, Mohan Poduval, was an actor in the play organized by the very doctor for their arts club annual function. I know there were rumours of foul play as he was the nephew of a suspended officer, but nothing wrong was found in our investigation."

"Do you remember the other accident that night?" Jane asked, leaning forward.

"Yeah, I said it was the deadliest night, didn't I? A jeep collided head-on with a tree, and the driver was seriously injured. He was transferred to the city medical college hospital, but he died a week later."

Their hopes took a sudden dive again. It felt like a curse; every crucial person they needed to find had died soon after their birth. Strange!

Ravi saw their faces and felt remorse for his blunt delivery. "I am sorry for being insensitive, but there is no proof it was your grandfather. I don't remember the details off-hand, but I will check it up for you."

Before he could add anything, another officer with a grim face, rushed to them and asked Ravi to report to the Sub-inspector's office at once. Ravi excused himself and got up instantly.

Jane could see him turning into an office at the far end of the long hall. A short, thin, sour-looking man in plain clothes was talking agitatedly to a heavily built officer who stood behind a huge desk, looking stern and surly. They both turned to look up to the reception as if they felt her gaze on them. Jane's attention was immediately on the man in plain clothes. There was something unsettlingly familiar about him. His thin face and piercing eyes sent a chill down her spine. He held her gaze for a second and then slammed the door shut. She saw the nameplate on the door, which read - 'Sub Inspector Sridharan Poduval!'

14. Police story

"Is the last name Poduval quite common here?" Jane asked Gopi with urgency.

They were back in the car, heading to the hotel. Jane's mind was racing. After head-constable Ravi left to respond to his boss's summons, a grim officer had dismissed them unceremoniously. His promise to follow up on their inquiry seemed rehearsed. He clearly wanted them gone.

But the name 'Poduval' had driven out everything else from Jane's mind. The coincidence was too glaring—Mohan Poduval, who died with Dr. Mathew, was the nephew of a dismissed inspector known for his grudge against Dr. Mathew. Twenty-five years later, another Poduval was in the same station!

"The name itself isn't common, but that family has deep ties to this town," Gopi explained. "The new sub-inspector, Sridharan, indeed is the son of the disgraced inspector and the cousin of Mohan Poduval. His father didn't handle the fall from grace well. He turned to drinking and became abusive. Sridharan who was only a teenager that time, outcast along with his father, vowed to restore his family's honour and became ruthlessly determined. He's a lonely soul, with no close friends in town or at work, but he isn't unjust either."

"What's just about sending us packing?" Jane fumed. "There was a plain-clothed man with him— sharp, mean, foxy looking. I've seen him before!"

"I couldn't see the office from where I sat. Maybe another police officer?" James suggested.

"I know head constable Ravi Nair. He is my neighbour. I could check," Gopi offered.

"Probably not immediately. Ravi seemed in trouble already, although I don't know why!" Jane said, frowning as she tried to recall the fox face, but the memory was fading.

They discussed their next move. The only lead left was

Dr. Mathew's family. Jane tried Joey's number again, to no avail. They weren't sure if Dr. Mathew's wife would welcome anyone dredging up old wounds, but they decided to take the chance. James called Lakeview International and booked rooms. Gopi happily agreed to drive them—finally his usual tourist route. He dropped them at the hotel to pack and went home to get his own overnight bag.

Jane felt uneasy. She insisted they pack everything without letting anyone know their travel plans. James thought she was being overly cautious but went along, not wanting to argue. He packed in ten minutes, his neatly folded clothes and belongings back in his suitcase. He smirked as Jane emptied her stuffed suitcase onto the bed and began repacking to make space for scattered items.

Seizing the moment, he called Olivia. She was glad to hear his voice, and their conversation flowed easily. He updated her on their plans.

"It sounds dangerous, with deaths and a police case. Can't you get a professional to help?" Olivia worried.

"Don't worry, darling. It's perfectly safe here. We're just searching for a missing person, that's all. I promise," he soothed.

James understood her concerns. Olivia, having seldom travelled outside Europe, found the police and systems of a distant country foreign. They were foreign to him too, despite his mixed heritage. But they were just pursuing a long cold case. Nothing more.

If James had known about the dangerous cogwheels churning in the background, he would have heeded the women's instincts more carefully.

15. Shakuni

The unexpected call jolted Shakuni into action.

Shakuni wasn't his real name, but everyone who knew him thought the name was fitting. Just like the crafty and devious character from the epic Mahabharata, Shakuni prided himself on his ability to weave complex schemes. The original Shakuni had poisoned the minds of his nephews, the Kauravas, inciting a feud with their cousins, the Pandavas. This conflict, driven by perceived injustice, culminated in the great war of Kurukshetra.

Shakuni himself relished his nickname. It spoke to his impeccable planning skills and foresight, allowing him to orchestrate events from the shadows. In his mind, he was a kingmaker, eliminating opposition with surgical precision before they even saw it coming. His actions were justified; like the Kauravas, he had been wronged and he was merely restoring balance.

He paced in his cluttered office, reflecting on the events of 25 years ago. He had believed the problem resolved, tied up neatly with a bow. The convenient way it had all ended seemed almost divinely ordained. Since then, he had built his new world brick by brick, becoming the rightful heir to fortunes he believed were his all along. He couldn't afford to lose it now.

What had he missed? He knew the old man had been in Kalpetta the day Poduval was killed. He had laughed when he heard of the old man's death, never linking it to the accident involving the doctor and Poduval. He believed Poduval was simply avenging his uncle. The police thought so too, covering it up quickly. Poduval was hot-headed, often acting without considering consequences. But had he been aiming to kill two birds with one stone that day?

Where did these kids come from? Why were they searching for the old man and a dead gynaecologist? Did

Poduval know something was amiss? Was that why he ended up dead?

Shakuni knew he had to stop this investigation before it gained momentum. Then, he could look under the carpet for any missing puzzle pieces and clean up as necessary.

An unpleasant thought belched up in his mind, un-called—of the skeletons in his own closet. Were the ghosts of his past biding their time, waiting to avenge their deaths? As they had with others before, one by one? Was his number finally up after all these years? Some sort of delayed justice? A shiver ran down his spine.

16. Destiny's guide

Gopi was keen to navigate the forest road before night-fall. He accelerated, the car cutting through the empty road flanked by dense forest, teeming with wildlife. Wild elephants and tigers roamed these ancient woods that spanned three Indian states, a sanctuary where nature still held dominion despite the winding roads that bisected it.

Gopi regaled Jane and James with tales of lone bull elephants in musth—an aggressive state driven by heightened testosterone—chasing vehicles, sometimes causing serious injuries and even death. His stories, rich with the wild unpredictability of nature, added a thrilling undercurrent to their journey. Fortunately, their drive was uneventful. They got sight of elephants on a couple of occasions, but safely away in the forest, peacefully munching on vegetations. Deer's and birds made their appearance all the way through. Once a pretty peacock came up displaying its resplendent feathers, much to their delight. The drive was enjoyable for the wide-eyed visitors and Gopi was the perfect guide pointing out locations interspersed with interesting bits of information.

As they ascended the narrow mountain road, the drive became a dizzying series of sharp turns. They were gaining altitude very quickly. Jane, feeling queasy, clung to a sickness bag. After what felt like hours, Gopi announced that the by-road to their hotel was just around the corner. The car pulled off at a viewing point just off the main road. Jane, desperate for fresh air, scrambled out and vomited. Once she felt steadier, she rinsed her face with cool water and took a few sips. It made her feel better. She walked to the viewpoint; the cool breeze gently caressed her tired face and swayed her hair. An amazing view of the valley greeted her, spreading out far below; the horizon had turned to gold in the twilight, and mirrored in the lake below with tall pine trees framing the landscape.

"That's the loveliest view I've ever captured," a deep voice remarked.

Jane turned to see a handsome man perched on a boulder, dressed all in black- a leather jacket over a roll neck t-shirt over black jeans, and boots. His thick, shoulder-length hair and smouldering stubble complemented his striking features. A DSLR camera on a tripod was pointed at the valley, a backpack open beside him, with an assortment of lenses.

"Was that view during or after I threw up?" Jane retorted; eyebrows raised.

"Definitely after," he laughed heartily, descending the hill.

James fetched his medicine bag and came to check on Jane. She declined the tablets, feeling better in the cool air.

"Hello there. I am Joey Kuriyan, Thank you for a masterpiece," the newcomer announced smiling.

"Are you a photographer?" James asked, eyeing the equipment.

"More like paparazzi," Jane quipped, noticing a powerful black motorbike parked nearby.

"You must be a celebrity, then?" he replied coolly. "But no, just a hobby. This is my favourite sunset spot. You just happened to barge into my frame."

He showed them the picture—it was the silhouette of Jane; her flowing hair framing her face, her head tipped a little, a bottle of water raised in her hand, in front of the breath-taking view of the valley under the golden sky. It was a beautiful shot.

"What do you mean by your favourite viewpoint?" Jane, intrigued by his talent, asked.

"My parents' home is just around the corner. This is the best place to watch the sunset," he said, gesturing towards a manor house down the road.

Jane frowned, "You live there?"

"No, my parents do. But I grew up here and went to a

boarding school in Kodaikanal," he explained. "I now live in Bangalore, managing the IT division of an American bank."

Astonishment spread across Jane's face, and she glanced at James. He hadn't made the connection - she realised seeing his pleasant but blank face. Had their luck finally turned a corner?

She quickly recovered and introduced herself. She registered his eyes widen a fraction on hearing her subject of study as Astrophysics. He shook her hand firmly, without taking his gaze off her eyes. She felt the assured confidence in his grip, an inviting acceptance in his manner.

"And here is my brother, a real doctor this time—Dr. James," she continued. She thought she saw a hopeful smile for a fleeting second on Joey's face as he shook hands with James. He surely had a pleasant face to match his name.

"Is your father the late Dr. Mathew Joseph?" Jane asked, no longer able to suppress the question burning in her mind.

Joey looked taken aback. "Now you sound like a stalking paparazzi! How do you know my father?"

It was James's turn to look overwhelmed and speechless, while Joey's gaze darted between them.

"We've come from Wayanad. Fr. John at the Mission hospital mentioned you and your father, as did Suleiman from Kalpetta Café," Jane explained.

"My father died many years ago! Why mention him now? Or me?"

"Well, we possibly share some history," James said. "Your father was our mother's gynaecologist. We came here hoping to find one of his old friends, Sr. Tina, a nurse who worked with him."

Joey's frown remained. "You came all this way to find a hospital staff member after so many years... but why?"

Jane noticed the sharp intelligence in his eyes, the way he quickly saw through their cover story. If they needed his help, they might have to reveal what they knew. How he would react was uncertain, and the possibility made her stomach tighten. They had only hunches, which could easily be seen as accusations of professional mishandling or worse, a crime. So far, everyone who knew the doctor, including their mother, had reacted with disbelief.

Would Joey help them unravel these mysteries, or would he walk away? She wouldn't blame him if he did—it was about his father, after all, a father he had lost as a child. Joey might not have any details, having been very young when his father died. But he could connect them with his mother. Their plan was rudimentary at best: show up uninvited and hope for the best. Perhaps fate had indeed brought them to Joey.

"You must be so close to have such a bond," Joey said, his voice tinged with envy as he observed the silent understanding between the siblings.

Jane smiled, noticing again his perceptiveness.

"We were born on the night your father died," she said softly, her eyes meeting his, hoping to convey the gravity of their situation.

James took a deep breath and explained their discovery about their parentage and the decision to trace their origins back to where they were born. He recounted the events they knew and how they believed the late doctor and the nurse held the keys to the truth about that Christmas Eve.

"All we've found so far are dead ends, literally! Some extraordinary fate brought you to us. We hope you can help us find some way ahead," Jane said, her gaze steady on Joey's incredulous face.

The story was indeed a lot to take in, and Jane wouldn't fault Joey if he lashed out, angry at the old wounds they were reopening. She watched him turn away from them, staring at the deep valley, which was being blanketed by the advancing darkness, his face full of untold emotion. She held a silent prayer... for his understanding; and his help....

17. Reflections

Wayanad, India: 26 years ago

"I think I could really fly if I just jump and flap my hands," insisted the little boy, waving his arms in the wind, mimicking the eagle soaring above. Deliriously happy to be atop the mountain, he took in the green valleys and the majestic forest stretching forever to one side. December brought cool, pleasant weather.

His father laughed, setting down his backpack and unpacking their picnic as usual: a flask of sweet warm milk, wrapped tea cakes, ginger biscuits, and a mix of fruits. Suleimanikka always prepared their picnic, leaving it ready to be picked up on their way.

Joey came running at the sight of the cakes, picking up the apple and setting it aside. "An apple a day keeps the doctor away..." he recited, finding the best escape route.

This brought fresh laughter from his father. "I'm a special baby doctor; an apple wouldn't dare keep me away from you, son!" He placed the fruit back on Joey's plate.

"I wish Mum could come with us too. I like the mountains. It's so nice here."

"Oh, but you know she doesn't like to wear muddy shoes like us."

"That's true," Joey agreed. "Only the mud-brave can come up here."

It was Joey's favourite time, and he always looked forward to their outdoor adventures whenever his father could find the time.

"You're so busy, Dad!" he said.

"I know... We don't have enough staff at the hospital. I can't send back the poor babies to be born elsewhere, can I?"

"No," Joey readily agreed. "I like babies. I want a baby

brother too, but Mum said I can't!" he said.

"Did she say so?" His father looked sad.

"Maybe you should get me one from the hospital. You said there are so many!"

"Maybe I will, if you can convince your Mum!" His dad tickled him until he laughed.

****

Six months later, one July evening, Joey found his father alone in his study. It was after another particularly long and bitter argument between his parents. His mother had stormed out, seeking solace with a friend, ignoring the torrential rain. His father sat in an antique chair; face hidden behind a hardcover book titled 'Annie.'

"Haven't you finished that book yet, Dad? I've seen you reading it so many times!"

Joey saw tears welling in his father's eyes. Maybe he was sorry for fighting with Mum.

"I'm re-reading it. It's a terrific book. You should read it too. Listen to this..."

He read a line from the book:

"The sun'll come out Tomorrow, so you gotta hang on till Tomorrow. Come what may. Tomorrow, Tomorrow, I love ya, Tomorrow. You're only a day away!"

"So, Mum will be okay tomorrow?"

His father nodded.

"Who's that other woman Mum was talking about? Is it Annammachi?" Joey couldn't think of anyone his dad could love enough to leave him behind.

"No, son, she didn't mean it. She was just angry."

Joey was sad. Grownups were complicated.

His mother was very pretty, resembling the film actors in the movie magazines she liked to read. His father seemed the only one unaffected by her looks.

"You know, you should call Mum Hemamalini sometimes," he said after a minute.

"Why?" His father looked surprised.

"She likes it when her friends call her that. I saw Hema-malini in Mum's magazine. She's very pretty!"

That prompted a faint smile from his father. "Real beauty is not about a pretty face. It's inside you, like your beautiful heart," he said, giving Joey a hug.

"Aunt Tina promised to bring me a comic book. Why isn't she coming to see me anymore?"

"She's busy. But I'll ask her about the book when I see her at the hospital."

"I heard Mum say, you're with her more than you're home!"

"I know. Your Mum is mad at me because I had to post-pone our holiday again. But I promise, this Christmas, we'll go together, and you'll get to see grandfather and Annam-machi too at the Old House."

"But Mum doesn't like the Old House! But I love it there! And Annammachi's special plum cake... And the beautiful, mighty Meenachil river... Oh, I can't wait for Christmas!"

****

That Christmas never came. No more mountain walks or picnics with his father to brighten his days. Time faded his memories and sorrows, but the gap left by his father never truly bridged.

He had clung to his mother, and to his surprise, she let him. They found comfort in the cocoon, with everyone around them caring for the young widow and her little son. "Gone too soon," they all said. They stuck together while she grappled with the new status quo.

But her old grievances soon resurfaced, turning into a monologue now, having lost their regular target to the moun-tains and six feet of earth.

"What a thoughtless husband he was, leaving us un-happy and poor. We could have been richer with his talent! And all the time he spent at work! How will we live now?"

"We could go and live at the Old House, with grandfather," Joey suggested hopefully, yearning to see it again and the mesmerising river beside it. Annammachi would surely make a plum cake for him if he visited.

"Ha... Old House. That's all there is! An old crumbling house with an old man and a cackling old woman in it!"

He didn't bother to mention the new mansion where Mercy's father lived. Joey would rather live alone in the forest than with the Grizzly Bear. He smiled at the thought – a secret name he had made up for his overbearing, pretentious grandfather after a particularly trying visit. Mathew had overheard him muttering it and had said he was spot on. The name stuck between the two of them. He never dared say it in front of his mother. She was temperamental; one wouldn't know if she would flip out or laugh with him like his father did.

Thankfully, Mum repeatedly refused to live with the Grizzly Bear. Maybe she felt the same as he did and would have laughed with them after all!

His mother found someone soon after who called her Hemamalini and wooed her with expensive gifts and attention. He was much older but very wealthy. Soon, they were married and moved to a handsome house in the hill station.

His stepfather, PC Kuriyan, was a practical man. He wanted a young, pretty, sociable wife with family connections, good for his profile as a businessman. His first wife had none of that. But he was clever and made his fortune in the hotel business. Their children had grown and moved out when she died after a short illness. He sought a new wife, and Mercy ticked all the boxes. He understood her well enough to keep her content.

He was fond of Joey, though not overly. Joey's brilliance and good manners impressed him. He gave him his family name and provided for him. He treated him like an adult. Joey didn't mind but felt he had lost his childhood along with his real dad.

Joey saw his Mum was busy with her new husband. She travelled with him on business trips, enjoying the new rich life she always felt she deserved. She dreamed of her son being competent, world-savvy, and polished, and sent him to an expensive boarding school. Joey saw it as abandonment, but he gradually adapted to the new life. The school wasn't bad, and he made friends easily.

Mercy stayed away from all family ties, including her own and her late husband's. Joey once heard her over phone, telling Annammachi not to bother visiting, as she would be away abroad. Joey couldn't visit them either, she repeated - he was attending a prestigious school camp all summer.

The only link to his old life was Suleimanikka's occasional visits, armed with special treats. He spread them on a blanket in the school grounds, just like his Dad did, and they reminisced about his father and their walks. Sometimes, Suleiman brought his grandson Samir. These visits kept his father's spirit alive and inspired Joey to be like him: likeable, respected, virtuous. Over time, he forgave his mother's apparent distance, thinking his father would have. "Tomorrow is only a day away..."

****

"I don't believe in fate. I believe one must make his own," Joey finally said, looking up at the twins.

"We're really sorry you lost your father," Jane said with compassion. "We don't know who our birth parents are or what happened to them. Not sure if that's better or worse."

The hidden emotions since she first spoke to Dr. Jones caught up with Jane, bringing a wave of uncertainty. What was their identity if they didn't know who gave birth to them? Were they orphans despite having a home and loving parent? Would they be okay if they went back without knowing what happened to their own children?

"Knowing is half the battle!" James said, echoing her

thoughts.

"My father used to say that!" Joey said.

Jane looked up, surprised. That phrase was her Mum's favourite too!

"What you said doesn't align with my father's character from my memories or anything I've ever heard about him. But I want to find out... Only to prove you wrong," said Joey with conviction, daring her to challenge him.

"We understand. Our Mum said the same about your father; she was incredibly grateful to him. Our assumptions are just vague thoughts... We have nothing else to go by," James said, desperation was evident in his voice.

Joey looked at him and then at Jane, conflicting emotions flashing in his dark, deep eyes, silence growing its shadows while he contemplated.

"I'll see if I can persuade Mum to see you. Where are you staying?"

"We're booked in the Lakeview Resort," Jane said, handing him her mobile number.

He left with a nod to her, jogging towards his bike. Jane thought about his parting gaze, his fathomless eyes were full of mystery!

18. The Manor House

Joey found his mother, Mercy, in her vast walk-in wardrobe.

Mercy, a glamorous woman who looked decades younger than her fifty-five years, knew how to maintain her appearance well. Her flawless skin and face were always complemented by expensive clothes specially fitted for her. She took immense pride in her appearance, more than most other things in life, and enjoyed the attention she commanded in her circles.

Mercy glanced at the glittering gown she had chosen for the evening party.

"I thought you didn't fancy going to Mrs Banerjee's party tonight," Joey asked, leaning against the doorframe.

"Oh, I have nothing else to do here. They will gossip about me behind my back if I don't go."

"That's sad, Mum. Why don't you find some real friends who could say it in front of you?"

"No such people exist, son... All tend to be jealous, especially if you are rich and pretty."

"It would be funny if you didn't mean it literally!" Joey shook his head, disappointed. It was always like this with her. She did not trust anyone. The so-called friends she chose were from the same flock, all with high social status and glamour. It all seemed vain to Joey.

"I have a couple of friends visiting from England who would love to meet you if you could stay back for dinner," Joey suggested.

Mercy was fond of anything foreign. She always pushed Joey to go and live abroad or make friends, which she considered a posh thing to do. He was counting on it to get her to talk to Jane and James.

"Really? Are they your old classmates from school? Children of that visiting professor... with blue eyes and blond hair? I was always fond of them!"

"No, Mum!" Joey rolled his eyes in exasperation. "Jane and James were born here but are visiting India for the first time."

"Ok, invite them over. I will ask to make something nice," she said, heading down to find the cook.

Joey was relieved by the quick success and called Jane to confirm. They were ecstatic and agreed at once. There was a tingle of anticipation. Joey smiled to himself as he stepped into the shower to get ready.

Dinner was grand. On Mercy's insistence, the cook had prepared a selection of sandwiches and brought in burgers and an apple crumble dessert from the resort's kitchen for the English friends, beyond their usual dinner. Mercy was disappointed by the absence of blue eyes and blond hair, but she warmed to their accented English, especially James's, which she instantly approved as proper Queen's English.

Joey had warned them of his mother's singularity towards everything foreign, so they had turned up in proper dinner jackets and a gown to play along. Mercy was forever complimenting the twins on their academic achievements and was quite impressed on learning that Jane did her PhD in physics from Cambridge.

"Joey had a fair flair in physics, but I discouraged him. It is so hard to find a career in that field in this country. Better to stick to medicine or engineering, with far more success ratio," said Mercy, with obvious conviction.

"India has two Nobel laureates in physics alone, and a successful space programme!" Jane glanced at Joey, who shrugged as if to say no big deal. She thought about the way his eyes lit up when she mentioned her field of study; so, there was that tiny connection!

"Not a great odd in a country of a billion people!" Mercy was the one who answered. "But I have forever wanted Joey to study in England. You have the best colleges in the world!

Joey eventually did his MBA at the London School of Economics, only after much persuasion from me. I assume that's how he met you two?"

The twins looked at Joey again, and he nodded assent. So, they went along with it.

"Have you got any family here?" asked Mercy, serving them the desserts.

"We were born here in Wayanad but have no family here anymore. Our mum knew Sr. Tina from the mission hospital. Do you know where she is now?" Jane asked cautiously.

Joey had asked them not to reveal their connection to his father, should it upset her.

"No," said Mercy. "I never really liked her. She was always chasing after my husband at work and then disappeared altogether when he died. She did not even come once..."

Mercy was on her fourth glass of wine by then and had started talking incessantly. Joey removed the bottle from the table surreptitiously and signalled to the servant to stop serving. Jane was the only one who noticed it, and he smiled at her apologetically. Mercy started complaining about her absent husband, who was away on business.

"If not business, he would be shut up in his farmhouse... I hardly get to see him nowadays! Just turning out like my first husband... he was crazy about his patients. This one is all about his business. Great goody-good thing, but who suffers? The abandoned wives! When Kuriyan first met me, he was head over heels, even though I was still married to Joey's father then!"

Joey's face went pale. Jane realised he did not know this particular detail before.

"You met him before Dad died?" he asked.

"Yes, don't you remember? We were all staying in his hotel for a summer holiday, and he came in to say hello to Mathew. Said he had heard a lot about the good doctor's exceptional talent and complimented him for having the most beautiful woman by his side. He even asked me to dance with him."

Mercy smiled at the distant memory.

"He was just fooling around, I knew of course. It felt good to get some admiration and wished my husband would take notice! I was much prettier then, but Mathew didn't care at all. How could he? I should have known; the saint doctor's heart was never his own but belonged to his precious Annie. But everyone only judged me!"

She finished her glass and looked around for the bottle.

"Annie?" The name ricocheted in Joey's mind, making him uneasy. "Mum, you are imagining things now. I have never heard about any of it before!"

Wine and his mum did not go well together, and he was embarrassed for her, especially in front of Jane. He should have anticipated this with the number of drinks she had!

"How could I? Your father wouldn't hear anything bad about her at all! Or her family! Mathew had grown up in his godfather's house along with his daughter, Annie. Maybe he couldn't marry her. Who knows, that would have been too uncomfortable for his godfather!"

"Dad's godfather? Who?" Joey asked, bewildered.

"Varkey John. He was the best friend and neighbour of Mathew's father in Kottayam, and they migrated to Malabar together in the fifties. Mathew had spent his childhood there. He never got bored of reminiscing the strange stories of Malabar whenever he met his father or his great aunt Annammachi. But I couldn't imagine surviving like that. Wilderness and diseases! And what is there to gain talking non-stop about that sorry life! I did try my best to avoid it and them altogether!"

Joey stared at her disbelievingly, but some clouds were clearing in his head, faint recollections peeping through from the time gone by.

"Why did he not come to meet us ever?"

"Varkey died a long time ago. Even if he hadn't, I wouldn't have wanted anything to do with him or his wretched daughter Annie. I still believe she was the one who had made my husband feel I was never good enough for him! He had said it to my face, not long before he died... He had come back from Malabar, all strange and sick, drenched in the incessant rain. He looked as if he was soaked and cold for the whole week, his bags were full of sodden, muddy clothes. He spent the week in hospital recovering from pneumonia, not talking to anyone. That week, back home from the hospital, we had a big row about your school admission. When Varkey came here asking for Mathew the very next week, I just plainly told him to get lost and to stay away from our life!"

"How could you behave that way to Dad's godfather?!" Joey was aghast.

"Varkey was behaving oddly, all tight-lipped and rigid, with overnight bags and odd things stuffed in his old jeep with a pretence of seeking some medical advice from Mathew. I had told him to find some other doctor, but he said he could only trust Mathew for his precious Annie! Blimey! You think I would be happy to bring more trouble to my own home!"

"Wasn't Dad angry?! You said they were close."

"We weren't speaking after the row. So, I did not bother telling him! Why would I? I was just a fool to even think I would find my 'happily ever after' by marrying the brilliant, promising, handsome doctor I was madly in love with, the one I fell for the moment I saw him the very first time. But I don't think he loved me back, ever!" she said bitterly.

Mercy got up abruptly and left the room. Joey stared at the empty doorway for a long while, unable to comprehend his own emotions.

"We are really sorry to have upset your mother," James apologised.

"It's not your fault. She shouldn't be drinking at all. She won't remember any of it tomorrow... Do not worry about it."

But Joey looked troubled. His mum's outburst had disturbed the pristine memory he had preserved in his heart about his father. He wasn't sure if any of it was true, or whether she was pulling off one of her melodramas she was so famous for.

"My mum dreaded keeping acquaintances with any of my father's family even when he was alive. She disliked them all with a passion. She considered them to be way below her social standard. She did not like Dad's friends either, including Tina, so there's a little chance she would have kept in touch with them."

"But what she said about Varkey ties with what we heard from the police constable Ravi and Suleimanikka earlier today. Your father was seen talking to the accident victim that evening. who died a week later. If he was your father's godfather, it makes sense that he attended to him in the middle of his work," Jane said thoughtfully.

"And if he had a daughter, that too fits with the narrative from the day," James agreed.

Joey was quiet. He was familiar with his mother's constant accusations; she did not trust anyone. He shouldn't take the latest one any more seriously than others. But why was it bothering him now?

They got up to say goodbye. Jane came over and gave Joey a hug; she felt responsible for leaving him in a gloomy mood.

Joey brightened up a little and promised to catch up with them in the morning.

19. Mirror, mirror

Mercy lay awake under the covers, staring at the ceiling. Sleep eluded her, as memories and regrets swirled in her mind. Mathew's disappointed face haunted her thoughts, a constant reminder of the past.

She first saw him on the stage at the inter-university arts festival. Drawn by his eloquent speech about social responsibility and community support, she found herself captivated by the very handsome Dr. Mathew Joseph, a post-graduate student at Kottayam Medical College. He passionately argued that humanity's survival depended on our unique capacity for compassion. She rolled her eyes at the competition's theme on the board: 'Survival of the Fittest and the Social Context.'

She waited for him to come off the stage after his speech, but he remained in the wings, cheering for the next speaker, a much younger woman—Annie Varkey. Annie articulated the necessity of women's equal status in society. The human race couldn't survive without women, she declared aloud; women have equal dreams and hopes for the world, to sustain and survive, not just men. Her speech was fiery, and Mathew was the first to congratulate her on her performance, giving her a high-five before she spiritedly returned to the audience.

Impatient, Mercy glanced at the contestant list again. Only one more speaker now, she thought with relief. When Adityan MK, a law student, was called, she seized her chance and approached Mathew.

"Hello, Dr. Mathew. My name is Mercy. I enjoyed your speech immensely. It was inspiring—you were brilliant."

Mathew smiled politely and thanked her. What a beautiful set of teeth! Mercy thought, adding it to her checklist.

"I'm an English literature student at Kottayam CMS College, very close to yours..." She flashed her most charming smile, knowing it usually worked.

But his attention was still on the girl, now listening intently to the slow, measured speech of a seemingly shy speaker narrating how education could empower society, how it could be the basis of survival for all. He was speaking about the literacy movement that could help the nation raise its base level by empowering its citizens...

To Mercy's disappointment, Mathew excused himself to join the audience. Undeterred, Mercy made it her mission to cross paths with him again, using common friends and social events to her advantage. She ensured she bumped into him at every party or function he was expected to attend.

Though she knew in her heart he didn't feel the same, Mercy persisted. She learned that Annie was Mathew's godfather's daughter, and they had grown up together in Malabar. Sensing his hidden feelings for Annie, Mercy's love turned into obsession. She reasoned that a talented doctor would need a well-educated, socially adept partner to succeed, justifying her relentless pursuit. Despite her father's insistence that she marry, as many of her friends already had, she resisted, enrolling in a master's degree course instead.

Her persistence paid off. At the post-graduation party, she watched gleefully as Annie stormed off after a rare row with Mathew. He remained, downing drinks in an uncharacteristic manner, detached and dazed. Mercy stayed with him after her friends left, seizing the moment to show him how madly she was in love. As dawn approached, doubts crept in. What if Mathew saw it as a mistake? What if he returned to Annie?

The next day, Mathew was sober but did not turn her away. He seemed comforted by her desire for him, as if her need anchored him amidst his turmoil. Mercy made him feel like the centre of her universe, expressing how long she had waited for him. As their relationship progressed, Mathew appeared to accept what fate had brought him, though Mercy sensed his lingering regrets. She ignored it, believing she could change his heart with time.

Mercy introduced him to her father, who was proud to have a genius doctor as a future son-in-law. He insisted on a quick marriage, not wanting his unwed daughter fooling around. Mathew, feeling rushed but resigned, agreed. He persuaded his father and aunt Annammachi to arrange the wedding soon, reasoning that it would be better to have company during his rural training. They married within months, Mercy's father making it a grand affair.

The honeymoon did not last long. Mercy wanted to show off her successful husband, now practicing earnestly. She wished to travel and experience the world, but her own world turned upside down when she found out she was pregnant. She cried all night, not wanting the burden of a child yet. But Mathew, a gynaecologist, refused to consider termination.

During her pregnancy, Mercy fell into depression, rejecting Mathew's suggestions for professional help. After the baby was born, things improved slightly. Mathew was a devoted father, giving her free time to restore her pre-pregnancy beauty and attend glamorous parties. However, their established routines left them spending more time apart. They looked like a perfect family but had grown distant, making Mercy question what had once obsessed her.

When Joey reached school age, a new argument arose. Mercy received an acceptance letter for Joey from a prestigious city school and wanted to move. He simply refused, not even listening to her well-thought-out plan for them, content with his rural job and its rudimentary pay.

He had been moody since his return from Malabar, that July recovering from pneumonia. Mercy, frustrated by his silence and detachment, finally confronted him.

"You're so stubborn, so inconsiderate… You never treated me right… Never loved me back as much I did. Now I know why. It's Annie, isn't it?" She yelled, throwing his book. "You're forever under her spell. Whenever you come back from your precious sweetheart, you seem convinced of your wife's worthlessness.... And you treat me like dirt!"

Mathew, touched by her accusation, screamed for the first time.

"Don't drag Annie into this! Our marriage was a joke from the beginning. Yes, you're right, I shouldn't have married you. We were never right for each other. You can leave if you want. Just leave my son behind. You can be free and live your life the way you want. This time, I won't come after you..."

His words, delivered with a finality she had never heard before, cut deep. Mercy stormed off into the rain, away from the pain and the failure that stared back at her.

20. Old tales

Joey slept restlessly, haunted by a recurring nightmare. He and his father were trapped in a car, hurtling towards a dark lake. His mother stood at a viewpoint, screaming at them. "You left me here alone... You never loved me... All these years... but judged me all the while!" Joey looked at his father, covered in blood but eerily peaceful. The car hit the water, and he felt himself drowning. The photograph he clutched to his chest floated away, the beautiful silhouette dissolving into the waves.

He jolted awake, the nightmare still fresh in his mind. The room was cloaked in darkness, but sleep eluded him. His head buzzed with fragments of yesterday's events. Long-buried memories stirred yet refused to take form. Driven by a need for something tangible to connect him to his father, Joey got out of bed and headed to the attic.

The dark space was a forgotten realm, coated in dust and cobwebs. Joey wrapped a towel around his face, trying to keep the dust at bay as he ventured in. Old furniture, toys, and picture books lay scattered about. His eyes lingered on a familiar picnic basket, memories flooding back.

There were no personal items of his father here; his mother had likely purged them. But a large cardboard box caught his eye. It was filled with Mathew's books, mostly medical texts and references, some so old they seemed like relics. It was interesting to think his Mum kept them though, maybe she thought it might come useful to him, she had long harboured a dream of her son becoming a famous doctor, to compensate his father's lack of ambition. James might find them useful, Joey thought dryly.

In the corner of the box, a collection of Malayalam classics lay hidden. He recognized the titles: books of Thoppil Bhasi - Aswamedham, Thulabharam, Ningalenne Communistakki; Indulekha by Chandu Menon, and few others.

The pages were filled with annotations and notes. There were also English books, including well-worn copies of Shakespeare. Joey remembered, his father was a fan of literature and had been the hospital's arts and literature club secretary. Joey carefully packed these into a smaller box and carried them to his room, seeking a connection to his father.

The box caught on the door handle as he entered, spilling the books and a thick layer of dust across the floor. He picked them up and noticed a small book that had instantly drawn him. Joey remembered his father sitting in the old grandfather chair, buried in this very book. The title read Annie.

Opening it gingerly, Joey found a note on the first page, written in neat, curved handwriting.

"Johny sent me this first edition from the States. He said I might like to see my name in print! I thought you might like this book for your next college play adaptation. Keep going my genius Shakespeare! And be true always... Love, Annie."

Joey stared at the note for a long time. Was it just playful banter between childhood friends, or did it mean something more? He had seen his father with this book many times. Did it hold deeper significance?

The phone interrupted his thoughts. It was his stepfather, Kuriyan. As usual, he was straight to the point.

"How do you know James and Jane Banks? I understand they're staying at our hotel. Your mum said they were over for dinner last night?"

"Yes, they're friends visiting from England."

"Do you know why the police might be interested in them?"

"The police?" Joey frowned. "Maybe it's about the missing person request they filed yesterday in Wayanad?"

"I got the impression they've irked someone high up. A normal missing person request doesn't reach the level I've heard about."

"Really? Who told you this?" Joey was puzzled.

"I can't disclose that, son. Just stay away from trouble."

"They're not trouble, Dad. They're just friends. But since you called, can you help me with something?"

"What is it?"

"You knew Mum when she was still married to my father? You knew him?"

A silence followed. When Kuriyan spoke, his voice was measured.

"Yes, I did. You stayed at my hotel for a holiday, and your father was well-known person. What's this about?"

Joey hesitated, lost in his thoughts.

"Nothing really. It just came up yesterday. She said she was unhappy then, and I wondered if she was looking for a way out."

Kuriyan paused. "You think I played a 'David and Uriah' trick and stole her?"

"No!" Joey said quickly. Perhaps too quickly.

The phone was quiet for a while, then he heard the strained voice of his stepfather.

"Listen, son. I might be a ruthless businessman, but I don't need to be that way in my personal life. I could have married anyone. After I learned of Mathew's tragic death, I proposed to your mother as she fitted the bill, that's all. She was happy to move on. There's no reason why she couldn't have been happy with your father then or now with me. But she's insecure and doesn't trust anyone for long. That make her forever spiteful, destined to drown in her own misery. There's not much you or I can do about it."

He paused, resignation evident in his voice, then added, "About your friends, I'd advise them to move on. You never know how sensitive some people can be, especially those in power."

Joey hung up, even more puzzled. He went to see if his mum was awake. She looked like she hadn't slept well either.

To his dismay, she had skipped tea and started the morning with a glass of wine. He tried to talk sense to her, but she was in one of her depressive moods.

"I don't want to talk about the past. I don't remember what I told you yesterday. Forget it—I was drunk."

Joey was silent for a while, disturbed and seeking clarity.

"Listen, Mum, I have to leave today."

She looked up in surprise. "I thought you had a couple of weeks' holidays?"

"I do, but I want to visit Grandfather and Annammachi in Kottayam. Would you like to come?"

"What for? I didn't like her even when she was younger. Now she must be ancient and crazy!"

"She's 83 and still whole. Grandfather isn't well. If not them, you could meet your father."

"I don't like him either. The most disapproving, heartless father one could have. I'm fine here, on my own."

Joey agreed with his mother about the grizzly bear, even if she refused to come with him.

Joey called Jane and James to convey what he had heard from Kuriyan. He didn't mention that Kuriyan wanted him to stay out of it. They were as surprised as Joey to hear about the ripples they might have caused. But why? Jane was cautious and said they should heed the advice and return. There wasn't much more to learn here. They could plan the next step on the way back.

On impulse, Joey asked if they would like to visit his grandfather and great-aunt Annammachi.

"They can tell you about my father and Annie if that's what you're after."

Jane and James agreed it was worth a try, they had nothing else to do here, with police or goons or both on their pursuit with no reason they could fathom. Maybe the distance and the impromptu plans are the wisest choices now. They arranged to pick him up at home. Gopi could drive them to

Kozhikode, and they could take a train if Joey was okay with that. He said it was fine—he would rather not drive the 320 KM to Kottayam.

His stepfather's advice echoed in his mind as he packed the little book with his belongings. Annie's note seemed to stare back at him, urging him to find the truth.

21. Dangerous times

Joey sat in the front seat with Gopi, while the twins took the back seat. Jane couldn't fathom why they would be in trouble with anyone, higher up or not—they hadn't uncovered anything substantial yet. Their searches had been mostly futile, save for a vague lead about a father and daughter possibly present on the day they were born. It could all be a wild goose chase.

Jane glanced at Joey's reflection in the rear-view mirror, noting a renewed determination on his handsome face. She was staring at his profile and his flowing hair, gently swaying in the wind, when she suddenly felt his sharp gaze return in the mirror, intent on her, his face fierce. She gave him a weak smile and turned away quickly to the passing mountain scenery, trying to mask the jolt she felt, as if she was on the path of a lightning.

James rummaged in his kit and handed her an anti-sickness tablet with a smug smile. She gave him a look of wounded pride but took it with a gulp of water, not wanting a repeat of yesterday's journey.

As the car reached steep slopes and sharp bends, Jane tried to ignore the growing unease in her stomach. Gopi seemed tense, glancing repeatedly in the side mirror. A bright orange truck with an ominous look, hauling a green trailer loaded with large barrels, was tailing them dangerously close. Joey looked back and froze. A giant of a man sat next to the rough-looking driver, both pointing at their car with menacing intent.

"Gopi, drive as fast as you can," He shouted. "Those crooks can't mean anything good for us."

James and Jane looked back, immediately alarmed by the truck's proximity.

Gopi accelerated, skilfully navigating the treacherous road. The truck also sped up, but their 4x4 was nimbler than the lumbering truck, allowing them to put some distance between the vehicles.

"We'll gain speed once we reach the forest road; it's a straight stretch," Gopi assured them.

But as they approached the section, his hopes were dashed by a queue of cars forming ahead. He overtook them, knowing the distance and intervening vehicles were their best defence. Joey saw other drivers hooting frantically, trying to warn them. Suddenly, they heard the unmistakable sound of an elephant's trumpet. A huge branch snapped in the cluster of trees ahead, revealing a gigantic lone elephant rumbling madly.

"What do we do?" James asked, panic in his voice.

"I find the ones in that truck more menacing than this one," Jane said grimly.

Gopi made a quick decision and raced forward. The road ahead was empty; incoming traffic had likely stopped, hearing the elephant's trumpet.

In seconds, they crossed the stretch near the raging elephant, which dropped the branch and charged at them.

"Run!" James screamed as the elephant trumpeted angrily, the sound deafening at close range.

Gopi saw the elephant gaining on them in the mirror and floored the accelerator.

Jane, always fond of wildlife, felt a raw fear unlike any other. She had always sympathised with the plight of elephants. But in that second, she saw the wild in all its fury, so close she could see the criss-cross lines on the hide. An oil-like substance secreted from its temporal glands on either side of the forehead making a downward path as if it was shedding tears... Its legs were wet and soggy. Her heartbeat raced out of control, faced with a raw fear. She felt the sheer terror and the savagery of the wild and was painfully aware of their tiny, fragile human frame against the might of a five-tonne beast.

Gopi was driving like crazy to add some distance. The elephant trumpeted again, its trunk raised menacingly, shaking its ears and tusks. But to their relief, it appeared to lose speed. Joey spotted a group of female elephants further in the woods, and the bull seemed to change its intent.

Gopi only slowed when they reached the waiting cars on the other end. Traffic had indeed stopped waiting for the danger to pass.

"That brute is still on the road. Wait until it moves off before crossing. It looked mad!" Gopi warned.

He sped up again, and no one spoke for a while, trying to steady their breaths.

"Why would they chase us in a truck?" James finally voiced the question hanging in the air.

"They were intending to kill us! But why?" Jane echoed.

Joey was silent. Of all the many trips he had taken on this route, even on his bike, he never had been on such a ride. Did Kuriyan know something more, that prompted the warning for Joey to stay away?

"Let's get off this road after the state border. I don't want to be chased by crazy trucks or mad elephants again today," Gopi said, his voice mild with relief, which brought a smile to all their faces.

He took a small side road and, after a few miles, stopped at a lonely eatery. He parked the car behind the shop, well-hidden from the road. Jane found an old-fashioned but clean toilet in a separate shed and was most relieved to find it in such a remote place.

The only menu item available was a rice meal with Sambar - a vegetable curry, but they all found it appealing.

"You're not really tourists, are you?" Gopi stated the obvious.

James looked at Jane. They owed him the truth, having put him in danger, more than once. Jane nodded.

"Gopi, we're looking for our birth parents. Hence the

detours to hospitals and the police," Jane explained.

"My father was their mother's doctor. He died the night they were born. I think something awful happened that night, not just a tragic accident as I was told all these years!" added Joey.

"Oh... did you poke a hornet 's nest too in one day!" Gopi looked concerned.

"What I don't understand is why someone's after us. We don't know anything yet, or do we?" Jane frowned. "Gopi, could you call Constable Ravi and check who was with him and Inspector Poduval? We need to know if this has anything to do with the police."

Gopi made the call and quickly disconnected, leaving everyone staring at him.

"He said he'll call back."

They waited for ten minutes before the phone rang. Gopi frowned at the unknown number as he picked it up. His face filled with trepidation as he spoke. All eyes were on him, anxious and confused.

"The call was from Head Constable Ravi. He insisted the whole conversation was strictly off-the-record. He tried to access the old files to find the injured man's identity. No files could be found in the computer. The IT desk said the Head Office requested to retrieve the archived files already, which is now marked as restricted. Only SP-Superintendent of Police-level officers have access. Inspector Poduval told Ravi to sit on it until further notice...."

"The man with him the other day was the Crime-Branch SP, Sunil Kumar. He sort-of warned me that the SP has questionable motives and powerful connections, so to watch-out."

Jane and James looked clueless; it was the first time they heard about a Crime-Branch.

"It's a specialist division in Kerala Police, investigating sensational, complicated, or undetected crimes. They have special powers and jurisdiction across the state and inter-states," Joey explained.

"What's sensational about a missing person and an accidental death enquiry?" James was sceptical.

"Unless there was a cover-up in the original verdict. If a review implicates the state police or its officers, it could become sensational," Joey said, more convinced.

"Ravi said officers were sent to your hotel last night. When they didn't find you, they traced us to Ooty. I had to fill the form at the border, and Lakeview Hotel was listed along with my phone number," Gopi added.

"My Dad might have been contacted by someone. He's a shrewd businessman with connections. Crime-Branch Cyber Cell can trace your phone number. That's likely how they found us," Joey said thoughtfully.

Gopi switched off his phone at once.

Bewilderment filled them. Extraordinary manipulations were happening behind their backs.

James called the Kalpetta Maria Mission Hospital and spoke to Father John. The police had been there too, asking about them. He told them the twins were inquiring about Dr. Mathew, their mother's old doctor, and that it was a social visit, not revealing their private conversation. James thanked him profusely and requested him to warn Sr. Girija. Father John assured him it was done.

Jane retraced their steps. Their request to the police was only about the missing person. They discussed Dr. Mathew's accident only to give context. But SP Sunil was already ordering the inspector around when they filed the report. He couldn't have known about the bogus report then.

A memory flashed before her eyes—a laughing couple, a man nodding curtly on his way out. Yes, she had seen him at Kalpetta Café. Had he overheard their conversation?

She shared her realisation with the others.

"We had talked about Suleimanikka seeing Dr. Mathew

speaking to the accident victim and driving out soon after. We wondered if the two accidents were linked and if there was a daughter at the scene. The police must have linked the two based on what we discussed at the café!"

Jane buried her face in her hands, feeling foolish. Someone higher up seemed threatened by their knowledge, enough to run them over. Really?! But why?

"What do they know? How are we even linked?" James said.

"We should move now before they catch up," Joey said urgently and asked the man behind the counter to pack some fruits, biscuits, and water. They might need rations for a dangerous wild goose chase, if it comes to that!

Gopi took them through inner roads and safely deposited them at the train station for the Express train to Kottayam, ensuring no one followed them, human or otherwise!

22. Hidden records

Joey had reserved an air-conditioned berth for them on the train. The one remaining seat in it was empty, leaving the whole cabin to themselves.

He called Annammachi from the train. She brightened up on hearing his voice and was ecstatic to learn he was on the way to her.

Next, he called Roshan, an old friend who oversaw the IT department of the state government. They had been friends since their engineering college days.

"I need information on an old police case. Can you help?" Joey asked.

"No, Joey, I don't have access to the production data. Security settings. You know the drills!"

"All I need to know is who accessed the file recently. You don't need to access the actual file, just check the logs! Please."

Roshan grunted non-committal. He got the specifics from Joey and disconnected. An hour later, he called back.

"I don't even want to know why you're interested in some high-profile case. All files recorded that week by the Kalpetta office are locked out. They were accessed from the SP office and the secretariat offices yesterday!"

Joey listened quietly, his expression turning serious.

Roshan continued with caution. "I don't know the content of the case file, but an attachment in it was labelled with the prefix KL13D2085, which is obviously a licence plate. I looked up the old RTO records for you. It belonged to a 'Varkey John', registered in Kannur district. That vehicle, a jeep, has no current record. That's all I have. And the headache to fix this security flaw of the system! By the way, if anyone asks, we only talked about our college alumni meeting this year!"

"Sure, we must meet up soon. I would like to see

Unniyarcha. Is she still in charge of it?" Joey listened and disconnected with a laugh.

When he looked at Jane and James, the laughter was replaced with a grave expression. "It is exactly what my Dad alluded to. The plot thickens. Somehow the secretariat office is interested in this case!"

"What's a secretariat office?" James queried.

"That's the state ministerial office in Thiruvananthapuram, the highest office of the government in Kerala."

"So, Constable Ravi was right! SP Sunil Kumar has connections to high offices!" Jane said.

"Roshan also traced the accident record to a Varkey John... my father's godfather Mum told us about. He was there at Wayanad on that fateful day..."

They all fell silent at the potential implication. Dr. Mathew indeed knew the accident victim—not just knew, he was family. And Annie? Was she there too? Did he leave the hospital for her? Was it the reason Dr. Mathew ended up dead that day? What really happened that night?

Dread spread across their faces. Death seemed to catch up with their destiny too after 25 years. Why else were they being followed?

The rails stretched ahead, hot in the sun. The train ran non-stop ignoring smaller stations, its loud horns doubling down its intent.

"Who is Unniyarcha? An officer?" Jane asked, curious. Determination replaced the fear in her eyes as she smiled at her companions.

"An officer?!" Joey laughed. "You could say that! She was a legendary warrior from the 16th century. She was the queen of 'Vadakkan pattu', a northern Kerala folklore describing her valour and her unparalleled skills with the Urumi—the lethal whip-like sword—in 'Kalarippayattu', Kerala's own famous martial art. In those times, rich people settled their feuds through combat, contracting Kalari warriors to fight on their behalf. These warriors, having trained all their lives, fought to the death for others."

"Really?! So not too different from the Roman Gladiators, or the English Hedge Knights if you think of it! History is not so unrelated even in seemingly distant lands. Human nature must be very much the same to act alike!" Jane exclaimed.

Joey nodded. "Our medieval history is filled with stories of 'Chaver'—the suicide squads who lived to die for a cause—to defeat the Zamorin, the ruler of the Kozhikode Kingdom. They died fighting during Mamankam, a festival organized by the Zamorins every twelve years. Those young men, some just in their teens, trained all their lives with the sole mission of reaching the Zamorin at the festival stage and killing him, hoping to soar past the thousands of sword-bearing soldiers surrounding the ruler. Never in history did anyone succeed, but they sacrificed their lives for centuries, upholding the ritual and community pride, attaining only the heroic death they knew was certain."

Joey smiled at the horrified faces in front of him.

"It was a long time ago. Now 'Kalarippayattu' exists only as an art form. We performed a play in college on the story of Unniyarcha. Megha, Roshan's wife, played the title role brilliantly. She had some training in Kalarippayattu, which was marvellous. I played her brother Aromal, and Roshan played the villain, Chandu Chekavar. In the epic, Unniyarcha rejected Chandu's advances. So, he betrayed them, causing the death of Aromal after a duel in which Chandu was Aromal's squire. A devastated Unniyarcha swore revenge, and later her son, Aromalunni, a ferocious warrior trained by his mother, fulfilled her wish and killed Chandu."

"Obviously, Roshan won over Megha to marry her in real life. We were planning a reproduction of the play for the class reunion this year, but Megha is pregnant now and out of action!"

23. Roots

Joey's grandfather's house was from a forgotten era, and it looked its age. The small house had a tiled roof and a long veranda that served as the reception, a narrow corridor leading to the small bedrooms. Coconut trees and banana plants dotted the land, gradually sloping towards the Meenachil river. The riverbanks were covered in a green canopy of bamboos and mangroves. The house seemed asleep and still, unaware of the stately mansions that had sprouted all around it with their manicured gardens and grand stature.

An old woman sat on a chair in the veranda, looking up now and then towards the long winding footpath connected to the main road. She felt disappointed every time a car went by without stopping. Her hair was white and tied in a loose bun at the back, her skin wrinkled all around her face and neck, her limbs skinny and dark, her eyes crinkled with age. She wore a plain white Chatta-Mundu—a loose V-neck cotton blouse over a long dhoti tied neatly with long flowing folded frills in the back giving it a layered skirt appearance. She had distinct large gold loops, worn on the top of the elongated earlobe.

When a taxi finally stopped and Joey alighted, Annammachi leaped up from the chair and came down the stone steps of the veranda with a new spring in her steps. Joey gave her a hug, grinning widely and trying to answer the volley of questions. Yes, mother was okay, sorry she couldn't come, work was fine, still in Bangalore and he got a couple of days with her!

Jane and James stood back and looked around. They were fascinated by the house, the land, and the view of the river. The roof tiles were blackened and covered in moss. They felt like they had travelled back to the past where life stood unchanged as if in a cocoon. They could hear the quiet and constant murmur of the water flowing effortlessly and the birds chirping. A grumpy-looking goat and its two kids stood munching the grass covering the grounds of the coconut farm. Chickens pecked the ground in no apparent hurry, taking time to peer at the visitors.

Annammachi waved at James and Jane to come close, and they were at once pelted with questions and monologues. Joey intervened. They were his friends visiting from abroad, and they could talk about it all if she only gave them a moment to breathe!

Annammachi rolled her eyes at Joey but let them all into the house. The simple white walls and the cemented floors were clean. The rooms had bare minimum furniture.

"Your grandfather is in the side room; he sleeps most of the time nowadays." She led them to a room beside the long, narrow veranda.

The room looked shabby but clean. The wooden furniture in the room was sparse and old. A tall shelf discoloured with age, and a battered armchair with long curvy arms. Joey noticed it, his father had a similar one in their Kalpetta house, they might have been part of a set.

"Are you still asleep? Joey is here finally!" Annammachi said cheerfully in a loud voice, shaking the old man awake.

He opened his eyes slowly. His movements were restricted and slow. His very thin body looked ancient and tired. His skin was all wrinkled as if a wave of ripples had passed through it leaving its marks permanently. He looked up to Joey who held his hand gently. It took a while, but the recognition brought a twinkle in his tired eyes. It was so remarkable from the rest of his appearance, Joey had an acute feeling, those eyes were a magical portal to his grandfather's old self, taking him back to the past... To the fantastic stories he had heard time and again, to the wisdom beyond his own.

Joseph patted his grandson affectionately. "I had forgotten the time... I can't remember very well. Actually, there is nothing I can do well these days!"

"Don't worry. We have a lot of time to talk. We will go freshen up and then we could talk all day long."

"Lincy...," Annammachi called out in a long tone.

A young woman came trotting to the door. She gave them a shy smile.

"Check they have everything they needed in the rooms..."

Lincy led them to the rooms at the back. There were two rooms, and the ceiling was barely high enough for James to walk around. Polished cement floors were cold to the touch. The larger room had twin beds and the smaller one with a single, all made up with clean linen.

"Bathrooms are outside," Lincy said pointing to the extension on one side. She gave them a stack of towels and hurried back, as another call rang out from the kitchen.

James placed Jane's bags in the single room and followed Joey to the twin room.

Annammachi served them all a hot breakfast, Appam—a pancake made with fermented ground rice and coconut, roasted in a deep bottom pan giving its peculiar round shape and texture—paper thin on the sides with a thick layer in the middle. It was accompanied with spiced egg curry and home-brewed coffee.

Annammachi was extremely cheerful to have someone new to talk to, which was hard to come by as they were getting older. They could see she loved to talk and made no effort to hold back on anyone's behalf. She lamented about the young people who no longer had time for old people and their old tales, treated them like the old furniture - creaky and out of fashion, taking up space.

"You will be surprised then; we are here specially for the old tales".

"Yes, Joey promised us great stories to bring us in. I am fond of history in particular!" Jane added.

"That's good then... Old tales are the only thing Joseph-

Chachan remembers nowadays. As he holds onto the past so fiercely, there is no space for anything new. He even forgets to eat if I don't remind him!" Annammachi peered at Joseph who was watching the twins with an odd expression. His breakfast stayed forgotten to prove her point.

"How did you two know our Joey?" asked Annammachi. She was so used to her brother; she was the one who often voiced what he was thinking before he made an effort himself.

"We came to see the land where we were born. Our mother wanted us to connect to the land and our roots, hence the trip. She had been in Malabar when she was young. When we met Joey, it felt as if our stories are all connected and we would get to know about ourselves through those same stories," said Jane.

Joey looked curiously at Jane. She said it all truthfully, yet not revealing anything. Did she guess what he was thinking since his mother's outburst in Ooty? He thought with some apprehension. He did not want to voice his doubts until he knew more.

"I told them a couple of your Malabar stories, and they were hooked," Joey said looking at his grandfather.

"It was a long time ago..." Joseph said slowly.

He had trouble remembering recent things, everyday things like days of the week, names of people he met recently or even to eat on time. He sometimes forgot Lincy, the kind-hearted niece who came every day to check on them and help with daily chores. But he never forgot the old tales he exchanged with Lincy's father. He loved to talk about their childhood, spent in that very neighbourhood, their momentous, adventurous travel to Malabar with his friend Varkey. That was a cherished memory he kept securely in his mind, when everything else was blurred around him. He always found those effortlessly, waiting to be called upon, like the shining polished brass mug on the table in front of him. It called him from afar, like old friends who never forgot their ways, even though a lot had happened since the time they had left to live apart, only biding time to rekindle their friendship, instantly and effortlessly. He sat back on his chair, taking a flight back, frames after frames flashing back at him willingly, of immense happiness and immeasurable heartbreaks.

— Part 2 End —

Therese Pal

Part 3

"The path from dreams to success does exist. May you have the vision to find it, the courage to get on to it, and the perseverance to follow it." - Kalpana Chawla

24. Promised Land

Kottayam, Kerala: 65 years ago

The LORD, the God of your fathers—the God of Abraham, Isaac, and Jacob—has appeared to me and said: I have surely attended to you and have seen what has been done to you in Egypt. And I have promised to bring you up out of your affliction in Egypt, into the land of the Canaanites, Hittites, Amorites, Perizzites, Hivites, and Jebusites—a land flowing with milk and honey.'

The first reading from the book of Exodus that Sunday breathed new energy into Joseph. He was excited as he repeated his dreams to his friend Varkey while they returned home from the Sunday mass. Joseph talked about moving to Malabar, a place he had heard about from friends who had migrated there. He had heard tales of vast amounts of land available at unbelievably low prices, perfect for farming. It was a virgin land with high yield, where people could become major landowners with their meagre savings. He was inspired by the legendary stories of adventure.

Anna, his sister, and Maria, Varkey's wife, walked with them. Maria wasn't convinced. Along with the rags-to-riches stories, they had heard tales of death and destruction by malaria and wild animals. Many had lost everything and returned empty-handed or broken-hearted. It was enough for her to drag her feet back.

"What do you think would have happened if Moses did

not listen to God and hadn't left for Canaan?" Joseph asked earnestly.

"He could have saved a lot of suffering! If you didn't know, Moses did not get to set foot in Canaan; he died trying!" Anna retorted. Anna, four years younger than him, often infuriated him with her quick tongue.

"You could say that... you will be happily married in a few weeks and won't have a care in the world about any of us and how we would live!" Joseph shot back.

"I told you; I don't want to get married into that pompous family. If my dear brother can get me out of the wedding somehow, then I could come to Malabar with you! You also don't have to put yourself in huge debt to arrange the wedding for me; we could buy double the land instead. Imagine the extra fortune it would bring!" she said.

Even the thought of living an independent life, away from social expectations, made her happy. It was a dream Anna had long harboured, while her friends mostly cared about marrying and settling down.

"Nice try, father set the apparent match in heaven. They are loaded so that you could have a life of a queen, even if they are a little pretentious! I would rather live with a debt and the wild boars than cross our father's path. Besides, you have the will of a tiger and an equivalent decibel level. I don't want to be in perpetual trouble!" Joseph turned to Varkey, who was now a step behind them. "What do you say?"

"About malaria and scary elephants? I totally agree with Anna, wise words!" replied Varkey with a smile.

"Come on... think of the positive side of it. The adventure we will have, the money we will make, and coming back victorious!" insisted his friend in exasperation.

Varkey did not want to think of leaving home behind or going to an unknown land, even if it wasn't a trapdoor with death lurking behind. But the economic situation was becoming increasingly difficult in the once rich and famous land of

Travancore—Thiru Kochi, in the south of India. The Second World War had far-reaching effects, even in distant lands, long after it ended. Food rationing was in place, and nothing was affordable, leaving everyone in unending misery.

Life was turning steadily harder for their families. Others often argued that being born into a highly reputed ancestral family like theirs was a privilege. But comparing the deterioration of the family to its current hopeless state made him think otherwise. Grand receptions mandated for each birth, marriage, and every other function in the family did not help. Not even death spared expenses: one was obliged to invite and feast family, friends, and the social circle to honour the dead. Daughters had been generously sent off after marriage with dowries.

Now, with the last of his sisters, Anna, to be married off, Joseph had to spend all his savings and some more, and he couldn't find any sustainable solutions in the foreseeable future.

Varkey was in better financial state, but the future troubled him equally. Varkey's great-grandfather had hundreds of acres of agricultural land. He had a big house that proclaimed the wealth and name of the family. He also inherited his status as being part of the Syrian Catholic family whose genesis supposedly dated back to the first century and was said to be privileged to become Christians from St. Thomas, the very apostle of Christ. Over time, those stories of origin had varied versions; still, its core message remained. It sang the greatness of those who had lived and gone, of the remarkable things they had done, and how imperative it was to keep the faith and traditions. It omitted those who faltered; the weaker branches went unknown, those who failed to uphold the prestigious but expensive way of life were not revered anymore. Varkey's family wealth had dwindled down over the generations, and maintaining his ancestral house was an expensive affair, which he knew he couldn't afford for much longer.

"There is no point in gloating about being good in mathematics if you don't use it in your own life!" Joseph said crossly. "You don't need a Ramanujam to calculate the mathematical progression of dwindling wealth. Our ancestors had lots of assets, but then they also had ten or twelve children to divide it into, if they survived to adulthood! It didn't take many generations to eat up the whole lot of wealth. Having as many children was considered a blessing! It wasn't a choice for our God-fearing Catholic ancestors to say no to such gifts of God nor to the man of the church who insisted it was such a good thing, although they didn't need to look after those brood of offspring!"

The logical side of Varkey's brain told him his friend was right. Maybe he needed a fresh start, away from all the family bindings and expectations. Maybe he ought to heed his friend and go see the land himself, sooner rather than later.

25. Shape of a dream

It was a scorching summer when Varkey and Joseph turned up at the temporary stage at the famous fairground—Kannur Police Maidan—looking for Rajan, their friend, and the young writer of the play. The ground was dry and dusty, having not seen a drop of water for months. But neither the heat nor the humidity stopped the big crowd who came to watch the play earlier that evening.

"We all call him Rajan Mash—that's t short for Master in these parts," said a helper boy, pointing to the young man packing costumes into a large tin trunk, his shirt dripping with sweat.

"There he is, our very own Shakespeare!" said Joseph, tapping on his back.

Rajan looked up in surprise, his face brightening on seeing the visitors.

"It's a long way from home. I can't believe you would come this far to watch my play!"

"I would vouch it's the best theatre adaptation I have seen of the illustrious book. You did justice to Thakazhi and his 'Chemmeen,'" Varkey patted Rajan with pride.

"Don't sweat even more than you are now, dear friend. We just happened to be here in Kannur, so thought why not support a struggling artist!" said Joseph, grinning.

"Ok, you deflated me enough, but why are you here?"

"We came to look up some land we were told was up for sale. What a waste of time! To think we travelled 500 kilometres to see a strip of barren land in the shape of a chilli. We can't even build a decent house on it, let alone farm!" Varkey looked disappointed.

"I am going to punch that evil Chacko. I knew he couldn't be so generous to me all of a sudden," Joseph was furious.

"You shouldn't have made fun of his choice of crop last year," said Varkey.

"But he was trying to produce wetland rice on a perpetually dry hill. I did him a favour!"

"So, you two are taking the plunge and deciding to move here then?" Rajan asked.

He did not think Varkey would leave his home and the history behind and move to a place where no one knew him.

"Not for this joke of a land surely, but if I could find my dream place, I might," Varkey said non-committedly.

Rajan thought for a moment.

"I have recently been to one of those old houses as part of my research on the traditions and history of the feudal farm system in Northern Kerala for a new play. The famous Korothu Mana is a historic and prominent family in these parts. They have been property owners for centuries. Not to mention, it is the family home of comrade VD, although he got disowned by them for his socialist movement and ideas!

But they are indeed afraid of the movement and believe the land reform bill would soon become a reality and they would lose their land. They are looking for buyers although they wouldn't advertise it to keep their pride and not appear weak or panicked!"

"Really?" Varkey and Joseph were instantly interested. They did not want this long trip to end up with nothing.

The next day, Rajan took them to Palari, a journey that involved two hours by bus on dirt roads and another ten kilometres on foot through coconut farms, river paths, and over narrow bunds built around the green paddy fields. Finally, they reached the grand house of Korothu Mana. It stood tall with two floors, revealing the abundance its inhabitants had enjoyed for generations. The long, high veranda, surrounded by carved teak wood frames, accommodated a smooth stone seating platform for at least two dozen people. Antique wooden chairs faced the vast grounds, and the huge mahogany main door was ornately carved with pictures of laden rice stalks over traditional grain-filled vats—a symbol of prosperity and a testament to excellent wood artisanship.

Sankaran Nambudiri, the oldest son of the feared family patriarch, came out to meet them. He had an arrogant and haughty air about him, looking at Rajan questioningly, all his manners screaming self-importance and snobbery. However, when Rajan introduced the visitors and patiently explained the grand family name and stature of Varkey, he turned courteous enough to offer them seats. When he learned, they had come to enquire about the land and had the means to buy it outright, he became earnest. Despite the grandeur of the house and estate, it did not provide him with enough disposable cash to accommodate his needs. It made sense to get rid of the land before it was taken away by the widely anticipated, dreaded land reform bill his own treacherous brother had championed.

"Ten years ago, Father wouldn't have considered selling even a tiny piece of our ancestral land, but times change. He hasn't seen to the upkeep of the land for many years. We don't have people like we used to for proper day jobs; they're all turning into communists now!" Sankaran said with discernible disdain.

Varkey looked at the large, plump, extremely pale-skinned, bald man with the protruding belly and thought about the non-existent days he himself had done a proper day's work. No wonder his younger brother turned against him and became a communist.

"The Padinjattu plot on the hill is over 100 acres. I intend to sell it all together; hence, I can't deal with small-timers and locals. After all, the buyers would be our neighbours, so I must give it some thought. Mind you, it is an abundant piece of land, once full of black-pepper plantations—a profitable one when European trade was at its height. But it's been neglected since then. You could bring it back to its former glory!"

The visitors smiled politely.

"Kunjelu...," Sankaran called out loudly.

"Thambran!"

A short, thin, dull-faced man came running and halted in the courtyard, his back curved low, his hands covering his mouth in an extremely subservient posture matching his answering call. Joseph glanced at Varkey surreptitiously, finding the comical figure reminiscent of a bygone era.

"Show these gentlemen the Padinjattu Mala land, the surveyor plotted for us last month," Sankaran ordered his servant.

Kunjelu waited for them to descend from the veranda and started walking westward. After a few minutes of walking, they saw a clearing through the trees. There was a huge pond, built entirely by cutting into the laterite rock. Two sets of neat stone steps led into the water. The deep, long pond was full of clean blue water, with fishes splashing around. An old, gnarled banyan tree stood guard on one side, its branches and roots covering the corner of the pond, its canopy extending shade over the water, its heart-shaped leaves wavering continuously in the gentle breeze.

"This pond is full even in the height of summer!" exclaimed Varkey, looking quite pleased.

"Indeed, sir, it is used by the family for their daily baths. And NO-ONE else is allowed in it," said Kunjelu loudly, as if to forewarn Joseph, who was heading towards the pond, from going any further.

"It must be overflowing during the monsoon?" asked Joseph, seemingly intent on ignoring the warning and taking a dip to beat the scorching summer and the tiredness from the long journey.

"Never beyond the top steps. The water drains into the river down below."

"There is a river?" Varkey was now excited.

"Yes, sir. The Padinjattu Mala is beyond the Palari river."

Kunjelu walked around the pond, giving it a wide berth

to demonstrate how to respect the unwritten sacred rules of the family, and marched ahead. The land began to slope downward, and shortly they could hear the flowing water. After a few more minutes of walking through a thick set of mangroves, they reached the wild, foamy river. It gurgled noisily around huge rocks, creating whirlpools here and there, rushing and slowing down. Unlike the Meenachilar they were used to back home, this river was narrower but fierce and untouched, still holding its force even in the summer. Beyond a streak of paddy fields, an inviting green hill rose, wild and formidable, fertile and virgin. A stream wound its way down, winding around the paddy fields to the river.

Joseph whistled happily and jumped into the nearest sandy pool created by the whirling current, splashing water all around, just like his overflowing heart. Varkey grinned at him; dreams had started to settle in his eyes too…

****

It had rained heavily over the Big House the night before they left for Malabar. Rainwater flowed noisily over the roof tiles into the tin gutters, pooling on the flooded ground. Water streamed down the small courtyard, joining the larger flow from the footpath above, changing colour to match and making its way between the tall, lined coconut trees. It paused briefly to form a whirlpool in an empty pit along the path before humming at the sight of the mighty river five hundred yards away. It revelled with all the adjoining streams, and together they joined the pregnant brown river, which constantly blushed at the newcomers while happily munching on bits of the defeated land on her sides.

The monsoon had made its impact known, raining all day into the night. It was late August already, but it hesitated to say goodbye for the year, lingering a while longer.

The rain mirrored the minds of the people inside, who lay awake listening to its constant roar, trying to drown their worried thoughts. They tried to comfort each other with words meant to pour hope and douse the flames of doubt. But it wasn't enough to defeat their combined fears. It was their last night to savour the familiar sounds and feel the surroundings that were so comfortable. Yet the thought of tomorrow hovered over their heads like giant bats, scaring off the little doves of sleep.

Thus, they would embark on their long journey to the Promised Land, the New Canaan—a land they hoped would flow with milk and honey.

****

"Four months after my marriage, Joseph-Chachan left for Malabar. They sold their houses and all belongings, packed what they could carry, and left with their dreams held close to their hearts. I still remember the dread I felt for them. None of us really slept that night, or the many nights after that," Annammachi sighed.

"I was never with the doubting camp. For me, it was a dream that was real and magical at the same time. As if... I could touch the giant bubble, radiating the most luxuriant rainbow, without making it burst into nothingness. It was a fairy tale for me, and I just stood admiring it for a long time," Joseph said in a feverish pitch as if the promised land still stood in front of him, with all its magic and beauty.

Joey smiled at the twins, seeing their engrossed faces, and winked to say, 'I told you so.' They had found the narration to be a window to a strange, yet familiar land, pulling them as if they were tied to it by some invisible strings of precious silk—a link which they weren't aware of until now and couldn't shake off, having found it now.

26. Malabar memories

An older man entered through the open front doors, carrying a large bunch of ripe bananas on his shoulder. He tied it safely with a rope hanging from the pantry ceiling, then came into the kitchen.

"These were waiting in my farm, perfectly ripe and sweet. The wretched diabetes won't let me eat any of them! When I heard your grandson was coming, I thought he might like them," he greeted warmly.

"This is Lenin Lona, our nephew and Lincy's father," Annammachi introduced him.

"Lenin?" James did a double take.

Lenin laughed at the incredulous young face. "My father was a communist, so he named me after his idol. Don't be surprised; you'll find many Lenins, Stalins, and Marxs here!" he explained, bringing laughter to the room.

"Kerala is home to the first democratically elected communist governments in the world! So, we have our own share of history too," he added more seriously.

"Lenin's dad, Lona my cousin, decided to join us after we found the dream land in Malabar," Joseph said.

"I was only ten when we went to Malabar. What an adventure that was! I was so excited."

"I forgot you were that young. You were a force even then!" Joseph's face brightened as they started talking.

This was a routine for them—to sit and talk about old times, as if time hadn't passed by them at all. The familiarity was there, and the comfort that came with the memories. It never occurred to them as repetitive. Youngsters often got bored of this rumination, their minds set in a different gear, not obliged to listen for long. Today was an exception; they hardly ever had a more receptive audience than Joey, Jane, and James, and it automatically pulled them into overdrive.

"Was it truly the Promised Land?" Joey asked.

"Yes, it was! A hard one, but adventurous. The vast barn building had been neglected for years, but we were able to repair and convert it into a solid, secure house—better than what many locals could afford. The abandoned pepper field had to be cleared to plant fresh crops. We still got a good enough harvest from the field to finance the heavy work on the land that first year. Migrating families were truly inventive. When rice was scarce, we replaced traditional rice-based meals with cassava, jackfruit, and various yams that grew well on those hills. It was said that cassava, originally from Brazil, was introduced to Kerala in the 19th century after a great famine. I can tell you; dried cassava saved us from going hungry during those long monsoon months," Joseph reminisced.

Beside them, Lenin beamed. "Nothing could beat cassava with the curry we made after our hunting trips! Varkey-Chachan's brother, Chandy, managed to get hold of a rifle—rudimentary and ancient but still working. He took over the role of our protector, made a watch-house on the tallest tree at the edge of our land to keep away wild animals. He often led hunting trips to the forest, bringing back enough meat for a feast along with many adventure stories. He truly came alive then, often narrowly escaping imminent danger. Predators roamed the forest. Wild elephants and venomous snakes could bring death. The mulchy forest floors and ground bushes were full of leeches waiting to drain your blood, competing with the mosquitoes. But with all that, a good trip could bring a feast for the whole hunting party and their families for a week. During the early monsoon, fish were abundant, often coming upstream from the river to the flooded paddy fields."

Jane shivered involuntarily at the mention of elephants. She couldn't imagine facing another one, let alone living among them.

"Varkey didn't regret leaving his life in Kottayam

behind?"

"On the contrary... He truly shined in Malabar. He was a natural leader. He organised the migrant community to create a community church, so they didn't need to walk miles for Sunday mass, baptisms, weddings, and funerals. He and the parish priest then led the drive for a local school. It was a godsend for all the local children. Before that, they walked hours to reach the nearest school in the next town, crossing the mighty Palari River. Most would skip school during the rainy season as the path became even longer with the lone make-shift bridge being a mile further. It took years more for Palari to get its first primary health centre. Hospitals only existed in the big towns and cities, not easily accessible for those living in remote villages," Joseph explained.

"It must have been hard for a community to survive without hospitals?" said James, understandingly.

"It was... I learned it the hard way. My wife, Penni, was the youngest daughter of one of the early migrants to Malabar. I met her while she was working on the farm with her parents. I fell for her the moment I saw her—muddy and sweaty in her work clothes, but with a sparkling human spirit! Ours was the first wedding in the new church, eight years after we moved to Palari. We had Mathew three years later. I should have taken better care of her when she was pregnant with our second child...But she insisted on staying home. Homebirth was the norm then; not many could afford hospitals those days..."

Painful memories filled his heart. The agony of the day they carried his pregnant wife, desperately trying to get medical help on that fateful monsoon day, still haunted him. The expected delivery had gone all wrong; the baby couldn't be delivered by the home-nurse. By the time they made their way to the hospital, she was falling in and out of consciousness, her body giving up on the unendurable pain. The rain had covered his tears, the thunders echoed his dread as he rushed through the narrow footpath, praying and promising everything he owned, including his life, in return for hers. He knew the bargain wasn't accepted by the supposedly merciful god; his wife had gone completely quiet in the dripping stretcher in the last mile. The doctor could only tell him it was too late for her and their baby girl.

Joseph was lost without her, drowned in sorrow and regret. She had brightened up his life so much in those short years, the rest of his life felt like perpetual darkness. He knew how much he owed to his friend Varkey and Maria for taking the young Mathew under their wings and protecting him from the anguish Joseph felt for many years. It was his mother's loss that made Mathew determined to become a doctor.

Annammachi sat beside him, quietly reflecting on her own life. She had traded the promised land for a promised marital home that was supposed to provide comfort. Instead, she endured an unbearable existence with overbearing relatives who crushed her free spirit. Her husband, lacking a voice of his own, offered her no support. Barbed words constantly murmured about her lack of propriety; her worth as a wife was questioned repeatedly as the barren months turned into years.

She despised the world's pronouncements of failure while her husband cringed around everyone, a cloud of smoke trailing him everywhere. Her life burned as fiercely as the cigarettes he couldn't live without. Eventually, it all made her bitter. The only way to survive in that suffocating environment was to be tougher than the biggest bully around. She stopped caring about what others thought or said, closing doors in their faces until she earned the nickname 'Asura-Vithu Anna'—the offspring of a demon sent to bring their end. She was made an example of how a headstrong bride could bring calamity to a respected family and destroy it. Everyone sympathised with her unfortunate husband. Anna made it a point to earn her tough-woman stature, ignoring all the jibes. When her husband died of a prolonged illness, his tobacco-filled lungs finally giving out, all she felt was relief. He had failed to make her feel anything good while alive, nor did he in death. There was nothing left in her to feel for him.

Tears filled Annammachi's age mellowed eyes as she looked at Joey. "I decided to move in here with Joseph-Chachan and Mathew when they came back to Kottayam and bought back the house. My husband had died a year before, and there was nothing to hold me back to his house. Mathew brightened up my world until it was all snatched away once again."

Joseph looked away, tired and weary. Joey insisted they take a rest; they would have time to talk later. Joseph retired to his room. Exhaustion caught up with him, and he closed his eyes, dreaming of his wife and son, so near yet so far away...

27. Weaving threads

"The house next door once belonged to Varkey. When he left for Malabar, he sold it to Rajan Mash. He made a new annexe on the land recently but maintained the old Big House with all its original features. Rajan Mash was already a prodigy artist and play director when he moved in. He is revered by many, recipient of state and national awards and quite famous. He still makes films, but only occasionally," Joey said as they walked across the path towards the river.

The river - Meenachilar - called out to him. He remembered his father splashing in the water joyfully the last time they visited together, a lifetime ago. They jumped across the stones to get to the big rock mid-way, half submerged in the river, and sat down. Jane put her bare feet in the water, and tiny fishes gathered round, covering her heels and toes, tickling her.

"I would be paying a hefty amount in a resort for this treat," Jane said, giggling, trying to keep her feet still, now hidden beneath a school of tiny fishes.

"It is so peaceful out here," James said, breathing in the fresh air and the views.

"Yes, I always loved to come here. This river could become mighty swollen and wild in the monsoon, the water level sometimes reaching up to the path near the house. They look so irresistibly inviting, these rivers, but they could also be a death trap to the untrained, with their hidden whirlpools and unexpected undercurrents!" Joey said.

"Wise words, young man!" an old voice called out. An elderly man in a long white kurta and pyjama was walking towards them, stepping carefully through the shallow water. His long beard and moustache were all white, as was his shoulder-length hair.

Joey stood up and greeted him heartily. "Hello Rajan Mash, great to run into you."

The newcomer settled onto another rock and smiled. "Good to see you, Joey. Long time no see. Anna talks about you all the time and forces me to look at the albums whenever I visit her. I have an inkling she does that more to keep herself from forgetting you!"

"It's been a while since my last visit." Joey introduced Jane and James to Rajan Mash.

He smiled pleasantly. "Hope you don't mind us sharing your quiet time," James called out, noticing the fishing rod and basket he carried.

"I occasionally like young company! It helps me get creative ideas. Besides, I am old; I live in the past most of the time, as it is now the longer stretch in my life than what is to come." Rajan Mash nodded good-naturedly.

"Congratulations on the recent national film award," Joey complimented.

"Thank you. Movies were so much better in the old days, and I liked the theatre even more—real talent, real stories, many of which were illustrious enough to cause or support a social movement. I grew up in the era of KPAC and Aleppey theatres. It was the golden time in Kerala's theatre history."

"Joey told us you bought your house from his grandfather's friend, all those years ago. You knew him well?" Jane wasn't one to let go of an opportunity, materialising right in front of her.

"Varkey was an ardent fan of theatre. He used to come and watch when I started directing plays, and we struck up a real friendship. He often invited me to stay over if I was taking part in any plays nearby. I loved his house the moment I first set eyes on it, a very historic house in this part of the state."

Rajan Mash sat there reminiscing; his fishing rod lay forgotten on the rock.

"I played a small part in your family history too, by leading Varkey and your grandfather to their destiny in Malabar,"

Rajan Mash said softly.

"Yes, we just heard about it from grandfather."

"They both liked the Korothu mana land. It was indeed a good deal, much bigger than what they originally bargained for. Joseph's cousin, Lona, decided to move with them to Palari. Varkey's older brother Chandy was also enthusiastic about joining them. Although everyone else thought it was a bad idea, in the end, he convinced everyone to take a bet on him."

"That's when you bought this house?" asked James.

"Yes. The Big House had a certain historic value, and I was fascinated by it. A rich uncle, an eccentric, crazy enough to believe in my dreams and my plays, helped me with the capital. This lucky house was the beginning of an ascent for me. I was able to build my own theatre company, giving us a base and a home. The house had outbuildings to accommodate artists who stayed over for rehearsals and local performances. We were able to recruit more women too in the group as they found it safer to stay over in a house with proper walls than the temporary sheds we managed in those days with a travelling drama group. We had to beg for accommodation for them with locals when we travelled. Hotel facilities and money were both tight in those days." Rajan Mash said. "Varkey and I stayed friends throughout our lives, although the distance and work made it difficult to meet often enough. But I had met him on the day, just hours before his fateful accident, though I did not know about the accident until much later. His son Johny called me a week later with the tragic news. We were all still in shock about Dr. Mathew and one of our own theatre crew..."

"You were there in Kalpetta that day?" All of them were astonished.

"I had my theatre group, Kerala Arts Club, in Kalpetta for the play we did for the hospital's annual day. It was Joey's dad, Mathew, who invited us to perform. I was so fond of him, you know, as I got to spend time with him when he moved back here for college. What a terrible loss for you and all the people he served selflessly!"

Rajan Mash stared at the flowing river, the morning sun's reflection broken and shivering, along with his memories from that fateful night.

28. Crossroad to the past

Wayanad, Kerala: 25 years ago

Rajan joined the late-night celebratory drink with his troupe, a tradition after every successful performance. 'Krishna Leela' had been a hit. The audience's appreciative claps echoed in his mind, a testament to their success.

No trouble from rowdy drunks tonight either, Rajan noted with relief. Sometimes, overexcited spectators would storm the stage, eager to manhandle the villainous characters or express their displeasure with the performance. He always made sure to inform the local police of his planned performances, just in case.

Most of the troupe remained in the makeshift camp, waiting for daylight to pack up and leave. A few, with other commitments, had departed earlier. Rajan understood the hardships his team faced—leaving their families and regular lives behind to perform in remote places with inadequate amenities. The pay wasn't great, especially for smaller venues like this. Many directors and artists were shifting to movies, which offered better pay and stardom for some. Rajan had dabbled in films but preferred the theatre for its vibrancy, closeness to the audience, and the immediate feedback.

Lost in these thoughts, Rajan was startled by a panicked shout.

"There's been an accident! Mohan Poduval's car is down in a ditch! And Dr. Mathew's!"

Rajan's heart skipped a beat. "Poduval? What was he doing here? He left hours ago! And Dr. Mathew? Oh no, not him, No..." Rajan's voice trailed off in disbelief.

He raced to the scene. The police were already there, cordoning off the area. Rajan approached an officer.

"I'm a long-time friend of Dr. Mathew, and Mohan

Poduval was working with my troupe. How are they?" Rajan's voice shook.

"Both dead, I'm afraid. We need to assess the scene before retrieving the bodies from the wreckage," the officer said, matter-of-factly.

Rajan's head spun. He leaned against a wall, trying to process the information.

Rajan called Poduval's family. His father's response was chillingly curt. "I predicted this. With the company he kept, he was bound to end up like this. I told him he was playing with fire. He was dead to me long before this."

Rajan was taken aback. Did he disapprove of his son joining the theatre group? It wasn't a reckless life! Rajan wondered if Poduval's father would even come to claim the body! Rajan then called Poduval's friend, Mahendran, who had initially introduced Poduval to him. Poduval had produced glowing letters of reference from some of the most well-known play directors. Rajan later discovered that Poduval had never worked with any of them; he had a talent for forging letters instead. Rajan had found him to be a mediocre actor, somewhat unhinged, but he had settled in and proved to be resourceful. Wealthy, he did not worry about timely pay cheques like the others and his possession of a vehicle was an asset for the drama group with limited resources.

Mahendran, the only son of the late Sankaran, responded gravely to the news of Poduval's death. He seemed shaken and panicked, his voice urgent as he asked how and when Poduval had died. Rajan could hear his intensified breathing through the phone. Perhaps he was just shocked by the sudden death of a friend.

"He called me this evening, but I wasn't home. He didn't want to leave any message for me! So, I just wondered..."

Rajan sensed that Mahendran was struggling to control his emotions, but there was something else in his voice... fear!

Rajan accompanied the police to break the news to Mercy. She showed no emotion, refusing to go to the hospital morgue.

"She's in shock," Rajan murmured to the others, looking to get some support to her. She wasn't close to any of the hospital staff, and her family lived far away. Then he thought of Varkey, he was Mathews's godfather and closest family. He tried calling his home number, but it rang endlessly. Then he remembered —Varkey couldn't be home; he had been in Kalpetta that evening. Rajan had seen him during the play, looking dishevelled and desperate to find Mathew.

Rajan stayed behind to complete the formalities with the police. It seemed to take forever. Then he received another shocking call, from Varkey's son, Johny. "My Father had an accident last week, he died from his injuries yesterday..."

Johny was frantic.

"When did you arrive from the US?" Rajan asked, grief freezing his voice.

"I got the news about Mathew, so I had come for his funeral. He was a true brother to me. I couldn't reach my father. When I went to the police, they were already trying to contact me. They had identified my father from the vehicle records."

Rajan's heart ached for him. He couldn't imagine what Johny was going through, having lost his father all too soon. And Mathew too. Everything was going wrong again...

****

Joey, Jane, and James sat in stunned silence, listening to Rajan Mash's strained voice recounting memories from the past. The elderly man seemed to age further with each word, his face etched with melancholy. His memories were vivid, as if the events had unfolded yesterday.

Too many pieces of the puzzle lay before them, each needing careful contemplation to fit into the bigger picture.

"You knew Varkey's family? His daughter too?" Jane

asked, her voice hopeful.

"Oh, the spirited young Annie, of course, I knew her," Rajan replied, a fond yet sorrowful smile crossing his face. "She was a fiercely independent soul, always questioning the status quo if she found it unjust. She would argue so much for her case, I had asked her once why she opted to study commerce rather than a degree in law! She said, 'The world is ruled by commerce, and the law merely protects it. The future will prove this even more.'"

His voice carried a mix of admiration and sadness.

"Sounds a lot like you, Jane," James said with a twinkle in his eye.

"My mum mentioned Annie but didn't know where she is now. Do you know?" Joey asked, leaning forward.

Rajan Mash looked up, startled. "Your mother didn't know? How come? Mathew was searching for her frantically, day and night, for a week, in the mud and the torrential rain…"

"What do you mean?" Jane and Joey asked simultaneously, their voices tinged with urgency.

"Annie, her mother Maria, and her aunt Alice were washed away in a horrific landslide at Palari, just six months before your dad died. They only found Maria's body; the other two were presumed dead…"

The revelation hung heavy in the air. Joey, Jane, and James exchanged glances, each processing the gravity of the news. The river's gentle murmur seemed a cruel contrast to the harsh truths emerging.

29. Back to Square One

The three of them watched Rajan Mash walk back to his house, his steps slow and laboured as if each one required significant effort. He had forgotten his fishing rod.

"I really thought we had something finally," Jane said, her voice tinged with frustration. "His narrative matched with what we thought about Varkey being in Kalpetta on that day. But Annie was dead six months before! Really?"

"I'm not sure why we always reach a dead end, quite literally," James lamented. "It almost feels like we are somehow killing off the people by seeking them!"

Their hard-found puzzle pieces seemed to fall apart again, creating a meaningless heap. If Annie wasn't the pregnant woman who was supposed to be at the hospital that day, they were back to square one. A heavy gloom settled over them.

"I don't like that Poduval guy! His shadow grows longer and longer," Joey said after some time. "He was the nephew of the disgraced inspector. Suleimanikka believed he was acting on behalf of his uncle—to get revenge."

"He had a legitimate reason to be there that day," Jane countered. "Rajan Mash said they showed no hostility at the backstage."

"He may not have had personal reasons, but if he agreed to do the deed for someone else, he wouldn't be showing off his intentions, would he? He was with Rajan Mash for only six months and had a record of forging letters. His character sounded fishy, especially given his father's and friend's reactions to his death," Joey argued.

"What about the police reporting it as an accident?" James asked.

"If the guy was related to police personnel, they are not likely to say anything else unless it was obvious," Joey replied.

"Maybe it was just Varkey at the hospital that day," James suggested. "Dr. Mathew might have accompanied his godfather and had the unfortunate accident."

"If that were the case, why wouldn't Dr. Mathew identify him and record it in the hospital records? Why would it be an anonymous entry? And why hasn't he mentioned it to any of his colleagues? He would have wanted the best care possible for him. And where did he go from the hospital without attending to his godfather?" Jane's frustration was palpable.

"You know, I had a fleeting thought," Joey said quietly. "With my mother's outburst and the shared history, they seemed to have, my father probably had an affair with Annie and you two might have been my half-siblings."

Jane registered the relief in his voice without commenting.

"Really?" James was perplexed. His thoughts usually marched in straight lines, opting for simple answers until an alternative became evident.

But Jane wasn't surprised. That particular thought had crossed her mind more than once. Usually, her mind worked out all the possibilities that could arise from a situation. She weighed them systematically before reaching any conclusion. She would often argue with James that the analytic approach helped one to be ready and proactive, unlike his ever-optimistic view. He would say her doomsday approach was unhealthy. Life was full of complexities, and one found peace in keeping things simple where possible. And, as usual, he remained optimistic that she would one day agree with him on the value of a simple mind!

"I don't think your father would have abandoned his own children if he knew," James said with conviction.

"Well, we can only guess what one does in a crisis. Let's go back; it's time for lunch already." Joey got up and extended his hand to Jane. She took it after a moment, and he pulled her up with a small smile. He picked up the fishing rod left by Rajan Mash; they could return it later.

Annammachi was instructing Lincy on garnishing the fish curry, which was bubbling in a traditional earthen pot on the stove top in the old kitchen when they returned. Mustard seeds spluttered in hot oil, shallots and curry leaves sizzled, and the aroma filled the air.

James was the most enthusiastic, enjoying the meal. He ate with his hands like a pro, smirking at Jane, who was rummaging through the cupboards for cutlery.

"Be a Roman when in Rome," he teased.

Jane mimicked a sword swipe, indicating she would rather be a gladiator. Or Unniyarcha with her Urumi to suit the plot. James grinned, knowing Jane could be adamant about her habits.

Annammachi served seconds to Joey, ignoring his protests. "You all need to eat more while you're young. Your father used to love hearty lunches, then he would go for long walks with Rajan Mash, talking non-stop about plays and movies. You wouldn't think they were of two different generations!"

"We met Rajan Mash earlier at the riverbank. He told us about Annie and her mother dying in a landslide in Palari," Joey mentioned.

Annammachi shrugged noncommittally. "Hmm... On that, I had my doubts though! At least for a while."

They all looked at her abruptly.

"No one ever found their remains in these 25 years, although the land had been rebuilt many times. Varkey stopped the search after they found Maria's body. Of course, he was in deep shock, not talking to anyone for days, sitting dazed in a corner. But he never accepted that his daughter had died. He died the same year, so I don't know if he knew anything different. Alice, Annie's aunt, was also presumed dead that day. But I could have sworn I saw her once in a passing bus near Kozhikode a few months after that. I couldn't do anything but stare in disbelief until the bus disappeared from my view."

They looked at each other, astonished.

"Did you not tell anyone?" James asked.

"No one would believe me. They said I might have imagined it or was going crazy. I don't know! I haven't heard of either of them all these years since, so I could have imagined it after all!"

"What about Johny, her brother? Did you not ask him?"

"That was the worst of it. We were his family when Johny grew up, although calls became less frequent after he went to the US. When I called him to ask him about seeing Alice, he got really upset. He might have thought I was making a game of it, telling people such stories! He wouldn't call us after that. We tried, but he wouldn't return the calls. Maybe such deep grief changes people. He lost all his family in six months."

Annammachi looked most remorseful. "I felt bad. I regretted ever telling him such a thing. We lost touch with him since. The number we had is no longer active; he must have changed the address."

"My father was close to Annie, wasn't he?" Joey asked.

"Mathew was very fond of Annie. She was born when he was just six years old, and they grew up together practically in the same house in Malabar. His mother had died two years earlier, my brother didn't really know what to do at home or with a young child. Varkey and Maria became more of parents to him. Mathew moved back here when he joined the Medical College to study medicine. A few years later, Annie also moved and joined Ernakulam Maharajas College. She used to spend most weekends here with us."

"Did he... Did they... Were they more than friends?" Joey hesitated.

Annammachi was silent for a while. "I don't know,

neither of them ever said anything of the sort. But they were really close to each other for most of their lives, apart from a brief period. When Mathew suddenly decided to marry your mother and move to Wayanad, Annie was angry. But then it went back to normal, although they did not see much of each other anymore. I thought it was because Mercy did not like him seeing Annie. She was too possessive," she looked at Joey apologetically.

"Oh, don't be sorry. I know she can be difficult at times," Joey said. 'Well, most of the time,' he thought privately.

"I still remember the last time Mathew visited us. Annie was here too. It was the Easter week, three months before the landslide. I think he had his college alumni meet or something. Annie came to stay with a couple of her friends. They were talking and laughing way into the night."

"Annie was here for Easter that year?" Jane asked, surprised. Joey saw the thoughts swirling in Jane's eyes, which were now focused intently on him. Easter was conveniently nine months before Christmas!

"Yes, Annie and her friends were taking part in the inter-college youth festival. We all sat and watched them rehearsing the dance the night before the competition. I remember feeling young again! Rajan too was here to watch the performance. He was so impressed; he asked Annie's friend if she would like to join his theatre group."

"Really? Who was that?" Jane asked.

"I think her name was Lakshmi or something and from a traditional family. They wouldn't have let her join a drama club or movies! It wasn't glamorous then, especially for women, with all the prevalent social norms and nonsense!" Annammachi looked disdainful. She was still inflamed about the norms that had tied her to societal expectations and suffocated her throughout her long life. She despised the judgment panels as much as those who used them to decide her life's path.

"Do you know where any of them are now?"

"No, when we lost our Mathew, we lost the entire world he brought to us too. Who would want to keep visiting some old people and tell them anything at all?" Annammachi's voice was filled with melancholy. She was dejected about the irrelevance her age had caused, making them invisible to those around them.

30. Fresh start

Jane and James took the time to call their parents. Both were anxious but relieved to hear their voices. Lissy pleaded with them to come back and abandon the quest, believing it was becoming too dangerous.

"We are making some progress, Mum. If we reach a dead end, we'll come back," James said in his most reassuring voice.

"It seems like a dead end already if Annie was dead before you were born!" Lissy exclaimed.

Richard intervened, handing them the British high-commissioner's number. "Call her if you need any urgent help. She is an old friend of mine. I've spoken to her already about the trouble you're facing with your missing person enquiry."

Lissy's worry echoed through the phone as she repeated her warnings about their safety. Jane sighed, feeling the weight of her mother's concern. Disconnecting the call, she sat frowning, her mind racing. If Annie was a dead end, what else did they have? Could they go on with just the instinct of Annammachi? Someone should have seen Annie if she were alive all these years?

Joey was rifling through his father's notes, hoping to find any names or contacts from those days. Finding none, he finally called his mother.

"I'm sorry, Joey. I didn't keep in touch with any of his friends from college. Two of his friends, Dr. Srinivasan and Dr. Moideen, used to visit Wayanad sometimes. I don't know where they are now. I tried to stay away from all that painful past, you know that" she said.

She sounded sober, and Joey felt reassured. He didn't want to worry about her constantly, but it was hard with her mood swings and depression, compounded by drinking. It made her unpredictable.

"Mum, I understand. It all must have been hard on you.

I'm sorry you felt alone and abandoned."

Suddenly, Jane jumped up, grabbing his phone. Her face was flushed with sudden inspiration.

"Hello, Mrs. Kuriyan. You said Dr. Mathew once came home from Malabar all sick. Do you remember when that was?"

"It was monsoon time; he had a bag full of drenched clothes. I think it was July, around six months before he died."

The importance of that question hit Joey and James, both looking at Jane with astonishment.

"Mum, Annie's mother died that week in a landslide, and Annie was presumed dead. Dad was there searching for them in the rain and mud. That's how he must have gotten sick. Didn't he tell you anything about it?"

There was a long pause. When she finally spoke, her voice was barely audible.

"I had no idea! I was so mad at him for being so uncommunicative. I couldn't read his mind, you see. He screamed at me when I cursed Annie, and it turned into a shouting match with neither of us listening. I stormed out of the house. I didn't speak to him for weeks."

Silence stretched on the line, everyone lost in thought.

"You said Dr. Mathew's godfather came a week after that?" Jane asked again with trepidation.

"Yes, that's true... No... Annie couldn't have been dead. Varkey was clearly seeking Mathew for her. That's why I got angry and didn't ask him in," Mercy said.

"Did you see her in the car?"

"There was someone in the car. It was stuffed to the brim, so I couldn't see inside properly, but I thought it was Annie. I deliberately didn't tell Mathew about the visit later because seeing them made me so cross. But he never mentioned Annie again..."

She paused again.

"If what you said is true, maybe he believed she was dead. He was never the same after... as if life had gone out of him." Mercy's voice had lost its edge, replaced by a hint of regret. She said goodbye and disconnected.

The three sat in silence, absorbing the information. It wasn't concrete proof, but it was as good as any they had, and it fit their original trail. Annie must have been pregnant, and Varkey took her to a trusted person who happened to be a gynaecologist too. Even though Mercy stopped him then, he must have gone back to Mathew for help when Annie was near her due date, when Rajan Mash met him in Wayanad. It all made sense.

"But why would he pretend his daughter was dead when they needed help the most?" James was lost in thought.

"Being pregnant before marriage wasn't acceptable here, not even now. It would have been a scandal of enormous proportion at that time. Pretending to be dead might have seemed like a better option," Joey said.

"If Varkey accepted his daughter and died trying to protect her and her baby, who is chasing us now, willing to kill us? After all these years? How could someone be so crazy?" James asked.

"To find that out, we need to discover the circumstances by which Annie got pregnant. Was it a result of a crime?... Or an affair with someone unfaithful or powerful?... In any case, someone didn't want the secret out then or now," Joey reasoned.

"If it was the former, or even an unwanted pregnancy, Annie could have opted for an abortion. It was legalised in India from 1971 under comparatively broad conditions," Jane said, having researched previously for possible scenarios of infant abandonment.

"You're forgetting that she and her family were devout Catholics. Many still have strong feelings about abortion, whatever the cause," Joey reminded her.

"That's crazy. How can we find out what really happened? Who can tell us anything when the world thinks Annie has been dead for years?" James asked, resigned.

"Either her closest friends or those who are trying to kill us before we reach them! Neither will be easy," Jane said, determination in her voice.

Joey ran searches on the two names his mother had given him, hoping they could confirm that his father wasn't the unfaithful one or that someone related to him was hell-bent on killing his new friends.

There were too many doctors named Sreenivasan and no relevant one for Moideen. He searched the college alumni group with no luck. He messaged the admin through the Facebook page, providing his father's and his friends' names with graduation year details.

Miraculously, the dutiful admin replied after a while. She found a Dr. Moideen, a consultant in a private hospital in Palakkad. She wasn't sure if it was the same person but provided the hospital's front desk number.

Joey called the number, and after much persuasion and referencing his late father, the call was transferred to Dr. Moideen.

"You're really Dr. Mathew's son?" asked a deep voice, lined with doubt.

"Yes, I'm Joey. Mum told me you used to visit our old home in Wayanad."

The voice softened at once.

"It's been so long. I was sorry to lose my best friend so tragically and to lose touch with you after your mother remarried. I'm so glad you reached out. There's so much I want to know about you."

Joey told him briefly about his life and whereabouts. Moideen was pleased.

"Did you know anything about my father's childhood friend, Annie Varkey?"

"Yes, I knew her. She used to hang around with us on weekends."

Joey sensed there was more left unsaid in that short statement.

"Was she more to my father than just a dear friend?" Joey asked directly, not knowing what to expect.

31. Unrequited love

Kottayam Medical College, Kerala: 30 years ago

On the very first day at medical college, Moideen met Mathew and Sreenivasan. Among the freshers who moved together like a school of fish, using the same defence mechanism to avoid the senior students and their infamous initiation rituals, which often caused humiliation and trauma to the guileless youngsters living away from home for the first time.

Mathew, noticing the anxious look on Sreeni's face, walked up to a professor, and struck up an animated conversation about the upcoming annual conference of surgeons, having noticed the leaflet the professor was carrying earlier. Srini and Moideen fell in step with them inconspicuously, providing an air of authenticity for the watchful senior students. It worked. They weren't bothered by anyone for the next few weeks; word spread that the three had some connection to the professor, and no one wanted to risk getting into trouble. The trio became friends in the process. Mathew was bright and articulate, Moideen was the class clown, witty and wicked, while Sreeni was the serious, studious type.

They were in their final year when Annie joined a nearby college. Cheerful, free-spirited, and a joy to be around, Annie quickly became the centre of attention. Many weekends were spent together, sometimes with Annie's extended group of friends. Moideen had long suspected a deep, unspoken connection between Mathew and Annie, although Mathew never voiced it aloud.

"I hear your Annie is quite popular at her college," Moideen commented one day. "Someone else will secure her heart soon!"

It was right after the inter-college youth festival. Annie had come with a group from her college, and men often crowded around her, clearly favouring the vivacious, ever joyful, and attractive girl.

"Surely not! Isn't she too young?" Mathew replied, surprised, but his face betrayed his conflicted emotions.

"Only for you. You've seen her ever since she was born!"

"My godfather thinks of me as his own son. I can't break his trust with any missteps on my part!"

"Not much difference from son to son-in-law!" Moideen encouraged. "It's not like you are related by blood or anything. It's perfectly legal!"

"Unless you fancy the rich girl who's hell-bent on capturing your attention. I dare say she's what you need, really, for a promising but poor doctor!" Srini added.

They had seen the new girl suddenly appearing in their circle wherever they went. Mercy was resourceful when it came to getting what she wanted, and Mathew had taken her fancy this time, above many other wannabe suitors. But Mathew hadn't even noticed her!

"Maybe what you need is an eye specialist. There's one I know in our class!" Moideen joked, bitter about the unfairness of it all. Why couldn't the rich girl take a fancy to him instead?

It was the first time Mathew came close to admitting his true feelings for Annie to his friends, and even to himself.

Annie had always been part of his life. He didn't know how to define that link or name his feelings. She filled him with joy, anticipation, fulfilment, and lately, some complex, unfamiliar emotions. What if she didn't think of him that way? He couldn't risk the bond they shared on this crazy idea.

Srini sided with Mathew, but he himself was forever the biggest procrastinator in their group, always finding ways to delay critical decisions until it was forced on him.

"Srini, you would have delayed your own birth if it were up to you! Don't lead Mathew down your rabbit hole!" Moideen said exasperatedly. "It's better to know than to live in doubt!"

But Mathew, ever confident and assured, bolted on this one dilemma. He kept silent about his growing frustration over his mixed feelings for Annie while she remained joyful and carefree around him. It made him more anxious, certain she wanted to keep the status quo between them.

Things changed on their graduation day. Moideen didn't know what went wrong or when. He and Sreeni were delayed for the after-party, tasked with dropping off their chief guest. The day ended in the most unexpected way for Mathew. They found him drunk and incoherent—for the first time ever—dazed and confused, wrapped in Mercy's possessive arms. At least, she looked smug and cheerful.

Mathew was in an even stranger mood the next day. He refused to speak about Annie or what had transpired between them that obviously stopped him in his tracks. Who could say for certain the mysterious ways of the fallen heart? No rhyme or reason stood a chance in the wild whirlwind of love, especially an unrequited love.

32. Key to the past

"In all those years, he never said anything about it?" Joey asked Moideen.

"No, he didn't. He married your mother soon after and seemed determined to move on. He was back to his old self after you were born. You brought him joy and the work gave him fulfilment. He often talked fondly about it."

"You met Annie after that?"

"Things returned to normal between them after some time, I think it was after you were born. When Mathew visited us in Kottayam, Annie would come along if she was in town. It was like old times. The last time I saw them together was at our alumni meet. We watched Annie and her friends rehearse for the dance performance until daybreak. Mathew was happy that day, so was Annie. It was the last time I heard his boundless laughter..."

Moideen's voice broke on the line, grief creeping in.

"The week after Annie died in the landslide, I went to see Mathew. He was in the hospital with a serious case of pneumonia. He had spent days searching for her in the ruin, soaking in the torrential rain, not listening to anyone. That's when I realised the depth of Mathew's feelings for her. I lost my friend that day, as if she was the spirit burned in his heart, and he was dead without it. He couldn't move on this time; he hardly spoke to anyone apart from his patients. My calls were rarely returned, and when they were, they were too short to make any difference. He wasn't himself in those six months until his sudden death..."

The line went silent for a long moment, the loss, despair, and grief enveloping all of them.

"I am terribly sorry to tell you all this, but you asked for the truth. That's the truth as I saw it..."

Moideen gave Joey the names of two friends who had accompanied Annie to the inter-college festival: Veena Nair, who later became a professor at Maharaja's College, and Lakshmi, a gifted dancer whose whereabouts he no longer knew.

Joey, Jane, and James went back to the riverbank to clear their heads.

"It would have all fitted if Annie did not die in the story!" Jane muttered to herself. The river flowed quietly in answer, willing to take away her disappointments.

Joey gave her a smile. "We could do a DNA test to see if we share a parent. At least one knot could be straightened. It's killing me not to know!"

Jane sat up straight, scaring the fish away. Knowing the truth would be helpful. Besides, it would free Joey from the constant doubts about his father's involvement. It must have been hard for him to disturb the memories of his long-lost father this way.

Joey looked solemn and determined. Going back and forth on what might have happened all those years ago was excruciating.

"It's a brilliant idea," agreed James. "It will remove one hurdle we need to jump." James seemed to respond to the pain he saw in Joey's eyes.

James reached out to Olivia's Bangalore colleagues to get the details of a reputed and confidential agency where they could do the test. He got two addresses—one in Ernakulam and another in Kozhikode.

Joey booked an appointment for the next day at the Ernakulam centre; it wasn't too far.

Meanwhile, Jane rummaged through her bag and brought out a card with the phone number of Professor Gopal Sreenivasan, whom they met at the Dubai airport. The professor had mentioned teaching at the same college as Veena Nair.

"Worth a try! He had promised to help!" she said.

Gopal picked up the phone on the second ring. He sounded pleased to hear from her.

"Hello Professor, hope you could help me. Do you know Professor Veena Nair from Maharajas College?"

"Oh, yes, Veena and I worked together for some years before I retired. How do you know her?"

"We were looking for information about a relative of ours, Annie Varkey. She was a friend of Veena's. Any chance you knew her too?"

Professor Gopal thought for some time, searching deep into his memory.

"Annie Varkey? I think Veena talked about her. She was the chairperson of the students' union one year, not a mean feat! But Veena said Annie died in a landslide in Malabar, if my memory serves me right. Was it really the same person?"

"Yes, the same. We came to know she was a long-lost relative of ours."

"She is long lost if dead for two decades?" prompted the Professor.

"I am only after the history, which could never be dead or lost!" she countered.

"You've got a point there. Ok, maybe Veena could help. I'll give you, her number."

"Thank you very much, Professor." She wrote down the details and disconnected.

Jane got through to Veena and told her they wanted to talk to her about her old friend Annie.

"I'm sorry, I'm visiting my family today. But I can talk to you tomorrow. If you would like to come down to the college, even better. I would like to meet Joey too; I knew his father."

Veena's voice was light and bubbly, with a slight southern sing-song accent.

Jane covered the phone and looked at Joey. "Could we meet her tomorrow on campus?"

Joey did some quick calculations. "We're going to Ernakulam for the test anyway. We could meet her around noon if that works."

"Tomorrow around 12 PM, okay for you?"

"Yes, it's perfect. I could get you the college canteen lunch to complete the experience," Veena laughed. Even her laughter was infectious.

Veena drove her shiny new car to her husband's family home. For once, she looked every bit like the seasoned college professor she was. Everyone who knew her, including her students, called her the perpetual wild child for her radical appearance and teaching methods. Outside of work, she was usually seen driving her 4x4 through some forest trail or in a pair of long sturdy boots, trekking. Today was an exception. The monthly ritual of the mandated stiff family dinner always made her uncomfortable. Her husband was coming directly, and the kids were grown and in college, finally glad to have excuses to skip the tenacious family gatherings. It meant she had an hour's drive all to herself.

The earlier call from a foreign-accented woman enquiring about Annie was unexpected and made her think of her friend after an awfully long time. Annie was a force; her influence was so fierce from the very first day they met. The five years spent with her had brought out the real Veena so vehemently, so unlike the former quiet, mousy, subdued self. She herself did not believe it was possible for one to change that much in a lifetime. She stared at the flooding memories, closing in like a swarm of bees, and there was Annie with her honey-sweet smile, filling the frame.

33 The art of mischief

Ernakulam, Kerala: 30 years ago

The long journey was draining Veena. Her mild headache had grown into a monstrous throb, fed by the clamour and clutter of the sticky, crowded bus. Heat and humidity competed to wear her down, and a wave of nausea lurked, waiting for the most inopportune moment. Every passing moment felt like an eternity, yet she dreaded reaching her destination—a new college and hostel filled with strangers, far from everything familiar. Her thoughts ran in a loop, a chaotic cycle her aching head struggled to process.

Once off the bus, she bought a cool sweet lemon soda, which calmed her nerves and eased some of the nausea. Her father was impatient, eager to finish the admission formalities and catch the night bus back home. Exhausted, Veena dropped her luggage beside the empty metal cot in her assigned room. Another bed, covered in bright sheets, with books and files strewn all over it, walls covered with a collage of powerful women of the world, indicated a roommate of distinct character. After a quick shower to wash away the dust and dirt, her headache dulled slightly. She eyed the bed longingly just as loud stereo music blared from the next room, reversing and amplifying her agony.

An attractive girl burst into the room, laughter still lingering on her face. She stopped, assessing Veena's pained expression.

"I'm Annie. Rough first day, huh?" she asked.

"Sorry, not feeling well after the long bus ride. I'm Veena," she mumbled, trying to smile despite the pounding in her head.

Annie left the room and soon Veena heard her loudly demanding the neighbours turn down the music. After some jeering, the music continued. Annie returned, locked the door, and pulled a small coin from her purse. She removed the bulb from her table lamp, placed the coin underneath, and switched it on. The lights went out, and the music stopped abruptly.

"Now you can sleep in peace. It'll take a while for the watchman to replace the fuse," she said simply.

Veena was glad her new roommate couldn't see her gaping mouth and awestruck expression in the dark. She went to bed with a huge smile.

The next morning, electricity was restored. Annie maintained an innocent face for their suspicious neighbours. Veena stayed close to her all day, benefiting from the good fortune that seemed to follow Annie. They got extra treats at breakfast, a good seat in the hall, and a lift to college with one of Annie's friends, saving them a long walk. Veena soon learned that Annie was a favourite among the teachers too, balancing top scores with myriad mischiefs.

"You want to come with me for a fun weekend?" Annie asked, stuffing her backpack a couple of weeks later.

"I don't have permission. My father won't approve," Veena said regretfully.

"Is he going to visit you?"

"Oh no, he's busy with his new wife! I have to wait for vacation to go home."

Annie listened sympathetically to the wishful tone, and then wrote a permission letter, forging Veena's father's signature with a flourish. "Who's going to know? You need some fun!"

Thus began the routine of weekend visits, the most fun Veena had ever experienced. If Mathew was free, they went trekking or swimming in the river. Annie often debated social justice issues with Mathew and their neighbour, Rajan Mash.

"Life is short. One must live it to the fullest," Annie would say, her infectious energy spreading to everyone around her.

One weekend, Veena's father made an unexpected visit to the hostel. Her brother called to warn her at Mathew's home. She and Annie rushed back, arriving just in time to see her father heading to the front gate. They jumped the back wall and overtook him to the reception area. Veena's heart pounded as she greeted her father. Annie, ever resourceful, tipped over a tray of papers at the front desk, successfully distracting the hostel warden. She then engaged Veena's father in animated conversation, charming him as she did with all parents.

Veena transformed under Annie's influence from a timid girl to a brave young woman, under the wings of Annie. For the first time in her life, she felt free, like a fluttering butterfly, out of the morbid caterpillar and cocoon phases of her life.

"Up for a night out? There's a famous temple festival I want to check out." It was Veena who suggested the latest rule break, surprising Annie. Hostel had strict rules against leaving the premise after seven in the evening.

"Looks like I'm a bad influence on you," Annie chuckled, agreeing instantly.

Veena handed her a black robe and hijab. "Borrowed it from Haseena. We don't want to be recognised, do we?" She winked, making Annie laugh.

They jumped the wall, donned the outfits, and walked briskly to the temple.

The man at the gate of the temple stared at the duo. Annie pulled Veena along to skip the gate and straight ahead. Veena giggled loudly on their near miss.

"Ah... We must not cause any religious disharmony!" Annie muttered as she took the robe off her in a quiet corner, away from the prying eyes of the festival goers, and stuffed in the bag.

"Yeah, remember not to kneel down and do a cross while you are inside, that would help!"

She often went with Annie to church on Sundays and Annie did the same for the temple visit with Veena, both were now well versed with the rituals although habits sometime showed up unknowingly.

The temple sight inside was worth the ride. It was beautiful, with hundreds of oil lamps lit up in rows along the temple walls. They both donned identical yellow sandalwood paste tilaks on their foreheads, fragrant Tulsi flowers in their loose, damp hair, and walked among the devotees, lighting more diyas. The evening was cool, and the devotional temple music added to the ambience. They moved around, avoiding visitors who were busy clicking pictures of the lights.

"That was a beautiful evening," Annie commented as they returned to the hostel. Veena agreed. The festival brought back cherished memories of her mother and their revered temple visits. It stayed as a memory after her mother fell sick and died, leaving her and her brother in misery. Her father had no time for small things and nostalgia as he was busy finding a new wife, rebuilding his own life.

The next day, the hostel guard smiled knowingly and handed them a newspaper. There it was, a report on the ongoing festival on the famous temple and a picture attached to it, young women lighting diyas at the temple. At the front of the row was the two of them, clear and beautiful, no mistaking of identity this time. They both cringed, this time Veena couldn't think how they could escape the consequence. Annie thought for a moment, she handed a note discreetly to the guard and took out the offending sheet from all sets of the paper, about to be distributed.

"They might see it elsewhere!" Veena whispered.

"Sure, but we can start the summer vacation a day early and go home today. No one is going to remember it after a restful holiday!" Annie said and took out 2 sheets of blank paper from her bag. She wrote in two permission letters to leave early in entirely different hands in less than 2 minutes...

34. Dinner schemes

Veena woke from her reverie as she parked in front of the enormous house, wiping the smile off her face. She counted the various models of luxury cars. At least she wasn't the last to arrive.

"You're finally here!" greeted a cheerful voice. A well-dressed man in his fifties, with waves of grey hair, took two steps at a time to reach her door. She smiled at her husband's grand gesture.

"So, you won your case, I take it?"

"Of course. When did I ever lose one?" he asked innocently.

"When you took the case for my father!"

"Oh, that was years ago. Your father didn't have a case to argue at all!"

"Is everyone in? Am I in trouble?"

"No. All are busy weaving cunning plans for the next election, I'm sure. They haven't noticed you're late!"

Men around the table were engrossed in heated discussions about the nearing election. Rounds of drinks and snacks had already been served. Veena took the side door to find her sisters-in-law in the kitchen, busy with last-minute additions to the elaborate spread under their mother-in-law's supervision. The matriarch looked severe, even at her advanced age, clad in a starched traditional cotton sari, her white hair tied in a small loose bun.

"On your own, still late?" she commented without preamble.

"I had a late class in college," Veena replied matter-of-factly.

She was never a favourite in this house and had abandoned the pretence of trying to win them over. To them, she was an outsider who had driven their son crazy enough to marry her without their consent. After many years and two grandkids, they relented and invited her over. They endured her presence only for appearances. The political climate was shifting, and her father-in-law needed the votes of a more liberal populace. They were good to their grandchildren; the only reason Veena decided to make amends and attend the family functions.

Veena and Krishnan privately thought recent political changes might have added favourable points for them. Their long-time friend Adi – the ever-popular Adityan MK – had joined the state ministry and was considered a future leader of the party. Krishnan's father, RP Menon, the Chanakya of his generation in politics, knew how to leverage such connections.

The discussion in the drawing room dragged on, the food grew cold, and no one dared interrupt. Her mother-in-law continued instructing the servants. Veena went upstairs to their room, always kept ready as if her mother-in-law expected her son to return home. Today, her husband was there before her, munching an apple from her bag.

"I'm so hungry, but no point. Sunil just arrived, and now dinner won't be before midnight!" he said with disdain, detesting his sister's husband with his excessive hunger for power.

Veena joined him, snatching some snacks.

"Didn't they want any criminal lawyer services today?"

"They have all the crime support they need! Sunil is filling the shoes; not sure he is serving the police or the crime! Best to avoid these dinners until the election is over!"

RP, a serving minister, always found a way to stick to power, even if it meant changing alliances. He had tried to bring Krishnan into politics, but he resisted. He continued practicing law, finding courthouses less criminal than his own family. The forced alienation from home after his unapproved marriage to Veena was a blessing in disguise, giving him the courage to say no.

"Remember Annie?" asked Veena. "I had a call from a young woman, a relative of Annie. She was with Dr. Mathew's son Joey. It felt like our best friends were calling for a reunion!" Veena's voice was wishful, and Krishnan squeezed her hand.

"Of course. Annie brought us together in the first place!"

"She knew I had a crush on you ever since you gave me a lift on that first day!"

"Adi and I used to come with you and Annie to Mathew's house for weekends. What a fantastic time we had then... And we lost both of them.... in the same year."

Both sat silently, lost in memories.

"It is some time since we met Adi; We should invite him for dinner one day," said Krishnan.

"Let's make it the same day as the family dinner. Your father won't be mad if Adi was the one keeping us away."

"Let's sneak out the back door and find dinner elsewhere!" he said, pulling her along.

There was some shuffling sound outside their door. Krishnan found his brother-in-law halfway up the stairs. "Good, I was coming to call you. Dinner time!" Sunil called out with uncharacteristic politeness which made them both frown.

The kitchen was busy reheating dishes. It took another half hour for her mother-in-law to call the men to the table and another two hours for Veena and Krishnan to leave, sleepy and tired from the long day.

35. Echo of the past

Maharajas College stood majestic, a testament to a century and a half of history, on the banks of the Vembanad Lake. Its grand campus had witnessed countless murmurs of youth, myriad social awakenings, wits, and frenzy. Tree-lined pathways mirrored the long corridors of the historic buildings—old but lively.

Just before lunchtime, Jane, James, and Joey entered the campus through its celebrated porch gates. Veena was in an empty office, waiting for them.

"You look familiar. Have we met before?" Veena asked in surprise.

"Not likely. We are in India for the first time," Jane replied, assessing the older woman. Did they look like Annie?

James looked as if he had read her thoughts. Did he feel the same compelling intuition toward this unorthodox woman?

"Maybe we are all recycled souls, close enough to leave a thread unbroken from a past life!" Veena laughed effortlessly bringing smiles on the youngsters' faces.

"How are you related to Annie?" She asked, her curiosity piqued.

"We are not sure yet," James said cautiously.

"What does that mean?" Veena frowned. She noticed the indefinable communication between the twins and Jane's reluctant nod in response.

"We think—only a thought at this moment—that she was our birth mother," James said with his typical frankness.

Veena raised her eyebrows, clearly starting to think they were either crazy or fraudsters. "That's impossible! She wasn't pregnant when I last saw her, and she died three months after that. I know for sure she hadn't any children before either. I was with her all those years. You are somehow misguided."

"We think she survived the landslide," Joey interjected.

Veena looked at him. "You must be Joey?"

"Yes. I assume you knew my father?"

"Of course. Your father was there all week in the rubble. All her neighbours and friends from our college were there, desperately looking for her. I attended her mother's funeral. All her family was there, mourning the lost."

"Did her father tell you? Did he tell you Annie was dead?" Jane asked.

"No...not in words. But he was in a state of self-denial, understandably. He was very fond of his daughter."

"The day my father died, six months after the landslide, Annie's father was in Wayanad. He had asked my father to save his daughter. We believe my father helped Annie that night," Joey explained.

"And we have reason to believe Dr. Mathew cared for Annie more than his own career and even his life in the end, to save her," James added.

"You all have surely gone crazy. May I ask how you reached this fantastic conclusion?" Veena listened quietly to their theories. She sat upright when they told her about the police and crime-branch response. She looked at their faces, measuring them, carefully choosing what to say.

"I am sorry about your father, Joey. He obviously loved Annie very much. He was such a gentle person anyone could fall for. But Annie—she never saw him that way and was oblivious to the change in his feelings as they grew older. Maybe he hated himself for being in that position and wouldn't dare to express his true feelings. I believe when he realised Annie did not reciprocate his feelings, he made a conscious decision to move on and give her space. He married your mother soon after his graduation."

"Do you know if anyone else was close to Annie?" Joey asked.

Veena hesitated. "It's funny. Half the boys in college

fancied her, but she deflated their advances with her self-deprecating humour and charm, making them her friends instead. She had that charisma. Even Krishnan once asked her out, but Annie put us two together instead, knowing I had a crush on him!" She laughed at the memory.

"Your husband is the famous lawyer Krishnan Menon, isn't he? The state transport minister's son?" Joey asked, having checked her details online.

"Yes, the very one! He is RP Menon's son—his only fault!" She smiled. "Thankfully, my husband and I detest politics enough to stay away from it as far as we can when it has become a family subsidiary!" she said with obvious loathing.

"You don't think my father and Annie were ever together? Maybe in later years?" Joey asked, his tone matter of fact.

"No, because Annie was... I know Annie's feelings hadn't changed towards Mathew!"

Veena paused mid-sentence and stood up. Jane sensed that she didn't say what she originally meant to.

Veena took them to the canteen for the promised lunch. She told them stories of Annie and their college days, the umpteen mischiefs they managed without being caught. She also recounted the gleaming accolades Annie had amassed along with her ingrained leadership qualities and passion.

Jane and James felt a kinship towards Annie, this unknown yet familiar person who may or may not be their mother. There were quirks in her they recognized in each other.

As they said their goodbyes, Veena promised to call if she found anything more...

Veena was restless after the twins left. Was it true? Did her friend survive? But she would have reached out, wouldn't she? Especially if she found out she was pregnant? Really? What did happen after the clandestine meeting? Did all hell break loose as they feared? If so, why was she left in the dark? Her head swam with confusing thoughts. Suddenly it felt as though nothing was really as it seemed for a long time. She felt foolish.

She dialled a landline number. An assistant told her he was in a meeting and assured her to pass the message to call back urgently. She left a voice message on his mobile phone and waited.

There was still no reply when Veena left the college in the evening. She was absorbed in thoughts when she opened her car door. She missed the tiny movement of the seats, adjusting automatically to the pre-set position controlled by her car keys. Otherwise, she would have known someone else had been in her car since she left it in the morning, causing the alteration. Only when she approached the busy road junction did she realise her brakes weren't working. She slammed the brakes repeatedly in panic, but nothing changed. The car continued careening towards the line of crossing traffic. Veena turned the steering sharply to the left, scraping hard against the compound brick wall to lose momentum. The car finally stopped, crashing into it. Flying bricks, dust, and broken glass heaped over its crumpled bonnet and roof.

As fate would have it, it was the same hostel wall Veena and Annie had jumped many times in their zappy student days to escape into a livelier world...

36. Arakillam

Some short miles away, a flurry of phone calls had set off a chain reaction that afternoon, each one escalating the tension and the stakes.

"You said they were searching for their missing grandfather! All I asked was not to lead them to any doors we don't want opened. How have they reached the heart of it all so quickly?" Shakuni's quiet voice was cold and sharp, an iceberg with the hidden depth of the menace it carried.

"I'll find out. Now that we know what they know, it should be quicker to trail." The caller tried hard to placate with the promise.

"Make sure you don't poke the wretched international press; two of them are British! The high commissioner has already made some noise."

"Of course..." came the cold assurance. The line went dead without any goodbyes.

Shakuni hurled his phone across the room, seething. How had this happened under his watch? The situation was more complex than he had initially thought. The risks had soared, threatening to unearth secrets and shift loyalties.

Immediate action was necessary to keep the status quo intact and to ensure unwanted truths remained buried. The quest had grown more tentacles, and if it all came together, decades-old secrets would surface, shifting alliances and fortunes.

She was supposed to be dead 25 years ago... too conveniently, before he had to do it himself. The old man was clever, just like Vidur. But the story was too real to doubt. What went wrong?

His strained brain brought up a scene from the revered textbook Mahabharata, of a time his namesake failed to kill the Pandavas, even leaving them with no clue of their failure itself... The other side had outwitted them.

The newly built palace of the Pandavas was burning, its occupants perishing within.

After losing everything in a game of dice, the Kauravas had offered the exiled Pandavas a luxurious palace as a peace offering, to placate the disgruntled public. It was a brilliant plan, meant to show Kauravas' goodwill while secretly plotting their cousins' demise. The grand palace was constructed with wax, designed to burn with everything in it.

When the flames subsided, seven bodies were found, accounting for the five brothers, their wife Draupadi, and their mother Kunthi. People mourned, including Pandavas' closest friend, Krishna. The Kauravas themselves shed bucket loads of crocodile tears and returned to their own palace, congratulating Shakuni on his faultless plan.

But the Pandavas had suspected the sudden generosity and discovered the trap of the highly inflammable walls. On the advice of their uncle Vidur, they had dug a secret tunnel beneath the palace before it was occupied. When the fire started, they fled through the tunnel, while an unfortunate huntsman, his five children, and the man sent to start the fire had perished.

The Kauravas were beaten at their own game, leaving them ignorant of the truth for a long time, which allowed the Pandavas to live in safety.

Shakuni now knew how his namesake must have felt upon realizing he had been outsmarted. The crocodile tears weren't just theirs; Pandavas' friends knew they were safe all along. He was certain now that Poduval knew the truth and the facade. It was a shame he died before passing on the message. The twins were the harbingers of his miserable end. His fall would be monumental, facing judgment not only for his sins but also for those before him. The ghosts of the past were closing in, ready to avenge. Unless he acted decisively, the secrets could spill everywhere. He had to strike before it was too late.

37. Spider net

Joey was driving the car he had borrowed from Lenin for the round trip. The cacophony of traffic noise and the incessant blaring of horns were punctuated by the deafening sirens of passing trains on the adjacent track, as if the angry trains were chasing to swallow the annoying traffic.

A furrow appeared on Joey's face as he stared into the rear-view mirror. "Don't look back now, but a black SUV has been following us since we left the college," he said to the twins, his voice tense. He sped up, weaving through the main road's traffic, but the SUV mirrored their moves, staying a few vehicles behind. Joey scanned the traffic, searching for more pursuers, but saw none.

He glanced at his watch and increased his speed. The SUV still trailed them, though Joey had put some distance between them. Suddenly, he swerved the car, darting in and out of traffic. Angry honks erupted from jilted drivers, the loudest from the SUV, but Joey didn't stop.

Jane saw his target: the rail crossing signal had turned red, the automated gates starting to close to make way for the whistling train, now sounding much closer. Joey accelerated and crossed the path just in time as the gates closed behind him. They didn't wait to see the expression of the SUV driver, who blared the horn furiously, and sped away. A few minutes later, a goods train with fifty or so wagons rumbled parallel to their road, blocking the SUV's path.

"Hopefully, we lost them, but we can't stay on the road. They might catch up or call for reinforcements," Joey said urgently, taking a sharp turn onto a narrow side road hidden by trees and bushes. After driving a mile without encountering any traffic, he turned into the open gate of a villa and parked in an empty garage.

"Darling... Come to the patio, coffee is ready..." a musical voice called out as they stopped the engine.

Joey flicked a switch to close the garage door, hiding them and the car from view. He also closed the gate for good measure. Opening a small side door that led to the back patio, he beckoned the twins to follow him.

The garden ahead had a well-tended lawn, bordered with various flowering bushes. Pots dotted the wide patio with an attractive sandstone floor.

"Hello, Unniyarcha!" Joey called out to the woman setting up a coffee tray on the patio table.

She looked up suddenly, knocking a China cup to the floor, shattering it. Joey stopped, giving her time to recover. Her anxious face turned into a brilliant smile when she recognized the intruder. The owner of the sharp face and intelligent eyes was heavily pregnant.

"Oh, dearest brother Aromal, you came to see your forgotten sister! It's high time you made the visit!" she beamed at him.

She looked quizzically at him when the twins came into view behind him.

"Hello, these are my friends, James and Jane, visiting from London. And this is Ms Megha Roshan, my friend from college and the dear wife of Roshan. We spoke to him from the train, you remember. They played the parts of Unniyarcha and her nemesis Chandu in our famous college play," Joey said quickly.

"So, it isn't a planned visit if your friends didn't know where they were going!" commented Megha.

Jane was impressed with her quick intelligence.

"No, it isn't. We were running away from a possible murderer," Joey said.

"You don't mean my husband, do you? He could murder you again off the stage if you brought calamity on your wake as you usually do!"

"Unfortunately, it is true. That's why I closed the garage and the gate, hope you don't mind."

This time, she looked at him seriously, realizing something was wrong, although Joey was casual in his comment.

"Have a seat. Roshan is on his way. I'll make some more coffee," she picked up the broken cup and hurried into the kitchen through the open French door.

Sure enough, there was a short honk. Megha opened the gate for Roshan, instructing him to park in the drive and not to open the garage. He came in with a perplexed look but beamed when he saw Joey, giving him a bear hug.

Joey introduced Jane and James.

"Thank you for your help earlier," James said, shaking Roshan's hand. "The police case file – Joey asked you for us."

"Oh... I was wondering why this bugger was interested in that! But why even you? You sound like a recent import... by your accent!" he laughed heartily.

Megha brought in coffee and biscuits, and they all took seats around the patio table. Jane sat next to the host on the wide-seated cane sofa.

"You won't believe what these two bring with them! We've been chased by a five-tonne elephant, a four-tonne truck, and a two-tonne SUV in the last two days!" Joey quipped. "We just escaped from the last one, right outside the rail crossing here. Life is never boring with them, I tell you!"

Megha's eyes widened in horror, while her husband sat up straight, his face keen. His life around computers and servers did not offer much of an adrenaline rush like the dangerous chases Joey described. He was hooked instantly. James explained the strange incidents that had happened around them since they landed in God's Own Country. Some dangerous aura was surely around them, but they didn't know for what.

"But we have our theories," Jane said.

"Definitely, you scraped something too close for comfort for someone!" said Roshan.

"But why? We came to look for our birth parents, whom we lost nearly 25 years ago; we don't even know who they were!" said James.

"People could take offence for things that happened thousands of years ago, just look around the world! Twenty-five years is still a short time," Megha was philosophical.

"I always thought my father died in an accident, but it doesn't seem that way anymore," Joey said.

"But how could your father be linked to their missing parents?" asked Roshan.

They explained what they knew so far and their theories.

"I had a thought they could be my half-siblings, but we are told that couldn't be true," Joey said.

"You trust this Veena woman then?" asked Megha.

"Don't know, she is a venerated university professor, and she was supposed to be Annie's best friend. Why would she need to lie to us?" Jane said.

"If she doesn't believe you are her children, she doesn't have any obligation to tell you anything!" Megha countered.

"Have you seen the driver?" asked Roshan.

"He had dark glasses and a beard. It didn't look real," Joey answered.

"But I noted the registration number," Jane handed her notebook with the number.

Roshan's face lit up; this was right in his alley. He brought his laptop along and searched the vehicle register. "That is registered to a Krishnan Menon in Ernakulam District."

"Veena's Husband!" said Jane and Joey together. They looked at each other in astonishment.

"But we never spoke to her before yesterday! And we only said we were looking for some information on Annie and nothing else yesterday. Today, the car was already waiting for us, as if pre-planned!" said James.

"You don't know if her phone was on or recording while you talked to her today, do you?" asked Megha.

"No, that can't be. I think the professor was genuine and spoke the truth," James said quietly.

Jane looked at him. She also had thought so before, but now she wasn't sure. Did they make a huge mistake in telling Veena about what they knew? Would all that now be passed on to the one determined to harm them?

Megha voiced the same concern. "Could either Veena or her husband have any reasons to stop you from finding out about Annie?"

None of them could think of any. They had all been good friends, from what they heard from Veena. But they knew so little...

"Advocate Krishnan Menon is the only one in that family not muddled in some ugly controversy, mind you!" said Roshan. "He openly refused to defend his own family in numerous court cases in recent years. I don't see RP returning him any favours," Roshan said.

"I heard RP was a ruthless politician. Didn't he disown his brother a few years ago for trying to contest for the party leadership?" Joey asked.

"Yes, and that hapless brother ended up dead under mysterious circumstances a couple of years later! RP was hostile to his son ever since he married Veena against his wishes. But Krishnan Menon and his wife are close friends from their college days with Adityan, our education minister. Things eased up with RP when Adi became prominent in his party and the government, tipped to become the next chief minister. RP clearly wanted to appear close to them, especially as he tries to cling on to his ministerial seat and keep his party's alliance alive," said Roshan.

"If this Adi was a friend of Veena's, then he might have known Annie as well. Being a minister and the next in line to be the Chief Minister, he would be powerful, wouldn't he?

As much to influence the police and have access to case records? A lot to lose too if unpleasant truths came out?" Jane asked thoughtfully.

They all looked at her suddenly.

"Of course, he could be! Also, if they were all friends then, she could have mentioned to him yesterday about some random people asking about Annie, their long-dead common friend!" Megha said.

"Yes, that's a possibility. The police files from the old Wayanad inquiry were accessed from the secretariat office this week and had been blocked for all others. Someone like him, with government power and connections, could make that happen," agreed Roshan.

"What kind of person is this Education Minister?" James asked.

"He is the nephew of the legendary leader VD, who fought with powerful landlords, including his own family, to bring social reform and rights for the labour class. A proper communist. He supported the land reform bill, which enabled scores of small-time farmers and farm workers to own the land they worked for generations. He was a charismatic leader who brought in lots of educated young men and women from all religions and classes to be interested in politics and government. Adi, his nephew, was one of them.

Adi has a seemingly good track record so far. He has shined in his role as education minister, a portfolio he insisted on owning, although more significant roles were available to him. He said education is the best tool available to create a brighter future generation and that without it, civilisation would be lost forever. At the least, he was well qualified for the job, unlike some of his predecessors. But we wouldn't know how things work in the background or if power has corrupted him over the years. Especially now, as he aims for the highest post available in the state government! You know what they say, power corrupts, and absolute power corrupts absolutely!" answered Roshan.

"So, we have a number of nominees for the villainous role with potential motives! Adi and RP for political gains, Krishnan and Veena for historical fallouts, Sridharan and Sunil from the police for abuse of power... Any other volunteers?" James said in a disheartened tone. The list was getting long!

"Veena is the connecting link to the top four. She would have some answers!" Jane said.

"If she is the one who tipped you off, you would be in great danger going back to her," Megha said.

Jane searched the name and found abundant references on Adi. Numerous contributions to education reforms were attributed to him. She focused on the 'Early Life and Education' section on the wiki page. He studied at the Maharajas College and then at the Government Law College in Ernakulam. Born as the elder son of Madhavan Nambudiri and Arya Antharjanam in an influential family in the village of Palari. He had a younger sister, AnandaLakshmi, and a famous uncle, VD—Vasudevan, the youngest brother of his father and a former Chief Minister. There was a helpful family tree on the page.

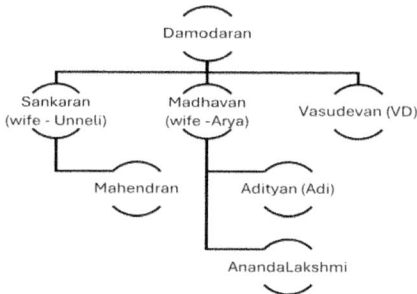

Damodaran

Sankaran (wife - Unneli) — Madhavan (wife -Arya) — Vasudevan (VD)

Mahendran — Adityan (Adi)

AnandaLakshmi

She opened the page attributed to VD to read more about the extraordinary political movement he led in his time and his accomplishments as a Chief Minister for a term. There was some mention of the time when he was accused of political insurgency. A sudden jolt hit Jane as she read the family section, which mentioned his older brother Sankaran of Korothu Mana, who died 25 years ago in Palari.

She read the section aloud. Joey had picked up her meaning a second before James.

"Sankaran of Korothu Mana! My grandfather bought the land from him in Palari, so Annie and Adi must have been neighbours!"

"Adi was Veena and Krishnan's college friend, so Annie must have been in college at the same time as him!" Jane added.

"And Sankaran died 25 years ago?! What's with that year with so many deaths?!" James said.

Jane searched again on Sankaran; his death was recorded in August, a month after Annie's presumed death, but there was no other information on him on any of the pages.

"Too many people and too many family connections. How anyone could remember all these!" Jane held her head in surrender. Joey had a rueful smile on his face and drew two more trees for her.

She laughed seeing that one was his own.

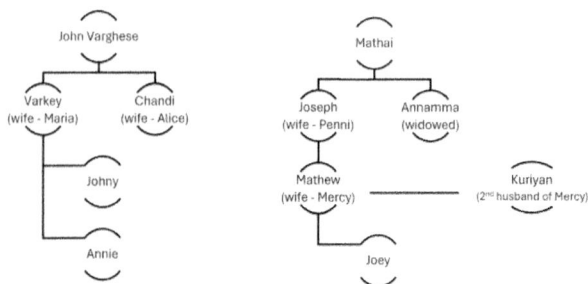

They stayed with Roshan and Megha that night. They decided it was best to leave their car in the garage to collect it later. Roshan agreed to arrange for someone to drive it in a day or two to Kottayam.

Megha lent them her own car.

"I am not using it anyway. My humongous bump already touches the steering wheel!" She said, pointing to her heavily pregnant self. "When we send yours to Kottayam, the driver could bring mine back."

****

A few miles away, another car was being recovered from the roadside by a scrap dealer. From its condition, no one would have guessed the driver escaped alive. Veena thought the same, resting in the private hospital room. It was only a miracle that saved her life; maybe her friend Annie was watching over her from that lucky wall! Was that her spirit or the living self, Veena didn't know!

38. Converging tracks

They left before sunrise, the road quiet at that hour. To their great relief, no marksmen followed them this time. Joey was driving; Jane and James were terrified of sitting behind the wheel. One needed a sixth sense to drive on these roads, a fact they had both agreed on their first day in Gopi's taxi. After two road chases in a week, they had vowed not to try.

James insisted Jane take the front passenger seat. "You'll feel better, and I can catch up on my sleep!" he said and promptly fell asleep within five minutes of hitting the road.

Joey and Jane sat in companionable silence. Jane glanced at him, studying his profile. He was focused on the road ahead, his face intent and pleasant. He felt her gaze and nodded with a smile.

"When will you get the test result?" Jane asked.

"The lab said one to two days. What do you think it will be?"

"I don't know. If it's a match, one quest will be complete..." Her voice trailed off.

"I don't think it will be a match," Joey said firmly. They both ignored the undercurrent in his voice. Jane could read the emotion hidden behind his dark eyes, but neither of them acknowledged it openly.

The national highway ahead showed signs of awakening. There were more early birds on the road like them, and a few big trucks. Thankfully, no one seemed interested in the small red sedan they drove.

"How's life in Bangalore?" Jane asked, changing the subject.

"It's great. I feel more at home there now than any-where else. I moved a lot during school, went to Mumbai IIT for my computer engineering degree, London for my MBA, and worked there for a while before returning to Bangalore.

My flat in Bangalore is my first and only home I've ever owned, so naturally, it became my hometown."

"Why is IT so popular in India?"

"The most popular profession in India is medicine, not IT. We have lots of doctors and surgeons, and most believe a medical job will never run out of demand!"

"So, James is in the right profession?" she mused with a smile.

"Sure, he is, and he can also claim he does some good for humanity!"

"I hope I can say that about my field of study! It often ends up too lofty and takes decades to prove or disprove anything. One reason I chose it is that it forces me to be patient!" She sighed.

"Physics brings answers to our biggest questions. Who are we, and how did we come to be where we are? I'm a fan of Stephen Hawking and Einstein... and of all the science fiction ever written, especially Arthur C. Clarke! You're lucky to work in the same field. What was your thesis paper?"

Jane looked at him in surprise. No one other than her research buddies ever asked her about her thesis. Not even James. Most ran a mile before she could complete the word "theoretical physics"!

"It was on Einstein's cosmological constant, introduced in 1917 to explain a static universe, which he later admitted was his biggest blunder when Hubble found out the universe was expanding. Fast forward six decades, scientists find that the expansion is accelerating, and the same constant could be used—although for entirely different reasons—now to explain the dark energy causing that acceleration! We ran simulations from Hubble telescope data to gather evidence and counted our lucky stars to have all the computational power and big data platforms available to modern scientists. It's an enormous help. Your chosen field, of course! Who could live without computers now?"

Joey smiled amiably. "Your original observation on Information Technology is true, though. IT is immensely popular and a major employer in the country. Enormous numbers of colleges have computer degrees and courses, not to mention the numerous local computer centres mushrooming in every small town, offering cheap classes often with a couple of old PCs and free or pirated software. In the initial period, the big software giants weren't too hard on licenses and copyrights in those tiny setups, but it enabled millions to train cheaply and find decent jobs and wages, raising so many households out of poverty. Many of these youngsters later became spearheads in the industry, helping those very corporations to grow. So, it was mutually beneficial in the end.

Governments also invested in the infrastructure and set up supportive policies, attractive tax exemption schemes for the IT industry in the '70s and '80s. The abundance of skilled, bright young talent makes it attractive for companies to keep investing in India even with the increasing costs over the years."

Jane was fascinated.

"I think the most coveted incentive for working in the computer field was the weather! Those early days, often the only offices with air conditioning were the rooms that held the computers, as they needed to be protected from overheating. If you worked with the computer, you had the most comfortable office you could dream of in a hot country like India!"

"I can believe that! It's warm here even in the midst of winter; I can't imagine the summers! It must be tiring," Jane agreed. "Back home, we complain about the rain and the cold and wait eagerly for the summer sun, but now I'm starting to miss those chilly days! Maybe the cold preserves us better!"

"It does. The British chose Ooty and Kodaikanal in the Nilgiri Hills for their cold climate and converted them into summer retreats to escape the intense hot weather in the plains. They still have some great old houses. It's a shame you couldn't see it properly. When the goons are off your back, I would like to take you back for a proper holiday!"

There was a promise and a wish in his voice. Although he tried to make it mild with a wink, Jane detected it all the same. Now, the future seemed as foggy as their distant past, overcast by presumptions and theories. Maybe there would be a time they could do normal things and be normal tourists.

Joey had questions about her work, life, and friends. Jane couldn't help but notice how keenly he listened to every word she said and seemed genuinely interested in knowing about her and, mostly, what she thought of her future.

"You learned Bharatanatyam? I wouldn't have thought so with all your academic focus. Amazing," Joey said when she mentioned she and her best friend Rita had recently performed in a dance drama production.

"Mum likes all that art and performance stuff; now I do it to keep myself fit. Do you know the poise you have to keep all the time in this dance form makes your body ache like you climbed ten flights of stairs at once!"

"I know, I once made a bet with Megha and tried to stay in the wretched 'aramandalam' posture. I didn't last even ten seconds! I still remember her smug face! So, I have enormous respect for classical dancers."

Jane burst into laughter, imagining the scene.

They talked about their favourite music, breaking into impromptu karaoke along with the car stereo. Delightful companionship made her forget the miles they passed. The morning sun accompanied them, rising steadily, brightening the road ahead.

Time flew by, and by the time James woke up, they had reached Annammachi's home.

39. One straightened knot

"I think we are missing some links with all of these events," Jane said, collecting bright pebbles shining in the clear water, smoothened by the river.

They were all back at the riverbank after a filling lunch fixed by Annammachi, taking stock of the events, they already knew to make sense of what was left to find out. It was going back nearly sixty years or so from the time Joseph and Varkey went to Palari. They needed to piece together these fragments to untangle the mystery of the missing Annie and the events leading to the death of Joey's father.

"If they took Varkey to the Kozhikode Hospital, and if Annie was in the same ambulance, she would have been admitted there too, right? Could we not check if there was a record of her there?" Jane suggested.

But Joey shook his head, looking doubtful. "Kozhikode Hospital is a medical college hospital; it is one of the busiest in the state. Finding a record from nearly 25 years ago would be as practical as finding a needle in a haystack!"

"But we found the record in the Kalpetta hospital!" Jane argued.

"Kalpetta Hospital is a small unit, and you were lucky to have Fr. John and Sr. Girija from that time still working there. Besides, they kept the records separately because of the exceptional circumstances—first the police case and then my father being one of their key staff. We can't expect the same from a medical college hospital with hundreds of patients every day unless you know someone higher up to prioritise the search."

James had to admit that even at his own hospital back home, it would be difficult to trace a random record from that long ago, even with a brilliant IT and record management system within the NHS.

"Suppose we have a brilliant IT engineer on hand with

equally brilliant friends... They should be able to hack into a simple hospital system?" Jane asked with innocence plastered all over her face.

"I suppose they could!" Joey grinned. "If the records are online... But most likely they would be in dusty old book registers. If they were keyed into the computer later, it would be in a cold archive or on hard disks/tape. In that case, you'd need a brilliant burglar too! You know any hobbits?"

"Just a hypothetical question, of course," she grinned back.

Joey's phone rang, a wave of emotions playing on his face as he listened intently. Jane looked at him worried.

"DNA results... it's not a match... not enough to make us siblings, either full or half," Joey announced, trying to mask his relief and failing. "I know it complicates the puzzle, but I'm glad my parents' story isn't tangled up in even more drama," he sighed.

"Of course, it is better this way," James said, looking thoughtfully at Jane.

She smiled at them with a nod, trying to erase the complex feelings and uncertainties etched on her face. She needed time to process it. Seemed Joey and James thought so too, and the pregnant silence grew with all the possibilities.

"Veena insisted Annie hadn't had a romantic relationship with Mathew. She was on the verge of telling us something but then decided not to. I noticed it then," Jane said, diverting the conversation to firmer grounds.

"Then it could have been anyone from her college or from Palari, or anywhere in between!" said James.

"That's a very small percentage considering the population of this country!" she sighed.

They all laughed at the odds. Then there was that companionable silence again, each delving into what this meant for them. James looked at Jane and Joey, both deep in thought. He then excused himself and hurried to the house insisting he need to call Olivia before she left for work.

Jane looked for more pebbles in the shallow water. Sunrays made shiny floating rings on her bare feet through the water, and her silky hair caressed her pensive face in the gentle breeze.

"So, what's the deal with James? Are you going to get a sister-in-law soon?" Joey asked after a while.

"I don't know. James never had any serious relationship until now. This one, they look besotted!"

"What about you? Someone smitten about you back home?"

"I can't even match my own expectations in life, let alone another person's," Jane replied, her voice faltering slightly.

Joey raised an eyebrow, sensing the deep feelings behind her words. "You know, high achievers like you often forget that perfection isn't a prerequisite for love."

Jane was taken aback by his observation and matter-of-fact tone. She looked at him and found only genuine interest. It made her lower her usual shield of defence while she contemplated the truth.

"I don't know really," Jane sighed. "Growing up, I was always trying to figure out who I was. James and I stood out, and people made sure we knew it. Mum was so at ease with herself, but I felt like a chameleon, never quite fitting in. Dad adored us all, but every time I looked in the mirror, I saw a misfit's face."

Joey watched her, sensing the weight of her words. "So, you tried to prove you belonged, in the only way you knew how."

"Exactly," Jane admitted, her voice softer. "Society seemed to measure us with different sticks and expected us to be grateful for the rather comfortable life we had, as if we didn't really deserve it. I pushed myself to succeed, to prove that I deserved everything I was given. It's a bit crazy, isn't it? Always pushing beyond the limits, never just... being."

She felt raw, saying the truth out loud. She had envied James for gradually growing up to accept the same feelings as part of his life, for being able to sidestep it to direct his compassion for others who needed it through his work and finding fulfilment, just like their mother. Yes, her work helped in a way, by recognizing the insignificance of human beings, the whole planet and the galaxy itself among billions of others. But she was never able to completely shut down the negative loops running in her head, seeking meaning and belonging.

She glanced at Joey, who nodded with understanding. "It isn't uncommon to feel that way. It's too evident in our continent than yours, perhaps for very different reasons—to make oneself noticed among the billions, not to be perished as common in the abundance of talents. But companionship should be different from all that. Are you seriously saying you haven't noticed a similar soul on your high-flying journey so far?"

"The only one I ever fancied took a plunge into political activism, rather than binding himself to any trivial notion of love and domestic life! That cured me of any fantasies!" Jane said, with no bitterness which really surprised herself.

"That's an odd tale. Now I would like to know more!"

Jane told him about Steve Chang and his higher calling. She twirled her hair with her fingers absentmindedly as she talked. Joey saw a rare glimpse of the vulnerability she carried beneath all that confident self. 'A chink in her armour! She couldn't take rejections very well...'

"Ah, you're not alone," Joey said, his tone light but with a hint of something deeper. "Even Buddha left his wife and son in search of enlightenment."

Jane let out a dry laugh. "Well, at least I'm in select company, ditched for the greater good. Lord Ram and now

Buddha too!"

Joey's eyes shifted to the water flowing below; the bitterness barely concealed in his voice. "Disenchantments can sneaks up in so many ways. My parents... their marriage was a disaster. I had vowed to myself not to repeat it, ever. Whenever someone hinted at getting serious, all I could see was that same chaos, multiplied... I'd be out the door before the conversation finished..." He chuckled, but it was a hollow sound. "Desertion is something I've gotten pretty good at too"

Jane thought of her parents, of James and Olivia, and then of her lonely self. Why was she shunning the effort she needed to put in? Why is it so hard to trust, to let her heart open to possibilities?

She saw Joey's reflection in the water, shimmering with the gentle waves. She looked up and saw his intense gaze, solely focused on her, a storm of his own, raging up in those hidden ocean depths.

She felt the familiar tension rising in her gut at the thought, shields rising again to cover the vulnerability. Buddha was right about one thing: desire was the cause of all the sufferings!

"Let's go... and talk to Rajan Mash? We need to find more of those puzzle pieces, before I can go home..." she said abruptly, turning away from him, packing the pebbles safely back in her pockets, leaving Joey to stare at her retreating form with a pained look in his eyes.

40. The Big House

James joined them to their walk to Rajan Mash. He couldn't reach Olivia, but he had spoken to Lissy. She took the news of the DNA test with a note of disappointment; Mathew's parental judgment could have slightly eased her pain of the error on her side, giving some authenticity for the swap. Besides, she had liked him very much, and his son Joey sounded exactly like him, which could have been great genes for her children to inherit.

"She was half joking and half wishing!" James said with a smile. Joey returned a self-deprecating smile at that, still rapt in thoughts. James looked at Jane and found her too lost in thoughts.

They found Rajan Mash on his veranda, reading a script. He set it aside and heartily welcomed them in. He asked his cook to bring them all hot tea and snacks and showed them around his house.

They were particularly drawn to the older section of the house, a testament to history with its vast wooden structures, predominantly teak and mahogany. Narrow corridors extended from the veranda, leading to smaller rooms on either side, each with raised steps and heavy wooden doors. The centrepiece of the mansion was a grand hall, its majesty still evident in the arched wooden ceilings supported by massive, intricately carved pillars, each seemingly fashioned from a single piece of wood. The twins found it difficult to envision Varkey sitting proudly in this majestic hall, contemplating leaving all this behind for an unknown, perilous land. Knowing that he had actually made that courageous choice deepened their admiration for the man they believed could be their grandfather.

James looked around, eyes wide with admiration. "This place is incredible, Rajan Mash."

Rajan Mash nodded, a faint smile playing on his lips. "It

was already standing proud when I found it. I've just tried to honour and retain its legacy."

Joey leaned in, curiosity flickering in his eyes. "Grandfather mentioned that you introduced him to Sankaran Namboodiri when they bought the Palari land. His nephew is the education minister now, right? Adi? Is he really as impressive as they say?"

"I do know Adi from my many trips to Palari and the capital," Rajan Mash began, his tone suggesting a cautious admiration. "He's one of the few good politicians left in this country. But then, how good can a politician really be?" He let the question hang in the air, a faint smile playing on his lips. "Politics is like a swamp of corruption and power struggles. It can drag down even the best intentions."

Jane leaned in, sensing there was more beneath the surface. "But Adi seems different?"

Rajan Mash nodded slowly. "Adi has never shown much interest in power for its own sake. Perhaps that's what sets him apart. His uncle, VD, saw something unique in him early on. Adi organized classes and events in every remote village, rallying the youth. It was incredible to witness. He told me he discovered his cause in those days, working tirelessly."

"But then he left it all behind?" Joey probed, noting the subtle shift in Rajan Mash's expression.

"Yes, he left it all abruptly and travelled across India for a while. It took a lot of persuasion from VD to bring him back," Rajan Mash replied, his voice tinged with something Jane couldn't quite place – regret, perhaps, or sadness.

"Doesn't he have any family of his own? There was no mention of it on the wiki pages or online," James said.

Rajan Mash smiled, a hint of irony in his eyes. "Adi always says he's married to public service. Not a bad thing, really. Plenty of 'public servants' seem to think their roles are family heirlooms. Power's a seductive legacy to pass on through bloodline. The survival instinct in our DNA bled into the human psyche!"

Jane's eyebrows knitted together. "But it seems like he got to power through his uncle VD, didn't he?"

Rajan Mash nodded slightly. "VD might have opened the door, but Adi walked his own path. After VD's death, Adi was pushed out of the party. That's when he started his own independent political party with a few like-minded individuals, working at the grassroots level to build it into a mainstream force. I remember seeing him in those early days, out in the villages, getting his hands dirty. His work spoke for itself; people couldn't ignore him."

Jane glanced at James, who leaned forward. "What about VD's family?"

"VD remained single all his life," Rajan Mash began. "His bride died in an accident a week before their wedding. She was a spirited young party worker and the sister of his comrade friend. VD's family, particularly his father and older brother Sankaran, were vehemently against the union because she was from a lower caste. VD left his family home after a final clash with them. There were whispers that his family might have had a hand in the accident, but nothing was ever proven."

"And his other brother?" James asked.

"Adi's father, Madhavan, was a kind man but grew up timid under the shadow of his father and older brother. He led a quiet life centred around the family temple, finding solace in prayers, rituals, and Vedic texts. His wife was different—educated and quietly determined. She ensured her children saw beyond their entitlement and power. She secretly facilitated their contact with VD, taking great personal risk. Adi once told me his mother was an unsung activist, working wonders from the shadows rather than from rooftops. He called her his silent powerhouse."

"You have been to Palari often?" Jane was curious.

"Recently, yes. I have been looking for a location for my

next movie—Indulekha. It is one of the oldest novels we have in Malayalam. I know Korothu Mana is an excellent match for what I have in my mind. Adi agreed to let us shoot there as they could use some of the funds for the upcoming election campaign. My team has been there already for a location visit."

He showed them a collection of photographs. The place indeed looked like from another world, ancient and sacred, strange and intriguing, intimidating and sleepy, all at the same time.

"We are doing some preliminary work from this week. Some of my crew is coming with me tomorrow. Mahendran, Sankaran's son, is now working as the personal staff manager for Adi. He said we could stay in the house as it is currently empty. For the extended crew, we will have the caravans brought in."

A sudden idea formed in Jane's mind. An unexpected opportunity to learn more and a path to proceed...

"Is it possible for us to join you? We've heard so much about the place and would love to see the house and Palari. Could you let us tag along?"

Jane's eyes met James's and Joey's. "What do you think?"

James nodded. "Absolutely. It sounds like an adventure."

Joey shook his head, a hint of regret and decision in his eyes. "I'd love to, but I have to return to work. Maybe I can swing by later if that's ok."

Jane turned to look at him, measuring his words and his determination, a faint disquiet stirring in her chest, letting it to sink into the quiet corners of her mind.

"I could add the two of you to the party, but you must pretend to be part of the crew. I don't want Adi to think I made their home a tourist place," Rajan Mash smiled.

"Of course, we could help. We can review your script to

give you a fresh perspective."

"Have you read Indulekha before?" Rajan Mash was keen.

"No, that's why I said a fresh perspective...," Jane laughed.

"Ah..."

"I have read Indulekha. In fact, I have a play adaptation script from my father, based on the very book, right here with me!" Joey said, looking in his bag and producing a stack of papers yellowed with age, notes scribbled along the sides of the typewriter text in Mathew's own handwriting.

Rajan Mash took it and looked through it. "I remember this, Mathew did that play at the college. There was a much-talked-about scene in it, Lakshmi, the actress in her character as Indulekha, slapped the pompous, rich, old, silly suitor after he tried to kiss her on stage, causing him to fall flat on his back. The audience liked it very much, evident from the spontaneous applause. Mathew later told me this wasn't in the script, and the rogue actor had misbehaved and got his due. These sorts of things do happen in our movie sets sometimes, usually off the screen, but equally a nightmare for a director and producer. Some come up with the silly excuse that artists live on the edge of emotions to bring their best, so some ought to lose control at some time!"

"I thought the script was brilliant. I always liked the original book; it has the similar grace and flair of Jane Austen's books, set in the 19th century Kerala. Chandu Menon portrayed the society brilliantly in his book as if in an oil canvas," Joey said.

"So, you read classics?" Jane had a curious smile on her face.

"Of course, I do read all sorts of books," Joey agreed with no resistance. Books were his steady companions after his dad's death. Kuriyan's Ooty house had good stocks of books which had helped him to take himself out of gloom to a different world, to live the life of someone else on the pages of those delightful books.

"You don't mind if I keep the script for a little longer? I could adapt some of it and credit Mathew in the movie if you are okay with it?" Rajan Mash asked, holding onto the old script.

"Of course. When I saw it, it reminded me of him, sitting in his study and writing notes late into the night. The thought of his hands moving steadily across these papers brought me great comfort and some precious memories. I realised I have only very few of them."

"I will just take a photocopy, and you can keep the original," Rajan Mash said. He too had felt the pang when he saw those papers, stirring the memories of a shared friendship and of loss.

****

"We have to leave tomorrow," Joey said to his grandfather and Annammachi, polishing off the last of the plum cake she made for tea. They had decided to leave as soon as possible; it wasn't safe if their hunters had traced the car to Lenin.

Joseph and Annammachi were sad to see the end of the lively days with Joey and his young friends. It would again be back to the gloomy days, which started and ended the same way, only tiredness and loneliness growing in between, with nothing new to look forward to.

"I promise to come back soon. Besides, James and Jane are going to Palari, your dreamland. They could tell you if the place is still the land of milk and honey or a wasp nest!" he said.

"Palari, you should see it through the eyes of those hopeful travellers who left their homeland with nothing but dreams. Then only you could see the promised land. Or it would look just like any other!" Joseph cautioned. "Many of us have made our life, working magic from that dirt. Life was

194   Therese Pal

hard, often dangerous. Mother Nature only intended the fittest to survive, and those who survived did so through arduous work, ingenuity, and the ability to adapt..."

41. Into the deep

Early the next morning, they were all set to start on their respective journeys.

"Call me if you find out anything more," Joey said to Jane, his gaze lingering on her a moment longer.

"I thought you had two weeks," she said quietly.

"Something came up. And I think some space and time will be of help to me right now... Maybe you too..."

The moments stretched, heavy with all they could not say, as the world moved past them in indifferent circles. The past clung like chains, anchoring them to the earth, their feet too heavy to risk a step closer.

James came to say his goodbyes. He shook Joey's hands with warmth while nodding to Jane's pensive face. "Please do try to join us later, if all ok. It would be a shame if our paths didn't cross again..."

Joey left with the hired driver Roshan had sent to drop off Lenin's car and pick up Megha's. He planned to ride to Ernakulam and take a flight to Bangalore.

James and Jane left soon after with Rajan Mash in his car. His cameraman Girish settled into the driving seat, letting loose his ponytail and preparing for the long drive.

On the way, Rajan Mash called Adi.

"Hello, Rajan Mash... Adi is away at a meeting. Anything urgent?" a soft voice answered after a few rings.

"No, it's okay, Mahendran. You'll do just fine. I just called to say we're leaving for Palari."

"Okay. I called the caretaker earlier to confirm the arrangements and your accommodation. All set and ready for you. Hope you have an exciting time!"

"Great, thank you. Any chance of meeting you or Adi there?"

"Not likely. It's a busy time with the upcoming election."

"Alright, I'll come see you in Thiruvananthapuram after

this trip. Thanks again for letting us use the location."

"You're welcome. It's for our benefit as well. We must meet the huge bill of the election expenses. You know how Adi goes on about keeping to a shoestring budget, as if that's what really happens in politics!"

"Well, all the very best with that," Rajan Mash said, then disconnected.

Jane looked outside at the passing scenery; they were already out of the city and navigating the national highway.

"Is it Adi's cousin? " Jane asked, her tone casual, but her eyes sharp with curiosity.

"Yes, He's Sankaran's son, who originally sold the land to Varkey and Joseph. Mahendran now manage Adi's official as well as personal matters. He arranged this location deal for us too."

"Really? We heard that Sankaran died around the time Annie died twenty-five years ago. Mahendran got his own fortune then?" asked Jane.

Rajan Mash paused, as if weighing his next words. "Not quite. His life and persona is shaped by complicated circumstances.

Four weeks after the landslide that killed Varkey's family, Sankaran was found dead in the family pond, among the roots of the ancient Banyan tree. Mahendran, who found him, was so afraid he ran back screaming. Allegedly, he saw a snake around Sankaran's neck, as if it strangled him. When everyone else arrived, there was no snake, though there was an unexplained scrape around his neck. The post-mortem said he died of a heart attack. Most bizarre. No one was sad about his passing, though; he was one of the cruellest and most bigoted landlords ever, like his father who had even worse record in exploiting common folks and women alike, passing the baton to his oldest son Sankaran."

"Curious," Jane said, her voice trailing off in thought.

"It was a strange and deadly period in Palari. I remember

it; Newspapers ran numerous articles on it then. Varkey lost three family members in the landslide. The next day, one of Annie's friend - Lalitha - was found dead in the swollen river. She left a note saying she couldn't live with the thought of her only friend buried alive under the mud; apparently, they were quite close."

"Two months later, Lalitha's father, Kunjelu, was also found dead in the Korothu family's Snake temple. Death was caused by a snake bite, from a King Cobra. The whole village believed the curse of the snakes was upon the family."

"Why the curse?"

"There's a backstory about that family. Everyone in the village knew it, so it's not exactly a secret. It was known that Sankaran fathered both Lalitha and her sister Radha. Their mother, Madhavi, was an exceptionally beautiful young woman from an extremely poor family, a tenant of Sankaran. He gifted the meagre house and land to her large family and forced her father to marry off his oldest daughter to his loyal servant Kunjelu to make it look proper and legal. Sankaran placed them in a plush house near his own, but he made routine visits to Madhavi whenever he felt like it. No one questioned him. Kunjelu was happy to oblige and found alternatives in the huts of workwomen from the farm.

Soon after the marriage, Sankaran gave Madhavi the duty of maintaining the famed Sarpa-kaavu, the sacred snake temple surrounded by an ancient grove with rare old trees and a stream flowing through the thick vegetation, undisturbed for centuries. Lalitha and Radha grew up in this setup. People believed the snakes were distressed by Lalitha's death and turned aggressive with vengeance."

"Really! Hostile snakes taking revenge by killing two people one after the other?" Girish shook his head in disbelief. "That's more dramatic than our movies!"

"Beliefs aren't always logical. There were six untimely deaths in the span of two months: three in the landslide and another three in unnatural circumstances. After these consecutive deaths, there were many folklores about sightings of snakes and ghosts. People heard ethereal voices echoing around the pond and the Sarpa-kaavu, so the place was abandoned. It's been reclaimed by the wild, adding to its paranormal spectacles."

The youngsters listened, intrigue sparking in their eyes. The story was thick with suspense – maybe the deaths were accidental, but they couldn't shake the feeling of something more sinister. Blaming it on a curse seemed too convenient, too neat. But with so many years gone by, any evidence of foul play would be buried deep, if it existed at all.

"Madhavi and Radha are still in Palari?" Jane asked, adding notes onto the family tree she had copied from Adi's wikipage.

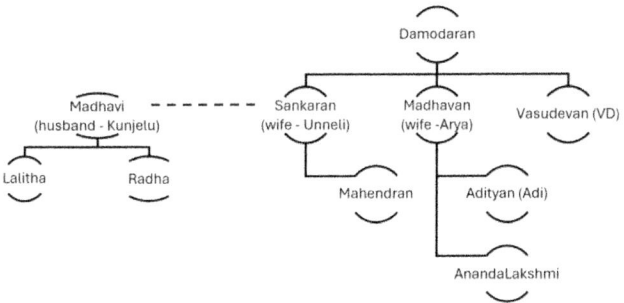

```
                              Damodaran
                                  |
        +-------------------+-----------+------------------+
     Madhavi  - - - - -  Sankaran    Madhavan       Vasudevan (VD)
  (husband - Kunjelu)  (wife - Unneli) (wife -Arya)
     +--------+              |             |
  Lalitha   Radha        Mahendran    Adityan (Adi)
                                          |
                                     AnandaLakshmi
```

"I don't know. Sankaran didn't transfer the property title to Madhavi and his kids, probably to keep them dependent on him. But with his death, everything was thrown into question.

Mahendran evicted Madhavi and Radha, partly to take revenge for the shame his father caused him and his mother with decades of gossips."

"He made his own sister homeless! What kind of man is he?" Jane was indignant.

"Mahendran was up against the wall by then, with no place to go. His father had sold off most of his inheritance already. He lived in the family home, which was legally owned by Adi's father. His grandfather was afraid of his older son's habit of losing family properties, so he had left the family home to his docile middle son.

Adi felt bad for Mahendran. It wasn't Mahendran's fault to grow up with such a father and grandfather. Unlike Adi, he never knew any other way. Mahendran mellowed later, without his father leaning over his shoulder. He still needed an income, so Adi gave him a job. After Adi's parents died, he relied more on his cousin, the only family member left. Mahendran proved his worth with his organizational skills and now handles most of Adi's campaign and schedule."

"I'm glad he got a second chance," said James.

"I've always believed in Karma," Rajan Mash said, his voice taking on a reflective quality. "Our actions shape our destiny. We're all given the freedom to choose our path – some walk a righteous road, others stray into darkness, and a few find redemption along the way. But no matter the path, it circles back. It's a reminder, a nudge to live rightly."

"It doesn't always look that way. There are too many sinners living comfortably. What's the karma in their case?" Jane asked.

"It may look comfortable on the surface. But material comfort isn't everything. Can you say for definite, these sinners as you call, suffer no internal torment and acute cognitive dissonance? The mental prison they are in, could be worse than physical pain or death they caused on others. Our soul needs a different kind of comfort, which comes from good thoughts and the well wishes of others. You can force someone to do as you please, but you can't control their thoughts. Only good deeds can bring that."

Jane's eyes narrowed slightly, probing for more. "If someone believes their actions are right, there's no torment, is there? "

"Maybe they could, for a while," Rajan Mash conceded,

his eyes distant, as if recalling old battles. "But not forever. The truth has a way of surfacing, like a stubborn weed. And fooling oneself... that's the hardest deception of all. We know our own truths, even if we hide them from the world. And that's enough to bring Karma knocking at our door. There is a phrase in Mahabharata: 'Dharmo rakṣhati rakṣhitaḥ', meaning dharma- righteous duty- protects those who uphold it."

Rajan Mash's gaze softened, his voice spiritual. "We all have a conscience. It's built above our common thoughts and beliefs. It's attuned more to the suffering of others and human emotions around us. And then there's death, the only certainty. We all face it. Death brings realization and regret, an end to a circle of life, even if one doesn't believe in an afterlife."

Jane hesitated, her scepticism evident. "We don't know what happens after death. That can't deter our actions in this life."

Rajan Mash leaned forward, his gaze locking onto hers, searching. "There will be that moment of reckoning. Humans fear the unknown, hence we constantly try to learn, to understand. Isn't that true for you?"

Jane felt the intensity of his question, as if he saw through her defences to reach her soul. She nodded slowly, realising he had touched a nerve.

Jane thought about the unknowns she was facing. There were too many. Too close to heart, even though she never admitted it. Maybe she was fooling herself that the answers didn't matter. What if one of the unknowns was death? Would she be afraid?

She saw her brother's reflection in the mirror, his smile reassuring. Maybe she wasn't afraid because of him. Whatever they faced, they had each other. They would go through it together, no matter what the unknown was.

42. Step back in time

Night had fallen by the time they reached Korothu Mana. The soft, distinctive music of traditional drums, Nadaswaram, and flute from the family temple accompanied them through the winding driveway to the vast courtyard. The house stood grand and imposing, a multi-storied Nalukettu with ornate mahogany doors and a wide veranda adorned with carved wood rails. Tiny flames flickered from the huge brass lamp, casting dancing shadows on the court-yard, while a diffused electric light at the other end reflected off the shiny black floor.

The caretaker, Murali, greeted them cordially. He was nearly sixty-five, tall and spindly, with glasses that seemed too large for his thin face. Dressed in a linen shirt and a white mundu with a golden Kasavu border, he had a pleasant, wel-coming manner.

"I've lived here most of my life. I'm a distant relative of Adi's mother," Murali said, lifting their luggage with prac-ticed ease. There was a hint of pride in his voice, but also a shadow of something else, a life shaped by this place's his-tory. "My mother died when I was ten, and I had nowhere to go. Adi's mother, took me in. She was kind, saw something in a lost boy. Adi... he made me the caretaker later on." He paused, a brief flicker of emotion crossing his face. "If you freshen up and come down, dinner is ready to serve."

The twins were captivated by the grandeur of the house, feeling as if it had risen from the pages of history, both sleepy and magical. James pressed the solid wooden doors of the bedroom, appreciating the cool, rough texture. Unlike the or-nate front door, these were plain but sturdy, exuding a closed-in, confinement feeling. Their rooms were a step back in time, with slanted windows framing the sprawling inner courtyard. Hall lights filtered through, casting intricate shad-ows from the carved wooden railings of the chuttu veranda,

Therese Pal

which enclosed the entire courtyard. Jane ran her fingers along the smooth, worn wood of the low seating platform that lined the veranda, imagining the generations who sat there before her. In the courtyard's centre, a Tulsi plant, fragile yet steadfast, stood on its ancient platform. The small lamps around it flickered, their light dancing like restless spirits in the night breeze, a silent guardian of the old house's secrets.

Adi's cook, Sukumar, served them a vegetarian dinner on the large, ornate dining table. The meal included steaming rice, sambar and Aviyal- curries made of mixed vegetables, Thoran - a dry dish made from pulses and finely chopped banana flower, and Kalan- a yogurt-based curry with cooked yam and raw plantain.

"A mini Sadya indeed. I enjoyed it very much," Rajan Mash thanked Sukumar, who was clearing the plates.

Sukumar's face glowed with pride. Around fifty, with a round belly and nearly bald head, he was awestruck in the presence of Rajan Mash, having grown up watching his movies on the big screen.

"Thank you, sir. It's all organic and home-grown, from our own vegetable patch and paddy field. Adi insisted on making us self-reliant on food, a program he wants to push across the state to reduce reliance on imported vegetables, which often come with loads of pesticides. An interest he inherited from his mother. I took over the garden after she passed away. Our fields produce more than enough for our own use, so we often sell the excess in Palari market."

Sukumar had grown up in Palari and had tried his hand at cooking at his uncle's local eatery after his academic aspirations ended with his third failure in high school. He took the position at Korothu Mana when their old cook left suddenly after Sankaran's death.

"We lost most of the staff that year; they left in droves," Murali added. "It was hard to find staff to work at the house after the consecutive deaths and the spreading stories of vengeful spirits."

Upstairs in her strange room, Jane turned restlessly in bed. Despite being tired from the long journey, she couldn't sleep. She thought of the generations who had lived and died in this old house, feeling she could hear their whispers through the stone walls. Eventually, she fell into a disturbed sleep, where the whispers grew louder, intermittently silenced by a forlorn, soul-stirring tune. She wanted to speak to the singer but found herself mute. She reached out to comfort her, but the floating mist around her hand formed an impenetrable curtain.

Jane woke up in the morning, more tired than before. It took her some time to orient herself. The walls were thankfully silent, with nothing to say to her in the daylight.

After breakfast, Murali took it upon himself to show them around the house. He guided them through the sprawling estate, his voice resonating off the cavernous walls. He paused at the south block, gesturing towards the grand reception rooms filled with ornate furniture. "This is the Thekkini," he announced. He continued down a corridor, his hand resting on a heavy wooden door before he pushed it open to reveal a storeroom filled with large wooden boxes. "And here is the Padinjattini, where we used to keep our most valued possessions."

At the centre of the block stood the Arappura, its floor elevated and ceiling low, forcing anyone inside to stoop. The room was packed with enormous wooden chests, some large enough to hold a person. Murali pointed to the largest one. "This big one is called a Pathayam, used to store grains for the entire year. The smaller ones held other valuables— metal utensils, plates, dishes, even books in the old days," he said. "Only the family elder had the keys. Everyone else needed permission to take anything out."

The room remained dim despite the overhead electric

lamp. The aged wooden panels and boxes seemed to drink in the light, their secrets well-hidden. The twins noticed a latch in the corner of the floor and glanced questioningly at Murali.

"That leads to the Nilavara, the basement storage room," he explained with a shrug. "I doubt the latch works anymore. It hasn't been used for decades."

Moving to the east block, Kizhakkini, they found the kitchen bustling with activity. The cook was busy preparing lunch, assisted by a maid who chopped vegetables. Outside, a deep well, covered with a net to keep out falling leaves, was accessible from inside through a wide window equipped with a pulley.

"That's the source of all the water we use in the house. I've drawn thousands of buckets using that pulley," Murali reminisced, smiling. "Thankfully, we have plumbing in the kitchen and bathrooms now." He drew a pail of water and poured some into their outstretched palms. The water was clear as crystal, naturally cold and sweet.

Finally, they arrived at the north block, Vadakkini, which housed a huge dining room and the bedrooms for the staff.

"This place is enormous," James remarked, his voice tinged with awe.

Murali nodded. "Yes, Tharavadu houses like this were built for joint families, accommodating many generations under one roof. Now, it's mostly empty. Adi and Mahendran spend most of their time in the capital. Adi suggested renting it out to keep the house useful and to generate income for its upkeep. Without that, maintaining these old houses would be a huge financial burden. Many old families go bankrupt trying to preserve their inheritance, too proud to commercialise it."

Outside, the air was crisp and cool. Rajan Mash stood amidst his location team, his eyes sparkling with excitement as he beckoned them over.

"Isn't it a great location?" he asked, a twinkle in his eye.

Jane nodded, her smile broadening. "Absolutely."

"It's so surreal," James added, his gaze sweeping across the landscape.

They walked westwards, with Girish occasionally pausing to frame imaginary shots and point out potential camera angles.

Soon, they reached the pond, a vast and stately expanse carved into the laterite rock. Nature had reclaimed it, ivy and weeds choking the pathways, old tree branches and roots sprawling over the water, concealing most of its banks. The water itself was barely visible beneath the thick overgrowth.

Girish, the cinematographer, frowned at the sight. "This could be such a focal point if it were cleared," he said, his voice tinged with hope.

Murali shifted uncomfortably. "It's a cursed place; no one really comes this way anymore," he whispered, as if afraid to awaken lingering spirits.

"That's nonsense. Rajan Mash told us the old story. Who believes in ghost tales these days?" Girish retorted, determination in his eyes.

He envisioned a thousand breathtaking stills around the pond. His mind raced with scenes of beautiful Indulekha on those steps, friends and maids around her, playful and charming as they rubbed turmeric and sandal paste on her skin before a bath. He could almost feel the weight of the best-cinematography award in his hands.

He turned to Rajan Mash, pleading. But the director only shrugged.

"I don't believe in ghosts, but I've seen how deep-rooted fears can cripple even the strongest minds. Primal fear can unravel a person completely," Rajan Mash explained.

James looked at him curiously. "I agree with your observation. I've seen medical cases complicated by beliefs and horror stories. London too has its own haunted house tour along those myths... Some honestly believe in them. An intriguing case study!"

Jane remained sceptical. Ghosts defied her logic, it was an amusing story at best. Yet, she held her tongue, the memory of her own nightmare from the previous night still fresh in her mind.

"I don't know. I will ask Adi and Mahendran. I need their permission to do anything about it," Murali said noncommittally. "I've lived through those frightened times. The locals have shared too many chilling accounts. I've seen the bodies of Sankaran and Kunjelu, terror frozen in their eyes... and the girl, bloated and blue in the river. Nightmares still haunt me, the soul-tearing melody   constantly echoing in my ears as if it happened yesterday."

It was clear to everyone that Murali would prefer to avoid this place entirely if given the choice.

43. New Malabar

Jane clutched the map Murali had drawn, her fingers gliding over the pencilled route that led them across the new concrete bridge spanning the Palari River. The car navigated through the early morning fog, the landscape shifting before their eyes. Dense forests gave way to cultivated fields, and a bustling town emerged from the mist.

James had suggested retracing the path Varkey and Joseph had taken on foot, but Jane, weary from a sleepless night, had vetoed the idea. The hill beyond the river, stretching miles over the paddy fields, seemed too daunting.

"I promise we can come back and cross the suspension footbridge later. It's scary enough to get your adrenaline pumping even without the hike," she said, flashing a daring smile. James, always game for her challenges despite the trouble they often led to, reluctantly agreed. The bridge was scary enough!

The town teemed with life. Shops overflowed with fresh produce, the air thick with the scent of spices and the sound of traders. Small tea-stalls and restaurants buzzed with activity, while a modern shopping mall drew in customers from every corner.

"Remember when they had to trek all the way to Palari? No transport at all?" James remarked, marvelling at the high-end cars on the streets.

"It's hard to imagine that! What a transformation!" Jane agreed.

Away from the crowded streets, they discovered a multi-storey hospital, a towering church spire, and the expansive high school compound. They decided to visit the church first, hoping to find information on the Varkey family. The Church of St. Thomas stood majestically on high ground, reached by wide steps flanked by terraced gardens. Flowering shrubs and evergreen bushes shaped like large candles adorned the path. The spacious round ground above was lined with grand Gulmohar trees. Inside, the church was equally stunning, with a decorated altar facing the vast circular hall.

"Mum says the first prayer in a new church has special significance," James said.

Jane smiled but joined him, making a sincere prayer to help them untangle the mysteries. Though not a firm believer anymore, she felt it was worth trying to unite unseen forces for their cause.

In the adjacent rectory, they met the parish priest, Fr. Dominic Kanikathu. When they mentioned their visit to see the town after hearing so much about it from Joseph, one of the first migrants to Palari, Fr. Dominic's eyes brightened with recognition.

"You see the land where we built the church?" he said, gesturing towards the church. "Most of it was donated by Varkey. He and the first parish priest, Fr. George Vellari, were the driving forces behind mobilising everyone to build the church and school. A few years ago, we celebrated the 50th anniversary of the church. We compiled a yearbook with all those amazing stories."

Fr. Dominic reached for a thick, bound book and opened it, revealing black-and-white photos of the first church and school. He pointed to a group photo from the blessing day, showing the people who worked on the project. There were Varkey, and Joseph in the group, even Lenin, all young and lean from physical labour, their faces glowing with a sense of achievement and happiness. Jane and James leafed through the pages, absorbing the history and the effort etched in every photograph. They bought two copies of the yearbook, one for Joey's grandfather, to rekindle his cherished memories.

Their final stop was Varkey's old house. Though they knew it was sold after his death, they felt compelled to see it. The house, larger than expected, stood proudly on a prime location in the bustling town. Surrounded by various crops and trees, the two-storey building had a tiled courtyard at the end of the drive. The stories from Joseph and Lenin had painted a picture of hardship and minimal comforts, but the house exuded an unexpected luxury.

The gate was locked, but Jane pressed the bell. The gate opened remotely, a middle-aged man came out to the veranda.

"Sorry to intrude. Are you the one who bought this house from Varkey John some years ago?" Jane asked with a charming smile.

"That would be my father. Not just some years, but twenty-five years ago. And not from Varkey, but his son Johny," the man clarified, smiling warmly. "My name is Karia."

The twins visibly relaxed. Karia clearly knew Annie and the family and seemed willing to share information. Their hope kindled.

"We are friends of Joey, Varkey's godson," James introduced themselves.

"Oh, my father knew Joey's grandfather Joseph. They all came to Malabar at the same time. Come on in," Karia invited them inside and offered them seats.

"We've come from Joseph's home in Kottayam. He wanted to reach out to Johny but lost his contact information. Do you have any way to reach him?" Jane asked, trying to remain hopeful.

"I'm sorry, kids. Johny seemed eager to sell this house and couldn't wait to complete the sale. It was a painful time for him. The agreement listed his correspondence address, but I'm not sure if it's still valid, its long time ago." Karia explained.

The twins had anticipated this. If Johny didn't want to stay in touch with Joseph, he likely hadn't kept in contact with anyone else.

They strolled through the land with Karia, the sound of the waterfall mingling with the chirping of birds called out to them. The water cascaded down the ridges of the hill, splashing into a small pool below before winding its way through a rocky path to join the Palari River. Stacked stone walls lined the canal, and scattered boulders marked the path of the water's destructive journey from that fateful day.

"I was barely twenty-five when the landslide struck," Karia said, his voice tinged with the weight of memory. "Annie's aunt Alice's house was right in the path of destruction. She had Annie and her mother over that night; one of them always stayed with her after her husband Chandi died a year earlier. It was the most horrific day in Palari's memory. Thankfully, we haven't had another landslide since."

Jane looked at him, her eyes filled with unasked questions. "Joseph-Chachan told us they only ever found Annie's mother," she said, her voice trailing off.

Karia nodded sombrely. "I know. Initially, we avoided this area, dreading what we might find. But after a few years, people went ahead and rebuilt the land. We haven't found anything. Maybe the remains were washed away to the river and sea with the first surge of water."

"Yeah, probably," James agreed quietly.

"I knew Annie," Karia continued, a faint smile touching his lips. "We went to school together. But unlike me, she excelled in her studies and went to college. I failed my board exams and joined my father in the farm business. We now own the spice factory in town."

Jane's eyes lit up. "Oh, you knew Annie? I heard she was quite a personality from a young age."

"She was, and she would have been one of a kind leader now if she had lived." Karia confirmed, a hint of nostalgia in his voice. "When she went off to college, she threw herself into the literacy movement in Ernakulam. VD led the charge, rallying the youth of Kerala. Annie was always by his side, helping to mobilise young people to launch the initiative in every Panchayat across the state. Those were golden days for our community. It wasn't just about education; it was about unity and sense of purpose. We put aside politics and religion, knocking on doors to find people who couldn't read, teaching them in our makeshift classrooms. Weekends were filled with local gatherings, dances, and dramas, a real community building effort. Many of the youth were college-educated but jobless, desperate to leave for the Gulf or anywhere for work. The literacy movement gave us a purpose, something to believe in during those tough times."

"Any of her friends still here?" Jane asked.

"Her best friend killed herself the day after Annie died. There was another friend AnandaLakshmi, a great dancer then, who studied in the same college as Annie. She married and moved to Bombay right after college, even before Annie's death."

"AnandaLakshmi? She was from Palari?" Jane asked, astonished.

"Of course. She is somewhere abroad now. She is also the younger sister of Adi, the minister!"

This revelation stunned them. How had they missed this detail before? The wiki page had said Adi had a sister named AnandaLakshmi, but they hadn't made the connection to Annie's friend. Adi was big on the education and literacy movement. If Annie was working with VD, she must have been working with Adi as well. The threads were finally starting to weave together. They ascended the hill with Karia, weaving through the plantation to get a better view of the waterfall and the river below. The land was magnificent in the golden sunshine, lush and green all the way down to the Palari River. The slopes were parted into small terraces, with various crops growing steadily. It was the result of generations of hard work and sweat, beginning with those few dreamers who dared to risk everything to come here and build.

Jane felt a sense of awe envelop her heart, truly understanding the dreams Varkey and Joseph saw the day they crossed the Palari River. She could see the result of what might have been just a vision for them then. The promised land lay before them, glorious and thriving, flowing with milk and honey indeed...

— **Part 3 End** —

Therese Pal

Part 4

"As you sow, so shall you reap." - The Bible

44. Evil's shadow

Back at Korothu Mana, activities were in full swing. To the total dismay of Murali, Mahendran had agreed to clear the abandoned pond and its surroundings.

"It's high time we reclaim the property from these so-called ghosts and get our grand home back in business. Stories don't pay the bills, Murali. Rajan Mash chose our place for a reason. This could put us on the map, bring in business. And with the election coming up, we need every bit of good press." Mahendran told Murali over the phone.

"I need to speak to Adi as well," Murali said, clearly uneasy.

"Oh, don't bother. I've already spoken to him; he wanted to do it for ages!"

A sense of foreboding enveloped Murali as he considered the daunting task ahead. When he approached the locals for help, none agreed to go near the pond, all too familiar with the stories and whispers that had circulated for years.

Finally, Girish stepped in. He called a contact in the movie business and arranged for some professional men to do the job. By lunchtime, six burly men arrived with a ride-on brush cutter that looked more like a bulldozer. In no time, they had cleared away the jungle surrounding the pond. They brought nets and baskets to collect and carry away the moss and debris accumulated in the water over the years. Overgrown branches of the Banyan tree that covered the pond were swiftly cut and removed. The famed steps around the pond needed some cleaning to bring back their colour, a task efficiently handled by the crew who came prepared with all the necessary cleaning equipment.

By evening, the pond was clear of weeds and rubbish.

Mahendran called again in the evening, this time via video call. Impressed by what he saw, he asked the team to resume work the next day to clear the outhouse he owned and the overgrown Sarpa-kaavu next to it. He vowed to make his house safe and liveable again, mentioning it was high time he found a tenant for it.

Locals who came to inspect the clearing effort, and partly to admire the machinery—a novelty in the village—chatted excitedly. Their curious eyes gleamed with fascination, though a few lingered at the edge, their faces etched with apprehension, whispering among themselves, casting wary glances at the pond, as if it might reveal its secrets at any moment.

When the twins returned in the evening, they were spellbound by the cleared pond, its water shimmering in the evening light.

Girish was ecstatic. "I'm going to add some lotus plants for the visuals. This place is serene. It's a sin to waste such beauty," he declared to anyone who would listen.

Rajan Mash kept to himself, away from the hubbub. He sat on a wooden recliner under the Banyan tree, reading his script and making notes, cross-referencing it with Mathew's papers.

Jane approached him, her curiosity piqued.

"You look happy," he remarked conversationally.

"Yes, we saw Palari town and the land. It's amazing."

"Promised land with milk and honey?" Rajan Mash had heard the description many times from Varkey and Joseph in the past.

"Indeed."

"Joseph would be glad you found it so."

"Girish's location looks stunning too."

"I'm sure..." There wasn't the conviction she expected.

"You don't approve?"

"I'm an old man, like Murali, tied more closely to the past. But I'm happy to let the youngsters decide on matters important to them rather than imposing myself."

James drifted from the group, the faint murmur of water calling him. The path was barely visible among the mangroves, supplying thick coverage to the ground. He pushed through the thick foliage, each step taking him closer to the river. The sound grew louder, turning into a constant roar as he reached the narrow opening to a thin strip of sand perched over the waterline.

A giant Banyan tree stood to the left of the path, towering over all other trees around it. The tree resembled the one next to the pond but appeared more gnarly. Its myriad of hanging prop roots were thick and crowded, like an ancient curtain, hiding its bulk body. It stood on a raised round platform, and beneath the roots were large, flat, smoothened black stones, covered in a blood-red stains—the red dye from Kumkum tree seeds.

James stared at the tree, feeling an eerie presence. He circled it, and as he did, a branch quivered. A flock of birds flew out, startling him. He peered around and saw a squirrel darting out of sight. The twigs remained still again, save for the shivering leaves in the wind.

James continued up the path to a clearing where bushes and trees had been cut back to provide access to the river. A lonely suspension footbridge lay ahead, swaying lightly in the mist from the gushing water below.

He marvelled at the view. The bridge, made of long ropes and a bamboo platform, looked strong enough. He noticed new bamboo shoots and ropes in places where the old ones were worn out. It was just wide enough for one person to pass, with side ropes bound at waist height and connected to the walking platform with a net of thinner ropes. There was no one around at either end. He took a tentative step onto the bridge; it held firm. Holding onto the side ropes, he began to walk across, adrenaline coursing through him as he looked down at the rushing water.

The bridge swayed more as he reached the centre. He gripped the ropes tighter, but the rocking motion increased dangerously. Panic rose in his chest, and he decided to turn back.

Turning around on the narrow bridge was tricky. The bridge rocked violently as he shifted, causing him to lose his balance. His left arm, already at an awkward angle, broke with a snap. He lost his grip and tumbled, his right hand grabbing the net, which tore under his weight.

As he fell into the river, he heard a piercing scream that drowned out his own, chilling him. He saw a flash of gold and white at the bridge's end where he'd come from—a stout figure covered in gold and white cloth, tumbling and a large gold chain swung in an arc, its golden leaf reflecting the last of the evening sun.

He screamed in pain as he hit the surface hard, his left arm searing in pain and useless. He kicked with his feet to stay afloat, but the current was too powerful. The banks seemed far away, rocks dotting the path, too smooth to grab. He was dragged downstream, scraping his legs and body. He struggled to keep his face above water, rolling to his back and kicking furiously. The stroking current pulled him under. His scientific mind knew what would come next: water would enter his airway, his larynx would close, water would fill his lungs, unconsciousness would follow it. His oxygen-starved heart would stop finally.

His head struck something, and he went under, holding his breath. The pain was excruciating, spasms wracking his body. In the midst of it, Jane's face flashed in his mind.

"I shouldn't have left her alone in this strange place." Sadness enveloped him.

Her face changed, deep wrinkles appeared on it, her hair floated around her, longer and peppered with grey. Her large eyes remained the same black, now filled with torment.

"That's how you'll look when you're old… I'm sorry I won't be there to see it," he said, his tears merging with the river. He willed the pain to end, hardly aware of his closing eyes. The last rays of the sun had vanished behind a curtain of darkness.

45. Deathly depth

"What was that?" exclaimed Jane, jumping up.

She had heard the scream, as if the water itself had cried out to her. She was sitting on a stone step, facing the pond talking to Rajan Mash. He was startled too.

Girish and his crew were on their feet, saying the sound came from the river. They started running towards it, and Jane joined them.

The locals huddled together, stunned, fear clouding their features. "It was a damned place. Only fools would disturb the sleeping spirits. Now damnation will be upon us all," they whispered and left in groups the opposite direction.

Rajan Mash rushed to the house for extra help.

Jane spotted her brother's lifeless form sprawled on a narrow strip of sand near the banyan tree. Her heart thundered in her chest as she sprinted down the slippery path, her feet barely finding purchase. James lay face down, motionless. The sight hit her like a punch to the gut.

"What do I do? What do I do?" she muttered, desperate for focus. She forced the panic down, knowing she needed a clear head. Images from years ago flashed before her eyes— their mum in the living room, calmly teaching them CPR, making them practice on a dummy until they were proficient. They were fourteen then, giggling and carefree. Now, there was no room for laughter, only urgency and tears.

She knelt beside him, tilting his head back, sealing her mouth over his, and pinching his nose. She blew into his mouth, counting each breath, her mind a whirl of fear. Five breaths. Then she positioned her hands over his chest and began compressions, pushing firmly, counting aloud to stay focused.

"One, two, three... Come back, James, come back," she pleaded, tears streaming down her face. Her voice cracked, but she pushed on, her hands steady despite her trembling.

Time twisted around her, each second an eternity. She felt the weight of every moment pressing down on her, the world narrowing to the rhythm of her compressions. "Don't leave me, James... please..." She kept on counting and pressing, keeping the rhythm, to keep her grounded. She refused to let go, ignoring the exertion, not trusting the help offered by the panicked faces around her.

After what felt like an endless void, James jerked, water sputtering from his mouth. He coughed, drawing in a shuddering breath. Jane let out a sob of relief, clutching his shoulders, her tears falling freely.

Girish rushed over, gently helping to tilt James sideways, allowing more water to drain from his mouth. James's breaths came more evenly, his eyes wide and glassy, trying to make sense of what had happened.

"I thought I lost you," Jane sobbed, clinging to him as if letting go would make him vanish.

James looked around; his eyes clouded with confusion. "I saw you in the water. You pulled me out?"

Jane shook her head, her voice trembling. "No, I found you on this sand bed. What happened?"

"I... I slipped from the bridge," he mumbled, his thoughts a foggy mess.

"You must have climbed up and then passed out?"

James didn't have an answer. The pain in his arm flared up, sharp and unforgiving. "I think my arm is broken."

Jane's eyes widened with worry. "Yes, it looks odd. And you're bleeding all over. What else is hurting?"

"Everywhere..." he whispered, touching the back of his head with his good hand. His fingers came away red. He wiggled his toes, relief washing over him—no permanent damage there.

"Let's get you to the hospital," Girish said, his tone brisk and authoritative. He had already sent one of his crew for help. They returned with a wooden plank, and Rajan Mash carried James's medicine bag and a bottle of water.

James, trying to focus through the haze of pain, directed Jane to fetch a painkiller and some emergency medicine from his bag. He didn't think anything else was broken but chose not to risk it. He accepted their help, allowing them to carry him on the makeshift stretcher to the car and to the hospital.

"You said you wanted to check out the hospital, so here's your chance," Jane tried to joke, her smile breaking through the tears.

James squeezed her hand with his good arm before being wheeled into the emergency room. "I'm grateful to be alive... Truly..."

****

Morning crept in softly, casting a gentle light across the hospital room. James lay awake, his arm encased in a cast and sling, bandages swathing his head, legs, and torso. His gaze lingered on Jane, who had steadfastly refused to leave his side, no matter what. In the dim light, he saw her form slumped on the chair in exhaustion, her head resting on her arm on the edge of his bed, and asleep. He thought about the last evening, all he could remember was the weathered face of his sister coming to him in the water, as if it was seared on his brain forever.

The wall clock read five o'clock. He reached for his phone, picturing Olivia in her pyjamas, preparing for a restful night. As he dialled, he could almost feel the comfort of her presence, the safety of home and the wistfulness of simpler life. Part of him wanted to be with her, away from this nightmare and the strange land. The accident had shaken him to his core, although he hadn't admitted it to anyone.

"I was about to sleep. I've been thinking of you all day," she answered, her voice a soothing balm.

"I'm glad. Maybe your pleasant thoughts brought me back from the jaws of death," he joked, but the gravity of his words hung in the air. He heard her sharp intake of breath and instantly regretted the blunts delivery. But he relayed the events truthfully, assuring her of his full recovery in no time.

"It's too risky there... You should come back at once. You could hire private investigators instead," she insisted, worry threading through her words.

"It all happened so long ago for any of them to make much sense. I'll be careful," he promised, though he felt the weight of her concern. After they said their goodnights, he stared out of the window, watching the early light filtering through the green mountains.

He imagined being with her, wrapped in the familiar comforts of home, far from the spectre of danger that loomed here. The thought of saving lives, not being a patient, tugged at his heart. Yet, the quest for his roots and identity burned brighter, making home feel a distant dream, without the answers he sought. The pull of his past was a powerful force, one he couldn't ignore despite the longing for the safety and solace of home.

46. Strange events

Rajan Mash arrived with Murali to see him in the hospital. James lay in his hospital bed, bandaged and weary but awake, and Jane sat beside him, her eyes red from lack of sleep.

"You two look better than I expected," Rajan Mash said, forcing a smile.

Murali's eyes darted nervously. "The household staff is in a frenzy. Whispers are spreading like wildfire."

"What for?" Jane asked, frowning.

"Murali's voice trembled. "They believe the scream from yesterday is an omen, a sign of evil things to come."

Jane's eyes hardened. "That scream saved my brother. We wouldn't have found him in time without it. I owe everything to whoever or whatever made it."

Murali's fear was palpable. "Please, don't dismiss it so easily. This is serious."

James, still groggy, looked between them. "You heard the scream too?"

"Yes," Jane confirmed. "It led us to you."

"I heard it too, a moment before I fell from the bridge. I had forgotten about it."

"You didn't make it, did you?" Jane asked with a faint smile.

"Of course, I screamed, but what I heard was far louder than my own. It wasn't a cry of impending death, but of torment. It was strange to hear it exactly before I fell!"

"Maybe someone witnessed your fall and cried out," Jane suggested.

Rajan Mash shook his head. "No one saw anything. And no one's come forward. In our village, people don't stay silent about saving a life."

The room fell silent, the weight of unanswered questions hanging in the air.

James's eyes narrowed as he recalled the details. "I... I saw someone at the bridge. Just a flash," he said, his voice tinged with uncertainty. "Someone stout, in white silk with golden lace."

Murali's complexion paled instantly. He gripped the back of a chair, knuckles white.

All eyes turned to Murali, who seemed to struggle with unseen memories. "Strange things have happened here," he began, his voice barely above a whisper. "Deaths... unexplained deaths. That vision of a man in white and gold, and the scream—this isn't the first time."

Jane and James leaned in, tension crackling in the air.

"The day Sankaran died in the pond, Mahendran heard a scream," Murali continued, his words halting. "He found his father lifeless in the water minutes later. Since then, many have heard the eerie, unnatural songs of a woman, especially on full moon nights. Stories spread of a man in white and gold and a woman in Davani... seen among the mangroves and the Sarpa-kaavu, around the pond and the river."

Murali's eyes darted around the room as if expecting to see the apparitions right then. "Locals say it's the spirits of Sankaran and his daughter, both taken too soon... unfulfilled."

The room grew colder, the weight of his words sinking in.

"We dismissed these tales as the imagination of frightened villagers," Murali said, his voice quivering. "Until another scream, another death. Kunjelu at the Sarpa-kaavu. People were terrified. And when Kunjelu's wife hanged herself three years later, it only confirmed their fears. Now, with that scream again... I can feel the wheels of dread and death turning once more."

Rajan Mash, his face set in determination, placed a steady hand on Murali's trembling shoulder. "I'll take Murali home," he said gently. "You two need rest. Please, be cautious. It's wise to stay vigilant in times like these."

When they were alone, Jane and James exchanged glances, each trying to make sense of the bizarre things they had heard.

Jane's concern for her brother was palpable, after the near-death experience he went through. "I still see your un-moving face whenever I close my eyes," she confessed, her voice trembling slightly.

James met her gaze, his expression softening. "And I saw your face, old and wrinkled, right before I lost conscious-ness."

Jane's heart swelled at his words, realizing she had been his final thought. She wiped away the tears that threatened to spill, refusing to let them fall.

"You saw me old? I always thought I'd die young, given my taste for danger!" she quipped, trying to lighten the mood.

James chuckled softly. "I saw your face clearly, then it changed to an older woman, but your eyes stayed the same. They say your eyes never age."

"And your teeth, until they fall out!" Jane teased. "So, how did I look old? If it's a premonition, I should take notes!"

"Old, wrinkled, with long, curly black and grey hair," James described with a smile, glancing at her flawless face and short, silky hair. "I remember feeling sad I wouldn't be there to see it."

Jane laughed, a warm, genuine sound. "But I'd be sad too if I had to see myself that old! I'm going to dye my hair and get Botox every few weeks, so you won't see me old and wrinkled ever!" she assured him with finality.

James grinned at her, their shared humour a balm to the day's tension.

"But what about this figure you saw? Murali makes it all sound like some mysterious, supernatural spirit!"

"I don't know, I thought it was a human at the time! I

only saw it as a flash as I turned, the bridge was rocking hard, then I was falling, and the scream took everything else out of my mind until I hit the water. Then it was a struggle for survival. Falling into a river was nothing like the pool lessons we had as children!"

"Do you think it was he, suppose it was a 'he,' who rocked the bridge?"

"It's possible. He was definitely close enough to the bridge to do so…"

"If it's a spirit, then it's an evil one! He wasn't the one who screamed?"

"No, the scream was high-pitched, more like a woman. And I thought the man was surprised as well, by the way he arched and fell backward on hearing it!"

James thought of the gold chain with its distinct banyan leaf, brilliantly reflecting the light. Jane was excited at this information.

"At least something definite and earthly than a shroud of white and gold, which was probably a Kasavu mundu or sari, all common in Kerala. Most people have one of those for special occasions."

"Possibly. Let's keep this bit to ourselves, just not to spook the owner."

She readily agreed.

"You know, I was thinking about all these deaths yesterday when you were out for counts," Jane said. "Now I believe all these deaths were connected and quite suspicious. Lalitha apparently killed herself the day after the landslide. By then only Annie's mother's body was found. They were still searching for Annie; she could have been found alive."

James thought for a moment. "Do you remember Mum telling us often that our mind can be our greatest ally or our worst enemy, that the course of our lifeboat depends on which of these guides us in critical moments. I think so too. Human minds are so unpredictable and vary so much. It is also about their frame of mind at any given time. One couldn't say how Lalitha took the news of a close friend's likely death and what was going on in her mind at the time. It takes only a second for us to make a drastic decision. From yesterday's experience, I can say the Palari river was less likely to give second chances once she jumped, or even if it was an accident. I know I'm just lucky to be alive."

"The river must have been much feistier in the monsoon, after the dreadful landslide," Jane shivered involuntarily, trying to swat the memory of James's still face from her mind.

"What if she was pushed, coaxed, or murdered? It could have set the course for what followed."

"But who would do that?"

"Sankaran or Kunjelu?" she suggested without much conviction.

"Why would they? And they killed themselves, out of guilt?"

"Maybe her mother killed them both and then killed herself!"

"After three years?!"

"It's a possibility!"

Jane knew she was on thin ice with that argument. "Then maybe someone else killed them all, like his son Mahendran, for money or title?"

"Rajan Mash told us Sankaran had already lost most of his wealth. There was no money for Mahendran to inherit by then."

"Maybe his cousin Adi? He's influential enough to put people to chase us or to order us to be removed from the quest. And he would have known Annie too. Passion, jealousy, revenge... any of it could be the reason if they had a history together..."

"Why would he kill his uncle and his other family?"

"Then the ghosts caused the death! There is a scream

and a shroud to prove it!" Jane said, frustration evident.

"Let's forget the old tales. It happened a long time ago…"

"I think it is relevant. If your accident was the result of sabotage, then there is someone out there trying to kill us. We have had too many close calls for it to be random. This time they nearly succeeded. We can't trust anyone…"

James saw the point in her argument. It couldn't all be random. That was sure.

"But what do they want?"

"It may be about what we are seeking. They could think we know too much already. Maybe we are closer to the truth than we know ourselves. We could be the only ones who thought Annie's disappearance and the deaths are all connected. Maybe they think we already made a solid connection. It happened one after the other with no clear explanation other than likely accidents, suicides, and a ridiculous ghost story."

James thought about the scream, how it chilled his heart more than the fall itself. He thought about the death he faced and the face he saw right before the darkness closed in. He was sure he was going to be engulfed in that blackness into nothingness forever. But how did he end up on the sandbank? The churning water that dragged him down was far from the banks as far as he could remember. Was there any extraordinary force at work that day?

"What do they think we know?" Jane was repeating herself to make sense of what they knew but failed to link.

"First, we know about Annie and Varkey, and we think it was Annie who gave birth to us in Wayanad, and Dr. Mathew helped her." Jane started listing. "That's an assumption still, but a possibility. They know this if they overheard us in the Kalpetta café and from the police records."

"Second, since Mathew isn't the father, there is a huge vacancy. Veena probably knows the truth."

"They would know it then if Professor Veena went to the other side," James said.

"Third, taking the other branch of enquiry, the man who died in the accident was the cousin of the police inspector. There are also historic abuses of power, tainted family names, and the possibility of involvement of someone higher up based on the obstruction of the case file access. Someone clearly wanted to hide something!"

"Enough to kill two people? After twenty-five years?"

"Don't you remember what Mum said? Family matters and vengeance could last through many generations. Think of all the wars from the dawn of time; most happened for revenge or to make or reverse history."

"Fourth..." he continued from her, "We were attacked since day two, at Ooty, Wayanad, Ernakulam, and now in Palari. I first thought they wanted to scare us away, but since yesterday, it has become more sinister. We should reconsider our options..."

"The only other choice we have is to stop and go back home. We would be no better than where we were at the beginning. What would we say to Mum and Dad?"

"If they knew what happened yesterday, they would want us to be back home this instant!"

But could she leave now... still not knowing? And how could she not? The terror still fresh from the day before, so real and imminent. She could not risk losing him again. But then what really happened to their birth parents and the babies they got swapped with? What if they were in danger too? Strangled in this strange and dangerous puzzle but with no inkling of the truth?

Her phone rang, and her face lit up involuntarily seeing the name of the caller.

"Hello there, I thought you forgot us altogether..."

"Not so quick, sweetheart... Have faith in the lasting impression you make on others. " said Joey.

"Hmm…. You think so ? Still?… With all the time and space, you sought?…. "

"Surprised ? Did it run differently in your universe?"

She smiled at the tone of his question. Unsure? Hopeful?

"Truthfully? We had our time warped here …. With all the dire news and death scare, could you believe?…" She relayed the incidents of the day before.

"It's getting worse," Joey whispered, sounding deeply worried. He checked his schedule and made a quick decision. "I'll be there in two days. Stay away from danger until then… promise me…."

"Sure, if only we knew where it would come from…"

****

The doctor came to check on James, satisfied with his recovery.

"There is no severe injury apart from your broken arm. You'll need the cast for a few weeks. The cuts on your head and body aren't deep. You were lucky."

"Thank you. Could I get discharged today? I think I can manage myself now."

"Better to stay for another night. I'll discharge you tomorrow. Till then, rest. And I'd be happy to give you a tour of our hospital later if it's of your professional interest."

"Thank you, that would be awesome!" James beamed at the older doctor. He had liked him instantly when they came in last night. Dr. Soman was efficient, knowledgeable, and charming.

Later that day, Dr. Soman took them around to show the hospital facilities. It was small, with limited staff, but efficient as a primary healthcare facility and first port of call for emergencies. He had arranged for an extra bed for Jane for the night as she insisted on staying. She was glad and her sleep was unexpectedly deep and dreamless.

The next morning, Rajan Mash came with Girish. He

looked tired and worried, and Girish was mutinous.

"Things are not going so well at the house," Rajan Mash said to their query.

"Another exodus of staff from the house. Murali is stressed. Sukumar is in bed with high fever for two nights straight, shivering and muttering incoherently."

"Now they want us out. They say my insistence on clearing the pond caused all these extraordinary events! Superstitious lots and heaps of nonsense! What do they know about the time it takes to find locations for a movie, and the months of planning? I am not going to leave just like that," Girish said adamantly.

"Let's keep it calm. They are all stressed, understandably. Mahendran is coming tomorrow. Let's discuss before concluding anything," Rajan Mash reassured him.

"Some of my crew came back late last night after running errands in town. They swore they heard ghostly singing from the pond," Rajan Mash told them. His tone was sympathetic. "Some of them are scared. We can't blame them; they've heard these sorts of stories all their lives. It's in their psyche to believe in ghosts and yakshis..."

Girish scoffed. Jane and James looked at him clueless. Rajan Mash sighed and told them about the folklore of yakshis. These mythical beings appeared as extraordinary, beautiful women with long flowing dark hair and snowy white saris. They would woo lonely travellers with their alluring songs, take them to their palatial homes with golden steps, and shroud them in a dreamlike sleep. Then they drank their blood. The splendid places the victims saw were huge palm trees, their remains often found beneath these trees in the morning.

"Those who grew up hearing these stories naturally add that angle when they hear extraordinary things," Rajan Mash said.

"Apparently, our house spirit visits on Pournami

nights—that's full moon nights! I would have thought they'd prefer new moon better, like mystical creatures of the dark, but no, this ethereal singer loves moonlit nights! And you know what? Tonight is full moon. I am going to catch them red-handed if yesterday's performance was only the dress rehearsal!" Girish was determined.

"They have some supporting facts for this belief. Sankaran was found dead on a full moon night in August. So was Kunjelu in September!" Rajan Mash said.

"Really?" James frowned.

"What about Lalitha?"

"She was found in the river the day after Pournami. That was in July, it would have been all dark and cloudy anyway with the monsoon season."

All were silent for a while, contemplating different things.

Jane didn't want to consider it as mere coincidence. She recalled a scene from a Shakespeare play she had seen long ago. "*It's the very error of the moon; She comes nearer the earth than she was wont, And makes men mad*...You know the word lunatic originated from moon, from the belief that changes in the moon caused intermittent insanity."

James's scientific mind reeled. If all the oceans could be affected by the phases of the moon, the human body, composed of 60% water, could also be influenced, although it was not yet proven. He had once read research on the impact of the full moon on people with bipolar disorder, suggesting that nerves synchronised with the lunar pattern could cause sleep problems, triggering manic episodes.

Rajan Mash spoke of numerous poems romanticizing full moons and the many movies shot in such settings, some even supernatural. Humans had been affected by the moon since ancient times, with gods, rituals, and traditions across the world tied to it.

Girish's thoughts had taken shape in visuals: a lovely

Indulekha in her traditional attire, jasmine garlands adorning her hair, holding the hands of her love interest, Madhavan, in bliss on the steps of the pond, enveloped in moonlight. His imagination went into overdrive, contemplating possibilities for his movie sets.

Finally, they all agreed to keep watch, to see if any merits to their collective thoughts.

When they returned to the house, conditions had escalated. That morning, Sukumar's dog was found dead under the mangroves. His condition worsened after hearing the news. James checked on him and found his face white as paper, his eyes red, and his temperature high. James sent him to the hospital with Girish. Dr. Soman would be able to help at the hospital.

Murali was edgy and worried. There was no cook at home, so he had arranged for food delivery from a restaurant for them all.

"What really happened to Sukumar? I didn't think he was easily scared," Jane asked Murali.

"Oh, but he is easily swayed... When the troubles continued after the deaths years ago, he wanted to leave, but I persuaded him to stay with an offer of double wages. It was hard to find any staff. Then things subsided, and nothing happened for months. He became emboldened. He helped Mahendran evict Madhavi from her house. Now he might think the spirits are after him! Finding his dog dead didn't help ease his fear..."

"I thought Madhavi died many years ago?"

"Yes, she did, again not a natural death. She hanged herself on the very tree over the pond. As per our belief, such souls wander and don't rest in peace. You need specific pujas to liberate the soul of the dead," he said with devotion.

"She had another daughter, didn't she? Where is she now?"

"Radha. She married and went with her husband to his

workplace; I think in Orissa or somewhere in North India. They came back a couple of months ago to his old house now, that he's retired. She often comes to Palari temple to do pujas for her sister and mother."

Jane was instantly interested and got Radha's whereabouts from Murali.

They turned to go to the dining room. James stopped suddenly, staring at the portrait on the far wall.

"Who is that?" James asked.

James was looking at a full portrait of a large, plump man with a round belly, wearing a traditional silk mundu-cloth with a wide golden Kasavu border and a veshti— a folded shawl—on his shoulder, covering his torso. A thick gold chain with a wide leaf pendant was partially visible.

James looked at Jane for a long second.

"Mahendran's father, Sankaran Nambudiri. This photo was taken a year before he died," Murali said with reverence, mixed with fear.

"He was feared even when he was alive," he said with resignation. "It is silly for me to fear even a portrait!"

Jane nodded to James. He saw the twinkle in her eyes, just like when she is struck by one of her sudden inspirations. "I love the antique gold chain he was wearing, so unique. I saw a picture of it in my dance class once. Is that rare?" She asked, admiring the picture.

"That is a family heirloom, passed from father to the son. Mahendran owns it now, he left it here in the house, not caring much about it. It probably reminds him of his father, whom he detested ever since I could remember."

"Could I see it? I could tell my friends back home I've seen one in real life," Jane asked earnestly, with a childlike enthusiasm.

Murali looked troubled but relented. He went to one of the shelves, used his key to open it, and took out an ornate wooden jewellery box. There were a couple of rings, but the central designated place was empty.

Murali looked pale. "I don't know where it's gone! Usually, it's here. No one takes it out anymore. I'll have to ask Mahendran if he put it in the locker or somewhere. God, one more thing to worry about!" Murali closed the box and shelf, sending them to the dining room for lunch, and excused himself to make a call. He came back, shaking his head.

"I couldn't reach him. He must be travelling. I'll have to tell him when he comes and brace for his wrath if it is indeed missing."

****

Night crept in leisurely, the sky clear on this last day of November.

"It's pleasantly warm, unlike home in November," Jane observed.

She, Girish, Murali, and Rajan Mash huddled behind a large mango tree, safely away from the pond but with a clear view of it. If there were spirits, hiding would be pointless, but if it was a mortal, they didn't want to risk being seen. Jane insisted James and Rajan Mash stay behind; one was recovering from a near-death experience with an arm in a sling, and the other was an octogenarian. Rajan Mash disagreed and said his age is an added value in these circumstances. James, unwilling to let his sister out of sight, agreed only after Murali reluctantly joined them, fulfilling his duty as caretaker despite the worry etched on his face. He brought a camp chair for Rajan Mash to make the wait more comfortable.

The moon ascended, bright and full, casting its reflection perfectly on the still water. Its light projected an aura of secrets, the dark craters and glossy edges adding to the mystery. The only sound was the constant chirping of crickets, their monotonous tone amplifying the tension.

Then, like a soft beam of moonlight, a melodious, solemn, and forlorn song echoed on the water's reflection, piercing their hearts and silencing the crickets. Murali, paralyzed with fear looked close to fainting.

Jane moved first, signalling Girish to follow. They stepped silently toward the water, following the haunting song, which abruptly ceased when they reached the steps. Girish switched on his powerful torch, illuminating the pond's wall and the truncated branch of the Banyan tree. They scanned the area; nothing moved. Rajan Mash and Murali joined them, their torches fanning light across the surroundings. The trees stood silent, unchanged.

They were bewildered. If not for the ethereal voice, they might have dismissed it as a dream, but the tune was hauntingly real.

"Look out!" Rajan Mash's voice cut through the silence.

All torches swung to where he pointed. A large snake slithered away into the mangroves.

"It's a rat snake, not venomous," Murali whispered, still trembling.

No other movement disturbed the night. The abrupt end of the singing left an eerie stillness.

"We need to get back home. There are venomous snakes around here, not just rat snakes," Murali urged.

They returned in silence, trying to make sense of what they had experienced.

James waited in his room, listening attentively as they recounted the events. He was as perplexed as they were. Girish, unusually quiet, showed no trace of his earlier confidence. None of them felt any wiser, just more muddled after witnessing the whispers firsthand. With nothing else to do, they retired to their rooms one by one. But sleep was elusive that bizarre night, leaving them tossing and turning, waiting for the sun to rise.

47. Unravel

The morning mist clung to the air, a cold reminder of the previous night's tension. Breakfast was a quiet affair, just toast, jam, and coffee, the absence of the cook felt keenly. Rajan Mash and Girish were taking stock of the project, considering alternate location options in case Mahendran decided to halt their work. Murali was busy making calls to find a cook and preparing for Mahendran's arrival with his entourage.

James wanted to investigate the haunted pond, so he slipped out with Jane. The pond and its surroundings were eerily quiet, showing no signs of the previous night's disturbances. The water was clear now, with the disturbed mud from the renovation settled at the bottom.

They scoured the area for any hidden spots but found nothing. Wildlife was active as usual, birds chirping and insects humming, but thankfully no snakes were in sight. They sat on the steps, puzzled. The stillness was unnerving, a stark contrast to last night's chaos. Each rustle, each ripple set their hearts racing, a reminder that danger lurked unseen.

"The voice sounded like it came from that corner," Jane pointed to a shadowy corner beneath the banyan tree. "It echoed from there," she whispered. "Even the scream the other day seemed to rise from the depths, not the river."

James watched a school of large yellow catfish swimming gracefully in the clear water. They swam towards the wall and then disappeared, only to return after a while, the formation still intact as if they took smooth turn in there.

"Did you see that? There must be a fairly large gap in that wall!" James exclaimed.

Jane moved closer, inspected the carved laterite wall, and found a gap large enough to fit through. She decided to explore it herself, not wanting to alarm anyone else until they knew more. Jane returned to her room and quickly changed into her Lycra top and leggings, layering her regular clothes over them. She grabbed a towel and a torch, stuffing them into a nondescript shopping bag before slipping back out. James kept an eye on the fish, confirming the gap's existence. He raised an eyebrow at her makeshift swimming costume.

"I can't swim in a bikini here! One thing more alarming than a ghost here would be a scantily clad woman!" she grinned and stepped into the water. "The water is warm!"

"Yes, the river too was warm, I would have enjoyed the dip if she wasn't so vicious!"

Jane took a deep breath and dived headfirst into the water, her powerful strokes propelling her toward the hidden gap. She slipped through it, disappearing from view. James waited anxiously on the shore.

Minutes later, her excited voice echoed back, "It's a tunnel! It leads upward to a carved space above the waterline."

James let out a breath he didn't realise he was holding. "How big is it?"

"The dry space is big enough for two people to crouch! Someone has been here before!" She inspected an old but clean towel that was left folded in a corner, and then there was another exclamation. "There's a crack in the wall, just an inch or two; I can see the pond and you!"

"I can't see you at all from here!"

"This tunnel goes towards the river. It's like an overflow chute. Big enough to crawl through!"

James was anxious. "Come back; we'll get someone else to look."

"Don't worry. I'll turn back if it gets too narrow or dangerous."

James counted the seconds nervously. Finally, Jane emerged, not through the gap in the water as he was expecting but ran up hill from the riverbank, covered in dirt and scratches but triumphant.

"The tunnel goes all the way to the river! The exit is hidden under thick mangroves, next to the banyan tree with the platform."

Jane took a dip in the pond to wash off the dirt. Once dry and dressed, they examined the hidden exit. It was close to where James had been found after his near drowning.

"The scream must have come through the tunnel, making it seem like it came from the water!" Jane realised... "and the ethereal singing yesterday... Someone must have been hiding there!"

James nodded. It all made sense. "But who was behind it?"

"And why. That's what we must find out."

They returned home, feeling lighter for having solved part of the mystery which troubled the locals for decades, though the larger questions remained.

A new face greeted them in the courtyard. He was over sixty, with greying hair and a pleasant demeanour.

"You must be Rajan Mash's friends. Good to see you," he said cordially.

"This is Mahendran, Adi's cousin." Rajan Mash introduced.

Mahendran did a double take when he turned to the twins, a gentle smile spreading over his face. Jane and James shook hands with him, surprised by his geniality.

"Sorry for all the trouble you've had. We usually offer our guests an unforgettable experience, renowned for our hospitality, right Rajan Mash?" Mahendran said.

"Of course, that's why I keep coming back!"

"Murali mentioned the local demand to stop the movie. Don't worry about that. Continue as planned. I will find out what nasty business is going on behind us. Let's hope it doesn't derail your shooting schedule."

Girish gave a cheery thumbs-up from the veranda.

"We have some information," James said, explaining the

cavity behind the pond's walls.

Astonishment spread across their audience.

"That's impossible! I've lived here all my life. We used that pond every day before my father's death!" Mahendran was overwhelmed.

"The opening from the pond was hidden behind the overgrown roots of the banyan tree. You couldn't have seen the gap with them. Even with that gone, no one would have noticed it really, it is three feet below the water line. James only found that because he was keenly observing the swimming pattern of the fish that went through there and deducing there must be a gap," Jane explained.

Mahendran regarded them with admiration. "Very clever indeed."

Rajan mash came forward to pat the twins on their back. "Well done. You have given us the fresh perspective as promised!"

Girish's excitement was evident, quickly shedding the uncertainty that had plagued him since their eerie adventure the night before. He insisted on verifying the tunnel himself, and in the end, they all returned to the pond.

Girish swam through the tunnel, following Jane's instructions.

Mahendran watched James; his brow furrowed. "You couldn't have checked it out yourself with your arm in a sling, could you?"

James shook his head. "No, Jane did."

Mahendran turned to Jane, a thoughtful nod accompanying his words. "You're really brave."

At the water's edge, Mahendran hesitated. After a moment, he took a deep breath and dived in, reemerging only after a minute, out of breath and visibly shaken.

"You, okay?" Rajan Mash asked, concerned.

"Terrible memories," Mahendran said with a shrug, trying to mask his discomfort. "This pond is incredibly old. To find such a hidden feature is astonishing... It's definitely man-made."

Rajan Mash mused aloud, "Both Tipu Sultan and Pazhassi Raja were active here in the late 18th century. This could have been a planned hiding place."

Girish emerged from the river side, grinning. "Seeing is believing. My world is righted again."

Jane couldn't resist a tease. "So, you had a night of belief in ghosts?"

Girish's smile turned sheepish. "Well, I blame it on overworked imagination!"

Mahendran's expression grew serious. "Don't feel bad. After my father's death, I believed something was amiss. We've abandoned much of our property because of it. Adi told me I was being silly, but I resisted all these years. We don't know who's behind this mischief. I'm not out of the woods until I find them."

"Any idea who that might be? Or why?" asked James falling in step with Mahendran as they walked home.

Mahendran shook his head. "Absolutely none! But you gave me hope and at least now I can calm my people. I must visit Sukumar to give him the good news. He needs some serious soothing," he added with a soft laugh.

"Do you know where your father's gold chain is? Murali said it was missing. I saw someone wearing it at the bridge, and I believe they were behind the sabotage," James asked quietly.

Mahendran stopped in his tracks, dismay and disbelief etched on his face. "Really? Wasn't it an accident? Did someone try to harm you? If so, It's indeed a crisis. We must be extremely careful."

He walked in silence for a minute, deep in thought.

"The gold chain is in the locker. I moved it after an antique expert told me its value. It seemed silly to leave it around, although I am not particularly fond of the heirloom.

But those jewellery styles are widely imitated and easily available in the market."

Back home, Murali was visibly relaxed, with Mahendran at helm and some breakthrough on the decade old puzzle, hopeful for better times. A young maid arrived with food parcels. Murali rushed to help her.

"Bhanu, you were supposed to be here an hour ago," he chided her for her tardiness.

"You say that sir, but what do I do? I had to stay back at Radhammayi's place, she is shivering with high fever since morning. She won't go to a doctor. What do I do? Vishnumaman is afraid of leaving her alone at night, so I often sleep at their house when he is away. He insists on that, as if she is a little baby... But what do I do? He had helped my Mum, when no one would do, so I had to listen to him. Didn't I? He had been away for three days. I couldn't leave her on her own with fever... what do I do? He would..." the maid wailed on.

Murali stopped her mid-sentence seeing she had no plan to stop. He sent her to the kitchen to get the plates.

"If you let her, Bhanu would talk for three hours, asking you, what could she have done, in every other minute," Murali explained, seeing Jane's curious face. "She is the distant niece of Vishnu, Radha's husband... you were asking about her before, Weren't you? Same one... Our dear Bhanu is a good soul, but no bell or break!" he said good-naturedly.

Mahendran chuckled at their banter.

"You should have a Bhanu in your movie, Rajan Mash; Quite an authentic character!" he said turning to Jane who was busy scribbling in her book. "Looks like Jane is already adding her to the script!"

"Oh no, just some notes, that's all", she hastily closed her notebook which now had a full family tree of Adi.

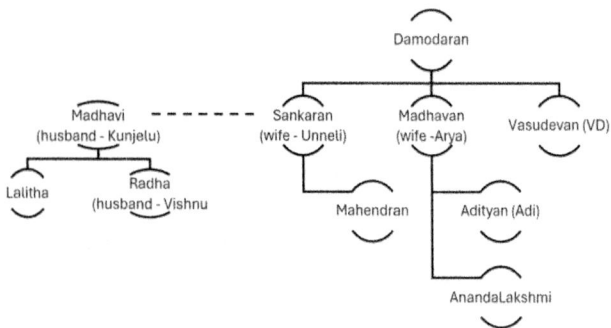

```
                                    Damodaran
                                        |
         ┌──────────────────┬──────────────────┬──────────────────┐
   Madhavi  - - - - -    Sankaran          Madhavan         Vasudevan (VD)
(husband - Kunjelu)    (wife - Unneli)   (wife - Arya)
        |
   ┌────┴────┐                    |              |
 Lalitha   Radha              Mahendran   Adityan (Adi)
        (husband - Vishnu)                      |
                                         AnandaLakshmi
```

Mahendran' phone rang. He frowned at it and excused himself. He returned after a while, with a grave face.

"Work never ends for me. I've got urgent errands for Adi. See you later, "said Mahendran with a forced cheer. He grabbed the key to his car, a nice-looking midnight blue Range Rover, and left with his assistants.

48. The missing link

After lunch, James and Jane left to explore Palari. Girish volunteered to drive them; his afternoon was free.

"I want to visit Radha first. I feel uneasy. Fever can be a killer if ignored," James said, grabbing his medical bag.

It took time to find her house. No one answered the doorbell. The front door and windows were closed and secure. Jane circled the modest single-story concrete house, which lacked decorations and colour. She pushed the back door, which opened into a dark, cold kitchen. Beyond the kitchen were two rooms, one little less dark by the faded light streaming through the heavy grills of an open window. A middle-aged woman lay on a double bed, bundled under multiple blankets, clinging to a pillow that smelled of sickness. Jane could hear her laboured breathing and, upon touching the woman's forehead, recoiled from the intense heat. The woman didn't respond to Jane's calls, only grunting and shivering with her eyes still closed.

Jane quickly opened the front door to let James and Girish in.

"It doesn't look good. Her pulse is too high," said James, taking out a stethoscope and a thermometer. Noticing the yellowness of her skin, he added, "Fever's too high, and her breathing's irregular. She's been sick too... I suspect the onset of jaundice. We need to get her to the hospital."

Girish carefully lifted the woman, leaving the bundle of blankets and dirty pillow in the bed and carried her to the car. James supported him with his one good arm and settled into the back seat next to her. Jane found a fresh blanket and pillow in the second room, using them to reduce the woman's shivering. She locked the front door from the inside and exited through the back door, pulling it shut tightly behind her. As soon as she got in the front passenger seat, Girish accelerated the car down the narrow country road towards the hospital.

Throughout the journey, the woman mumbled incoherently. James kept her steady, administered some medicine, and applied a wet towel to her forehead to reduce the fever. She looked gravely ill.

Girish crossed the bridge into town and slowed down. "We should inform her next of kin before taking her to the hospital, shouldn't we?" He asked Jane.

"Of course, you're right. I forgot to leave a note in all the rush. If her husband is back home, he'll be tearing the house apart looking for her! We practically kidnapped her!" Jane replied.

"You don't have Vishnu's number, do you?" James asked.

"No, I only got the address from Murali earlier. But I'll call him and ask... If he doesn't have it, Bhanu should... Oh, my phone has no network..." Jane said.

Girish handed his phone to her. She dialled Murali's number, but it was engaged. She waited for a few minutes and tried again, still engaged. She kept trying until finally, she got through.

"Murali, do you have Vishnu's mobile number?" she asked.

"Oh, don't bother, I called him already. He was on a bus to Palari. He should be in town in an hour, maybe earlier if he found a taxi. I hope he keeps his mind," Murali replied quickly. His speech always sped up when he was stressed.

"What do you mean?" Jane asked, confused.

"Where are you? Stay away from that place; it's already crowded with people, and the police are on the way!" Murali warned.

"I don't understand... Tell me what happened."

"You didn't call me about the fire at Radha's house? Bhanu's mother called ten minutes ago and said the house was in full blaze. No one could go near it! My phone has been ringing non-stop. Everyone thinks the spirits got the last of the family too. I don't know what to think. A couple of hours ago, I was so elated and at peace," he trailed off.

"What in the hell is going on in this place!" Jane was shocked. She opened her mouth to say where they were, but then stopped abruptly. Alarm bells rang in her head.

"Oh, we didn't know that... We were just driving through the countryside and are now close to the town. Strange affair, indeed. Thank you for letting us know. Please give me Vishnu's number anyway. We could give him a lift if it helps," she said.

She stored the number on her phone and disconnected.

James and Girish exchanged anxious glances during her conversation. She conveyed what she had heard from Murali, and both were astonished. Radha was still mumbling in her delirious state, unaware of the uproar.

"So, we three are the only ones who know for sure that Radha is still alive and well... or nearly!" James said, looking at her crumpled form.

"Yes, and the fire couldn't have been an accident; I'm sure of it. That house was dark and cold like a tomb when we left it." Jane said.

"What do we do?" Girish asked, eyeing the road ahead to the hospital.

"First, we should keep this knowledge to ourselves if we can. She's in danger, and probably us too," Jane said. She shivered as a series of scenes flashed through her mind: James's lifeless face, a chasing SUV, and a dangerously close truck.

"We need to get her to the hospital, though," James said, frowning and covering Radha completely with the blanket.

He took Girish's phone and called Dr. Soman. Thankfully, he picked up without delay.

"Dr. Soman, I need some help, most urgent and discreet

if you could...." He spoke earnestly for a minute, describing the situation. He then listened, thanked him, and disconnected.

"Girish, could you please take the car to the underground car park reserved for doctors?"

Dr. Soman was waiting there with a wheelchair. They transferred Radha, covered her with the blanket again, and took her through the lift to the top floor.

"It's our minor operation theatre. We rarely use it as we send patients to the city hospital for surgeries," Dr. Soman explained.

He took charge, moved Radha to a bed, set up a drip line, and took a blood sample to send for tests. "This is nothing illegal, is it? I'm doing it as a favour from one doctor to another," he asked James.

"Of course not, just a precaution for her safety, given the circumstances," James replied.

Jane was busy on the phone at the far end, apparently giving detailed instructions. She returned with a satisfied look.

"I spoke to Vishnu. He's still on the bus, terribly upset and panicked. When I told him briefly that his wife was safe, he didn't believe it, as if he knew she was in great danger. I told him the need to be discreet. Somehow, he understood better than I expected. I asked him to get down from the bus at the stop behind the factory. It's a quiet place. We can pick him up there without anyone seeing him," she said.

Then she left with Girish, taking the blanket. They parked their car on a side road behind some unused sheds. Jane was satisfied there was no one around. They heard a bus passing by and stopping ahead. A minute later, a man came running towards the car. His face was criss-crossed with age lines, his hair white and unkempt, with a tired and haggard look about him. His eyes were full of despair, a permanent resident, and fresh worries seemed to deepen the lines on his face.

"Vishnu?" Jane stepped out to meet him.

He nodded, doubt and fear in his eyes.

"You're telling the truth, aren't you?" His voice cracked; desperation clear.

"Yes. Your wife is safe. Dr. Soman is looking after her with my brother. I don't know what's really going on, but we thought it was better this way, to be discreet... Come on, we'll take you to her."

"Thank you. Thank you ! You have no idea how much danger there is... you have no idea..." he murmured repeatedly, almost to himself.

She looked at him, questions in her eyes, but decided it wasn't the time. She guided him to the back seat, asked him to lie down, and handed him the blanket to cover himself. He complied her without any question. They reached the room through the car park and the lift in a hurry.

Vishnu ran to his wife, hugging her tightly, still unable to believe she was alive and safe. With the fluid in, some colour had returned to her, and she was no longer shivering or mumbling.

"I think she's out of immediate danger, at least medically," Dr. Soman told them.

"No, no. She's in great danger. She can't stay here. They are all powerful people, capable of anything... She can't stay here... We've got to move..." Vishnu interjected.

"What people? What danger?" James asked.

"I can't tell... But I must take her to a safe place... And she needs her doctor too..." Vishnu kept repeating.

None of them could make sense of it, but they sensed the gravity of his request.

James looked at Dr. Soman.

"She's stable enough to move. But she would need to be under observation. I won't know if she has any underlying issues until I get the blood results," he said.

"Her doctor is expecting her in Kozhikode. She knows her condition. She'll be safer, away from here…" Vishnu insisted.

Jane and James didn't fully understand the nature of the danger, but their gut confirmed the imminent risk. They may unravel some of the mysteries in the process, having joined by an invisible thread of being the target of recent attacks.

Dr. Soman didn't want trouble in his hospital. It was thus decided to move quickly. Girish, though clueless, was up for an adventure. He had to go to the city to check the equipment anyway and could drop them on the way.

"That's fine. We'll get a taxi back from there," James said.

Jane nodded. They could do with a car of their own for the next few days. She called Gopi to check his availability. He was free and happy to meet them at Kozhikode. He could free up from his other shorter rides if needed for the next two days.

"Where's Sukumar? We need a ruse if someone saw us coming to the hospital," Jane said.

"He's on the first floor, second room. He's fine now. Mahendran came to see him after lunch, Sukumar's spirits seemed to be lifted considerably after that! I offered to discharge him today, but he begged me to delay it for one more day, said he slept better in the hospital!" Dr. Soman said with a smile.

, "Indeed. Though I'm not sure he was looking for THE spirit especially!" Jane said.

They all laughed at that.

Jane went down the stairs with Girish. The room was empty. Girish called out to the restroom, getting no reply. Jane asked the duty nurse, a burly man with a kind smile.

"I saw him taking a walk down the corridor after lunch. He's fine, don't worry. The doctor said he would be discharged soon," he said.

They thanked him and went back by the lift. They got Radha into the car on the back seat with a makeshift drip setup. Vishnu sat beside her, gently holding her. James took the seat on the other side with his medical bag squeezed on the floor under the seat.

The journey was long. James kept checking Radha's vitals in case of any decline. Her breathing was easier, her pallor better. Vishnu watched them with a guarded expression, troubled and tired.

The road twisted narrowly around the hill, one side dropping steeply to a winding river far below. Across the river, the land rose again into another, lower hill. Jane's eyes were alert, scanning for any trailing or oncoming vehicles, but the stretch of road remained deserted.

"There's a new highway on the other side of the hill, much more convenient for getting to the city. Hardly anyone uses this path now," Girish explained. "I thought we might benefit from the lack of attention."

"If there's any specific danger, now's the time to tell us," Jane said seriously, turning to Vishnu. "We need to avoid any risk with your wife on board."

Vishnu's face went even paler. He held Radha tightly as she stirred, opening her eyes slowly. His touch was tender, gentle.

James checked her temperature. "She's improving," he said with a relieved smile.

Radha looked at him, recognition flickering in her eyes. James instantly felt a strong pull towards her, his mind still processing furiously for the source of that connection.

"You're the doctor..." she said, more of a statement than a question.

"Yes. We found you at home, very sick with a high fever. You're better now; the drips should help you regain strength." He felt relief seeing her recover.

Vishnu gazed at Radha's exhausted face, her frail form

nestled in his arms, her breathing still shallow. She was alive, thanks to these strangers' kindness.

"We were incredibly lucky they found you when they did, Radha, really lucky," Vishnu said, his voice thick with emotion. He turned to James. "I can't thank you enough. I thought I'd lost her, and my entire world with her. The agony when I heard about the fire..."

Jane nodded, understanding his fear. She had felt the same when she found her brother not breathing by the river.

"I felt my world collapse, just like before... They say lightning rarely strikes twice, but they do... I couldn't face that same hopelessness again..." Vishnu's voice trailed off, as if speaking to himself.

The twins looked at him with concern.

"I was once engaged to Radha's sister Lalitha... We were in love, happy and looking forward to our future together. Then she was gone. All my hopes were dead too the moment she was found dead in the river. In the weeks that followed, I decided to join her. But Radha was there that day, like a guardian angel sent by her sister... to save me. I wouldn't be here, without her."

A stunned silence filled the car. Vishnu stared out of the window, his face taut with distress.

James replaced Radha's drip, aware of her gaze on him. "You saved me..." she said softly.

"Not more than you saved me," James replied calmly. "You were the one who pulled me out of the river, weren't you?"

Jane looked at him, astonished. He smiled, the realisation dawning on him since he first saw Radha. The certainty solidified as she regained her strength, as if he had known it all along. His final memory before losing consciousness was seared into his mind, and her gaze had brought it to the forefront, revealing the obvious truth.

"You were on that tree, weren't you? I sensed it then,

even if I didn't fully understand."

Radha nodded. She had seen him walking down the path from the pond, his steps drawing her focus despite her uneasy mind. As he approached the middle of the rope bridge, she noticed the man at the end, deliberately rocking it to trip him. The sight triggered her own dreadful memories, sending terror coursing through her. She had screamed, a primal release that startled the saboteur, who froze and then fled.

Seeing James struggle in the river, she had instinctively dived in, to the familiar water, navigating the tricky patches and whirlpools to reach him. She pulled him to the sandbank just as the crowd arrived, then discreetly retreated to the tree, watching as they revived him. She had cried silently, feeling his sister's anguish within herself, that had broken a dam of grief and sorrow, and the terrible sense of loss.

"Thank you... I owe you everything for saving him." Jane's voice trembled with gratitude.

"You did the same for my wife," Vishnu said. "I believe it was pre-written...."

Jane turned to her brother, puzzled. "James, you said you thought I pulled you out of the water. You mentioned it right after you came round."

James's brow furrowed. "Yes, your face was the last thing in my mind. But then, it changed. You looked older, but your eyes... they were the same."

He paused, glancing between Jane's questioning eyes and Radha's weary yet familiar gaze. Both pairs of deep, dark eyes mirrored each other, a startling realisation sinking in.

"Oh..." he murmured, astonished. Jane followed his gaze to Radha, a feeling of serendipity enveloped her as the similarity finally dawned on her.

They exchanged a look, an unspoken understanding passing between them. The air seemed charged with destiny, as if the threads of their quest has been aligning willingly in front of them. James and Jane felt a surge of exhilaration, sensing that they had one more piece of puzzle sliding in place.

Radha remained lost in her own memories, unaware of the silent revelation that had just unfolded around her. Then she told them her story.

49. Cruel fate

Life wasn't kind to Radha. Ever since her memory began, she carried the burden of the shameful circumstances of her birth. Her father, Kunjelu, despised her and her sister, scolding them for every petty thing. Her mother, kind but evasive, often met her questions with silent tears. Eventually, Radha stopped asking.

Kunjelu transformed to a mule, whenever Mahendran's father, Sankaran came around, tiptoeing around him. Radha and Lalitha feared Sankaran, retreating like snails at the sound of his commanding voice. Occasionally, he brought presents, new dresses, or sweets, which their mother handed to them with a rare smile in the morning.

Curious and clever, Radha learned to listen without being seen. It protected her from Kunjelu's beatings and the cruel jokes from others. As she grew, she understood the gossip: Sankaran was their real father. This knowledge in fact pleased her; being the child of a feared, wealthy man felt empowering to her; so much better than being the offspring of the spineless Kunjelu...

Lalitha hushed her. "Don't ever talk about this. You are just ten, You don't understand. You'll only bring more trouble to Mum."

Radha rebelled against the demeaning looks and whispers. Lalitha was too afraid to stand up for her own good, she decided. Her first act of defiance was to jump into the pond when Sankaran's wife and others from the high family were bathing. She decided the unwritten rule forbidding access to anyone outside the family didn't apply to her anymore. Though no one confronted her, the report reached Kunjelu. Incensed, he charged at her with his polished cane. Radha stood her ground and pushed him down the steps. Caught off guard, he fell to the courtyard with a scream.

Madhavi, hearing the commotion, dragged her

daughter into Lalitha's room, bolted, and locked the door behind them. Kunjelu's pounding on the door continued all day. Madhavi ventured out only when Sankaran's booming voice echoed outside. To their relief, Sankaran only chuckled.

"I like the spirit in that girl. More like me than you! I'll order Kunjelu to behave; he should know his place better..."

Things improved for them after that day. Though Kunjelu remained livid and irate around the three of them, he no longer dared to punish them physically. This emboldened Radha, who openly refused to follow his commands and often ignored Lalitha's pleas for restraint.

A year later, Mahendran's mother died, sparking rumours of Sankaran's involvement. Lalitha and Radha, however, found unexpected invitations to Korothu Mana during festivals and special events. Mahendran ignored them, but Adi and AnandaLakshmi were friendly. AnandaLakshmi, the same age as Lalitha, studied Bharatanatyam together with her at Raman master, while Radha took classical music lessons.

Korothu Mana always bustled with visitors. AnandaLakshmi often invited Lalitha for sleepovers or to practice dance. Lalitha's school friend Annie also came over some time, and the three had become close friends. Radha felt resentful as she was not privy to these gatherings in an equal grace, being eight years younger.

Despite her mother's strict forbiddance, Radha's fondness for the pond never waned. The big pond, with its inviting blue depths and calm, cool water, called to her every time she passed it during the sweltering summer. She was an excellent swimmer, a skill she and Lalitha had perfected in the dangerous Palari River. They had taught themselves to swim in a secluded alcove of the river, right below the dense trees in the Sarpa-kaavu, where no one frequented. It was part of their ritual of hiding away as they grew up, whenever Sankaran was visiting their mother. They ventured into the wilder part of the river when no one was looking, especially when it rained and kept everyone indoors. It eventually made them both excellent swimmers. They never mentioned it at home, fearing backlash from Kunjelu, who never liked anything they genuinely enjoyed.

One summer day, Radha, craving the water, dived into the pond when no one was around. To her horror, Sankaran's voice boomed nearby. She hid behind the banyan tree's roots and accidentally discovered the tunnel—a secret escape route.

Radha convinced a reluctant Lalitha to explore the tunnel, feeling triumphant at her discovery. It became her magical hideaway, a perfect spot to watch the family without being seen.

One day, hidden in the tunnel, Radha overheard Arya discussing AnandaLakshmi's secret relationship with Siva, Raman Master's son. Sankaran, furious about the match, had forbidden it.

"I wouldn't mind Siva; he's a good-natured boy and Adi's friend. But Sankaran forbade Lakshmi from seeing him. My husband, of course, wouldn't dare defy his older brother, so he pulled Lakshmi out of her dance classes."

"Sankaran's such a hypocrite," muttered Arya's companion. "He has an open affair with a married woman and even fathered her kids. Where's the family honour in that? And yet, he's fine with arranging Lalitha's marriage to Vishnu, Siva's brother."

"He follows a different set of rules. Powerful men in this family always had their discretions. Sankaran's father was no different. To him, Lalitha is Kunjelu's daughter and can marry a dance master's son. Lakshmi, though, carries the family name and can't marry below her status. He wants her to marry Mahendran's friend from an old, wealthy family. Lakshmi told me she'd never marry him; he misbehaved with her during a college drama, and she slapped him. Now, he wants revenge for that public rejection."

"Why let those girls in the house at all? Teach him a lesson."

"It's not the kids' fault. It wouldn't matter to him if they stayed away. He allowed them in because I insisted for years. It's their right."

Hidden, Radha felt a surge of warmth towards Arya. She wished her own mother could be as bold, instead of always crying and submitting to Sankaran. She promptly confronted Lalitha about the letters she carried, suspecting they were from AnandaLakshmi.

"Nothing for a fourteen-year-old to know," Lalitha snapped. "Stay out of it, Radha."

"Sure, the swan of Damayanti," Radha teased, running off.

It didn't take long for events to take a more serious turn. Right after the Vishu festival in April, Sankaran abruptly called off Lalitha's engagement with Vishnu, ignoring Madhavi and Lalitha's pleas and tears. Vishnu was furious, shouting at Sankaran that he had no right to interfere in their lives. Sankaran then turned up at their home, accompanied by Mahendran and one of his friends, and burned it down. The incident was hushed up with hefty bribes to the police. Radha, however, pieced together the puzzle: Vishnu's brother Siva was missing, along with AnandaLakshmi.

Radha's eavesdropping at the pond paid off soon enough. She overheard Sankaran and Mahendran discussing AnandaLakshmi and Siva's clandestine marriage in Ernakulam, with Adi and Annie as their witnesses.

Sankaran's voice trembled with rage. "It's all VD's doing. He's corrupted the next generation, right within our family. He'll see the end of everything we hold dear! And Adi, with that Varkey girl? I shouldn't have given him my land. Now it's full of those migrants... Nothing left for us."

"Adi and Annie are VD's disciples, pushing his literacy

movement. Wait for the inter-religion marriage next!" sneered Mahendran. "They have allies in your own roof! Lalitha is friends with both Lakshmi and Annie. She must have known their plans, all the while pretending to be innocent and naive."

Radha shivered. She knew Mahendran disliked them, but to incite his already enraged father against them.

Despite her rebellious nature, Radha was fond of her sister. She often took the blame for Radha's mischiefs, bearing the brunt of Kunjelu's punishments. Lalitha was her solace, especially when their mother sank into her depressive moods.

She ran home, rushed into Lalitha's room to warn her off, but found it empty. Frantically, she gathered all the letters and hid them in the attic just as Sankaran barged in, dragging a terrified Madhavi.

"Where is Lalitha?" he barked.

"She went to the temple," Madhavi whispered.

Sankaran ransacked the room but found nothing. "Tell her she's not to meet that disgraceful friend of hers or go anywhere until I marry her off. I don't want any more rebellion!"

Madhavi nodded, knowing better than to argue. Sankaran turned to Kunjelu, who stood quietly in the courtyard, ordering him to keep Lalitha in check. Kunjelu nodded, a decades-old habit of submission.

"Tell your rebellious daughter too. I don't want her defiance!" He shouted at Madhavi.

Radha, hidden from view, waited for Lalitha by the Sarpa-kaavu. She pulled her sister aside as soon as she arrived, recounting everything she'd overheard.

"I've hidden all your letters. Be careful with Annie. If Sankaran sees you near her, he'll kill you."

Lalitha wept silently, looking lost and timid. Radha hugged her tightly, trying to console her.

With Lalitha practically under house arrest, Radha became her messenger, but she read all the letters discreetly, learning the fate of Vishnu's family. Sankaran's revenge had led to the breakup of Vishnu's engagement and the arson of his home, causing Raman master's stroke and subsequent death. Lalitha poured her heart out to Vishnu, begging him to stay calm and not seek revenge. She planned to escape before being forced into marriage, insisting on taking Radha and their mother with her.

Radha was stunned. Her quiet, timid sister was planning to elope! Perhaps love did make people brave. She felt a warm glow knowing her sister cared enough to take her and their mother along with her.

She scrutinised Vishnu when handing him the letter. Tall and strong, with an angry, hardened look since his father's death, he wasn't very communicative, collecting the letter with a frown. She left him to read it in peace, promising to return the next day for a reply. Now she felt she had a stake in the game, she would do all she can to help.

50. Keystone

Summer had yielded to monsoon. Torrential rain became the norm, and the Palari river was at its wildest. Elders spoke of it as the worst rain year in their memory. Kunjelu was often out in the rain, directing floodwaters away from the grand house.

The rain paused one afternoon in July after three days of downpour. Radha, cooped up inside, was bored. Lalitha handed her a letter for Annie and pleaded for her to deliver it.

"I'd have gone myself, but I promised to be at the temple with Adi's Mum tonight. Adi is expected back from Bombay. I'll bring you sweets if he remembered." She cajoled, "If there's a reply, please bring it to me there. And be careful on the bridge; the river must be overflowing."

Radha agreed, crossing the roaring Palari river. At Annie's house, she overheard arguments between Annie and her father, usually the best of friends. Annie's tear-streaked face greeted her at the door.

Radha quickly handed over the letter, sensing Annie's disappointment at seeing her instead of Lalitha. Radha already knew the content, having read it on the way. Lalitha had written that she would be at Adi's house this evening, hoping to speak with him.

Annie looked at her worryingly, hesitated a moment, looking at the envelop she had held in her hand. She went to her room to add an extra note and handed it to her. "Thank you, Radha. Please bring me a reply. Our phone line is dead after the storm. Tell her I couldn't reach out."

Radha crossed the river and climbed the tree, hiding behind its curtain before opening the letter. Inside was a brief note to Lalitha, asking her to hand over the second envelope to Adi personally and as soon as possible. Radha's curiosity fought against her guilt. She knew Lalitha wouldn't have opened it herself. What if the information implicated them? She had to protect them both. She opened it and read it twice in disbelief.

"Adi, we agreed to keep our marriage secret for the uproar it would cause. But I had to remiss on that decision today, at least with my family. I am pregnant. know it would be as shocking to you as it was for me, but it is done. Now I have had time to process it, I am not overly worried. Hope you would see it too and we could work out a plan together. I am as hopeful as ever. Hope to see you soon... Love Annie..."

Hearing voices around the corner, Radha quickly re-sealed the envelope and hurried out of her hiding place, running all the way to the temple. Anxiety and guilt gnawed at her. This revelation was even more explosive than the news about AnandaLakshmi and Siva. Instinctively, she knew it could cause much bigger problems. The thought of Sankaran made her shiver.

She spotted Lalitha coming out of the temple, with a sour-looking Mahendran and his friend nearby. Discreetly, Radha fell in step with Lalitha and handed her the letter.

As Lalitha read the note, her face went extremely pale. Radha realised her mistake—she had forgotten to put Adi's letter in the second envelope, and that was what Lalitha had read first.

"Annie asked for a reply," Radha said to the still-shocked Lalitha. "I'll wait outside the window of the Well room." Without waiting for a response, she ran past her, not wanting Lalitha to see the guilt on her face.

She waited long in the corner, hearing clatters from nearby windows and doors. Finally, Lalitha whispered from a window, pale and shaken. Radha could sense something was wrong. Lalitha only shook her head and passed her a letter addressed to Annie. As she was turning to go, Lalitha mimed to her – RUN. Then she was gone.

Radha did as she was told this time. She ran, past the

tree and past the bridge before stopping at the gates of Annie's house. Her heart was beating so fast. Something was
wrong! Was her sister in any danger? This time she did not
feel any guilt to open the letter. Adi's beautiful handwriting
revealed the grim message.

"Dearest Annie,
I am at a loss for words. I understand what you are go-
ing through. The situation at home is dangerous; my
uncle is livid after finding out we were the witnesses to
Lakshmi and Siva's marriage. He set fire to Raman
master's home afterward. If he learns about us, he will
do the same to your father's house, whether we are
here or not. This could spark nothing less than a com-
munal riot in Palari. Your father is a prominent leader
in your community and has influence equal to my un-
cle's, unlike Raman master. No one could silence the
aftermath; no bribe or power could stop it. Knowing
this, we have to make the ultimate sacrifice to protect
the people we love. It kills me to say this, but I implore
you to terminate the pregnancy. We can be together
when the time is right. Please keep this news to your-
self for the sake of our loved ones.
With all my love...Adi"

Radha was shaking by the time she finished the note.
For the first time, she realised she was too young and naive
to understand the complexities of the choices others made
in their lives. She couldn't imagine how Annie would feel
reading this note, and she didn't want to know, that too for
the first time. Knowledge wasn't always power, she thought;
it also had the power to drown you.

Her feet were unsteady as she resumed her walk. She
handed the letter to Annie and left without another word.
She was worried about Lalitha. Why had she indicated for her

to run? Returning home, she told Madhavi that Adi's mum had invited her to stay with them that night because some puppet artists were visiting. She ran out before Madhavi had time to ask any questions.

Night fell, the full moon peeking through clouds. Radha quickened her steps, searching for Lalitha in all the usual places. She heard noises from the outhouse and peeped in, terrified to see Lalitha being pinned to the wall by Sankaran, her face swollen and bruised.

Radha screamed, drawing attention. She ran towards the pond, staying in the shadows, hiding from the footsteps and shouting behind her. She dived into the pond and swam up the tunnel, reaching the haven. She heard light footsteps on the steps. Relief washed over her when she saw Lalitha, who had managed to escape in the commotion. Radha urgently called to her, urging her to hurry. But to her horror, Lalitha stopped abruptly and turned decidedly away from her. In seconds, Sankaran appeared at the water's edge. He saw Lalitha standing defiantly in the water. His face twisted with rage, his eyes bulging and devilish in the moonlight, he lunged at her. He grabbed her by the neck and forced her underwater with all his strength. Radha froze behind the stony wall, her body stiff as a rock, unable to make a sound as she watched her sister's body go limp after minutes of frantic struggle. Her eyes were locked on the unfolding horror, unable to look away.

Kunjelu was the first to arrive the scene, a cruel smile playing on his lips as he watched. Mahendran's friend, whom Radha had seen earlier at the temple, came running and stopped at the edge. He surveyed the scene, then suggested they dump the body in the swollen river; it would be carried far away, leaving no trace. Sankaran nodded. Without a word, Kunjelu picked up the lifeless body and carried it down to the river. The rest headed back towards the house.

Radha's mind had shut down, unable to process the

horror. Darkness crept in as heavy clouds obscured the moon. She collapsed to the ground, unconscious, as the rain began to pour down with vengeance.

****

Radha shuddered as if in seizure. Shocked silence prevailed in the car after that horrific narrative.

James checked her pulse, finding it high along with elevated blood pressure. He administered a mild sedative, and Radha gradually relaxed, her vitals stabilising.

"I think the memories were too traumatic for her, even now," James said. "It was abject horror to witness at such a young age."

Vishnu held Radha close, tears streaming down his face. He spoke urgently, as if shedding a long-held burden.

"No one realised Lalitha or Radha were missing the next day. In the early morning hours, chaos erupted in Palari due to a massive landslide that had washed out much of the Padinjattu hill. Many properties were destroyed, and the entire village was searching for survivors. By noon, Annie's mother's body was found, and hope for finding others dwindled, though the search continued.

Madhavi had been searching for her daughters, but no one cared for her distress amidst the larger disaster. I was away and only returned at noon to hear the dreadful news. My worry grew frantic. By nightfall, someone found Lalitha's body miles downstream in the Palari river. Sankaran presented a suicide note, claiming to have found it in her room. It was Lalitha's handwriting. My world turned dark; hope and happiness vanished.

Everyone believed Radha was dead too. But to our surprise, she returned the next morning, covered in mud. She was dazed, her eyes unfocused, showing no tears or expression, like a mute, wooden doll. For weeks, she wouldn't talk. I tried to get answers, but she only stared into the distance. She spent hours in the Sarpa-kaavu, her only companions being the snakes. Other times, she wandered around the pond and river path. Madhavi, overwhelmed by her own grief, couldn't care for her.

I fell into depression. The thought of Lalitha giving up on me tore my heart apart. Her death felt like my own death sentence. Scattered memories and guilt tormented me, cursing my inability to save her.

Destiny, perhaps, led me to the same place where Radha was hiding when I decided to end my life. She screamed when she realised what I was about to do, the first sound she made in weeks. She kept screaming from behind the curtain of hanging roots, then started crying, hiding her face on her knee, as if a dam of grief and horror broke open. All I could do was sit there and wait for her to calm down. Eventually, she told me what she had seen that day and how Lalitha died."

He stopped abruptly, tears streaming down his face, the memory still raw and painful.

"All the traumas scarred her mind. She grew out of her childhood as a battered and withered soul the night her sister died. Days and nights lost their meaning. She transformed from an inquisitive, rebellious butterfly to a wingless moth; colours and happiness drained from her life. I didn't want her to end up in an asylum with no one to care for her, and her mother was burdened by her own depression. I married Radha the day she turned eighteen to take her away from this cursed place and the painful memories. Madhavi held on long enough to see Radha leave before succumbing to her miserable life. The grief we shared brought us together, and in a sense, we saved each other. I never broke my promise to care for her."

He turned to James; his eyes serious.

"You must have guessed; she's bipolar and needs constant medication to stay grounded. I never intended to return, but after I retired, she insisted on coming back to perform the rituals for her sister and mother. It was unwise; this place brings back all the awful memories, causing her to relapse."

James nodded with understanding. It explained a lot, and he didn't want to peel any more scabs off the old wounds.

Jane sat quietly, absorbing the information, haunted by the horror of it all.

Girish stared at the road as he drove, his mind picturing a dark collage of horror and trauma, evil and spite. "We're nearly there," He called out, straining to keep his eyes on the road illuminated by his headlights.

Vishnu looked relieved. Radha appeared stable, and he hoped she was out of immediate danger. James nodded his assent.

Jane was silent for a while before following another line of thought. "Your brother and wife, where are they now?"

"He's abroad, running a dance school with Lakshmi. I didn't want anything to do with him. He started the events that made me lose my love, our father and our home. When Lalitha died, he was busy building his own life," he said with detachment.

Something flashed in Jane's memory. "Siva and Lakshmi... running a dance school?" She chewed on it, the words echoing in her mind. Then she remembered. An elegant face, a graceful man standing next to her. "You look just like my daughter," an affectionate voice had said in her ears.

Astonished, she picked up her phone and went through the pictures. She pulled out one of Siva and Lakshmi, Jane beaming beside them. She showed it to Vishnu.

"Is this your brother and sister-in-law?"

Vishnu looked at it, surprise flashing on his face. "Yes, that's them, although I hadn't pictured them being that old. So, you met them already? Maybe it was destiny again!" A tinge of sadness crept into his voice.

Jane looked at James, amazement mirrored on both their faces. 'It was all there! … right at the beginning…'

They reached the hospital without incident. It was a smaller hospital with a mental health department attached. The staff took Radha to the treatment room. James briefed the duty doctor about her condition and the treatment she received so far, ensuring she got the best care. He also met her psychiatrist, a bright woman with kind eyes. With Vishnu's permission, he spoke about the recent events, and the possible repercussions Radha might face. The doctor nodded in understanding, thankful for his help.

James felt deep gratitude and protectiveness towards Radha. She had saved him from certain death, and she was their kin.

Jane called home to update her parents. A lot had happened since they last spoke. Lissy was worrying again.

"It's dangerous to stay there any longer. Please come back," she pleaded. "You know enough now, who your parents are. That's enough for me."

"We need to know what happened to Annie… and the other twins." Jane said.

"We can help. I've asked a friend in the US to search for Annie's brother, from the information you gave us earlier. We can continue the search, away from the present danger," Richard insisted.

"I think that's what we'll have to do eventually. But one thing you can help with now is meeting Siva and Lakshmi. They'll be in Paris for the show. See what they know. She would help if she knew we are her kin."

Richard agreed, glad he could take some action rather than waiting with worry at home.

Jane walked to James, who was talking to Girish already in his car.

"Could you please keep Radha's whereabouts and her past story to yourself? I think she and Vishnu are still in danger. It's better if no one knows about them, just yet."

"Of course," Girish nodded. "I understand."

They weren't sure how much he understood. He was a movie man, after all. They might have a special skill to link stories!

Jane and James waited for Gopi, alone in the waiting room.

"So, you think Radha had some hand in the deaths of Sankaran and Kunjelu?" Jane said it as a statement rather than a question.

James looked at her. He wasn't surprised she reached that conclusion. She had, after all, a very methodical mind.

"I don't know. She was only fifteen then. She was likely present at those locations based on what we heard, her usual hiding places. Sankaran died of heart failure. Radha was most alike Lalitha. If he saw her suddenly, at the very place he killed her, he could have had a heart attack caused by fright. It's rare, but it can happen. Kunjelu died from snake bite in the disused well in the Sarpa-kaavu. No one knows how he fell in. We only know Radha spent much time there."

"Why wouldn't you ask her?"

"She's gone through enough horrors in her life. I couldn't judge her for whatever happened to those evil people. If I don't know what happened, I don't have to report it."

Jane nodded. Even if she was sure of Radha's direct involvement, she would have acquitted her on the basis of self-defence. If Sankaran had guessed Radha was anywhere near that night, her fate wouldn't have been any different from her sister's.

'But someone had guessed it today, considering the attempt on her life. Maybe the same one was chasing them, to prevent them from disturbing the skeletons in the old closet.'

Night had fallen. Thick clouds obscured the stars, and the atmosphere was heavy and humid.

Jane looked at James. Most of the puzzle pieces were

falling into place; part of their question was answered, although they still needed confirmation. They didn't know how they truly felt about their supposed birth parents. It could wait until they had time to process it all. At least they knew where to find one of them. Knowing he had rejected them before they were born, they weren't sure they wanted to meet him now. He would most likely deny their existence, being a rising politician with much to lose. Would he attempt to harm them for power? Maybe... they didn't know him at all.

"What do we do now?" James asked.

Now that they had heard half the story, how could they confirm it? Would they have to confront Adi to know the rest? Wouldn't that be as crazy as walking into a lion's den? If they knew what had happened to Annie and the other set of twins, they could go home without meeting him. They had to find out... for the sake of their parents waiting back home.

51. Malevolence

Gopi was late.

Jane switched on her phone to check for any messages from him. A few notifications popped up, and it rang immediately, displaying an unknown number. She frowned as she answered.

"Hello?" Jane's frown deepened at the familiar voice.

It was Veena. She put her on speaker for James.

"I'm so glad to finally reach you!"

"Why?" Jane's voice was cold. She wasn't sure of Veena anymore.

"I promised to call with any updates. I needed to confirm the possibility of your theory before sharing anything. I owed it to my friends..."

"What do you mean?"

"Annie couldn't have changed her mind about Mathew because... she was in love with Adi... For a long time. She told Mathew on his graduation day. The reason they drifted apart."

"Last time we met, you didn't mention anything about Adi." Jane's voice was steely as she replied, her eyes narrowing in suspicion.

"It wasn't my secret to tell. He's a public figure, and it's his right to decide whether to discuss his private life. I've been trying to reach him since we spoke, but my messages didn't get through. This morning, I met him in person."

"And?"

"He admitted they were secretly married after Siva and Lakshmi's pre-planned wedding. Adi and Annie saw them off on a train to Bombay. They knew they couldn't be seen together until the dust settled from Siva and Lakshmi's elopement. But they couldn't bear the separation with such looming threat, so they had exchanged vows and garlands privately, symbolising their union, a true Gandharva marriage.

They never told anyone, wanting to keep it private until they could repeat it publicly. I didn't know until today."

"Last time we met, we were followed from the college, and that car belonged to your husband. How can we believe anything you say?" Jane persisted.

Veena didn't sound surprised.

"My husband's car was at his father's house that day. I suspect foul play; I had a brake failure on my new car after meeting you, leaving me stuck in hospital until now. I couldn't reach Adi over phone. Whether you believe me or not, Adi insists he didn't know Annie was pregnant. He was on a train the night of the landslide, returning after seeing his sister off to Europe. I know this for sure because Krishnan was with him to help Lakshmi with the visa and paperwork—he returned with Adi. The train was delayed due to rain, and Adi only reached Palari in the morning."

"You don't have to take my word. Adi is on his way to Palari to meet you. Murali told him you were there. He's in great pain and doesn't know what to believe anymore. I wish he'd told me about the marriage 25 years ago; I'd have understood his lonely life choices since losing Annie."

"When will he arrive in Palari?" Jane asked carefully, not wanting to reveal their location.

"He should be there by midnight. He was near Kozhikode when he called me last."

"Okay, speak to you later," Jane disconnected quickly and switched off her phone.

"Do they know we're in Kozhikode?" Jane frowned.

"They couldn't have! We were right here in the open if they wanted to find us."

"Adi is on the way to Palari to meet us. What if it's a trap?"

"What if she's telling the truth? He couldn't have received Annie's letter if he was still on the train. Maybe we should meet him, then we can go home finally," said James, convinced.

Gopi's car screeched to a halt in front of them. He got out with a welcoming smile and opened the front passenger door for Jane.

"You'd better sit in the front," he said with a grin. "I washed my car this evening!"

"Is that why you're late?" Jane asked, rolling her eyes.

"Oh no. You two are the reason. Since Ooty, I'm paranoid about being followed. I thought I saw a flash of the same truck far behind; it made me afraid. I took long loops to make sure I wasn't being followed."

Jane and James looked at each other in astonishment.

"You're sure?"

"Yes, I didn't want to fall prey again. I left my old phone at home too!"

They set off at once. On the edge of town, they stopped for food. Hungry and exhausted, they devoured the hot, spicy egg-puffs—the only thing available in the small café. The roads lay empty; only a single car, a black Innova, passed by as they waited.

They got back into the car, only to see an ominous truck approaching—bright orange with a green trailer, bearing a local number plate. They recognised it instantly from Ooty. For a moment they froze, but the vehicle rumbled past, taking the same road as the earlier car.

"I think we should stay back," said James.

"But that black car carried a flag in the front," Jane murmured, the unsettling detail clawing its way out of her subconscious memory.

"Ministerial cars usually have a flag. But they often come with a huge convoy, complete with road closures and all sorts of gimmicks. I saw a 25-car convoy last month and had to wait two hours on a busy highway because all traffic was stopped to let them pass! Our ministers act like they are god's own, and the people who vote for them are destined to wait on them!"

Gopi was inflamed again, his discontent with the broken political system flaring up and momentarily pushing the orange truck out of his mind.

"Indeed? I was under the impression such opulent displays were the purview of American presidents. Typically, our British ministers avail themselves of public transportation," James said.

Jane shushed them suddenly as another car went past. This time, it was a midnight blue Range Rover. Both Jane and James were flabbergasted. Gopi looked at them with confusion.

"That's Mahendran's car! Adi's cousin and PA! So, the black car must have been Adi's!" Jane told Gopi.

"Why would his team let a truck go in front of them? That is never done!" Gopi insisted.

"This is getting worse. If Veena's right, the real culprit could be someone else—and Adi's the one in danger. We must go after them... Gopi, let's move," said James.

Jane's brain was running on autopilot with various scenarios. She still wasn't sure how wise their move would be. Gopi hesitated too, but James urged him. "We would maintain a discreet distance. Given their position ahead of us, we should be okay this time."

"Provided there isn't another convoy of trucks behind us!" Gopi said. But he started the car.

Jane kept a watch behind them. There was nothing coming as far as she could see, no headlights piercing the dark night. They had passed the town area and were now on lonely, steep roads with no streetlights or shops. They couldn't see the other vehicles for some time until they reached the top of the hill. The road began descending through hairpin bends, and they saw three sets of headlights far below. Gopi switched to low-intensity lights, which only covered a short patch in front—a dangerous move on such a winding road. He slowed down to a snail's pace to see where he was going without giving away their position. They could still see the other cars as the road bent and wound over the hill.

Then it happened. The truck sped up and hit the black car from the side, tipping it over the ridge and down the slope. Gopi stopped their car abruptly and switched off the lights completely. They watched in horror as the stricken car rolled downward, its headlights illuminating the bushes and trees until they went out with a pop. The truck moved on without stopping and disappeared around the corner, to the other side of the hill and the valley ahead. Not knowing friend or foe, they waited for the Range Rover to reach the accident spot. The car stopped for a minute, as if assessing the damage, then, to their astonishment, sped on and disappeared around the corner, leaving the wreck in complete darkness.

Jane and Gopi sat in silence, their moth open, horror in their eyes. James's emergency training kicked in. He pulled out his phone, but there was no signal. He shook them both to get them out of their trance, checked their phones too, none had any signal. So, the plot was well planned.

"We need to get there... soon," he urged Gopi. He listened and started the car, driving to the spot. Gopi angled the headlights toward the wreckage. James found a torch in Gopi's overnight bag and jumped out with his medical kit. Jane followed.

The car had fallen sideways, with all its airbags deployed. The driver's door was smashed inwards, blood streaked across the sides and pooled over the shattered glass. A man in uniform was trapped behind the bent door and the seat, unmoving. James checked his neck for a pulse, the only part he could reach. The man was already dead. Jane came up behind him and, with difficulty, turned off the ignition key. There was only one passenger in the rear seat at the other end. James carefully reached him, avoiding the shattered glass and mangled metal. The man appeared unconscious, covered in debris, his white shirt stained with blood. James was relieved to find a pulse; he was not dead, at least for now. James called out but received no response. By the time he pushed away the airbag and removed the seat belts, Gopi came running down with an improvised stretcher, a thick blanket tightly folded and secured around two sturdy poles. They carried the passenger to their car, laying him on the long seat in the back.

"What about the driver?" Jane asked, trembling.

"Nothing we can do. We'll call emergency services when we have a signal," said James.

Gopi reversed the car and drove at maximum speed. No other cars came their way. The sky was cloudy, no stars visible.

James was in emergency doctor mode. The man was breathing on his own — a good sign. His pepper-grey hair was matted with blood, his body covered in cuts and bruises. James rummaged through his medical kit, cleaned the wounds, packed them with sterile gauze pads, and applied firm pressure to staunch the bleeding. Jane helped by securing the dressings with roller bandages.

She looked at the man's pale face and held his hand as he tried to speak. "You've had an accident, but you're safe with us. We're taking you to the hospital," she reassured him.

"Vijayan, my driver?" His voice was low but calm.

Jane only nodded, not wanting to upset him. She was touched that he asked about his companion first.

"What's your name?" she asked gently.

"Adityan," came the soft reply.

So, it was their father, if what they had heard was true. James patted her shoulder and gave Adi a reassuring smile.

What a way to meet a parent for the first time, was the thought that passed simultaneously through their minds.

"Can you feel your feet and arms?" James asked,

checking for signs of spinal injury.

Adi wiggled his fingers and toes, wincing with pain.

"You'll need proper support for your neck. For now, I've improvised with clothing to keep it immobilised," James explained.

"My vision is blurred... I can't see clearly."

"It may be from the impact — possibly whiplash or concussion. Don't worry, we'll be at the hospital soon, and they'll take care of you properly."

To his credit, Gopi reached the Kozhikode Medical College Hospital in record time. Empty roads helped. Ministers could have faster journeys without convoys if they invested in roads for all, he said aloud, even amidst the chaos.

James had intended to keep Adi's identity a secret for his own security, but that attempt was in vain. The staff immediately recognised him as they transferred the patient to the emergency room. There was a considerable change in their attitude and a marked increase in their response speed. Adi was wheeled into an examination room right next to an operating theatre, and a couple of senior doctors arrived to take over from the junior staff. James found himself explaining his medical background, how he found the patient at the accident site, his initial diagnosis, and the treatment given. He called one of the senior doctors aside, 'Dr. Sunny' according to his name plate, and requested additional protection for Adi, as he believed his car had been targeted, though he did not mention any names. The doctor was surprised but called the hospital office to arrange for VIP security.

Unable to leave Adi, they waited in the visitor's room that night, curled up on uncomfortable chairs. Gopi had left earlier with a packet and detailed instructions from James, promising to be back in a couple of hours. The long room was filled with rows of chairs, and anxious relatives and friends milled around even at this late hour. Accidents and emergencies seldom respected the clock. Some people clutched small glasses of weak tea from the hospital canteen. This reminded James of the task of informing Adi's kin, an ironic term, considering they now suspected he was their father.

Jane called Rajan Mash from the hospital phone.

"Is that you, Jane?" Rajan Mash's voice was filled with unusual panic.

"Yes, what happened?"

"Are you safe? And James?"

"Yes. But what happened?" she asked again, impatiently.

"Girish... His car... He had an accident. I thought you two were with him..."

Shock ran through her spine. James looked at her in astonishment.

"When?" Jane's voice was close to screaming.

"The accident happened a few hours ago. The police just called. He's in critical condition..."

Jane's heart sank. She decided not to tell Rajan Mash about Adi's fate, if Mahendran was indeed heading to Palari... The less he knew about Adi, the safer they would be.

It must have been right after Girish left them at the hospital. The attack was meant for them, given what they'd learned. Devastation and anger engulfed Jane and James, and they couldn't shake off the guilt. Girish's only fault was helping them.

Not knowing who else to call without adding further risk to Adi or themselves, they decided to call Veena. Adi had obviously trusted her, and she and her husband would know what to do. Jane told her about what they had seen and suspected. Veena was shocked and promised to join them as soon as possible.

"Stay low and keep safe," she advised.

Dr. Sunny returned to update them. Adi had broken ribs, an arm, and both his legs. His neck had serious impact injuries, along with various cuts and bruises. He was being treated in surgery. The police were informed and, on their way, to talk to them.

As if on cue, important-looking police officers moved past the waiting room towards the operating theatre. Jane looked at James. They didn't want to talk to the police yet, not before talking to Adi. Especially when they suspected Adi's family's involvement in the attempt on his life. They didn't trust the police either. It was funny how things turned out since the first conversation they had with Gopi on public's trust on police!

They quietly exited the waiting room, heading towards the corridor. The hall was empty, patients and relatives asleep. A young woman with a flask came from another corridor.

"Excuse me, is there an exit at this end of the building?" Jane asked, catching up with her.

The woman's eyes widened. "Jane, is that you?!"

James recognised her too—the young woman from the flight.

"Of course! My dad's admitted here. I was getting him some tea. He wakes up incredibly early, old habits!" she said with mock annoyance but a bright smile.

Jane and James remembered Anita mentioning her father's illness.

"Oh, what a surprise!" Jane said. "How's your dad?"

"He's much better. Hoping to get him home today. Would you like to come in? He'd be happy to meet you."

"Of course," Jane said, pulling James along. A ray of hope ignited in Jane's mind, bringing a broad smile to her excited face. Anita had told them her father was retired from Kozhikode Medical College Hospital! How could they have forgotten this valuable information?

It was a small room with no luxuries. But the man sitting on the bed was remarkable, with a serious face and a presence of his own, despite his tired appearance from the illness and hospital stay. He was already dressed in a white shirt and black trousers, perhaps another habit from his working days. His grey hair was neatly combed back, and his eyes were sharp.

"Dad, this is Dr. James and Dr. Jane, who helped me on the plane. My father, Dr. Chandran Menon," Anita introduced them.

"Ah, it's a pleasure to meet you. A friend in need is a friend indeed. Thank you for helping my daughter. Call me CM," he said graciously.

His handshake was strong, his voice booming.

"Anita says you retired from this hospital," James noted.

"Yes, that's correct. I was the principal of the college for ten years, and the head of cardiology department before that. I have spent long years of my life here, so I insist to come here when I am ill rather than any private hospital. I get to see a lot of old friends."

James and CM talked medical interests and experiences. CM turned to Jane with an apologetic nod.

"I didn't mean to ignore you. Your brother is brilliant," he said with a smile.

"No worries. It happens whenever I'm with his doctor buddies," she said, smiling.

Jane then told CM about finding Adi and bringing him along. CM was thoughtful.

"Politics is more polarised than ever. We used to debate all day without resorting to hatred and violence," he said.

"We think there's more at play here than just politics," Jane replied. "It could be linked to events from two decades ago, which is why we're here. We need information quickly before we get caught in the tornado that's already in motion. Do you know anyone who could help us find hospital admission records from twenty-five years ago?"

CM looked at her curiously. The request seemed odd, especially coming from such young faces. James sensed the need for clarity. He explained their search for their birth parents, their belief that Annie was their mother, and that she may have been taken to the hospital in critical condition on the day they were born.

"We don't have all the supporting evidence, and we can't go through formal channels without alerting someone. We believe she was in the intensive care unit, and that's where we lost her trail. We need to know if she survived and what happened to the babies."

CM studied their earnest faces and his daughter's hopeful expression. He considered for a moment and then nodded.

"I'll ask the hospital admin if they have archives from that long ago. If they do, I'll sign off on your request."

He called a desk number, spoke for a minute, then waited briefly before turning back to them.

"You might be in luck. The hospital administration department is on the fourth floor, the night manager said he could help if you get there before his shift ends."

They thanked him and Anita and hurried at once towards the lift.

52. The weight of grief

Oceans away in Paris, Richard and Lissy watched a flawless stage performance. Richard had contacted the event manager through Rita and arranged to meet Siva and Lakshmi after the show. They congratulated the pair backstage, then walked together to a reserved room near the venue, away from the boisterous cast and crew.

Lissy smiled at the renowned artists, who were humble and polite. As Richard explained the extraordinary situation and why they wanted to meet, she saw a sea of emotions play across their faces. They listened patiently as Richard recounted the various facts Jane and James had uncovered in their quest for the truth about their parentage.

Lakshmi's eyes widened, then filled with tears. "I remember the pretty girl in the dance costume," she said, her voice trembling. "She reminded me of my own daughter."

"My brother has loved Annie forever, and I know he still does," Lakshmi said through sobs.

Although they grew up in the same place, Adi and Annie had attended different schools and moved in different circles. Their relationship evolved from rivalry to love after the memorable inter-college competition. They shared a passion for the state-wide literacy program, which strengthened their bond. To avoid trouble at home, they kept their love hidden.

Annie and Adi were the official witnesses for Siva and Lakshmi's marriage, arranging everything to get them out of trouble. Lakshmi's uncle had planned to marry her off to Mahendran's friend, Mohan Poduval, who sought revenge for a public humiliation. Her uncle had played it down as her naivety and Poduval's boisterous nature- nothing a marriage couldn't fix. Lakshmi would not have had the courage to escape if it wasn't for Annie. She, a force of nature, wouldn't let her to succumb to the pressure. Adi too wanted his sister and friend to be safe and far away.

For twenty-five years, they all believed Annie had perished in the landslide. Lakshmi had cried for weeks for her friends and for her brother Adi, who was left heartbroken and inconsolable by the news.

"If Adi had known Annie was pregnant, he would have protected her," Lakshmi said, her voice trembling. "He was the most resourceful man I've ever known. He couldn't have written that letter; he only reached Palari after the landslide. It must have been Mahendran's idea, with his friend Mohan Poduval who had an exceptional talent for forgery."

Siva sat silently, weighed down by guilt. He held himself responsible for the fate that befell his father and older brother. Because of his elopement with the daughter of the grand house, his brother's engagement to Lalitha was broken, and their home was destroyed. He had inadvertently ruined his brother's life while saving his own. His repeated attempts to reconnect with Vishnu had been met with silence; grief and guilt thickening the icy barrier between them.

"I am guilty of stealing the happiness and life from my own brother... All these years," Siva shuddered. Lakshmi sobbed leaning on his shoulders, unable to add any words of comfort.

Lissy and Richard felt their pain as their own, as if they were guilty of the same crime against Annie and Adi, though unknowingly. And there was the grief for their own, for the children they lost...

****

The night manager, Satyan was waiting for Jane and James. He led them to the archive room. Dusty tapes and files filled the shelves.

"Here," Satyan said, pulling out a tape from the specified date. "Let's see what we can find."

As they scrolled through the records, disappointment washed over them. No mention of Annie or Varkey.

"Wait," James said, pointing to an entry. "An unnamed accident case on that date."

They cross-referenced the file and found a later entry for Varkey John, deceased from multiple injuries sustained in a car accident. His son's address was listed as Johny Varkey, Palari.

Jane's heart raced. "Varkey was here," she whispered.

They continued searching, scanning through entries of deliveries and newborns. No Annie, no unnamed entries either. Just when they were about to give-up, James stumbled on a name that caught his attention. "Tina Mary, age 23," he read. "Admitted with post-delivery complications after the stillbirth of twin girls. Discharged with medication and advised to revisit in two weeks.' There was an address in Kannur.

Grief gripped them both, rendering them speechless. Tears welled as they grieved for the loss of their parents back home. A loss hidden for years because they had taken that space—their parents' love, sacrifice, and dedication. They had been like cuckoo birds in an unsuspecting cowbird's nest. The thought of telling their parents that their faint hope of finding their own children was now extinguished brought fresh pain and disappointment.

They thanked Satyan for his help and left clutching the paper with the address of Tina Mary, their only lead left to pursue

.

53. The last link

The flight from Bangalore was delayed by half an hour. Jane and James waited with Gopi in the car. Joey was one of the first to emerge.

"Hello, strangers," he greeted them with a broad smile, his face alight with renewed determination.

"Since you're not our sibling, it's probably apt," Jane replied.

"Hope you're as happy as I am about that!" Joey's eyes sparkled as he clasped Jane's hand for a firm handshake. She felt a warm charge pass between them, her cheeks burning. Joey settled beside her in the back seat, a knowing smile spreading as he noticed her blush.

James turned from the front seat, his brows raising slightly at their flushed faces. Jane looked away, pretending to check the traffic. He shrugged and updated Joey on recent events, emphasising the significance of their next lead.

"We have an address. We believe it's Sister Tina, your father's old friend."

They arrived at the house, but no one answered the bell. Open windows at the back suggested someone might be home. Jane circled the house, only to freeze in terror as a massive black dog charged at her. James rushed to her side, knowing her fear of dogs, but Joey reached her first. The Alsatian barked menacingly, but Joey stood firm.

A woman called back the dog, catching its collar. "I'm sorry. Jacky isn't dangerous, though he looks and sounds it."

"It's my fault," Jane said, still shaken. "I came round when no one answered the bell."

The woman, in her early fifties, wore a simple salwar kameez. Joey felt a faint recognition. "I'm Joey. You knew my father, Dr. Mathew, from the Kalpetta hospital. You used to bring me comic books."

A smile slowly lit up her face. "You've grown into a fine

young man!" She gave him an awkward hug, barely reaching his shoulder.

"Good to see you, Aunt Tina. This is Jane and James Banks. We believe you and my father helped deliver them the day he died. We need to know what happened..." Joey's straightforward approach was necessary; they needed answers.

Tina clutched the wall for support, her face a canvas of disbelief, then guilt. She saw their anxious faces, eyes full of questions. She invited them into the bright living room, excusing herself to fetch drinks, perhaps to gather her thoughts before she faced them.

When Tina returned, her face was set. She took a deep breath. "You deserve to know the truth. I'll tell you what happened that night, as much as I know, " she began.

****

Dr. Mathew had been called from his holiday to attend to Zubeida Suleiman, who was in critical condition. Tina assisted him in the emergency caesarean, saving both mother and baby. They had barely finished when Mrs Lissy Banks was brought in, unconscious, her waters already broken. The foetus showed no sign of life. Lissy had a stillbirth, two girls, almost full-term but not lucky enough to survive. Mathew had stared at the tiny beings, willing them to live, knowing how precious this pregnancy was. Tina knew he cared deeply for Lissy, ever since she first came to the hospital with her aunt, the mother superior of the convent.

Suddenly, a commotion erupted outside as an ambulance arrived with an injured man. Mathew recognised the voice and had rushed out. To Tina's surprise, he left in his car without a word. He returned shortly with a heavily pregnant woman. Refusing help from anyone but Tina, he was near hysterics—something she had never seen before.

The woman's condition was dire: weak pulse, heavy bleeding, and bruises indicating a bad fall. She clutched

Mathew's hands, begging him to save her child and find the baby a safe home, as if she knew she wouldn't survive.

"Who is she?" Tina asked, bewildered.

"Annie," Mathew said, voice trembling. "My godfather's daughter, my childhood friend. I thought she died in the landslide six months ago. I told you about her before."

Tina knew Annie was more than a friend to Mathew—she was Mathew's only love, although he never said that aloud, ever. That night, they delivered Annie's twins: a girl and a boy. Despite the stress endured by their mother, the babies were born healthy. Annie, however, was in critical situation, near to death than life. Mathew insisted on transferring her to the medical college's intensive care unit and urged discretion, fearing for their lives.

"It's Annie's father in the ambulance. They were attacked today." Mathew said bitterly.

As the ambulance was about to leave, Mathew discreetly got Annie inside. Then, to Tina's horror, he handed her a baby basket with Lissy's stillborn babies.

"Trust me," he said calmly, his earlier panic replaced by determination. "This way, her babies will be safe and loved, away from the imminent danger. That's what she asked me when I rescued her from that damned house. It's the least I can do for her. A promise to keep…"

"Don't worry," he assured her. "I'll set the records straight once the danger passes."

He followed the ambulance in his car, keeping an eye out for the enemy he had seen lurking around, waiting for his chance. He had vowed to not let that happen…

****

Tina admitted the two patients to the emergency care at the medical college hospital. To her relief, Dr. Mathew had phoned ahead and arranged for urgent care with his friend in the hospital. She used her own name and address to keep Annie's whereabout discrete, while leaving the older man unidentified as before. She waited for Dr. Mathew, but he never arrived. The following morning, a call to Kalpetta hospital brought devastating news—Dr. Mathew was dead. Fear gripped her. Was Annie next?

Annie stayed in intensive care for nearly a week, her condition uncertain. Tina left countless messages for Annie's brother, Johny, using the number Dr. Mathew had given her. A call to Kalpetta hospital revealed Lissy and the babies had been discharged the next day. Tina was reeling, unsure if Dr. Mathew got a chance to tell them about the babies. What could she say to Annie now? She feared endangering everyone by revealing too much.

Annie eventually regained consciousness, only to be told about her stillborn babies by one of the doctors. Her condition deteriorated again. Finally, Tina received a reply from Johny, Annie's brother, who was in the city, searching discreetly for Annie. She took him to see Annie, only after he proved his identity.

Later that evening, Johny brought Annie's aunt, Alice, to the hospital. Alice had endured weeks of nightmares, not knowing where Annie or Varkey were. Returning home from a shopping trip to find no one there, she had rushed to Dr. Mathew's hospital, only to learn he was dead. Weeks of frantic searching had taken their toll. Despite being grief-stricken upon learning about Annie's babies, Alice put on a brave face for her niece.

It took days for Annie to recount the events of that harrowing night. "It was Mohan Poduval who attacked us. The demon had followed father after overhearing him talking to Mathew at the hospital earlier that day. Mohan Poduval has been obsessed with Lakshmi and went into a rage when she escaped his grasp. He knew Adi and I had helped her to escape and took his revenge on us. He even somehow knew I was pregnant..."

She paused, eyes distant, reliving the moment. "I knew

I had to act fast. I slipped out of the house to draw him away. But I lost my footing and fell hard in the ditch. The shock and the fall... it caused heavy bleeding. Father chased after him, following in his car."

Her voice broke. "Poduval was too cunning. He forced Father's car off the road. I saw the impact, but I couldn't move. I screamed and no one heard me. I lay there in the ditch bleeding, terrified for my baby and my father."

Tears filled Annie's eyes as she continued. "Hours passed. Then, like an angel, Mathew came, calling my name and found me. I could barely answer. He kept me calm and rushed me to the hospital. I made him promise to find a safe home for my child — far from danger. I was sure I was going to die that night."

Her voice went soft. "I survived, but I lost them all — everyone I loved. They died because of me. And my cursed love..."

It was another day when Annie spoke about the day, she left Palari. Her face was twisted in pain when uttering Adi's name. "Adi's letter, it felt like a death sentence. I could feel his coldness beneath all the logical explanations — abandoning me and our baby. He couldn't have hurt me more with razor-edged knives than with those cleverly written words. It hung like a final judgement on me, our baby, and even the very idea of us. How could he write that without even facing me? My parents' faces went pale when they saw it; they were hurt and angry. They asked if I wanted to terminate the pregnancy, as Adi had suggested. But I couldn't end the life that symbolised the love I once thought we had."

She buried her face in her knees, arms wrapped tightly around her legs, her hair cascading like a veil. Tears streamed down, soaking her hospital gown.

Her voice wavered. "That evening, Father sent me to Wayanad, to a safe house. Alice Aunt came with me. But fate was so cruel. A landslide took Mother along with the house.

To punish for my sins..." Her face hardened. "My friend died too thinking I was buried dead. I wish I had. The mud would have weighed far less than this guilt and grief. It was my fault, all of it." she sobbed.

"When I heard Mathew died in an accident along with Poduval, I knew it wasn't a coincidence. I know Mathew had tried to protect me. He died for me and my baby, just like father. But I lost my baby too. Then I found out I was carrying twins. Twisted joker of fate had thought my pain wasn't enough, so it had to double it at the end".

Annie collapsed into her aunt's arms, sobbing uncontrollably. "My life is a curse. I wish I didn't exist..."

The pain of her loss was blinding, the chasm of darkness was bottomless, the only way forward was downwards, to the heart of the misery. Alice and Johny held her tightly, offering silent comfort. They shared her pain, and her grief.

****

"Johny and Alice were immensely thankful to me," Tina continued with a sob. "They said they won't forget it was me who brought the last hope to them. Their Annie was alive only because of mine and Mathew's action. They were reeling from repeated tragedies and losses in their family, desperate to get Annie away from it all, to help her forget and start afresh. But I felt suffocated, not being able to tell them the whole truth."

Tina sighed deeply, her voice trembling with emotion. "Finally, I told Johny."

"He was miserable," Tina continued, her eyes distant with the memory. "He felt terrible for his grief-stricken sister. Together, we tried to trace Mrs. Lissy Banks, but she had left the country. The given contact was of her dead aunt, leaving no relatives or link."

"What could we have said to Annie?" Tina shook her head. "'Your children are probably okay but with someone else thousands of miles away, who obviously think they are

290   Therese Pal

their own!' Neither of us had any idea how it would affect Annie's strained mental condition and her weakened physical state. Didn't know how she would react at that stage. And if the news somehow leaked out, none of us would be safe, reversing all the safeguards Mathew and Varkey had paid with their lives. Johny thought of his young sister's future. Their parents had a world of dreams for her, and she was on the way to achieving it all until that moment of madness. Now that fate had intervened... She could do a fresh start without the burden of the past... Once she weathered the storm of grief."

Tina paused, looking at each of them intently. "I felt conflicted and afraid. I knew I could lose my license, livelihood, and probably my life if the news got out. So, I agreed with Johny and walked away from it all, with a heavy heart."

She continued, her voice softer now, "Johny took Annie and Alice with him to the US. 'A new place and new people could bring her old self and her spirits back,' he had said to me the night before they left. I thought the same for myself. The Kalpetta hospital had brought fresh trauma to me; the place was not the same anymore. So, I found a new job in Dubai and moved away from it all.

Johny was right. I was finally able to see the brighter side, knowing I helped save a young woman's life that night, and that was what mattered most in my line of duty. My dharma. But I never forgot those two tiny babies I had held that night and often wondered about them."

Tina looked at her silent audience, her eyes moist with unshed tears. "It was fate that brought you to me today. It was pre-written that we meet, so I could tell you your story... about the events that changed your destiny...."

Everyone was in a sombre mood when they got back in the car. The pieces of the puzzle had finally fallen into place, revealing the events of that fateful day. They could now see Dr. Mathew's desperate attempt to save them from the imminent danger embodied by Mohan Poduval aka 'Putana', the aptly named demon. His mind must have been racing, thinking of ways to fulfil his promise to Annie, to find a safer place for her babies. In that moment of peril, he must have thought of Lissy Banks—a kind soul he trusted. He believed she would make a wonderful mother, capable of filling their hearts with love as much as their real mother would.

"I can imagine what Dr. Mathew went through that day," James said, breaking the silence. "A doctor's first duty is always the safety of their patients. He wouldn't have wanted anyone to know about Annie or her children's existence, especially given the circumstances of their parentage. After what happened to Varkey and Annie, he must have decided not to record their presence at the hospital and get them away from it all."

Jane nodded, the logic settling in her mind. "Mohan Poduval was supposed to marry Lakshmi," she added. "He had reason to hate Annie and Adi who helped Lakshmi to get away. That connects the events to Wayanad driven by his twisted obsession and desire for revenge. He indeed overheard Varkey's conversation with Dr. Mathew and followed him with the intent to kill Annie. We know he followed the ambulance later, and Mathew tried to shake him off to protect Annie and Varkey. The police were right if that's what really happened."

She glanced at Joey, who sat quietly beside her, deep in thought. "Your father cared for Annie all his life," she continued softly. "He had the moral right to decide the best course of action for her children in that moment of danger. And... he saved us with his life... Our lives came at the cost of your loss."

Her voice trembled as she held Joey's hand gently, trying to convey her emotions. Tears welled up in her eyes, reflecting the grief and sadness for Annie, Varkey, and Dr. Mathew. In the rear-view mirror, she saw James's face mirroring her own feelings. He reached out to her and Joey, their joined hands trying to stem the grief and loss they felt in their hearts. Tears fell freely, as if an underground lake that had remained forgotten for a quarter of a century had finally broken its barriers. Life had flourished above it, nourished by its hidden depths of sacrifice and their combined blessings.

****

Richard and Lissy were stunned when they heard about the events. Lissy's sobs were audible when they told her about the stillborn babies. She was deeply saddened to hear about Annie and the danger she had faced, and Dr. Mathew's quick decision to save her babies.

They took their time processing the information, quietly and sombrely. They felt their family bond was forged from heartbreak and loss, strengthened by selfless sacrifices and love, tested against the forces of evil and hatred.

"It was destiny that brought us together," Lissy said, wiping away her tears. "I will be forever indebted to Annie for this precious gift—our treasured family, our dream."

Love and life had charted different paths for them all, only to bring them together in this moment. There was profound grief for a lost father, but also relief knowing Annie was safe somewhere, may be thousands of miles away, a half-turn of the earth in time. At least they knew where to find Adi. James's discrete DNA test with Adi's blood sample obtained on the day of the accident had confirmed their assumption. He was only a few miles away, their fates already intertwined as if by some cosmic connection. It was time to meet him…

54. Bittersweet

The hospital parking was full. They circled a few times before finding a spot far from the entrance, right at the exit. It was Gopi who alerted them, a splash of midnight blue hidden in a secluded corner, its engine still warm. Dread washed over them, and they sprinted toward the hospital.

In the corridor, they nearly collided with Veena. She was in wheelchair helped by Krishnan.

"Who is with Adi?" Jane asked urgently.

"We were there until five minutes ago. Just stepped out for coffee. There's a police officer guarding the room. No one is allowed in without clearance from the chief medical officer," Veena explained.

"Mahendran's car is in the car park," James said, his voice tense. They rushed to Adi's room.

The police officer outside the room frowned at their approach. "No one allowed in without permission."

"Did anyone else go in?" James demanded.

"Who are you to ask?" The officer raised an eyebrow.

"They're family," Veena said, catching up. "I can authorise them."

"Only a nurse went in, just now," the officer replied.

They burst into the room, ignoring the officer's protests. James spotted a uniformed figure by the bed, fiddling with the saline feed. The man, wearing a surgical mask and large glasses, bolted for the window and jumped out before they could stop him.

James quickly disconnected the feed from Adi's arm, checking his vitals. Jane pressed the call button, shouting at the officer to chase the intruder. The officer hesitated, confused.

A stream of nurses and doctors rushed in, taking over Adi's care. The visitors were pushed outside. James reluctantly followed, recognising Dr. Sunny from the previous day among the medical staff.

They waited anxiously with Veena and Krishnan, shaken by the events. Gopi and Joey returned, having lost the intruder.

Half an hour later, Dr. Sunny emerged. "No major harm done. We're still assessing the content of the tampered saline bag. Extra security has been added."

After a couple of hours, James and Jane were allowed in to see Adi. He was awake, resting still on the raised bed. His gaze was deep and sharp, his presence undiminished by the barrage of bandages, cuts, and grazes. No-one said anything for a minute, Adi and the twins appraised each other, with fixed glances and curious faces.

"I hear you saved my life... twice," Adi said, his voice a deep drawl, stronger than the previous day.

"One time for each of us," James replied with a smile.

Adi smiled faintly. "I can't remember the car rescue well. I was coming to meet you. Veena says you two might be my children..."

Neither Jane nor James had planned how to broach the subject. Adi's directness took them by surprise.

"What do you think?" Jane asked, her face hard and unreadable.

Adi studied her for a long moment. "I recognise that style, and some resemblance."

"To whom?" Jane pressed.

"To someone I cared about, a lot," Adi said, looking away. Sadness tinged his voice. "But I lost her a long time ago. I couldn't comprehend your story."

"Maybe you did lose her. Maybe you abandoned her. You wouldn't be the first to abandon the mother of their children," Jane retorted, bitterness lacing her words.

"I never abandoned her. I never would," Adi said calmly, though an undercurrent of anger simmered. "If she was alive, she would have contacted me. In all these years... the Annie

I know would have reached out to me."

"She wouldn't if she believed you abandoned her when she needed you the most. I wouldn't, if it were me," Jane said, her voice hard.

Adi stared at Jane, silent.

James looked at the pair with concern and a flicker of uncertainty. Then he made a decision and recounted what they knew. Adi's composed facade cracked, emotions flickering across his face.

"I never knew Annie was pregnant. I never got her letter. I couldn't have sent such a reply; I was on a delayed train that night. Mahendran told us about the landslide the next day when he came to pick me up at the railway station. If you knew how my world had gone dark at that moment..." he paused, trying to regain his composure, emotions splaying on his face. Minutes passed before his voice heard again, just as a whisper to himself, "I was at the site, searching for her in the rain and mud.... All week..."

"But Annie received a letter through Lalitha. Radha delivered it. Annie didn't want to terminate her pregnancy, so she went away with her aunt the same day, which saved her from the landslide," James explained, his voice softer.

Jane frowned, recalling Radha's mention of Mahendran and his friend Mohan Poduval, being present the day Lalitha was killed. What if they confiscated Annie's letter and forged one from Adi? She voiced her suspicion, her anger on behalf of Annie evident.

They all saw then the cunning plan for what it was. The letter aimed to ensure that the unborn child, who would tarnish the family name with yet another scandal, would be terminated at the earliest opportunity, effectively breaking the couple apart in the process. In turmoil with panic and helplessness, she must have believed the letter. Annie wouldn't reach out to Adi, if she believed he had abandoned her to fate. She blamed herself for the deaths of her parents, her babies, and her friend. The greater loss could have hardened her feeling to an unbroken determination to never ever contact Adi again!

James told him about Annie's ordeal, Varkey's efforts to protect her, and Dr. Mathew's rescue.

"She thought she lost her babies. She felt responsible for the death of her loved ones. She wouldn't have contacted you with that knowledge. She denied herself any more pain, even if she doubted the veracity of the letter later," Jane said, sadness replacing the bitterness.

Adi felt a knife twist in his heart. His family had betrayed him. They hid it from him all these years; his own uncle and cousin made an absolute fool of him. He should have known; VD had warned him about the cold hearts around him. The thought of Annie surviving hadn't even crossed his mind. He had suffered for so long, silently burying it all in a deep corner of his heart.

He closed his eyes; tears he thought long dried surprising him. He had buried that, along with his love, under a mountain of earth and mud. The last time he cried, the torrential rain had masked the relentless stream of tears from anyone's view.

When he opened them, he saw hope in the form of two determined young people—his children. And somewhere, Annie was alive and safe. That much was enough for him now to gather his strength …

"Thank you for finding me. I didn't know I was lost. Perhaps I did some good karma to call you my children," Adi said, his voice choked with emotion.

James and Jane, tears in their eyes, moved to embrace Adi, taking care not to disturb his broken body. He gently patted their cheeks and hair, tears flowing freely from all three.

55. Chakravyuha

The rest of the day passed in paranoia. The hospital was swarming with police, no one without explicit permission was allowed in, and a guard remained in Adi's room.

James and Jane visited Girish in the ICU. He was still in critical condition but stable, which brought them some comfort. He lay sedated, connected to numerous machines. Jane squeezed his hand gently, silently conveying her warmth and appreciation for his friendship.

The next day, James and Jane spoke with Adi when he was awake and able to talk, though their conversation was brief. It focused mostly on Annie. Efforts to trace her, who had seemingly disappeared after moving to the States with her brother and aunt, had so far yielded no results. Richard's inquiries had hit a dead end.

Adi promised to use his government contacts to see if she had ever returned to India, but he wanted to clear the murky waters in his own circle first. He was unsure how many of his associates were linked to Mahendran or had been swayed by his influence. Adi had trusted Mahendran implicitly until just yesterday. Now, Mahendran was out there, free with no concrete charges against him other than his car being spotted at the accident site.

At noon, a police officer arrived to update Adi on an urgent matter. Jane, sitting outside, recognized him immediately and sprang up, her voice accusatory.

"You're Sub Inspector Sridharan Poduval...," she said.

"Is that a crime?" the officer responded, raising an eyebrow.

James joined her, blocking his entry. "You can't go in there."

"Why? You have your grandfather in there?" he mocked. "I have clearance from security and the medical team. It's an urgent matter."

He crossed past them with steady steps, Jane and James followed him into the room with steely resolve.

"It's a police matter," he said curtly.

Adi calmed the officer and permitted the twins to stay. The officer's sharp eyes twinkled as he observed the warmth between Adi and the twins. A genuine smile appeared on his rough face, unexpectedly.

"If you insist, sir. After all, it matters to them too."

The news the officer delivered was shocking.

"Your household staff, Sukumar, had an accident early today," the officer began, his tone grave. "He was driving Mahendran's car when a truck hit him near Wayanad. He didn't make it, but he gave a statement before he died."

Adi's eyes narrowed, his jaw tightening as he processed the information. "And what did he say?" His voice was steady, but the undercurrent of urgency was unmistakable.

" Sukumar said he was Mahendran's shadow, his man on the inside, for years..." the officer explained. " Mahendran knew your every step. Thats how he could redirect Government funds quietly, whispers in the ears of the right officials bought what he wanted, could turn the windfall for his own benefits."

Adi's expression shifted from confusion to shock, his eyes widening as the realisation hit.

The officer nodded. "Mahendran's money bought him friends in high places. Sukumar was his eyes and ears, making sure Mahendran stayed one step ahead of any suspicion, and also the dealer of his dirty deeds when he needed that."

"How did I not see this?" Adi muttered, more to himself than anyone else.

The officer continued, "Recently, Mahendran got wind of two British youngsters poking around an old case involving the deaths of Mohan Poduval and Dr. Mathew. This had the makings of a political storm. His associate, SP Sunil Kumar had tipped Mahendran promptly."

James and Jane exchanged a glance.

"Mahendran ordered Sukumar to scare off the young people," the officer explained. "A truck was sent to chase them in Ooty, but that obviously failed to discourage them. When they reached out to Veena- your close friend and also Sunil's sister-in-law, Mahendran panicked. He engineered an accident to keep Veena from contacting you. Its only luck that she survived at all."

Adi clenched his fists.

The officer continued. "Indeed. Mahendran was surprised and alarmed when Sukumar called him and revealed that the same kids were at his home in Palari with Rajan Mash and his crew. He went ahead and gave permission to clear the pond. He wanted to use the old legend as a backdrop for his plan to remove them from the scene, this time for real."

Adi's eyes widened in shock. "But Mahendran truly believed in the legend after the string of deaths years ago!"

"Yes, that's how Sukumar knew how desperate Mahendran had become; When Sukumar found James near the river, he sabotaged the bridge. But an eerie scream had frightened him, and he abandoned his subsequent plan to poison them. He fell ill with fright that day, convinced the curse was real."

Adi shook his head, a mix of anger and disbelief on his face. "And Radha?"

"Mahendran somehow realised the ghost they feared all these years was Radha. His anger, built over decades, fixated on her. He believed she held the key to his downfall and sent Sukumar to start a fire at her home. Meanwhile, Mahendran planned to delay you, knowing you were heading to Palari. He was determined to keep you from meeting the twins at any cost."

Adi's expression darkened. "So, it was Sukumar again at the hospital?"

"Dressed as a nurse, Sukumar tampered with your saline feed but was caught before he could do more harm. Mahendran was furious but told Sukumar to meet him at the Wayanad bypass with the pretence of keeping an alibi. But all he met was the ominous truck."

Adi's face was grave as the officer finished.

James and Jane were stunned. They hadn't realised the full extent of the danger they were in. Their quest had triggered a chain of events that could have ended with their and Adi's deaths.

"Sukumar gave all this away willingly?" Adi asked, sceptically.

"He did," the officer confirmed. "He knew he was dying and knew he was double-crossed by Mahendran. He recognized the truck that hit him! It was the very same he himself arranged earlier for different outcomes!"

"What about Mahendran and Sunil?" Adi's voice was laced with anger.

"Sunil is arrested. The chief minister insisted on it. Sunil claims he only passed information for government business. He dealt with me first on that." the officer said, his tone tinged with frustration. "He was adamant about keeping the case closed. He tried to appeal to me by saying further investigation could tarnish my late father's memory. I told him plainly, I didn't care about that. My father did the damage himself, and it is an old story. He then instructed me to keep an eye on the foreigners, questioning their true motives."

He glanced at James and Jane, then to Adi. But he continued in his formal tone.

"Mahendran is still at large. He's exceptionally clever, leaving no trace that could tie him to the case if it went to court. If he had managed to silence Sukumar, there would be no solid evidence against him. He must have suspected someone had seen his car at the accident site, which is why he sent Sukumar in it before his death. His plan only failed because Sukumar lived long enough to tell his tale. We're trying to locate the truck to gather more evidence."

"Thank you, Inspector, for coming directly to me. Please keep any details about the two British nationals off the record for now, if you can. I don't want to put them in any more danger than they already faced..." Adi said with a grave face.

Inspector Poduval stared at the twins for a long moment, his expression thoughtful. "Krishna brought down his uncle Kamsa after all," he muttered to himself.

"What did you say?" Jane asked.

"Never mind. I have an update for you as well. I am sure, you already knew the man from the Kalpetta accident wasn't the person you submitted the missing report for."

The officer's gaze was knowing, and Jane and James knew they hadn't fooled him really with their pretence. But he continued in his measured professional manner.

"Nevertheless, I have done some inquiries. The retired army officer, Abraham Varghese, spent his final years in an Ashram in the Nilgiris, near Kodaikanal. After finding spiritual healing, he gave up drinking. I heard he was remorseful about abandoning his only daughter. He made some police inquiries about his sister, Sr. Frances, and his daughter, Lissy. However, his request came a few years after the nun's death, and there were no records of Lissy's whereabouts to provide him. He only lived a few more months after that..."

He retrieved a brown-paper-covered parcel from his bag and handed it to Jane.

"These are his diaries. I recovered them from the Ashram for you. Your mother might find them valuable..."

Pride coloured his voice, and Jane realised with regret and relief that he wasn't the villain or brute she had imagined but truly an honest officer! The exact opposite of his cousin Mohan Poduval.

She opened the parcel to find four diaries, filled with numerous letters, all dated and addressed to his daughter.

Finally, there was something tangible they could share with their mother. Amidst all the heartbreak and sadness, there was some good news for Lissy. She would be relieved to know her father had turned a corner and had wanted to see her before he died.

"Thank you, sir, for your dedicated service. We truly appreciate it," she said sincerely. James raised his hand in salute.

"I will close your missing person inquiry with that remark. We like to believe we are actively fulfilling the true Janamaithri intent," he said with a rare smile before leaving the room.

Jane handed the diaries to James and rubbed her eyes, feeling overwhelmed with emotions.

Adi's face too was filled with unfamiliar emotions— "I'm sorry for putting you both in danger. I promise to find Annie, and I sincerely hope we can do it together. To return her to you would be my atonement, for all that grief I caused knowingly or unknowingly. For being so blind to the sins of my own blood. I'm grateful to your parents for raising you so well. I couldn't have done a better job."

Adi did not want to make his connection to the twins or Annie public for fear of further attacks. The political world could be even more unforgiving than familial honour and revenge. Adi shuddered, looking at James's bandaged arm, realizing they had nearly been killed seeking him.

"You both get home to your parents safely. I will come and see you once I get out of the hospital," Adi insisted.

Jane noted Adi recognising their home being still with Richard and Lissy and felt thankful for it. She couldn't handle any higher claim at the present, whatever the facts were. Knowing was indeed half the battle, and they had won that round. Now they ought to decide whether the past they inherited must define the future or not…

They said their goodbyes with embraces, sharing the

overwhelming emotions.

****

On the phone to Richard and Lissy that evening, Jane and James discussed another expedition, to find Annie, this time to the US.

"She had suffered immensely, and likely still unaware of our survival. I think we ought to seek her, the very least, to lighten her burden." Jane said with conviction.

Richard and Lissy sighed with resignation; they knew how determined their children were, once they set their minds. At least they now knew their story and their roots, answering the immediate question of identity. Rest could follow its pace.

"Now we are coming home mum...", James said cheerfully.

"Yes, in time for our family Christmas and our birthday," Jane added.

Their hearts were still anchored where home was—with Lissy and Richard. Nothing could have changed that...

56. Homeward

Joey accompanied them to the airport, uncharacteristically quiet throughout the journey. At the terminal, James and Gopi went to find luggage trolleys.

Joey turned to Jane, took her hand in his, looked deep into her fathomless eyes, determination set in his own face, a clear reflection of what he felt in his heart.

"Jane, before you leave, I need you to know how I feel about you. I believe, you came into my frame that day for a reason. In the short time I have known you, you've have taken root in my heart. I've finally found what I've been searching for years. Words can't express how much you mean to me..."

Jane looked at his earnest face, seeing all the unspoken words there. Her heart leapt against the restraints.

"We live in different continents... Long-distance relationships don't work well for me, and with the baggage we carry... I, I ..." She struggled to articulate the conflicted feelings.

"No distance is too great to keep me away from you. We will find a way. Our lives have been different yet intertwined so deeply, much before we were even born. I've realised I've been carrying the wrong baggage all along. I am my father's son, who gave his life for the one he loved. That's my promise to you—to love you until the end. I come to believe destiny was written for us to be together and not our parents, and I now know their blessings will carry us forward.

And you, you were born from unconditional love, surviving against all odds and obstacles. You are the daughter of a remarkable woman who never gave up on you, and a distinguished man who kept his love alive even when he believed all was lost. You were raised by two loving parents. You couldn't ask for a better inheritance than that. You don't have to run away from your own heart anymore..."

Jane felt the promise in his words, resonating deeper than any dreams she had ever held. Her eyes filled with unshed tears; her heart suddenly full. She couldn't ignore the jolt that passed through her when his fingers wrapped around hers.

The intensity of his gaze made her forget the distance between them, thawing the frost of resistance she had built around her heart. She tiptoed and tenderly kissed him. Joey returned it fervently, enveloping her in an all-consuming embrace, the restraint on the pent-up emotions finally broken. Vague dreams began to take clear shapes in their minds. For that moment, the world melted away, leaving just the two of them nestled in clouds, wrapped by rainbows. The wind fervently echoed their declaration...

Nityaṃ tu mama mānase sarvasmi kṣhetravartini...

— Part 4 End —

Epilogue

"She walked out as if from the sun itself, her eyes reflected the fiery blaze, testament to the steely resolve she held, fiercer than the 'Agni Pariksha'- the trial by fire, they demanded of her, as if her purity could be any less than the wild-fire burned within her. It was ignited on the day she was abandoned, in the loneliest of places, on her weakest physical condition, in the most fragile state of mind. There, it had set hold of her, to protect her unborn child, the very essence of existence and survival known to the living beings. It burned on, through the day her twin sons were born, the rightful princes, but in the meagre setting of an Ashram, through the testing and tiring days of single parenting, through the intense education to make them the men they ought to be, men of great strength and integrity. And it had intensified to an all-consuming blaze, on the day she met him again, the king of all kings. She wasn't any more a weak woman he had abandoned for the sake of his own kingdom, but a force, emboldened by a life of self-determination, flanked by her brave, regal sons at her side. She had gone through the fire many times in the decade passed, coming victorious every time.

The majestic king was most remorseful, forever broken hearted, still bound by the rule of law he thought above anything else.

"I did not have a choice. For I am the king, who should lead by example. I could only sacrifice what belonged to me, and not the integrity of my country, of which I was born to lead. That was my destiny; written for me from the genesis..."

"You always had the choice my Lord... You always had... You could have left all that for me, the way I left my world to go with you to the end of the world for long fourteen years, being your trusted shadow in rich and poor. You had once left it for the honour of your father's oath, you could have left it once more for the oath you made to me on the day you

married me." Tears mellowed the fire, but the embers still glowed. "You could always have thrown away the rule book you have made for yourself.... You could have left this world of power for me... You could have loved me... the way I loved you..."

She turned away and embraced her sons for a final time. She blessed them with the all the goodness that came from a selfless, sacred motherhood, to last for an eternity. She knew her karma was fulfilled here. It was time for her to embrace her own mother, of immeasurable source of solace, forever loving and caring. After all, she was the daughter of Mother Earth, the goddess off infinite endurance...

Jane woke up with a start, dropping the envelop from the seat. The plane cruised over the clouds, homebound. Annie smiled at her from the scattered photos on the floor, young and vivacious, still unaware of any fire or fury.

.... The End...

Therese Pal

Acknowledgments

My deepest gratitude to Abhi, my first reader who started the book with all the scepticism in the world but ended up unable to put it down until 3 a.m. to finish the last chapter. That alone gave me the first true hope that this story might live beyond my desk.

To Jia and Josh, for debating endlessly with me about the characters—their flaws, or lack thereof—and pushing me to make them better.

To my family, who could connect with the story through our shared inheritance and memories. You are forever keystone of my life and my story.

To my friends, for enduring the lengthy, unpolished first draft and offering feedback and encouragement.

To Keith and Soom, for your generous help with editing.

And finally, to OpenAI, for the final polish. I wrestled with the absurdity of entrusting the product of my labour, that has been in the making for fifteen years or so, to an AI tool. But my engineering curiosity won out. I wanted to see what it could truly do with a real, original work. The result, a surprisingly competent editing assistant—so long as you never let it near the story itself!

References

This story draws upon a wide range of cultural, literary, and scientific sources that have shaped its themes of love, legacy, and identity. Among them:

- **The Mahabharata** – attributed to Vyasa, the epic of duty, love, and fate, whose timeless lessons echo through generations.
- **The Ramayana** – Valmiki's epic of exile, devotion, and moral struggle, resonating with the choices of family and destiny.
- **The Bible (Genesis, Exodus)** – as a meditation on origins, promised land, inheritance, and the search for truth.
- **A Survey of Kerala History (A. Sreedhara Menon)**- influential book on Kerala history comprehensively covering the geography and history of Kerala.
- **Sushruta Samhita (Sage Sushruta**) - an ancient Sanskrit text from 600 BC of Indian medicine and surgery that systematically details surgical techniques, medical knowledge, and Ayurvedic principles.
- **Annie (Thomas Meehan)**- The hopeful spirit of Annie that can help you overcome any challenge, no matter how difficult your circumstances may be.
- **Indulekha (O. Chandu Menon)** – Depicting pioneering Women characters from 19th century Kerala who dared to choose love over forced family traditions.
- **Vadakkan Pattu** – the Northern Ballads of Kerala, oral traditions celebrating valour, betrayal, and the bonds of kinship.
- **Chemmeen (Thakazhi Sivasankara Pillai)** – a Malayalam classic weaving love, superstition, and the rhythms of Kerala's coastal life.
- **Aswamedham, Thulabharam, Ningalenne Communistakki (Thoppil Bhasi)** – books and plays that

brought social movement to the forefront in 20th century Kerala, with KPAC and Alleppey theatres pioneering the field.

- **Malabar Stories (Vaikom Muhammad Basheer and others)** – tales of Kerala's landscapes, humour, and humanity that capture the pulse of everyday lives.
- **Albert Einstein's Theory of Relativity & the Cosmological Constant** – inspiration from science and the search for universal truths.
- **Indian Nobel Laureates in Literature & Science** – from **Rabindranath Tagore's** poetic works to **C.V. Raman's** scientific discoveries, symbolize the depth of Indian thought across disciplines.
- **Kerala's literacy movement** – a pioneering social initiative that mobilized communities and government support to achieve near-universal literacy, making it the first fully literate state in India by the early 1990s.
- **India IT industry Vision** – began in 70's and 80s , driven by Dr. Vikram Sarabhai, Dr. Raja Ramanna, Dr. A.P.J. Abdul Kalam and Narayana Murthy and supported by Indira Gandhi's government.
- **First democratically elected Communist government in the world** —formed on April 5, 1957, in Kerala India by Communist Party of India (CPI) with E. M. S. Namboodiripad as the Chief Minister.
- **Omanathinkal Kidavo – (Irayimman Thampi)** -a lullaby with vivid imagery composed in 19th century, expressing mother's deep love and affection.
- **'Nityaṃ tu mama mānase sarvasmin kṣetravartini'** - Sanskrit verse translate to: 'You are in my heart always, present in every part of my being!'

Map of Kerala –For illustration only

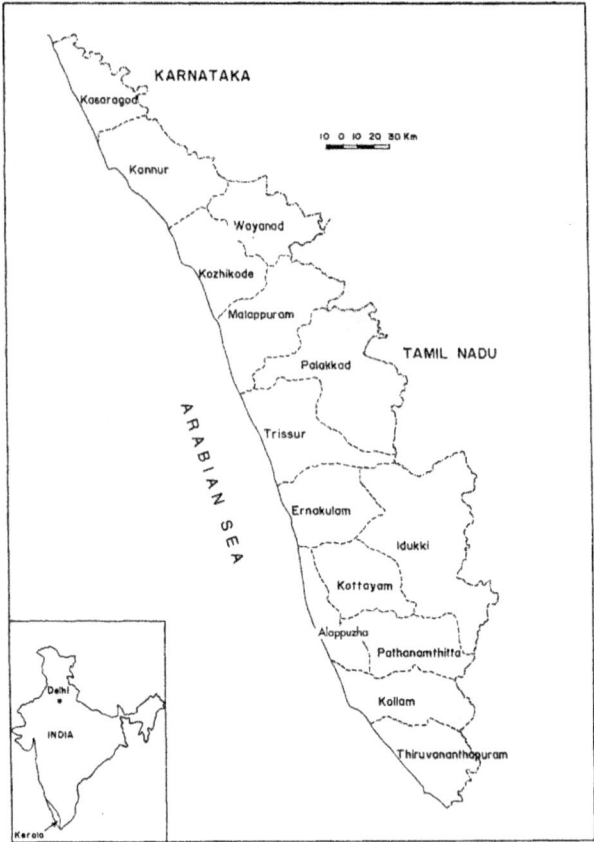

Therese Pal

Jane's notes on Family Trees

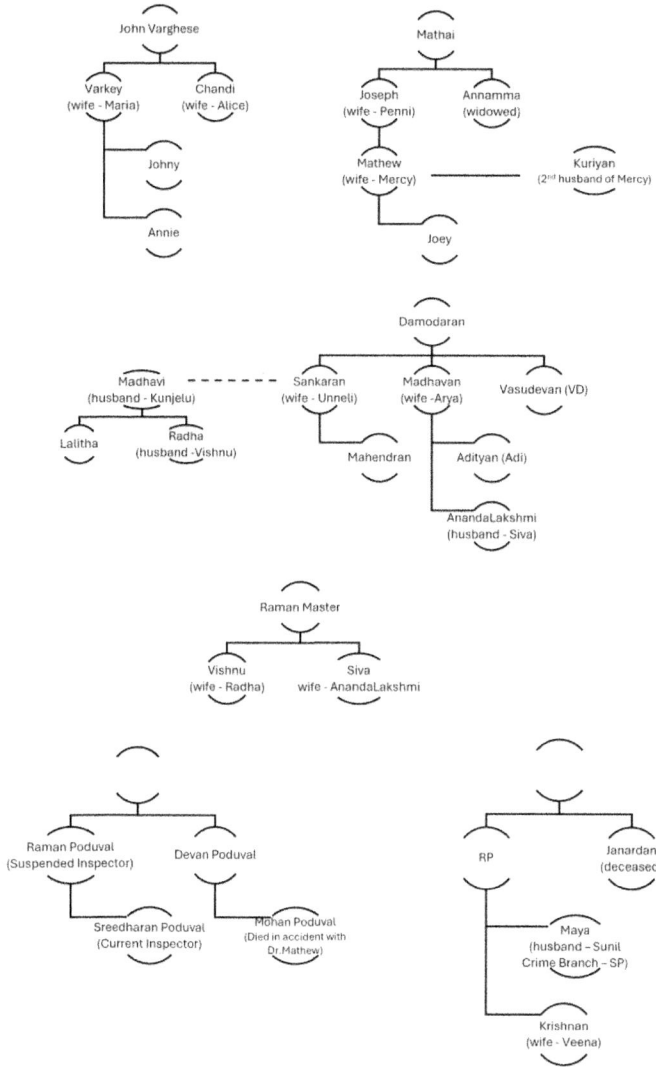

Jane's Sketch on Palari

Therese Pal

Printed in Dunstable, United Kingdom